A black shape rose
from the open sarcophagus . . .

"You can't hurt me!" Siria said, but her voice trembled.

Staun bent down and picked up the Sword of Light, but he did not use it against the Undead Lord; he didn't even look at the black thing. Instead he hefted it and took a step toward Siria.

She swallowed. Maybe the Undead Lord *could* hurt her—he couldn't harm her directly while she wore the armor, but the Sword of Light could probably hack right through the mail.

And even if it couldn't cut the magic armor, it could cut her exposed throat, or split her skull.

"Staun," she said, "drop the sword! *Please!*"

"Woman," Staun said, in a strained and unnatural voice, "you are all that stands between the Undead Lord and his freedom."

From "Arms and the Woman" by Lawrence Watt-Evans

MARION ZIMMER BRADLEY
in DAW editions

SWORD AND SORCERESS I–XVIII

THE DARKOVER NOVELS
The Founding
DARKOVER LANDFALL

The Ages of Chaos
STORMQUEEN!
HAWKMISTRESS!

The Hundred Kingdoms
TWO TO CONQUER
THE HEIRS OF HAMMERFELL

The Renunciates
THE SHATTERED CHAIN
THENDARA HOUSE
CITY OF SORCERY

Against the Terrans—The First Age
REDISCOVERY
THE SPELL SWORD
THE FORBIDDEN TOWER
STAR OF DANGER
WINDS OF DARKOVER

Against the Terrans—The Second Age
THE BLOODY SUN
HERITAGE OF HASTUR
THE PLANET SAVERS
SHARRA'S EXILE
THE WORLD WRECKERS
EXILE'S SONG
THE SHADOW MATRIX
TRAITOR'S SUN

SWORD AND SORCERESS XVIII

EDITED BY

Marion Zimmer Bradley

DAW BOOKS, INC.
DONALD A. WOLLHEIM, FOUNDER
375 Hudson Street, New York, NY 10014

ELIZABETH R. WOLLHEIM
SHEILA E. GILBERT
PUBLISHERS
www.dawbooks.com

First Printing, May 2001
1 2 3 4 5 6 7 8 9 10

DAW TRADEMARK REGISTERED
U.S. PAT OFF AND FOREIGN COUNTRIES
—MARCA REGISTRADA.
HECHO EN USA

PRINTED IN THE U.S.A.

ACKNOWLEDGEMENTS

A Passage of Power © 2001 by Diana L. Paxson
Lessons Learned © 2001 by Kati Doughery-Carthurn
Kendat's Ax © 2001 by Jan Combs
The Tower of Song © 2001 by Howard Holman
The Needed Stone © 2001 by Denise Lopes Heald
Armageddon © 2001 by Lisa Silverthorne
The Land of Graves © 2001 by Dave Smeds
Light © 2001 by Susan Urbanek Linville
In the Sacred Places of the Earth © 2001
   by Dorothy J. Heydt
The Glass Sword © 2001 by Richard Corwin
Bed of Roses © 2001 by The Waters Trust
Sword of Peace © 2001 by Lucy Cohen Schmeidler
The Fall of the Kingdom © 2001 by Mary Soon Lee
Arms and the Woman © 2001 by Lawrence Watt-Evans
The Stone Wives © 2001 by Michael Chesley Johnson
Tiger's Eye © 2001 by India Edghill
Raven-Winds on the Snow © 2001 by Pauline J. Alama
Little Rogue Riding Hood © 2001 by Rosemary Edghill
The Queen in Yellow © 2001 by Gerald Perkins
Magic Threads © 2001 by Pete D. Manison

CONTENTS

INTRODUCTION 1
by Elisabeth Waters

A PASSAGE OF POWER 3
by Diana L. Paxson

LESSONS LEARNED 23
by Kati Doughery-Carthum

KENDAT'S AX 35
by Jan Combs

THE TOWER OF SONG 48
by Howard Holman

THE NEEDED STONE 69
by Denise Lopes Heald

ARMAGEDDON 90
by Lisa Silverthorne

THE LAND OF GRAVES 94
by Dave Smeds

LIGHT 112
by Susan Urbanek Linville

IN THE SACRED PLACES OF THE EARTH   134
by Dorothy J. Heydt

THE GLASS SWORD   151
by Richard Corwin

BED OF ROSES   164
by Elisabeth Waters

SWORD OF PEACE   181
by Lucy Cohen Schmeidler

THE FALL OF THE KINGDOM   192
by Mary Soon Lee

ARMS AND THE WOMAN   197
by Lawrence Watt-Evans

THE STONE WIVES   214
by Michael Chesley Johnson

TIGER'S EYE   227
by India Edghill

RAVEN-WINGS ON THE SNOW   245
by Pauline J. Alama

LITTLE ROGUE RIDING HOOD   265
by Rosemary Edghill

THE QUEEN IN YELLOW   287
by Gerald Perkins

MAGIC THREADS   297
by Pete D. Manison

INTRODUCTION
by Elisabeth Waters

LAST night I was reading the page proofs for *S&S XVII*, starting with MZB's introduction. She wrote about the theme of the anthology (every year stories seem to cluster around a theme, sometimes so closely that we get two or three stories on the exact same subject) and about the chaos in her personal life, with her house being torn apart to replace a disintegrating foundation, forcing her to live elsewhere. There were two things she was looking forward to: moving back into her own home, and seeing what sort of theme *S&S XVIII* would end up with.

Tragically, she never managed the first; her home is still a construction zone. She did, however, live long enough to read nearly all of the manuscripts submitted for *S&S XVIII*, long enough to see three themes develop in the piles of manuscripts. The themes can be described as follows: impossible tasks and invading armies, learning about magic, and finding your true self or true path.

Thirteen weeks ago today I sat in the local hospital and held Marion's hand while she died. Six weeks after that, my father, whom I loved very much, died suddenly and unexpectedly. Under the circumstances, it's not surprising that I decided to use "Impossible Tasks and Invading Armies" for *S&S XVIII*.

Editing the anthology is not an impossible task; Marion chose the stories, and I've done final lineups and drafts of introductions for her approval for at least the last five years. It's a bit strange not to have her here to approve them, but she spent twenty years training me and drumming her prejudices into my head until I can scarcely tell her likes and dislikes from my own. I've been known to define an editor as "a collection of prejudices," but as long as the editor's prejudices match those of her readers, they'll keep on buying her books. It is my hope that I have been sufficiently faithful to her teaching that this volume will look just like all the ones that were done when she was around to supervise my work.

I wish she were still here, and not just to double-check what I've done. I miss her dreadfully. But the best way I can honor her memory is to finish the work she started and left uncompleted, and I intend to do that to the very best of my ability.

A PASSAGE OF POWER
by Diana L. Paxson

Diana L. Paxson gave her first work to Marion to critique, rewriting it until eventually she sold the first novel of Westria. Since then she has published twenty books, the most recent being *Hallowed Isle,* an Arthurian novel whose paperback version will appear in two volumes: *The Book of the Sword and Spear,* and *The Book of the Cauldron and the Stone.* She has just completed *Priestess of Avalon,* a collaboration with Marion.

Diana has never failed to turn in a story for *S&S.* Here's her latest one.

HORSES were galloping, hoofbeats drumming out the compelling rhythm of trance. Bera twitched to the beat, even as she realized that her body was tangled in the folds of her cloak. She strove to recapture the dream, and glimpsed a broad plain. Now the horses were disappearing into the distance, but she could still see the black mare. She recognized the spirit that helped Groa, who had taught her the arts of *seidh* that were the magic of the North.

"Don't leave me alone!" her dream self cried, but the horses did not return.

Bera watched until the scene dislimned in a jumble of images. When it was gone, she lay still for a little longer, waiting for her heartbeat to slow. It had felt like a dream of power. Bera wondered if the old Voelva had sent the black mare as a messenger.

If so, she could no longer remember the message, only the tide of emotion that had carried it, as if something tremendously important were slipping away. She sighed, rubbed the sleep from her eyes, and fought free of the cloak. Achtlan was up already, stirring porridge in an iron pot and talking to Haki, the old thrall whom Bera had inherited with the horse and cart when Groa retired. The Irishwoman's black hair shone auburn in the light of the fire, or perhaps it was her aura of power. It was hard to imagine that only a week ago she had been a thrall as well.

It was now just past the solstice, and during the short summer nights it was no hardship to sleep on the ground, but Bera had no desire to do so until a trading ship on which Achtlan could take passage back to Britain came to the harbor of Nidaros.

"Well, it's little choice we have about it," said Achtlan as Bera stretched the kinks from her muscles. "The gold my master gave to pay my passage will not be lasting for many days at the inn."

Achtlan's hand went to her neck, as if to make sure the thrall ring was no longer there. In Irland she had been a priestess of the goddess Brigid, but when she was a slave, she had suppressed her powers, and still needed reminding that she was free to use them once more.

And what about my *powers?* wondered Bera. *Why cannot I find the meaning of my dream?* Suddenly she smiled. "Indeed, I know of one hall where we are sure of a welcome, for the wisewoman who was my teacher is living there."

Halvor's farm at Raumsdale lay in the hills beyond Nidaros. By the time they turned up the road past the old mounds, the sun was sinking behind them. Bera frowned as she saw the new runestone that had been set up next to the howe of the ancestor of Halvor's line.

Halla, who ruled the servants here, came hurrying out of the door as Haki reined the horse to a halt in front of the hall. A confusing play of emotion touched the woman's face as she recognized Bera, settling finally to sadness.

"You're here—I dared not hope the message would find you so soon. She is still alive, though the gods alone know for how long. . . ."

Bera felt something congeal in her gut. "Is it Groa?"

"Last night," Halla said more gently. "We found her slumped in her chair, barely breathing. We put her to bed, but she has not regained her senses. We were hoping there might be something you could do."

Bera slid down from the cart, feeling suddenly stiff and cold. To fare through the Otherworld in search of a wandering soul was part of the craft that Groa had taught her, but some souls did not wish to be found. Groa had retired from her work as a wisewoman when she no longer had the stamina to work with the spirits. The last time Bera visited, the older woman had seemed content to sit beside the fire and spin, watching her daughter, who was being fostered here, grow.

She followed Halla around the side of the feasting hall. Raumsdale was an important farm, and there was a separate outbuilding for couples and another for the unmarried women. She blinked as they passed through the doorway to the darkness within.

Already she could hear the slow rasp of breathing from the box-bed at the end. The flicker of a seal-oil lamp lit the face and the russet hair of the thrall-woman who had been left to keep watch. Bera stopped, smiling as she saw it was Devorgilla, whose twins she had helped to deliver the first time she came here. Achtlan came to a halt behind her, looking around her with interest.

Groa had been a wealthy woman. Hangings of wool embroidered with scenes of ritual and processions of worshipers kept out draughts from around the bed, and the linen sheets were fine and soft. Bera picked up the lamp and bent over the bed. Groa's breathing stayed slow, steady. This was not the closed face of sleep, she thought with a sinking heart, but the slack features of a body that had been abandoned by its soul.

Groa could have been felled by some convulsion in the brain, she thought, giving the lamp back to the servant and passing her hands above the body to sense the flow of energy there, or it could have been her heart that had given way. If the damage were too great, it might be better if she did not return to her body again.

"Does she take nourishment?" she asked, stepping back again.

"When we dribble a little broth between her lips, she will be swallowing," said Devorgilla, "but she does not move."

"The body is wanting to live," said Achtlan. "This I have seen, in a warrior with injured head."

Devorgilla stared as she heard the Irish accent, but she kept silent, waiting for Bera to reply.

Bera sighed. "The power of the heart was the first to be given, and is the last to go, when the body cools."

"She still breathes—" pointed out Halla.

"Yes . . . So there may still be something left for her to do. . . ."

"Can you speak with her spirit?" Devorgilla asked then.

"I do not know," Bera said honestly. Then, seeing the despair in the girl's eyes. "Does it matter?"

"The Voelva no longer worked magic, but she was still respected," Halla said in a low voice. "She had become fond of Devorgilla, and spoke of buying her freedom from Halvor."

"Is he unwilling?" asked Bera.

Halla's face changed. "Ah, then you will not have heard—he was killed at Rastarkalf."

"I saw a runestone next to the old mound," said Bera.

"That is Berglind's doing," answered Halla. "Her son is still with the king, and she is ordering all things according to her own will. She could not go too far while Groa was able to bear witness to her deeds, but now—"

"Oh, my lady," Devorgilla burst in. "Before witnesses, Halvor declared my children free-born, but me he was keeping a thrall. And now the lady Berglind is saying she will sell me, and my poor babes not eight years old until this fall. Always she has hated them—who will be defending them if I am gone?"

Bera grimaced. At least she now understood why Halla had been so happy to see her, and why she was so anxious that Groa should recover. It made sense that Berglind would not want to see the estate divided between her son and the twins, who by law were entitled to a share as well. Her own grief, that the woman who had been the mother of her spirit should pass out of the world without even a word of farewell, meant little compared to the three lives that were at stake now.

"I will try—" she said heavily. "But I can promise nothing." She looked down at the slack face on the pillow, feeling as if all her own magic were locked away in that unresponsing head as well.

Dinner in the hall that evening was a somber affair. Berglind was too careful of her own reputation to refuse hospitality, but it was obvious that she wished Bera far away. *I bested you before, old woman,* thought Bera, returning her glare, *do not cross me now!*

But even as the thought faded, she knew it for empty defiance. In the three years since she had returned from her initiatory vision and taken over her teacher's role as Voelva, she had seen Groa rarely. She had learned to work on her own, and done it well. But, always, the knowledge that her old teacher was *there* had been an invisible support and consolation.

Only the presence of the twins lightened the gloom. Alfhelm had grown brown and sturdy, his sister as fair-skinned as her mother, with a ruddy glint to her hair. They were accustomed to Berglind's hostility, and their father had been away from home so often it was no surprise they did not grieve for him.

Indeed, their greatest sorrow seemed to be for Groa, whom they had known as a kind foster-grandmother, especially after her own daughter had been married off to a chieftain who lived several days' journey away. They had asked, very sweetly, if they could help.

"I could rub your shoulders," said Alfhild. "Groa always liked that, when her muscles cramped up after she had been spinning all day."

"And I could rub your feet," put in Alfhelm. "She liked that, too."

Bera nodded, blinking back the tears as she remembered how many times she had been the one to rub her teacher's feet or her shoulders when the strain of travel bore hard on old bones.

"When I have done something to merit it, you may do the same for me," she managed to smile.

She could feel the older members of the household watching her, waiting for her to perform some miracle, or sourly certain there would be none. She wanted to hitch up the old horse and ride away, but her will stood silent sentinel against her feelings, and it was will that drove her back to Groa's bedside the next day.

Ordering Devorgilla out, Bera sat down beside the cupboard bed where the sick woman lay. No—she told herself—the dying woman. She picked up the limp hand. It was warm, the skin dry and smooth. The bellows of the lungs still pumped in air, and the valiant heart still pushed blood through the veins.

"Groa, mother of my soul," she whispered. "Listen with your spirit, if your body cannot hear. Come back to us, wise one. Devorgilla's twins need you." After a moment more words forced themselves free. "*I* need you. Forgive me for not coming to visit you more often. I wanted to prove I could succeed on my own. But I walked in your shadow—I spoke with your authority. Who will care for my words when they know I am alone?"

There was no reply, no tremor in the slack features, nor any change in the atmosphere around her. Bera's lips twisted in scorn for her own self-pity. Groa had lived a long and honorable life. If it were not for the danger to Devorgilla, her duty would have clearly been to say farewell and let Groa go. But need compelled her. If Groa would not come to her, then she must follow her into the Otherworld.

"*Sithi Thor . . .*" she murmured to the god who protected her. "Thor aid me to work this seidh . . ." She closed her eyes.

For the first moments Bera was acutely aware of her other senses: the pop and hiss of the fire, the rough wool of the blanket beneath her hand. Then the sequence of long, slow, breaths sent consciousness inward. She sank into shadow, the memory of the firelight against her eyelids dwindling to a glowing point which gradually disappeared.

As always, it took an act of will to shift from this state to begin the work for which she had come. Gently she extended her center of awareness toward the older woman, noting and passing the physical body, its envelope of life force thinned so that it was scarcely greater than the flesh it surrounded, seeking the spirit within. One could touch the thoughts of a sleeper so, or someone in trance, but this time there was no sense of presence at all.

Groa has gone . . . she thought. *Her body still breathes, but the spirit is already far away.*

Well, she had not really expected it to be easy. With an inner sigh, Bera withdrew her consciousness to her own center and began to reconstruct the landscape of her dream. There was the rolling plain, and now she saw the Worldtree rising through its center like the axletree of a wheel. Satisfied, she took her bearings, and called to Brunbjorn, the great brown bear who was her guide and helper in the inner worlds.

For a few moments the scene blurred, and then she became aware of the massive presence of her ally beside her. She rarely saw him clearly—rather it was the overwhelming sense of "bear-ness" that told her he had arrived. She felt his inquiry, and the tolerant amusement which was characteristic of the beings of the Otherworld.

"Old friend, we have a wandering spirit to find. Show me where to go—"

"It is the old woman, yes? I cannot find her, but maybe I can find the ones who guide her—"

Bera had a sudden image of a feasting hall where all the fetches sat at long tables together, drinking ale and trading anecdotes about their human fosterlings. Embarrassed, she shut the picture away, but she felt Brunbjorn's amusement deepen and knew that he had caught it all the same.

Images swirled through her awareness—a black pony mare with flowing tail, a white owl skimming the treetops, a seal that sported in the waves. She sensed others as well, but she did not know their names. As the bear sent out his summons, Bera added her own calling.

"Blackmane, Mousebane, Seasinger, hear me—help me to find the one you guard!"

It seemed to her then that she heard an echo of hoofbeats, and glimpsed in the distance a dark figure speeding over the plain. She ran toward it, but it grew no closer. After a time she halted, listening to the hoofbeats recede as they had done in her dream.

"She does not want to be found—" said Brunbjorn. *"Mousebane tells me that she fears to be forced back into*

her outworn body. She is between worlds now, not among the living, and yet not truly free."

Bera felt grief tighten her throat, and knew that in her heart it had been her own need, not that of Devorgilla, that had impelled her to this quest.

"Mousebane," she called again. *"Listen. You know I would never wish your lady pain or harm. Tell her—"* she choked, forcing the next words out through stiff lips, *"tell her she is free to go. . . ."*

In the next moment it seemed to her that she stood in the midst of a great stillness, as if every creature in all the worlds had heard those words. What had she done? The intensity of her emotion whirled her backward into her own body again.

Bera opened her eyes, head still spinning, to find herself sitting by Groa's bedside, with the older woman's unresponsive hand still clasped in her own. She peered at her face and saw no change. *Perhaps,* she thought bitterly, *I imagined it all.*

Gently she laid Groa's hand atop the coverlet and went out the door. Devorgilla and Achtlan were just outside, chattering cheerfully in the Irish tongue. She paused beside the Irishwoman, who looked up, her face sobering in sympathy.

"Is she dying, then?"

"I think so," Bera replied. Devorgilla covered her face with a low wail and Achtlan reached out to pat her arm.

"I see that she will be mourned. Was she then so wonderful?" They had known each other long enough now for Bera to hear the unasked remainder:—*"What has this woman made of you, who hold my future in your hands?"*

Bera sighed. "Men always speak of the dying as if they had no flaws, but if I called Groa perfect, I would be self-deceived. She could be most generous, and the gods know, she was kind to me. But her care was above all for her craft and those things that served it, and she could be harsh and thoughtless when her interest was not engaged."

"And she was strong in magic?"

"Oh, yes—" Bera laughed a little. "She commanded a host of spirits. More than once men accused her of sorcery in her younger days."

"Well, and has not the same been said of many a *bean-drui* in my own country?" said Achtlan, and Devorgilla nodded agreement.

As Bera crossed the yard to the hall, she saw Berglind coming from the weaving shed with a length of folded linen in her arms. Even on an ordinary workday Halvor's widow was wearing a head-wrap of crimson silk embroidered with threads of gold. It did not flatter her rather doughy features at all.

"Is the old woman dead yet?" asked Berglind.

Bera stiffened, then an answering anger flared. "Is the wolf-bitch so eager for carrion? What good will Groa's death do you?"

"One less mouth to feed is a gain," said Berglind. "And the use of the building, and the labor of my thralls. It was my husband who agreed with Jarl Sigurd to keep her here— no one ever consulted *me!*"

You bitch, thought Bera, *you've hated me ever since I stopped you from killing the babes Devorgilla bore to your husband, and transferred your hostility to Groa, because I was not here.*

She drew herself up, pulling the shape of her fetch around her, and knew, from the widening of Berglind's eyes, that instead of a short, solidly-built young woman with curly brown hair, she was sensing a great brown bear rearing up on its hind legs in rage.

"Groa cannot speak against you," she growled, "but I am here, and I will see that you do no more or less than the law and the oaths that have been sworn require."

"But of course," answered Berglind, recovering, "that was always my intention. . . ."

Silenced, Bera glared as the older woman stalked away. For she had spoken truly, and as things stood now, no one could gainsay her right to deal with Devorgilla in any way she chose. She watched until Berglind had disappeared into the hall, then turned and walked swiftly toward the hillside behind the hall.

Long ago, when Bera had been an unwanted girl-child herding her father's cows, the hills had been her refuge. Like the twins, she had been the daughter of an Irish concubine, and when her father died, her stepmother had tried to claim her as a thrall. It was inevitable, Bera realized, that she should take the threat to Devorgilla and her children personally. It was Groa who had rescued Bera, taking her to train in the arts of prophecy. Now she must do the same for Devorgilla.

At this season most of the cattle were still in the high pastures, and on the lower slopes the grass grew thick and green. Presently, she passed into the shade beneath the mixed forest of pine and fir. When she emerged, muscles loosened by the exercise, there was a breeze to go with the sunshine.

Before her rose the folds and ridges of the true mountains. Turning, she could see Raumsdale spread out below her, the thatched buildings of the farmstead tucked into the hillside and the gentler slope of the home fields and the green hump of the Ancestor's mound. In the distance, hazed by the smoke of Nidaros, she glimpsed the gleam of the sea. Seagulls circled over the farmyard, yammering insults as they fought over scraps from the midden heap. From here, both the farm buildings and the woman who ruled them seemed very small.

Bera sat down with her back against an outcrop of smooth stone and let her eyes close. Here, the bones of the earth were close to the surface. Bera reached for that solid strength, willing all the tension of the past days to sink into the soil and dissolve away. Men and women died, and passed from the world, but two things remained, the reputation gained during their lifetimes, and the holy earth that received their bones.

Men will remember Groa's deeds, she told herself, *they will remember her magic, and her words of prophecy....* Few women in this world could boast of more. Whether Groa lived for one more day or many, it was now, Bera knew, that she was saying farewell. She felt the hot tears sting her eyes and rested her head upon her knees, letting them fall.

The sun was only just beginning to sink westward when Bera started down the hill once more, but her belly told her that she had been away for some hours. Her eyes were swollen and her throat raw from weeping, but the emptiness within her was not entirely hunger. The storm in her spirit had passed.

As she descended the hill, she realized that the world around her was less peaceful. More than once she missed her footing, as if the earth had moved. The forest floor was dappled with shadows that slid across her path like an owl on silent wings, but when she looked up she could see no bird. Yet some creature was there, for she heard a muffled drumming, almost like hoofbeats, that moved beside her through the trees.

Even from the hill she could see an unusual number of folk gathered in the yard. As she approached the farmstead, they stilled, staring. The anticipatory tightening in her gut became an ache. The farm folk were looking at each other, searching for the right words.

"The Voelva is dead," she said flatly, and saw eyes widen at this demonstration of her powers. But it did not take a Seidhkona to know what simple observation could reveal.

"Yes, Lady," answered Halla. "She ceased to breathe just after the sun passed the daymark for noon. Men have gone up to the grave field already to prepare the ground. The women have cleansed the body, but we thought that perhaps there was some rite. . . ." Her words trailed off, and Bera's lips twitched in a grim smile.

She had heard the stories, too, from Groa and others, of Voelvas who were more powerful in death than they had been when living, and malevolent, if they thought they had been wronged. These people wanted her protection, even Berglind, who had come out of the hall when Bera arrived.

One of the horses in the pen snorted and an idea came to her suddenly. Groa was not likely to haunt Raumsdale—but Berglind could not know that. Bera eyed her speculatively and saw the woman's glance shift away.

Berglind will be expecting trouble . . . she knows she is doing wrong, thought Bera. *Groa would not help us while still she lived, but in death she may be more useful.*

"Indeed, it is so," she said loftily. "I wonder that she did not leave you instructions, but perhaps her powers told her that when the time came for her passing I would be nigh. If a Voelva is not satisfied with the manner of her burial, there can be great danger, for with death, all her magic is unbound."

"We treated the body with reverence, and left a lamp burning," stammered Halla. "What else should we do?"

"For three nights she must lie, with her staff by her side, wrapped in her blue cloak and wearing all her magical gear, while the burial chamber is being prepared."

Relieved, men and women scattered to their work, until only Berglind was left, staring at Bera across the yard.

"Make use of Devorgilla while you can," Berglind said

finally. "By the time the old woman is buried, a buyer for the thrall will be here."

With an effort, Bera kept herself from reacting. "Will you send the children to be fostered with their mother's new owner?"

"Oh, no—" Berglind smiled mirthlessly. "My son is now their guardian. Alfhild and Alfhelm will stay here."

And will they live until they are old enough to claim a share in their father's property? wondered Bera. Folk might have their suspicions when the word came, but many children died. The twins, with no other kin to ask questions, would simply be two more. If Bera had possessed any money, she would have tried to purchase Devorgilla herself. But the horse, the wagon, and the thrall Haki, along with the skills that Groa had taught her, were all the wealth she had.

That night, clouds drew in. The air had an almost autumnal chill, and the big yew tree below the hall rustled uneasily. Voices grew lower and folk began to look over their shoulders. At times, when the wind blew louder, Bera would pause, eyes closed and fingers twitching in a warding sign.

"What are you listening to?" they asked, and "Is some spirit near?"

But Bera only shook her head. Achtlan, who knew as well as Bera that it was only the wind, lifted an eyebrow.

"Why should Groa's ghost be walking?" the Irishwoman asked quietly. "Did not you say she had a liking for the people here?"

"She did. But if harm comes to any, she may haunt them indeed!"

"Ah—It is the woman of this house that troubles you. Will you work seidh against her?"

"I do not wish to—that would be to betray Groa's teaching. But I will frighten her if I can," Bera replied.

As the hours of darkness drew on, Bera began to feel a little anxious herself. Some of the strange sounds were the work of Achtlan, who could come and go unnoticed while Bera's mutterings held everyone's attention. But several times she heard a pony's snort or the sound of hoofbeats when the Irishwoman was in the room, and when she went outside for air, a dark shape passed between her and the sky and she heard the mournful cry of an owl.

"Mousebane?" she whispered into the darkness. "Are you there? Will you speak to me?"

The owl hooted once more, but all that Bera could sense was confusion and loss.

In the morning she saw shadowed eyes and pale faces around her. Berglind said they should put Groa into the ground immediately, but Bera shook her head, and it was clear that in this matter the farm folk would obey her rather than their lady. One soul-part left the body with the breath, but there was a more subtle energy which must be given time to understand its changed state before the flesh was confined in a grave.

"And besides," she added, "the men are still building the funeral chamber. Groa would be insulted if we put her body into the bare ground."

That day she spent preparing the gravegoods, and though Berglind clearly coveted the embroidered bedcurtains and some of the other gear, she dared refuse nothing. The second night was much the same, and on the day that followed the men worked with a will, so that by sunset the wooden funeral chamber had been completed and rocks heaped around it, ready for the interment the next day.

That night was stormy. The lamps flickered wildly, sending odd shadows dancing across the wall. Bera began to wonder if she had been wise to delay the burial. The unsettled feeling she had noticed when Groa died had increased a hundredfold, as if the great tapestry of life that was Midgard was beginning to fray. Just after midnight, she took her own staff and went out to face the storm.

The waning moon flitted in and out of visibility as gusting winds drove clouds across the sky, the wild wargs close on the moon-god Mani's heels. Bera had always known that the world was full of spirits, but now the wights were rioting about the farmstead in such numbers that even ordinary folk could sense them. No wonder they were afraid.

Groa always told me to be careful what I asked for, lest it come upon me, she thought as she turned to face the blast. *I spoke truth without meaning to. Groa's last days were peaceful, but she has left us a dangerous legacy.*

She wondered suddenly if the spirits would be placated when they put the body into the ground, or if she herself would have to find, somehow, the strength to bind them. As if she had spoken, a new gust of wind came howling down upon her. Instinctively, Bera swung up her staff, rocking against the pressure on her body and her soul. She had thought she knew her teacher's familiars, but these were older powers, long suppressed but not extinguished, and all the more powerful because they had been so long denied.

"Begone!" she cried, "You are no responsibility of mine!" In the moment of respite that followed she ducked back into the hall.

As one of the menservants barred the door behind her, Berglind stood up, her face contorted by fear and pale even in the light of the fire.

"I can still hear them! The trolls are out there! You must stop them!"

"I *must?*" Bera flared back, fueling her own anger with her fear. "I owe nothing to you! When the sun rises, I can ride out of here and leave you to deal with the powers of the Unseen on your own!"

Now the rest of the household was pleading with Bera

to save them, blaming Berglind for angering her. The older woman looked around her nervously. Singly, she could command her servants, but they were becoming a mob against which she could not stand.

"You want to be paid? How much?"

Bera stared at her, possibilities unfolding within her awareness at dazzling speed. She could feel Achtlan's gaze upon her. Silence grew in the hall.

"Devorgilla . . ." she said at last. "Give me the thrall-woman and a fee to foster her children."

"You will take them away?" said Berglind when a long moment had passed.

Bera nodded. "What they may do when they are grown, I cannot promise, but you will be free of them until that day arrives—"

She could see Berglind weighing the possibility that the twins would never return to claim their heritage against her chances to make away with them if they stayed. Then a new gust sent wind whirling through some chink in the walls and struck a spray of sparks from the fire.

"Very well—" Berglind said harshly. "You will have them when you have laid the Voelva and all her fetches to rest."

If I can . . . Bera nodded, painfully aware of the glow of approval in Achtlan's face, of Devorgilla's grateful tears and the twins' shining eyes.

Groa, she sent up a silent prayer, *help me to remember your teaching, for you are the only one who can help me now!*

Taking up her staff, she marched sunwise around the hall, singing out the rune of Thor, who keeps the balance between humanity and the elder kin, and drawing it in the air with her staff. In her mind's eye she could see the runes, bristling outward like a hedge of thorns, and as she completed the circle she felt a change in pressure, and knew that this part of the farmstead, at least, was safe from the storm.

Morning brought little change, though the light lessened imaginary fears. In the end, it was only Berglind who had the courage to accompany Bera and Haki as they bore Groa's body to her howe beneath a lowering sky. The long grass on the ancestor's mound lay flat as the wind passed over it, alternately silver and green, but Groa's unfinished grave gaped dark as the gate to Hel as Haki reined in the horse and the wagon came to a halt.

"Unhitch the horse, Haki. The howe is high enough for the wagon to fit inside. Let Groa travel to Freyja's hall in state befitting her station, so they will know she was no common spaewife, but a Voelva."

"But mistress, how will we travel?" Haki blinked at her, his old face creasing in confusion.

"I cannot take a wagon on the whale-road, and it is oversea to Angleland that I mean to fare, to take Achtlan and Devorgilla home. I am giving you your freedom, Haki—I call Berglind to bear witness. You can take the horse and go back to that farm where the shepherd's widow liked you so well."

He shook his head, unable to answer, but the tears in his eyes were from joy. In silence they rolled the wagon into the dark opening, and Bera leaned over to place a last kiss on Groa's cold brow. Then they shut the wooden door and began to pile rocks up around it. Others could complete the work of covering it with earth, to match the Ancestor's mound.

"Snow shall cover you, rain shall fall upon you, long shall you sleep . . ." Bera murmured, signing the grave with a rune of protection. "May the holy gods keep you, until it comes time for you to be reborn."

Blinking back tears, she turned to face the wind. Berglind regarded her sourly.

"You have freed your thrall, but until you fulfill your part of our bargain, I will not free mine. The stormwind still blows, and even I can sense the wights that whirl around us."

"I know it," Bera said quietly. "You must promise that if I succeed you will release Devorgilla and the children, whatever happens to me." Berglind grunted agreement, and Bera picked her way over the stones until she stood atop the mound. "Now, for your souls' sakes, stand away, for the spirits I am calling will not submit easily to be bound."

Bera's hood fell back as she spread her arms wide, and the wind plucked her hair from its braid and sent it streaming behind her. Taking a deep breath, she closed her eyes.

I survived when the spirit-bears dismembered me. I can do this . . . she told herself, seeking the core of her own power. *Brunbjorn, oldest of allies, stand with me now!* She swayed a little as she felt the bulk of the great bear behind her. Then, with an act of will, she let down her defenses and reached out to the storm.

To Mousebane she called, and felt the mighty swoop of his descent on an owl's silent wings. Seasinger came from his home in the oceans, seal-shape wet and shining, and with their help she began to summon the others, coaxing or commanding, using every word of power Groa had ever taught her, and all the strength at her command. There were more than she had ever dreamed of—troll-shapes and beings of light, spirits of ancestors, and things that had no form at all, but only power—all the wights with whose aid Groa had made her magic.

One by one they came to her, and passed through her to the world within. She could feel her soul expanding to welcome them. When she was finished, one only still eluded her, and that was the black mare who had served the Voelva longest and been the spirit shape of her soul.

Blackmane! Blackmane! Without you, how can I carry the power? She waited, trying to remember the tricks she had used to bring in the horses when she was a child. Her father's ponies would come to a handful of grain, but what did a spirithorse desire?

At the edge of awareness she sensed a dark form. Trembling with need, she shaped all her longing into an apple and held it out on the palm of her hand.

Blackmane . . . she breathed, and heard at last the sound of hoofbeats, as freely and in love, the black mare came to her.

LESSONS LEARNED
by Kati Dougherty-Carthum

This is Kati's second story in this anthology series; her first was in *Sword and Sorceress X*. Since then, her life has changed dramatically, with a marriage, job, and child entering the picture. She currently lives in Washington state with husband David and adorable toddler Sarah. She teaches English and drama part-time at a junior high, working week-on, week-off so she "can spend more time at home with the kidlet." She says that she truly enjoys working with young adolescents; she finds that they're still enthusiastic, especially about more creative endeavors, and she can't wait to show them the story and prove that there *is* a writing world outside the classroom! She currently has several students working on their own fantasy novels, so she feels that it's time for her to catch up!

This story was made possible by a husband who asked every day for a month, "How are you doing on that story?"

THE ornate door closed with a thud. A slight figure sagged against the carved surface, sighing quietly. She shook her head, then crossed the room to the huge oak bed, stepping out of her shoes and tugging the gold circlet from her bright auburn hair. One by one, jewels dropped to the dressertop—two rings, a necklace of sparkling stones, an ornate brooch of an unusual design and weight. She placed the headpiece on the nightstand—

—and froze, a scream caught in her throat, as a hand

shot out from under the bed and grabbed her ankle, pinning her foot to the floor.

"I'm disappointed, Highness," a low voice growled. A dark shadow rolled out from beneath the high bedframe, still trapping the slender leg. "Very disappointed."

"Caytin!" gasped the Queen, falling back on the goosedown comforter, one hand pressed to her throat. She drew in a deep, shuddering breath. "When are you going to stop? I don't think my nerves can take many more of your attacks."

Caytin glowered at Dylas, hands on her hips. "'My nerves can't take it,'" she mocked. "If you don't learn to react quickly, instead of turning to stone, it's not your nerves that will have the brunt of it." She sat on the edge of the bed, pulling off her work gloves with short, angry tugs. "Your left foot was still free. Back-kick your ankle into my wrist. Twist and grab hold of something solid. SCREAM, for stars' sake. Or, better yet, check under your bed when you come into the room. Always be aware of your surroundings."

Dylas sighed and began pulling pins from her elaborately styled hair. Thick red locks tumbled across her shoulders. "I know, I know. You're only doing this for my own good. But all the time? When do you even have time to work on your swordcraft? It seems like whenever I let down my guard just a little, you're there to rub my nose in it."

Caytin slapped her gloves against her roughened palm. "Not rub your nose in it," she said quietly. "I do it because I want you to be safe. Now, when you let down your guard, I'm there—to remind you, and to protect you. But what happens the time I'm not there, and someone else is?"

"Well, if you're not there to protect me, the truthseer is—or should be." Dylas gestured toward the dresser impatiently. "Nothing. Not a buzz, not a whimper. What good is a magic amulet if it doesn't warn me when I'm in danger?"

"True danger, Highness, not these tests I set for you. It knows I mean you no real harm. But this is just what I keep warning you about. You depend on others too much—other people and other things. 'Magic' will not always be there to protect you, and neither will I. You need to learn to stand on your own."

Dylas reached over and grabbed her hand. "I'm sorry. I am working on it, but you know how hard it is to break old habits. I've always felt safe here, just like I feel safe in your workshop."

"It's in that safety that you are most vulnerable."

"My goodness, Caytin, this is really bothering you," Dylas exclaimed. "Your hand is just trembling!"

Caytin pulled her hand from Dylas' grasp and tucked it in her lap. "Just cold, that's all," she said roughly.

"Well, if that's what the problem is, I have a beautiful soaking tub with your name on it. Go scrub that soot off and warm yourself up. There's a robe next to the tub; don't worry, I have plenty. I'll call for a late supper and have the fire stoked." She pushed her friend toward the bathing room. "Go on, take your time. It'll take me forever just to get out of these ridiculous court clothes. I'll be warm and cozy in my nightwear by the time you finish, and we can talk until moonset."

"Won't the court find this gossip-worthy? You know how much the ladies disapprove of our friendship."

"Let them gossip. I refuse to avoid you just to placate scandal-mongers. After all, we've been friends since birth—and I am the Queen, you know."

Caytin bowed low, glancing up with an ironic glint in her eye. "Whatever you decree, Highne . . ." Dylas lifted a shoe threateningly, and Caytin laughed. "I'd love to, heartsister."

*   *   *

The fire burned to embers. Caytin stared at the ceiling, listening to the soft steady breathing of the sleeping heir. Holding her hand out, she glared at the tremors that licked at the surface of her wrist. She squeezed her eyes shut, chanting silent prayers in her head. But no goddess answered. The trembling remained.

Caytin cursed, flinging her apron across the smithy. Her latest weapon hissed in the brine bath, slowly losing its glow. "Another wasted effort," she muttered, scrubbing at her eyes with shaking palms. She drew in a shuddering breath and sat on the stone bench.

"Knock, knock," sang out a familiar voice. Caytin crossed her arms quickly, tucking her hands away from view. Without waiting for an invitation, Dylas ducked through the entryway. Her bright hair hung in a thick braid down her back, reaching past her waist. She was dressed in riding clothes.

"Care to join me for a quick jaunt through the woods?" Dylas grabbed Caytin's elbow and pulled her to her feet, cutting off all protest. "Now, if I can slip away for a short ride, you can certainly spare the time. Don't make me issue a royal decree!" She led Caytin out of the smithy to the stables, where two horses waited patiently in the paddock.

"Only two?" Caytin said dryly. "What about Mirno?"

Dylas grinned. "Afternoon off. I told him you were all the guard I needed for this ride."

"Perhaps not the smartest choice, heartsister," Caytin replied, but the young queen had already turned away. The stablehand helped Dylas onto her saddle, then turned to give Caytin a foot up. She stared at him blandly, one eyebrow quirked, then grasped the pommel and swung herself into the saddle, grunting a little with the effort. "Thank you, Kalo," Dylas said to the stablehand, who bowed and backed away from the gate. The two women turned their mounts and trotted out of the paddock.

Once away from the palace grounds, they broke into an easy canter, heading toward the Royal Forest. The afternoon sun warmed the air around them and glittered off the surface of the lake. The rich scent of fresh-turned earth and ripe berries clung to the light breeze. Dylas turned her face to the bright sun, closing her eyes and drinking in the warmth and light. Twisting in the saddle, she called out, "Last to the Sacred Grove has to clean the stables!" She nudged her horse with her heel, holding tight to both mane and reins as she bent low over the horse's neck. Ignoring the protest behind her, she urged her mount faster and faster until they were galloping across fields turned golden by sunlight.

Once under cover of trees, she slowed to a trot. Sunlight dappled the forest grounds in leaf-broken patterns. Birds called in the canopy overhead. "Isn't this beautiful?" she called over her shoulder.

"Aye, innit?" a rough voice growled. Dylas jumped, startled at the unfamiliar voice. Turning slowly, she saw a hulk of a man, with wild hair and wilder eyes, leaning against the trunk of an evergreen tree. He was dressed haphazardly, in rags of every color and description. And he was not alone.

Caytin watched the fast-disappearing figure of the queen and cursed roundly, using every common phrase and several made up on the spot. Without strength in her hands, she could not possibly control her horse at that fast a pace. She looked at the forest, the only location not yet protected by her magic. Too many hiding places, too much darkness—danger lurked, and Dylas was headed straight toward it with a gleeful heart. Should she follow, or ride back to the castle grounds and seek help? With a longing glance toward the distant spires of the castle, she turned her horse to the trees and urged it faster, trying to diminish the distance between herself and the queen. Too late, she glimpsed a movement through the field in front of her. The horse reared up, pitching Caytin backward. She clutched at the reins, but they slipped through her fingers. Unable to catch herself, she fell with an agonizing thud.

"I trust you are aware that you are trespassing," Dylas said firmly. She sat straight in the saddle, digging her nails into the smooth leather to keep her hands from trembling. She hoped she sounded calmer than she felt. Caytin had been right behind her. She would ride up any minute, send these ruffians on their way without a thought, and the two would have a daring story to tell. Wouldn't they?

"Oi, trespassin', is we? Listen ter the fancy lady, gents!" He roared with laughter, followed a half-second later by the four men ranged in a semicircle behind him. He nudged the thin, narrow-eyed fellow to his left. "Drop to yer knees, Sorin! Pay 'omage to the rich lady 'oo trusts we knows we're trespassin'!" Laughing again, he strode to Dylas and grabbed the reins from her hands. "Mebbe the lady 'uld like to see just 'ow much trespassin' we 'appen to be doin'."

"She'd find it right proper, Fennis," agreed Sorin. The others nodded, glancing at each other out of the corners of their eyes.

Dylas opened her mouth to protest, then snapped it shut as the other men spread to both ends of the trail, effectively blocking her only means of escape. She pulled her cloak tighter, silently cursing herself for leaving the clasp at home. She didn't need her magic token, she'd thought. Caytin would be with her. She listened intently for horse's hooves on the forest floor, but the only sound she heard was the breathing of her captors and birdsong from a distance. Think, she raged silently. You're on your own now. What would Caytin do?

* * *

Caytin blinked. The sun was lower in the sky, spreading shadows across the field. Goddess only knew how long she had been unconscious. She lay on her back, rocks digging into her legs and neck. She turned her head and spat out dirt and blood. One leg, twisted painfully under her, warned that she wouldn't be going anywhere soon. She struggled to an upright position, ignoring the shafts of pain radiating from her shoulder. The horse, well-trained, stood quietly a short distance away. Whatever woodland creature had spooked it had not been enough to make it abandon its rider. A soft clucking brought it to Caytin's side. "Here," she muttered, tying a knot in the reins, "a riderless mount should bring somebody." Reaching up, she twisted the reins around the pommel of the saddle and slapped the horse on the rump. It leaped forward and began trotting toward home.

"Welcome to our 'umble abode," boomed Fennis, pushing aside a veil of branches and then releasing them as Dylas rode through. He roared with laughter as the branches slapped across her reddened face. She reached up to push them away, surreptitiously breaking off a few twigs. As soon as they had left the trail, Dylas had begun leaving small clues to follow out, if she ever escaped. Her captors, delighting in the humor of face-slapping trees, had failed to notice.

A pile of branches leaned against a large tree trunk. Fennis ducked inside and returned with a length of rope. "Bring 'er over 'ere, lads," he crowed. "Can't 'ave our first guest runnin' out on us." Dylas blanched at the sight, but gritted her teeth and straightened her shoulders. There was no time for weakness. All she had were her wits.

The tavern door opened with a crash. A handful of patrons looked up as the young man rushed through the doorway. He glanced around, then headed toward the man sitting in the far corner. "Mirno?" he asked breathlessly.

"Aye," the man growled. "Who are you, and what's your business?"

"Kalo," he gasped. "Stablehand. Queen and blacksmith went for a ride today. One horse returned. No rider. No queen."

Mirno pushed back from the table, a grim set to his jaw. "Show me," he barked, and followed the panicked stablehand outside.

Dylas pulled against the ropes around her wrists. It was no use. The knots were good; they would hold. She watched her captors in the fading light. Fennis had emptied her saddlebags and they were passing around the contents, cheering at the meager wealth. A handful of coins, dried fruit and nuts, some leather goods—Dylas thanked the goddess that nothing inside had tied her to the throne. Now, they merely thought she was a wealthy lady of the court. If her royalty became known, who knows what measures they would take to ensure their fortune?

Any escape would hinge on freeing her horse as well. Even with the element of surprise she knew there was no way she could run fast enough and far enough to outstrip her captors. She had one chance, and one chance alone. She would wait for her moment, and act.

Caytin bit back a scream. A rough hand was shaking her by the shoulder. "What happened? Where is she?" Caytin blinked the sleep from her eyes and tried to focus on the figure in front of her. A bright sunset blazed behind his head, obscuring his features. "It's Mirno," he said impatiently. "Where's the queen?"

"Forest," she said. "Too fast for me to follow, and then my horse spooked and threw me. Something must have happened—she should be back by now. Find her."

"How long ago?"

"Don't know. Hours."

Mirno mounted his horse and jerked a chin at the stablehand standing behind Caytin. "Kalo will take you back. The physician is waiting in the stables. I hope you are the only one who needs his services."

Caytin leaned heavily on the young man as he helped her limp to the waiting horse. *So do I,* she thought wearily. *So do I.*

Dylas smiled shyly at the thin, ragged boy who stood guard over her. The sparse hairs on his chin approximated a beard; the attempt at a manly look only underscored his youth. He was easily the youngest of the group. He smiled back, then narrowed his eyes and turned his head. The others were gathering wood for a fire and food for the meal; it would soon be full darkness. Dylas leaned forward. "Excuse me," she said.

The young man jumped, startled. "What you want?" he grunted.

"Well, um, this is embarrassing, but . . ." Dylas scuffed a shoe into the dirt. "I'd been riding most of the day when you found me, and, well . . ." She stopped, looking at the ground.

"What?" he said impatiently.

"Well, I had a full water flask before I left, and now it's empty, you see . . ." Dylas watched as a slow flush crept up his mottled face. "I'd rather not take care of it right here, in the middle of your—your home."

"Yes. Well. 'Ere you go." He hauled her to her feet. "Bushes right there."

"My hands? I need them to—"

"Right!" he cut her off abruptly. "Turn 'round." The boy pulled the knots loose and Dylas tugged her hands free, shaking them to get some feeling back. "Right there," he repeated, pointing at a stand of bushes on the edge of

the clearing. "Two minutes, tops. And no foolin' 'round."
Satisfied, he leaned against the tree and began picking at
his fingernails.

Dylas stepped quickly behind the bushes and glanced
around. Her horse was at the other side of the clearing,
reins tied inexpertly to a branch on a tree. Behind her was
the direction from which they had come, complete with
broken branches to signpost her path home. She sidled toward the edge of the clearing.

Snap! A twig beneath her foot cracked in two. The guard
whirled in her direction. "'Ere now!" he bellowed. "Just
where are you goin'?"

Voices raised in the distance as the others caught on to
the situation. Heavy footsteps crashed through the underbrush toward the clearing. Dylas raced to her captive horse,
slipped the bit and reins off its head, and pushed it to the
edge of the clearing. Suddenly, rough hands grabbed her
from behind.

"Yer ain't leavin'!" Dylas struggled in the boy's grasp.
The others would be back in just moments. She took a
deep breath, then raised her foot and slammed the heel
down on her captor's instep. Howling, he began jumping
up and down. Dylas wrenched one arm free and drove her
elbow into his chest, leaving him gasping for air. The distraction was enough. She pulled free and grabbed the pommel of the saddle, hauling herself onto the horse's back.
With a quick prayer to the goddess that her mount was
trained enough to follow directions without a bit, she urged
it out of the clearing and toward freedom.

The angry voices thinned out as she rode through the
forest as fast as she dared. Even in the dimming light her
broken branches stood out as beacons. When she could no
longer hear her captors behind her, she slowed. There was
no use in injuring her horse on unfamiliar ground.

Suddenly, voices filled the forest. She started, then relaxed as she realized they were calling her name. "Over here!" she yelled.

"Your Majesty!" Mirno urged his horse off the trail and into the thick underbrush. "Just a moment and we'll save you."

Dylas laughed as Mirno rode through the trees to her side. "You're a bit late," she chided.

"Late, your Majesty?" he said.

"I've already managed to save myself, thank you very much."

"Ah. I see. So what exactly happened, Your Majesty?"

Dylas sobered. "I was waylaid by five very unpleasant men. No," she said, holding up a hand, "I'm not injured. They wanted money, not a monarch. You'll find them back in that direction. Capture them, but do not harm them. Hold them under guard until tomorrow, then bring them to court. I'm sure it will be a shock for them to see who will decide their fate."

"Caytin!" Dylas rushed past the protesting physician to her friend's bedside. "Are you all right? What in the goddess' name happened?"

Caytin swallowed hard. "My horse threw me."

"You're the best horsewoman in this kingdom. What aren't you telling me?"

Caytin stretched out a hand. Even in the dim light of the sick room faint tremors were visible. "Remember when you asked why I didn't use my magic more often?" Dylas nodded. "This is why. It has pulled the strength from my hands. I couldn't hold the reins. They were useless. I'm useless."

"Don't say that."

"I couldn't even protect you. Every night, bespelling this land to guard you and keep you safe. I thought, if I couldn't be there, at least my protection would serve. But I failed you, and so did my protection."

Dylas took Caytin's shaking hand in hers. "Every night?" she murmured. Caytin nodded, fiercely biting back tears. "And this weakness—is it—permanent?"

"I don't know."

"Then time and rest will begin the cure, and we will work together to complete it." She kissed Caytin's hand and placed it back on the bedcovering. "You're wrong, you know. About failing me. You weren't there, it's true. But your protection was."

"No it wasn't. The forest was beyond my reach."

"Perhaps your magic didn't follow me into the forest, but your teachings did. I didn't turn to stone. I didn't wait to be saved. I depended on myself. No guard, no magic amulet, nothing but me. Thank you." Dylas smiled and brushed Caytin's bangs off her forehead. "Sleep well and peacefully, heartsister. You have given me more than you will ever know. I do have one favor to ask, however."

Caytin quirked an eyebrow and waited.

"I think I've passed this final exam with flying colors. So no more sneak attacks. Agreed?"

Caytin smiled and closed her eyes. "Agreed, heartsister. Agreed."

KENDAT'S AX
by Jan Combs

Before Jan started school, she kept her sister awake by making up stories aloud after bedtime. She didn't get around to writing her stories down until high school, where she wrote during the boring classes to keep herself awake. (I remember that trick, but I generally wrote letters instead.)

She has sold several short stories, the first of which was "An Equitable Division" published in *Marion Zimmer Bradley's Fantasy Magazine,* issue 23 (Spring 1994).

She has lived all over the United States, from border to border, coast to coast, moving "at the whim of my husband's employers." Now, when she is not writing, she is an aircraft design drafter and configuration control expert in Wichita, Kansas, where she lives with her husband and a herd of tame sesquipedalia that take every opportunity to get into her work, but are otherwise harmless.

WHEN Martine and I reached the Kendat gates in midafternoon, the massive oaken portals were shut. The two of us had shared the road for a few months, a juggler and a bard combining talents for common gain. Kendat sat at the crossroads that was a divergence in both our ways and our relationship.

Footprints and wheel ruts led around the western side of the ditch, which ringed the high stone walls built of the stout red sandstone of the region. I asked, "Does this lead to the postern gate?"

Martine shrugged her shoulders; I straightened my skirts and turned to follow the path. As we followed the side path, she took up the argument she had belabored for the past three leagues. I did not listen; I knew I would go north on the morrow. She had a firm engagement with a troupe of players in the south, but did not want to leave me to travel north alone.

A shepherd and his flock joined us at the postern gate. He knew why the main gates were shut and cheerfully shared the information. "Be the ogre comin' to destroy the town again—tonight, mebbe the night after."

"I definitely will be staying only the night," I told the gatekeeper, who carefully wrote this information into a ledger of legendary proportions. "Is professional entertainment frowned on here?"

"No, ma'am. We've several fine inns that hire traveling players from time to time."

Martine, who had been there before, asked, "Are they still using the Square of Kendat's Ax for market?"

The guard assured us that the market was where it had always been. The goatherd offered us no further help, but led his flock out of sight. Martine led us the other way down a well-paved street. We ambled past neat stone houses, some set back from the street behind small lawns or roofed in slate to distinguish them from their neighbors. The few richly dressed passersby rarely looked up from their own feet; most everyone else glanced at us with curiosity, nudging one another or covering their mouths to make comments as we passed.

Attaining the nearly empty market square, we walked between stock pens, past the farmers' stalls and merchants' booths, most of which were unattended or shuttered, to the center of the market area.

I sat on the curb that surrounded the central dais. Martine said, "Performers use the dais for their shows when the market judges aren't judging a case."

"Kendat's ax?" I gestured with my thumb at the enormous weapon standing on its haft on at ornate pedestal, the centerpiece of the dais. If the original Lord Kendat, the local hero of the nearly mythical Yimld Wars, had actually wielded this ax, he had been of ogrish ancestry.

"That's what they call it, although I doubt the venerable Lord Kendat ever saw the blasted thing. It plays merry hob with performances in the round and puts the wind in the wrong quarter for juggling eleven times out of a dozen, as well." Martine took this bit of natural history as a personal affront.

"Is there a fee for using the dais?"

"Wasn't when I was here last. The guard would have said, had things changed."

"Not necessarily. If you don't mind, I intend to draw a crowd." I was willing to chance a fine after all the backtracking because of the closed gates.

She gestured at the few people in the square. "Do your best. I think it will be a small one."

After weeks of traveling together, she still did not believe in my bardic powers—even as she used them to her own advantage. I brought my harp from its case and tightened the strings, tuning them as I went. The beautiful harp I had made to sojourn with was broken long ago in a bar fight; this one, although with scant ornamentation, held a fine, sweet tune.

I struck a chord and then a second. I began the tune of "Hamelin's Piper." The chorus first, and then the verse, I sang the story of the piper's revenge. I closed my eyes and watched the power glimmer behind my eyelids as it rose and spread. I felt it touching all who heard my song— touching, drawing. A half-dozen children had come to sit on the ground in front of my feet before the second chorus ended. Their elders stood back some, but they had come. The power spread beyond the sound of my harp. It drew those who felt the power without hearing the song, as sometimes happens, into the sound, and then into the square. I began another tune, continuing the pull until my audience had grown to a half-hundred people, then damped the power slowly. These people would tell their neighbors of our show. That would be as sure a pull for the morning performance as bardic power.

I felt Martine rise to join the entertainment. She started, as usual, with three wooden balls—red, yellow, and blue. I played a gentle accompaniment to her patter, using the power in the tune to hold back the wind as she sent the balls hurtling back and forth. Now Martine pulled hoops from her toy box and set them spinning on her arms as she juggled the balls. She juggled the hoops; she juggled balls and hoops. She added clubs to balls and hoops and juggled them all, all the time telling news from both far and near. As a finale, she had one of the youngsters at our feet throw hoops to her, putting each one into the cascade in turn. It is impossible to juggle more than a dozen hoops; Martine juggled two dozen, three, with my help. Martine accepted my help for this, as she accepted the wind shielding: she never mentioned it.

She threw the hoops as high as she could, one by one. As they came down, she bounced them off her forehead so that each one landed over her outstretched foot. She bowed to the audience and gestured toward me. I sang a short rousing tune and announced our next performance while Martine took our collection bag through the small crowd. I finished with an instrumental reprise of "Hamelin's Piper." We collected enough coins for supper and lodging.

"Just what did you have in mind to rid the town of Kendat of its ogre?" Martine asked as we followed our noses to the nearest sausage stall.

I smirked. I had not chosen my opening song for subtlety. As Martine had asked loudly enough to turn heads our way, I answered as loudly, "If the authorities want our help, they'll seek us out." I lowered my voice. "Truly Martine, I haven't a full plan, and what plan I have would depend a great deal on your personal courage. I wouldn't want to put your life on the line before discussing it with you."

"Tell me."

"I want you to teach the ogre to juggle."

Martine stood dead still to stare at me. "That's going to kill an ogre?"

"Learning to juggle nearly killed me."

She began to grin. She had taught me to juggle a bit, enough to produce a three ball cascade, but the skill was hard won. Martine delighted in teasing me about the learning experience.

While weighing the quality of the available inns against the contents of our purse, we ran across a delegation of the authorities who had heard our offer to rid the town of its bane. The largest, a woman dressed in severe black in vain hope that the color would reduce her size, spoke for them. "We have prayed to Lord Kendat for deliverance from the ogre that would destroy us."

Martine allowed me to speak for both of us. "I know little of your Lord Kendat." Of course, I knew the legends, but the council woman's reverent statement made hero into saint. "We might be able to perform such a service for you—for a price."

"If you rid us of the ogre, you may stay free at my inn for a week, nay, a month."

"What good would that do us? We are travelers; we have no wish to wear out our welcome before we have earned enough to travel to the next town." By the look in her eyes, I knew she had taken this as an insult.

Unfortunately for this discussion, my words were unvarnished truth. Had I wanted to stay in Kendat, I would have found a way to do so before entering the gate. I had never asked Martine her feelings on the subject, but if she differed with me, she could speak for herself.

"Oh, indeed. You would not even stay one night at my inn, the most luxurious in town?"

"Although your rooms must surely hold unparalleled comfort, madam, we need a place to rest while we discuss our strategy, for which we intend to pay good coin. After the ogre is dead is time enough to reap our reward."

At this the innkeeper offered goods in exchange for our services. I turned down a year's supply of cheese and ale; I fended away other offers of perishable goods. I refused an offer of stoutly woven linen and woolen cloth; we had no means to carry such goods, nor any inclination to turn merchant-adventurer. Finally the burghers offered us gold. After viewing the gold at the moneylender's office, Martine and I agreed to a price for the task.

I said, "You must provide light for us before the main gates."

The spokesburgher said, "The ogre can see in the dark. Lights only annoy it."

"The poor, wee thing will just have to be annoyed. Without light, we won't be able to see what we are doing. While I can play my harp anytime, Mistress Martine doesn't fare so well in the dark. Besides, everyone in town will turn out to see the show. There's an opportunity for vendors of food and drink."

"We can certainly provide torches in that case." Her eyes glittered as she exchanged glances with the other townspeople. "Many would like to see the end of the beast that haunts our nights."

Martine grabbed my arm. "What are you thinking? If people watch the show and we are unsuccessful, they will be in as grave a danger as ourselves. Would the profit from a few pasties and tankards of ale make up for injuries and death? This will not be an entertainment—and especially not for small children."

"If the people want to watch, they'll do it from the top of the wall. I know you would never agree to have them any closer to the performance area." The burghers agreed to this compromise readily. Martine merely shook her head wearily.

"We will need the use of Kendat's ax," I told the towns-people. After much outraged huffing and puffing and promise of retribution to follow desecration of their holy relic, the burghers agreed to our terms.

We arranged lodging at an inn near the main gates where we could work out the soon-to-be fatal act in a secluded kitchen garden behind the stables. As I explained exactly how we would rid Kendat of the ogre, Martine listened carefully. She pulled out her clubs and juggled them as she thought the situation through.

"I can do that. One thing bothers me, though. Why should we allow the people to watch? Do they not understand that if anything goes wrong, the ogre will bash in their gates as soon as it has dealt with us? Have they looked at the places near the gate where the stone is weakened from the ogre's previous forays? Shouldn't we at least discourage the young children?"

Martine and I had argued over censorship before, and agreed to disagree on the subject.

"No. Do you remember telling me of your mother's lingering death when you were young? You knew that your father and sibs gave her every comfort as she lay dying. Yet you, the youngest, did not leave her side until the end. How would you have felt if they had kept you away from her? We will allow any of the townspeople to watch, because even the small children have a right to see the ogre's end."

She threw her clubs into the air again, but they made only two circuits before she agreed to her part in killing the ogre—a few more circuits occurred before she agreed to allow the audience.

Before sundown, the burghers had Kendat's ax leaning against the wall to one side of the gates; a few sacks of malt and some iron wagon tires sat beside them. Torches lined the top of the curtain wall and a space as large as the entry square directly outside the gates, which were closed once more. Martine and I sat on the opposite side of the road from the ax sharing an open air supper of meat pasties and small beer.

The townspeople ranged themselves along the top of the wall. The wealthy innkeeper and her family stood directly over the gates, the other worthies of the town to either side. They were held, not by the weight of humdrum in their day-to-day lives, but the too real drama of life or destruction to be enacted this evening.

The ogre came shortly after sundown. He was not as tall as a mountain—as the potboys at the inn claimed—but he was half again the height of the tallest man I had ever seen. To enter Kendat by the gate he would need to bend at his waist. He wore untanned hides as a loin cloth. His hair and beard were long and tangled. If he had ever bathed, it had been an act of one of the more merciful gods.

I played "Old Bangem," brought up the wind shielding, and prayed for strength. I also separated a few strands of the power, wove them into a net of curiosity, and threw it over the ogre. The ogre stopped to discover what we were about, his hands at his sides. I breathed a bit more easily, but continued to play.

Martine began her exhibition. Her toys cascaded into the air with her cheerful words. The people watching from the wall applauded. Although only a few had seen the show before, Martine varied the feats that she performed. She passed along the news of the surrounding countryside as she juggled.

"Now," Martine said, "I'll need a volunteer for my next

feat. You, sir, step over here." She waggled her clubs invitingly at the ogre, who looked startled and apprehensive. His mouth flattened suspiciously, which did nothing to hide the hand-length tusks that jutted from his lower jaw, pointing toward his puffy eyes.

Martine nodded at him encouragingly and handed him a stack of hoops. "Take these, sir. I see you've a bit of muscle on you. What I want you to do . . ."

I did not listen to the patter. I raised the shielding as high as I could so the hoops would fly high and true. The ogre, puzzled, tossed the hoops one at a time to Martine, who sent them into the air again. The hoops reached their apogee and came down again, swinging up again at the juggler's touch.

The ogre, finished with his part of the act, leaned upon his club, his attention on the show. I stood, but continued to play as Martine bounced the hoops from her forehead to her foot. I approached the ogre.

"You know, you did that very well. Martine has taught me to toss two weights from hand to hand. She says she won't teach me anymore, that I'm cack-handed. I wager you would do much better."

The ogre flicked a quick look in my direction, but made no comment. Martine had put the hoops down in favor of a scimitar, a blown glass globe, and a rag doll. The mismatched items went into the air as easy as could be. At the end of the cascade she bounced each item off her forehead into her hands and placed them into her toy box. The scimitar came down last, the most delicate part of the act for me, as the blade had to bounce flat rather than edge on. Martine bowed to the applause and picked up the money that the townspeople threw from the walls. I handed her a square of linen to wipe her brow.

"You're in fine form this evening, Mistress Martine. My friend here thinks he would like to learn your trade."

The ogre drew his head back, startled that I would say

such a thing in spite of my earlier flattery. I gushed, "No. Don't be shy. I saw the way you watched. You know, you might want to try some of the simpler things right now. Martine, show him how to do the first cascade. I just know you'll have him doing it in a minute."

Martine grinned as though we entertained a village child rather than a being that might have stepped from a nightmare. She looked at the ogre closely, then nodded. "He couldn't use my hoops and clubs. I noticed that his hands are much too large when he handled my hoops just now. Oh, but he could start with these malt sacks. They are ideal for a beginner anyway as they won't roll away if dropped."

The ogre accepted the malt sacks; bewilderment showing in his small, dark eyes. Yet, he watched Martine very carefully, and I enhanced the ogre's coordination until he tossed the bags of malt in a simple cascade for several minutes. Martine praised him highly.

I added my acclaim to my friend's. "You know, you're quite good at that for a beginner. Much better than myself, for instance. You could learn a few more feats and join us on the road. It is a great life to lead—always new things to see."

The ogre looked up at the silent townspeople. "No. I am ogre. I do not play such games."

I have never held with those who claim that all sentient beings have souls. However, the priests argue that, as ogres are of human stock, they must have souls and the basic wherewithal to understand right from wrong. I thought perhaps the town's problem with the ogre could be based on a misunderstanding. If he thought the townspeople were playing games with him, not dealing honestly, perhaps I might forge a compromise before someone got hurt. I said, "Someone told me that an ogre wanted to destroy this town."

"That be me."

"Why would you want to destroy this town? Did someone hurt you here?"

"No. Just like to tear rocks down and take what I want."

"If the townspeople gave you what you wanted would you be willing to leave the town and the people be?"

"No. They would not give me what I want. Asked them before, I did. I like the taste of man-brain."

The shock of his words hit me as though he had put his fist into my stomach; I had to look away for a moment. When I could look at our opponent again, he grinned at me, showing all his yellowed teeth.

"Sorry you feel that way, old chum," Martine said. "Here let me show you hoops. We can use these tires."

She soon had the ogre bouncing the iron rings from head to foot. I took up my tune again to enhance the ogre's juggling skills. To this day, I cannot tell you how I managed to breathe at the same time. The lesson continued with Martine alternately praising and cajoling until the moment came to try the mixed cascade. A malt sack, an iron hoop, and Kendat's ax each went into the air. Martine's voice soothed and suggested as the disparate items circled from hand to air and back.

"Steady. Now, starting with the malt sack, throw each item up as high as you can and bounce them on your forehead onto the ground at your feet as you did with your last cascade. Ready, now."

The malt sack went up, then the club. My power pushed the club past the malt sack, and the ax beyond that. Martine continued her soothing drone. I looked to the walls. The townspeople stood, enthralled.

I wished I could spare even a bit of power to manipulate the crowd, to send them all away for Martine's sake, but the ax had reached the limit of its flight and was descending. I had to ensure that it would not turn in its path.

When the task was complete, the gates crashed open. The townspeople carried Martine and me on their shoulders to the market dais to watch as they replaced Kendat's ax. Several people asked when they might hear the lay of how Kendat had protected his people again. I used that as an excuse to seek my solitude.

Martine followed me to the suite that overlooked the stable much later. She dropped the sack holding our reward on the desk where I was writing and set a mug of ale within my reach. "Have you made us heroes yet, my lady?"

"I'm sorry, Martine. Did you want to be a hero?"

"No." She grinned. "Heroes are expected to pay for the drinks. Who is the hero, if I am not?"

"Lord Kendat, who heard the prayers of his people and guided two anonymous strangers to be his hands."

"Ah, then, he can buy the next round of ale. I've already bought a round for each of us. May I hear your tune?"

I sang the whole tale from start to finish: a goodly lay, well crafted and suitably balanced. Martine applauded.

She cocked her head to look at me from a different perspective. "You're still welcome to come with me. I haven't taught you the cascade of four. Besides which, I hate the thought of dealing with the wind without you. Still no? I suppose you'll sing your new tale all through the north before summer's end."

"I wrote it out to take with you for any musicians you might meet in your travels." I had never objected to her coming along with me, but I was just as happy that she had apparently decided not to press her arguments about going south.

She nodded and stood to rummage in her toy box, settling things into their places for traveling. "The road being what it is, perhaps we'll meet again. But not, I think, in Kendat. Perhaps you'll help me with flaming torches then."

"You can't hold the outcome of this evening against the whole town, Martine. If you meet me here in Kendat

next autumn, I'll help you with your torches, Mind, I want
to head west then."

"All right, in Kendat, second full moon of autumn, then
west." She took out four hand-sized sand bags, made a
cascade, then tossed them to me one at a time. I caught
the bags and put them into a cascade as easily as Martine
ever had, but they faltered after a few passes. My mind
had already turned toward the north and the morrow.

THE TOWER OF SONG
by Howard Holman

Howard Holman was born and raised in Northern California and has lived in the small town of Durham since the age of three. He first knew he wanted to be a writer when he met authors of children's books who visited his school when he was in the second grade, and this desire was later reinforced by frequent journeys to the lands of Oz and Narnia.

In 1998, Howard earned his Master of Arts degree in English from California State University, Chico, to accompany his Secondary Teaching Credential in English and Technical Writing Certificate. He is working on two novels, one fantasy and the other science fiction.

EVEN though an autumn chill lingered in the mist-shrouded half-light of the forest, the crowd remained warm, huddled next to the Tower of Song. It was magic which radiated from the Tower's stormy walls, magic as old as memory in a land that survived on magic. The structure itself was tall but still dwarfed by the giant redwoods that surrounded it, its foundation embedded deep into the ground as if it was made of tree roots. Its stones had been molded by the magic of the long forgotten Great Ones, each piece placed carefully to insure its longevity. The only openings were a large wooden door at the base, which could be entered by any Challenger, and a balcony above them which only opened in the presence of a Royal Bard.

And that was the problem. It had been over a century since the last Royal Bard died, yet no bard had entered and survived the Tower of Song. With no Royal Bard, the magic and legends were being forgotten, lost behind the Tower's walls, and the Darkness with its Dark Things was engulfing them.

No one knew what the Tower measured or how to pass its test. They only knew those who didn't pass were never seen again. Hundreds had tried and failed, lost in some disaster devised by the Great Ones which most felt was slow and painful. Some thought the ground would open up and suck the aspiring bards in. Others believed the magic turned the Challengers into part of the stone Tower itself. Still others felt a dragon or even fiercer monster was pulled from another dimension to devour them. Whatever happened, it had happened to every bard who had failed.

The Tower of Song was the source from which all magic was replenished, yet no one knew how to use it, and the once vast and endless supply of magic was dwindling.

Fananon the Musical, generally considered the most talented bard in the Land, had entered the Tower the previous morning. He had arrived at sunrise, golden clothes sparkling in the red-yellow light as the sun attempted to penetrate the ever-swirling mist. Swung over his left shoulder and carefully protected by a leather case was his Stradivar harp, made by the elven harpsmith of the same name from a single branch, nearly matching the legendary Angel Harp of the Royal Bard. A look of supreme confidence shone from his long face, and he stared at the Tower with calm anticipation.

The bard was followed by a large crowd, and the buzzing talk was interspersed with cheers. Finally, finally a bard would escape the Tower of Song, bringing with him the secret to the magic, helping the king restore the Land.

Fananon stopped before the large wooden door at the Tower's base, and the crowd which had grown to almost five hundred cheered, chanting his name. The bard held up his hand, and soon everyone was quiet. Taking the Stradivar case from his shoulder, he lowered it to the ground and lovingly removed the instrument from its leather covering. With a few soft words, the small images of a man surrounded by a crowd appeared above him, illusionary actors in the musical tale he was about to sing. Soon the bard's audience recognized the man as Fananon himself, and then some pointed and laughed as they saw themselves surrounding the illusion of the bard. Pulling the harp to his chest and placing his fingers on the strings, Fananon began to play immediately, the Stradivar never needing to be tuned.

> *This tale begins with a man who goes out,*
> *To fight against Darkness, his mind free of doubt,*
> *To the Tower he'll go and challenge the test,*
> *Of course he will pass, for he is the best.*

And so the song continued, and the crowd was entranced by his flashing clothes and elven harp and the illusion which acted out the story in the air. When he finished, there was a silence as the illusion faded, and then the crowd erupted into applause. Fananon was indeed the best bard ever.

Finally, finally a bard would escape the Tower of Song, bringing with him the secret to the magic, helping the king restore the Land.

And so he had disappeared into the Tower almost an entire day before, the door closing and locking behind him. He had not yet returned.

As the sun began to shine faintly through the melting mists, the Tower started to glow a dark blue. There was a clanking like a castle gate being raised, and when the clanking stopped, the Tower's bottom door unlocked with a click.

The crowd kept their tired eyes on the balcony thirty feet above, where they expected Fananon to arrive triumphantly as the first Royal Bard in over one hundred years. But there was nothing, only the dripping of condensation on the leaves and trees.

Fananon, the greatest bard in the Land, had challenged the Tower of Song.

And failed.

The crowd had melted away, grief and despair washing over their silent faces. The hope which had filled them and sustained them through the night flickered and vanished. It was all over. There was nothing left which could stop the Darkness from soon overrunning the Land.

There remained before the Tower one young woman of about sixteen years. She wore a simple brown tunic and leather breeches and held nothing either in her hands or in her pockets. She just stood there, unaware of the climbing sun or the slightly diminishing mists. She stood there looking at the Tower, contemplating its meaning and what might lie within. Finally, with a sigh of resolve, she reached over to the door and turned the handle.

"What are you doing there, lassie?" a gruff voice called out. Startled, the girl released the door handle and turned to discover the voice's owner. She was met by an old man in bright green robes leaning heavily on a long oak staff. And around his neck she thought she saw a silver necklace which burrowed beneath the front of his clothes. The stranger's wrinkled face was filled with a large smile, and his blue eyes twinkled.

There was something about him that almost set the girl at ease.

Almost.

Not getting a response, the man spoke again. "You aren't thinking of going in there, are you?"

The girl glanced at the ground nervously. "I . . . I was just trying to figure out a way to help, that's all. The way people talked, this is our only hope."

"It is," said the old man matter-of-factly.

"How are you so sure?"

"Only the Tower's magic can stop the Darkness, and only a Royal Bard can bring the magic from the Tower. It's that simple."

"Oh," said the youth.

"What's your name, child?"

"Erin, sir. I'm the youngest child of Galadrin. He's gone off with the army to fight the Dark Things. So have my two brothers. I wanted to go with them, but my father wouldn't let me. He said I'd get in the way."

"And that's the reason you've come to the Tower?"

"Well, kind of. You see, my grandmother—she used to be a bard—she's been training me to enter the bards' guild for several years now, and she insists it's important to have bards on the battlefield. They can entertain and encourage the troops. They can record what happens so that it will be remembered and learned from. But when I asked to go with him, my father said bards are useless, like he always does, and wouldn't let me come. I wanted to show him he was wrong, that bards are important."

"Hmm," said the green-robed man, studying the girl. "I agree with you. Barding is indeed an admirable profession, especially for the reasons your grandmother gave. But more importantly, it takes a bard to pass the test. I noticed you were about to take the test yourself. Tell me, what makes you think you could survive the Tower of Song?"

"Well, I've had singing lessons, mainly from my grandmother, and most think I'm pretty good. I can carry a tune, and I thought maybe I could really help. I guess I'm just tired of staying on our farm, needing protection like my mother and sister. I have to do something."

"The Tower of Song is no place for independence-seeking children, lassie," said the old man. "You don't just get a slap on the hand if you fail."

"I know."

"Besides, no one even knows what the Tower's test measures. What makes you think you could pass?"

"Well, if a bard must take the test," said Erin, "I assume it measures the bard's abilities to sing or make illusions or play a musical instrument."

"Do you have an instrument?"

"No, just my voice."

"Your current wardrobe does not evoke any special emotions. Any outlandish costumes?"

"No."

"Can you do illusions?"

"A few simple ones, but nothing spectacular."

The old man shook his head. "Well, if you can't do any of those things, what makes you think you have a chance of passing the test?"

"Well," hesitated Erin, "I've thought about that, and I've been thinking that Fananon could do those things better than anyone in the Land, yet it didn't help him. Maybe the Tower needs someone who has a lot to learn, a lot of potential, someone to be trained as the Great Ones wish her to be trained."

"Or maybe Fananon just wasn't good enough," added the old man.

"Still, I think I can manage," she answered defensively.

"Think? Lassie, there have been two hundred twenty-six before you who thought they could pass! They aren't here anymore!" Erin's brown eyes widened as the old man's voice grew unexpectedly louder. But he quickly realized he was scaring her and paused a second to regain his composure. "Please," the old man continued in a much calmer but no less urgent voice, "don't waste your life on a doomed endeavor."

The young woman looked up the Tower wall to the balcony. She could hear her father's protective tone in the old man's request. "Defending the Land is not the job of a little girl," her father had said. What she wouldn't give to be up there with the crowd cheering as she brought back the magic to the dying Land. What she wouldn't give to see the look on her father's face as he realized his daughter could do more to stop the Dark Things than his two sons or himself. Despite the old man's warning, she wanted to take the risk.

"Tell me, sir, what will happen if no one passes the test?"

The old man hesitated a moment before answering. "We will be destroyed, of course, eventually. But does that mean you should waste your life? Maybe you could practice and then come back when you're older, more experienced."

"Better now than waiting for the Darkness."

The old man thought about Erin's last statement and eventually nodded his head in sad agreement. "It's your choice, of course, but don't make it because you 'think.' Believe completely in yourself or forget it. There'll be no room for second-guessing inside."

"How do you know?" asked Erin. "How do you know so much about the test and the Tower, anyway? Who are you?"

The old man studied her face for a moment, and Erin thought for a second she saw a hopeful expression, but then he shook his head, turned around, and began walking away. "I'm nobody to concern yourself with, lassie," he muttered, "nobody at all."

The old man hobbled stiffly, leaning awkwardly on his staff until he disappeared around the Tower. Erin suddenly felt like he had something important for her to know, something crucial he wasn't telling her, and she ran after him, circling around the structure until she came back to the door.

The old man, whoever he was, was gone.

Erin looked again at the Challenger's entrance before her. In her mind, the old man's warnings lingered for a few moments, but they were quickly drowned by the remembered cheers of the crowd who had applauded Fananon yesterday morning. But this time the cheers were for her.

I need to do something to prove to myself that I'm more than just another helpless victim of Fate, she thought, more than the helpless girl my family sees. For the first time in my life I want to make a decision for myself. I want to give a reason for my grandmother's belief in me.

Before she could change her mind, she opened the door and went in, letting the door close behind her.

It locked with an echoing click.

The silence in the Tower of Song was complete. No sounds permeated the gray walls of the structure as the click of the locking mechanism faded to nothingness, trapping Erin within. As the door closed, the last flicker of light was also extinguished, washing the room in darkness. Stale air filled the Tower along with a smell of burning metal she could not place.

A dark cloud of doubt began to creep across Erin's mind. This was nothing like she expected from the greatest source of magic in the Land. Something was wrong. Maybe the ancient tales hadn't been true. Maybe the Tower of Song was just an evil icon hidden behind a tale of glory.

She had to get out of there.

Erin turned and grabbed for the door handle but was surprised to find her hands on the warm stone wall. Frantically she searched along the wall, fingers moving blindly across the surface. But it was no use. She couldn't find the door. Turning away from the wall, she leaned back against it and forced herself to relax. The room felt empty and huge in the complete absence of light, but at the same time the darkness seemed to be suffocating her. She told herself to remain calm. There had to be a way out.

As Erin peered into the darkness, a small blue glow appeared in the center of the Tower floor, sudden and bright and penetrating. It grew quickly, rays of light reaching outward from an ever-increasing source. Erin held her hand up to shield her eyes from the brilliance.

As the blue, orb-shaped glow grew it began to take form, first legs and torso, then shoulders, arms, head. Finally the reaching lights retreated into the being which continued to radiate, its form nebulous and flickering at the edges.

Erin cried out in surprise. "It's you!"

It was the old man from outside the Tower, this time dexterously holding his staff in his left hand.

The old man smiled. "Greetings, friend Erin. You have entered the Tower of Song and by doing so agreed to accept its Challenge. I am the spirit of Trillo, last of the Royal Bards, and it is my duty to administer the test until a suitable replacement is found."

Erin's mind grasped about wildly as she tried to comprehend what she was seeing. Trillo had died over a century before, so what was he doing in the Tower? Or for that matter, why had he been outside it? Then she noticed that his necklace was hanging outside his robe. On the end was a large, glowing, silver key. She wondered what it opened . . . or locked.

Trillo continued. "The Royal Bard is the one person in all the Land who can unite the people against the evils that threaten us, so the position cannot be filled by just anyone. As the Guardian of the Magic and the Keeper of the Tower's Legend, he, or she, must be pure of heart and pure of motive. It must be determined that she can faithfully and fairly use the Tower's magic, and that she will never use it for any purpose which the Great Ones did not intend. This test will determine if you can meet these requirements, and whether or not you will be my successor as Royal Bard."

The doubt Erin had forced from her thoughts outside the Tower flooded into her mind as if a dam had burst. The full weight of what she had undertaken crushed her like a falling boulder, forcing her down the wall, and she landed in a heap on the floor.

"Second-guessing yourself?" the old man asked, a look of sadness on his glowing face. "Even though I'm not supposed to, I tried to stop you, but you chose not to listen. Your only options now are to pass the test or die."

Trillo then extended his arms upward, and balls of blue flame shot from his out-turned palms. The two globes of light began twirling around each other as they made their way to the top of the Tower. Erin followed them with her eyes as they finally reached the top, melting into the ceiling well over one hundred feet above her. There was a cranking noise, like a chain moving across a gear, and a screeching sound.

And then the ceiling slowly began to drop.

Erin's eyes flashed down to the image of Trillo as she realized what was happening. She was going to be crushed.

Trillo's face took on a placid look of indifference. "You must use your bard abilities to stop the ceiling from falling. If you have not been crushed by tomorrow at this time, you will become the Royal Bard."

"And if I can't figure out how to stop it?"

"Then I will wait for the next person who comes to take the test." Before Erin could say anything more, Trillo quickly faded to a single point and then went out, leaving Erin once again in darkness, only the sound of the clanking chains far above assuring her she was not dreaming.

Erin suddenly began to hyperventilate, and she had to force herself to calm down. Trillo had warned her before she had entered that she had to believe in herself, and she did. Besides, there was no choice in the matter. She either figured out the test or died. And she would never forgive herself for failing because she didn't try.

After a few minutes of her eyes adjusting to the darkness, it occurred to her that she could see the ceiling as it inched down the walls. The ceiling and walls were glowing faintly now, an odd bluish-white light that seemed bright but didn't provide much illumination. She decided to go around the wall once more in the faint light with the hope of finding the door she entered. Standing up and leaving a shoe as a marker, she carefully felt every stone along the edge of the room, hoping to come across a hidden latch or to dispel an illusionary portion of the wall. But there was nothing. She put her shoe back on and sat down to think.

The idea there might not be a test, the Tower only a well-constructed trap shrouded in ancient legends, suddenly crushed Erin's mind. But she quickly shut her thoughts to that possibility. There had to be a way to escape, she told herself. She had to assume the test to be true. And if it were a true test, there had to be a way to pass it.

Her first thought was to use magic. The entire Tower, from its glowing walls to disappearing doors, was the very heart of the Land's magic, the well from which all magic was drawn. It was therefore logical to think magic could solve its test. Considering this idea, she stood up and went to the center of the Tower floor where the ghost of Trillo had vanished.

Erin was no Fananon whose illusions took on a life of their own. Her illusions were simple, black and gray and white versions which did not really help her storytelling. But they were the only magic she had.

Concentrating, Erin waved her fingers nervously above her head. Soon a new light appeared, dull and gray, and it began to take the form of a large hand. It had no details like wrinkles or even fingernails and took on more of the appearance of a glove stuffed with cotton, but Erin was pleased. With beads of sweat beginning to roll down her forehead, she took one hand and thrust it up as high as she could reach. The illusion also began to rise, floating up toward the descending ceiling. In a few minutes the two met, Erin praying it would halt the blocks of stone. As they touched, the ceiling began to glow brightly, almost blindingly, and the hand was absorbed instantly into it, zigzagged arcs of blue fire rippling outward like a hand plunged into a still pond.

The abrupt disappearance of her illusion, like a strong wind that suddenly stops, caused Erin to tumble to the floor where she lay facedown and exhausted. Had she stopped it? Slowed it? She turned over onto her back and looked up. The ceiling was brighter and bigger.

And moving faster.

An image of Fananon using his magic on the ceiling entered her head. If her own weak illusions caused the ceiling to drop a little faster, what had Fananon's illusions done? The best bard in the land may have been dead in the first ten minutes. Erin shuddered at the thought as she lay on the stone floor. She knew she had to keep thinking about how to get out of the Tower, that she was slowly running out of time, but after the intense exertion of casting the illusion, a wave of exhaustion began to wash over her. She knew she would never pass the test if she couldn't concentrate, so she decided it was okay to shut her eyes and rest, but just for a moment or two.

Erin next remembered waking suddenly, several beads of salty perspiration dropping heavily across her lips. She did not know how long she had been in the Tower. The warm walls which had comforted her as she waited outside the previous night for Fananon now made her hot and uncomfortable. She looked up at the circular, glowing ceiling as it continued to descend. It was well over halfway down now, she decided, and she again felt like the walls and ceiling and floor were suffocating her.

Sitting up, Erin soon caught her breath, and then she forced herself to think again about her predicament. Well, it wasn't the illusionary magic which allowed a bard to pass the test. She wondered if it was the music of a special instrument which halted the ceiling. She doubted it, though. Trillo had mentioned hundreds had challenged the test, and she was sure that almost every instrument would have been used.

Erin shook her head. If hundreds of the most talented bards in the Land had failed, how did she ever think she was going to survive? Anyway, whether the key to the test was a musical instrument or not didn't matter because she didn't have one, so she would have to find another answer.

Unless the instrument needed was a voice.

But it couldn't be that easy, Erin thought. You couldn't just sing and expect to pass. Obviously what she sang about had to be old and important. She searched her memory for the oldest story she could remember, thinking perhaps one of the ancient songs was the answer. Most of the old stories weren't really known by anyone anymore, but she did recall one particular story scrawled in the back of one of her grandmother's books. Rising to her feet and remembering the best she could, Erin cleared her throat, steadied herself, and began to sing.

Ralon the Brave, he set out one day,
To capture the beast that had started the plague.
He rode across rivers and mountains and hills
With only his horse and a very strong will.

As she sang, the words did not seem to go with the tune she remembered, but she continued to sing the most difficult music her vocal cords could handle. After a few minutes she looked up expectantly only to find the ceiling growing even brighter.

And slowing down!

Excited, Erin began to sing faster and faster, increasing the range and jumping between octaves. Could it be this easy? Was it just a matter of singing fast, going from treble to bass and back again? Was this the only requirement of a Royal Bard? Erin smiled to herself. She didn't know how, but she had figured out the test. It was only a matter of waiting . . .

And then something awful happened.

Her voice cracked.

Even the best trained bards could not sing for very long, especially at the rate and range Erin was having to use to slow down the ceiling. That was why they carried instruments and performed illusions, so their voices didn't have to do all the work. Erin had not had the money or years to complete her training, so even though she was good for her age, she was not nearly perfect.

At the crack of her voice, the note wavered and the ceiling screeched to a stop. Erin didn't move or breathe. Had it stopped for good? She remained perfectly still, fearing the slightest motion might start the ceiling's drop again. She thought if she could just stand there unmoving she would survive. She would have a chance. She would pass the test.

But just when she thought she was all right, the chains hidden within the walls began to clank and the ceiling dropped again.

It was moving faster than ever. Her singing had only delayed the inevitable.

Tears filled Erin's eyes as she collapsed on the ground in disgust. She felt so tired in the Tower's sweltering heat.

Curse that ceiling! This wasn't a test, it was a torture chamber! In a sudden, frenzied mixture of exhaustion, fear, and anger, she removed her shoes and threw them, one after the other, at the glowing, blue-white ceiling.

Before she could even think of ducking as they fell back, the shoes disappeared into the ceiling, small lightning bolts of blue flame again rippling outward, as they had done when she had used her illusionary hand. But these shoes were no illusions, and a sickening fizzle accompanied their disappearance followed by a small puff of acrid smoke.

It smelled like burning metal.

Erin just sat there in disbelief. So this was what happened. She remembered that acrid smell from when she first entered the Tower, and the clanking sounds just before it. At some point the ceiling had come down on Fananon, erasing him from the world. Then the ceiling had slowly been raised and made ready for the next Challenger.

For her.

Erin crawled over to the wall and slumped back against it. She had tried everything. It wasn't magic or the story she told. Possibly her voice could have stopped it, but she didn't know anyone who could have kept singing like that for almost an entire day. Erin wondered how long she had been in the Tower. It might have been one hour or ten, but it didn't matter anymore.

As acceptance of her failure sank in, Erin stopped following the ceiling as it continued its descent, its glowing surface slowly closing in. Instead her thoughts wandered beyond the confines of the Tower and back into her past. The voice she heard was clear and warm and loving. It was her grandmother's. Her grandmother used to sing her to sleep when she was young, and when Erin was old enough, she had memorized her grandmother's songs so that she could sing along. Erin smiled as she remembered

the first one she had learned, and unconsciously she began
to sing.

When I sleep and close my eyes,
Someone always is close by.
When everything is cold and dark,
My family will be in my heart.

She continued to sing it over and over. There were only
two stanzas, and the music was simple and soft; she sang
without thinking.

Slowly, ever so slowly, she drifted into unconsciousness.

"Erin? Erin?"

The cobwebs slowly began to break free as Erin awakened. She felt as if she had just slept through a fever, her
cheeks and forehead incredibly warm. As she rubbed her
eyes, she looked around apprehensively. She appeared to
be in the Tower still, but the room was now lit brightly
with soft candlelight, and everything else had changed as
well.

Everything.

Where once the gray stones stood bare, there were now
rows upon rows of shelves filled with bound books. Tables were placed around the room, each covered with flickering candles, quills, bottles of ink, and stacks of vellum.
The door she had entered was once more against the wall,
and a stairway she didn't remember spiraled upward,
twirling into the ceiling in the center of the circular room.
And in the middle of everything, a large armchair was
placed, covered with a soft crimson material.

And in it sat Trillo with fingers tapping and eyes smiling, this time in solid form.

"Well, lassie," the man began, his face void of the magic
blue that Erin had remembered, his robes once more an

emerald green. "Are you going to just lie there on the floor
or are you going to get started? You have so much to
learn!" The old man leaped up from the chair with unexpected energy, the staff he had leaned on when Erin first
met him nowhere to be seen.

Trillo quickly helped Erin to her feet. "I'm so pleased
for you, so pleased!" He helped her over to the crimson
chair which she gently fell into. It was soft, such a nice
change from the stone floor.

Trillo's large smile quickly put Erin at ease. "Of
course," the old man continued, "we'll have to get you a
green robe, and some new shoes by the looks of it, but
that will have to wait. Now . . ." Trillo was about to say
something and then paused, as if it was right on the tip
of his tongue but he couldn't get it out. "What was I supposed to do? Oh, yes, the key." Carefully he removed the
chain and key from his neck and gave it to her. "This,
dear lassie, is the key to the Tower. Guard it well."

Erin put the chain around her neck. The key was bright
silver, large and heavy. "Thank you, but how . . . ?"

"No, no talking. You'll make me forget." Trillo ran, half
tripping, over to a wall shelf and pulled an item down.
"Here, this is yours." Trillo tossed the object to Erin. It
was all she could do to grab it. Looking down, she found
in her hands a small, golden harp carved into the form of
an angel. Erin recognized it immediately.

It was the Angel Harp, instrument of the Royal Bard.

Erin stared at the harp in disbelief. She looked up
quickly at the ceiling, wondering how she had escaped
being crushed or vaporized. The ceiling looked normal,
void of the glowing magic, and it seemed stuck at about
thirty feet. She could have sworn it had been closer last
night, but it had been dark. She looked over at Trillo with
a questioning expression.

Trillo smiled, talking like a man whose feet were being
tickled. "You have passed the test, and the Tower of Song

has been returned to the people! There are four levels to the Tower now, the top your living quarters, the other three filled with the Land's histories, the tales of the Great Ones and not so great ones, the stories of the magic which sustains us. You must master it all and go forth, singing what you have learned."

Erin was speechless, and she could only gaze about the room. She tried to take everything in but found her thoughts jumbled with disbelief. Trillo recognized that shocked and puzzled expression and knew he had some explaining to do.

"The Tower is the source of magic," the old man began. "Aye, that is the Legend of the Tower. And it's true that the Tower makes us stronger as a whole, but it's not the source from which all magic is taken, nor is it that which holds back the Darkness. It is more like a lucky rabbit's foot, or a rubbing stone, or a magic feather. It gives to the people a belief in themselves, a belief which cannot waver if we are to continue to hold back the Darkness."

Trillo paused for a moment, looking up as if reading notes from invisible pages. "During the Great War, the Tower truly was the source of magic. The Great Ones, who originally were a group of simple historians, were the first to unlock the arcane threads of magic, as once man discovered fire. This discovery they shared with the people, and those first taught its use became the wizards who fought the first war against the Darkness with its Dark Things. The Tower was the rallying point, and later the symbol of the victory that was won.

"Then from this Tower where the Great Ones dwelled they began to write the stories and histories of the Land, and people from everywhere followed the example, writing lyrics to melodies to describe the battles people fought, the lives people lived, the feats of strength and valor and cooperation. And so the bard profession was born. All the stories found their way into the Tower's books, sifted through and categorized and bound into the large volumes you see on the shelves."

Erin followed Trillo's hand as he motioned to the book-covered walls. There must have been hundreds of colorful tomes.

"People began frequent journeys to the Tower," continued Trillo, "and every evening one of the Great Ones would come out on the upper balcony and read from the stories. The stories and, over time, the Tower itself, represented to the people everything that was strong and good. Was it any wonder that the Legend of the Tower grew?

"This troubled the Great Ones, however. As you'll find out as you read the oldest of these books, they debated whether to allow this belief to continue. It was a debate which lasted to the last days of their centuries-long lives. In the end they felt it was important that the Legend of the Tower be continued. Realizing their time was short, their last action was to set up the position of Royal Bard to maintain the Legend and to administer the test to find each successor."

"But . . ." Erin said, looking skeptically at the ceiling, "but why was I chosen? How did I pass?"

"Aye, I was just getting to that, lassie. Well, the Tower is no longer needed to teach magic. The wizards' guild, and later the bards' guild, took over that role. But the Tower remains steeped in history and legend. To the Royal Bard is left the job of spreading the Tower's stories across the Land, assuring the people the Tower is once again theirs, bringing our people together so that the Darkness may be defeated once more.

"And to do that, the Great Ones had but one requirement for the Royal Bard. He or she needed only to be able to tell these stories clearly and simply so that the young may remember them, and the old may remember them again."

Trillo took hold of Erin's hand in both of his, a wistful smile on his face. "Your comforting, memorable little lullaby, lassie. That's what did it. Anyone who can use words like that would make a perfect Royal Bard."

Erin blushed. "My lullaby?" So that was it. The answer wasn't flashy clothes or elven harps or colorful illusions. The answer was a simple little lullaby taught to her as a child by her loving grandmother.

But Erin couldn't accept that. It sounded too simple.

"Trillo," she said, searching for the words, "You say the Tower isn't the source of magic, that it just contains stories."

"Aye."

"What I don't understand is how telling these stories will stop the Darkness."

"Aye, it sounds too simple, I know, but it's the simple things that have the most power. Tell me, how many people would have believed you could pass the test?"

Erin thought for a moment. "Probably just my grandmother."

"Aye, your grandmother," nodded Trillo. "Not your parents. Not your brothers or sister. Not the hundreds of people who watched Fananon two days ago. You carried only your grandmother's belief in you, and that was enough.

"And just as your grandmother was enough for you to overcome your despair, the Tower will do the same for the entire Land. The wizards will believe the Tower replenishes their stores of magic. The people will believe victory is possible. And this belief in the Tower of Song, a belief carried in the stories you tell, will defeat the Darkness once again."

Defeat the Darkness. Erin smiled at the sound of it. And the way Trillo explained it, it actually made sense. She could do this, she decided. She was going to be a good Royal Bard.

Finally, finally a bard had mastered the test of the Tower of Song, bringing with her the secret to the magic, helping the king restore the Land.

Erin stared up at all the shelves and all the books. There

were three of these rooms? How was she ever going to learn it all?

"Erin, lassie," said Trillo softly, "I know you'll want to get to work, but you have one responsibility before you begin." The old man, even as he pointed up the winding staircase, was beginning to fade. Erin's first impulse was to grab for him, but for some reason she knew it was of no use. There was only room for one Royal Bard in the Land. Trillo had told her what she had to do. His long job was done. Smiling, Erin began her way up the stairs to the balcony, carefully cradling the harp in her arms.

Stepping onto the balcony, the cool, fresh air gently kissed her face, and mid-morning sunlight filtered through the trailers of mist. Allowing her eyes to adjust to the sudden, natural light, Erin saw that the forest was empty, over a day having passed since Fananon's failure had been confirmed. No one ever expected someone would pass the test again.

"Play, lassie, play."

The voice of Trillo was distant and faint. Turning around toward the stairs, Erin watched as he faded from sight. There was a look of satisfaction and relief on the old man's face.

As Erin turned back to the balcony, a sudden thought hit her. She had never played a harp. But before she could worry, Trillo's words echoed again in her head.

"Play, lassie, play. "

Erin began to play, her fingers somehow finding their way across the strings. Almost immediately the mist dissipated completely, letting the sun's rays strike the Tower unhindered for the first time in over a century.

"I am the Royal Bard," she thought to herself.

Her grandmother would be so proud.

THE NEEDED STONE

by Denise Lopes Heald

Reno-based author Denise Lopes Heald's speculative fiction has appeared in *Sword & Sorceress XI*, *Marion Zimmer Bradley's Fantasy Magazine*, *Absolute Magnitude*, and other fantasy and science fiction magazines and anthologies. She is the author of the novel *Mistwalker*. Denise is most grateful for both MZB's rejection and acceptance of some of her earliest work.

I RAN through gray nothing, lungs aching. Behind me, boots pounded on ancient wooden planks. I needed help. Could I steal energy from the bridge for my fading protection spell? Nay, not from this cursed span.

But a man's dark silhouette loomed out of the bespelled fog that hovered over Daemons Bridge, and I flung my own spell through the night, tripped the man, dodged his fallen body, ran on.

In my wake, shouts and curses sounded as Wizard Keep's guards tumbled over the man I'd downed to block their pursuit. Now, if I was fast—

The bridge planks boomed beneath a new onslaught of running feet. They came from Citadel Isle, and must be the High Sorceress' troops. Had a sorceress sensed what I'd pried loose from Wizard's Keep and sent soldiers to claim it from me? More likely, the sorceress' guards were only taking advantage of this excuse to brawl with the wizards' troops or imagined the Wizard Guard was invading their Isle.

Usually, the high magickers' squabbling delighted me. Trapped between their forces, I gritted my teeth and sprang onto a railing. Daemons Bridge had been magicked two eons past. I had no power to rival a Daemon master's, not yet.

I leaped, and the black damned Darn swallowed me. Water filled my nose. Bubbles geysered. I sank, kicked off my boots, then stroked out, my muscles already stiffened by the cold, my spells spent and fallen away. I mustn't fail—

A sinuous bolt shot up my body and scales scraped flesh from my bare arms. I floundered and choked.

My cloak ripped away, and I was free again. Something trying to make dinner of me had missed, but would return. I kicked for the surface, needing energy to reweave my protection spell. Why had I jumped in the water? Why not crouch like a mouse and disappear into the fog? Because the college wizards were aware enough of my pilfering that by now they'd surely armed their guards with countercharms to my simpler magics.

A pale eye loomed above me. Death stared.

My thoughts turned to the recently stolen ring jammed on my thumb. Beneath its pewter cap pulsed all the power I needed to fight off man or beast . . . if I knew how to use the ring stone. But I didn't, nor did I know the use of any other of the stones I'd stolen in this city during the last two years. All the usable stone power I possessed resided in the tiny chip inside a stud, a birth gift from father, that pierced my right ear. Just now, that meager energy wasn't enough to save me. Yet, releasing the ring stone's power, even if I could master it, would draw the attention of beings more dangerous than river serpents. Better I drown than become a magicker's thrall.

My lungs fought to breathe. I held them closed and

grasped after that well of damnation which drove me to such insanity as stealing fire stones, spells, and charms from high magickers. My hate radiated great force.

The serpent's teeth nipped my toes, but the beast veered off as if it tasted poison. My protection spell had formed again. I laughed. My magic was gaining power! But my body wasn't. Where were the bridge's supports? I could follow them to shore—

A blow struck my spell barrier, shattered it, drove me toward the river bottom tangled with a monster.

One that wore clothes?

Arms grabbed me, and I punched the man's stomach, couldn't believe a watch guard had courage enough to follow me into the Darn. Someone must have pushed him.

My magic-powered fist drove against muscle, not armor. Maybe this wasn't a guard; perhaps it was the one I'd tripped in order to block my pursuers. His arms went limp and floated upward, releasing me. I stroked off, desperately needing to get my head above water. But the man's fingers floated over my breasts. He hadn't asked to be involved in my escape, yet was now—surely now, since I'd driven the breath from his lungs—drowning. If I let him die, it was the same as killing him.

I needed magic, needed air in my inadvertent victim's lungs and mine, needed to keep the circling river serpents at bay, needed not to fail father.

Teeth raked my calf, sending agony up my leg. I knotted my fingers in the man's hair and kicked off hard against a sinuous monster body.

Hot energy bled from between my bare foot and the river serpent. The serpents were full of power.

I kicked the thing again . . . could work a spell . . . what was it? A thought spell, a knowing spell. I knew the monsters possessed strength, and I knew it would come to me.

I didn't know how much would come. My body melted. The water boiled. I choked, had gasped and was drowning.

I thought about air, thought about glass globes. Globes? Breath filled my lungs, not water. I gulped more air, my vision glassy as I gazed by spell light at golden snakes and ruby-red fishes, gleaming green tentacled horrors and argent-shelled turtles with razor beaks.

The man's weight tugged against my arm. His head was inside the bubble I'd formed about my own head, but he wasn't breathing. I punched his chest.

The blow, though weakened by its passage through cold water, was powered by magic. It drove him back, and I heard—strange sound inside a bubble—his ragged gasp, heard another breath, knew that he lived. With my hand anchored in his collar, I avoided the gazes of the serpents outside my protection spell and stroked upward.

My head broke water into dark air. I floated and breathed with the man's head resting on my chest.

Where was I? Torchlight flickered along the river wall. We'd floated clear of the fog at Daemons Bridge. Wizard Keep, on its island, curved off to my right. On the opposite shore ran the long straight rock foundation of the Sorceresses' Citadel. Which domain to chance? I hated sorceresses most of all, but their citadel was nearest.

I sculled to the river wall and scrabbled at a ring. It was iron, set there to keep unwanted magickers like myself off the isle. The metal burned my spelling soul until both my grip and my protection spell failed.

Scrabbling at slime-slick stone, I swallowed water, would drown after all.

A blow struck my leg. Serpent, I thought. But the man I'd saved kicked my calf again as he arched up, grabbed the iron ring I'd let loose of—a simple man like him wasn't hurt by iron—and dragged us onto a stone landing.

We coughed up water and emptied our stomachs into the Darn. When I gathered my senses, I realized night had turned to deep murk and dawn was likely to catch us in the open. I wobbled to my feet, but the man I'd saved blocked my way up the landing's narrow steps.

He struggled to his knees, squinted and blinked, choked up more foul water, and finally said, "Help me."

I considered knocking him back in the Darn to clear my path, but he'd saved me at the last. So I grabbed his elbow, braced my back against the river wall and steadied him while he struggled to his feet.

"Th—there's st—still t—time." His teeth chattered. "We c—c can f—find her be—before it's too late"

"Wh—what y—choo s—s—say?"

"F—find my si—sister. You owe me."

My teeth ached from bouncing off each other. "I s—saved your life. I owe you n—nothing."

"Th—this is the last morn. T—today they'll enth—th—thrall her."

I tried to squeeze past him, but my feet slipped on stone made slick by our dripping clothes, and I grabbed his arm for balance. He grabbed me back, towing me up the last few steps and tucking me beneath his heavy arm.

"She's but a babe," he said. "Hasn't seen a moon cycle yet. I'll smash their isle before they can have her."

I tried to pull free of the madman. His story tore at old wounds, but I couldn't let one child stop me. I had entire holds to save from enthrallment, children by the hand count to protect, my own family . . . And I hadn't many more dawns to spend at it myself. Mira's last message said father was ill, and father was ancient, me a child of his failing years. My sixteen brothers were good men, but didn't know how to fight sorceresses, wizards, daemon summoners, plague callers, rot spreaders, or any of the rest who served the great magickers' wills. I needed to get away from this man, get on with my thieving. If I just found the right power stone, I could keep father alive.

My head spun, and the strength I'd stolen from the river serpents faded all in a breath. While I swooned, my

mad companion swept me along the river wall right up
to the sorceresses' side gate. I tugged at his wet clothes,
needed to make him hear me. "I can't go in there."

He wobbled, a towering dark figure against a gray sky
gone pink at its edges. "Why? It's a college for women."

"Don't act the fool." My chattering teeth nipped my
lower lip, and I tasted blood. "I'm no magicker apprentice."

"But you magicked me from the river."

"And I'll magic you back into it if you don't let me
go. I'm no use to you. Charm your sister out with your
sweet tongue." I tried to pull free of him while dredging
for spell strength from his touch. "Let me go."

He only knotted his fist in my shirt where his flesh
didn't touch mine, where I couldn't get at his body's energy. Then he tucked us into darkness beneath a tree that
grew between the walk we'd followed and the stone plaza
that encircled the sorceresses' towering citadel.

He said into my ear, "Will you take pay to find her?"

I thought about the wizard's ring on my thumb and the
other fire stones sewn into my undergarments. They held
so much power . . . but for all father's training, I didn't
know how to use them, which is what cursed me and my
family. Father, after a lifetime of siring sons from witches
and sorceresses, finally begot me on a sweet common lass,
who was, for the sin of loving my father, killed at my
birth by the High Sorceress' hate spell. Maybe, because
I, of all father's children, had the magic he needed to
make me his helpmate and replacement, the High Sorceress' death spell was meant for me, too. But father used
all his strength to protect me. So giving all my life to my
family was only fair payment on the debt I owed him and
my mother. Except—I didn't understand power stones.
Father touched them and knew their use. I touched them
and saw only madness. So, my powers were too simple
to save my family, and father—despairing, weakening—

sent me to the city to be trained by his enemies, hoping he'd live long enough for me to survive my enthrallment, come into my own power, and then—his most desperate hope—that I not be turned to evil, but return to protect my people.

I came to the city as he asked. But seeing the thralls—blank-eyed, slack-jawed, and tortured—who walked the city's streets by the hundreds, I knew that I would never ever let myself become one. Instead, I apprenticed myself to a thief. Anyway, learning that trade was faster than learning—if I ever could learn—how to free myself from a magicker's enthrallment, and thieving presented me with a new plan. Perhaps the fault in my understanding was not that I didn't understand stones, but that none of father's spoke to me. If I could steal one attuned to my own powers, then I could return to save my family. Was the stone in the ring now on my thumb the one?

A shake forced me from my helter-skelter thoughts. The cold was stealing my mind, made it difficult to focus on the man holding me prisoner.

"Listen." He spoke out of shadow. "You're a woman. That's all I need, just a woman to get inside."

I groaned. "Nay—"

His grip tightened until pain shot through my numbed shoulders as he lifted me nose-to-nose with him. "Just think of her, her eyes round and green, dark lashes, dark hair, fingers long and beautiful. She weaves like our father did, can knit anything whole again."

Something in his words struck me as odder than all the rest of the insanity he spoke, but I couldn't grasp the thought, only sensed his need grasping at me. I needed maybe to kill him after all, mustn't be caught. . . .

Look. He mindspoke me.

How had he done that? I possessed thought-protection spells—woven by father, the type that weren't weakened by my current exhaustion—spells which wizards had failed to crack. My eyes opened wide. A magicker of some sort or a seer he was. I tried to calm down. Maybe he was just so simple a mindspeaker, with no power to force me to do anything, that my protection spells didn't recognize him as a threat. I kneed his groin.

He half-blocked the blow, at the same time falling away from it, so my knee impacted with no real force. He grunted, but his grip never slackened and his presence in my mind glowed brighter still. *Think,* he said, *no one will notice another thrall in those halls.*

I threw hate at him. I was not a thrall.

He let go of my body and mind-stepped to the edge of my consciousness where I knew he couldn't read all my thoughts, let alone control them. But he didn't leave, only waited in the shadows of my sight and thought. He was no simple mindspeaker. I felt too much strength in him.

I need your help. He folded down onto stone.

I turned to leave. But, by touching my mind, he revealed his own to me. So I knew he meant what he said. He would die before he saw his sister enthralled. I tried to look away, didn't want any more pain. But truth was, we'd both come to this city to save family.

He touched my shirt hem. "Go into the citadel. You'll seem like a thrall with me inside your mind, and no one interferes with another's thrall. I can find Tania if you just get my mind inside the outer wall's protection spells."

I hugged myself against chill. "No. I won't be any kind of thrall. You just wait. Someday your sister will grow strong enough to free herself. Let it be. That's the law. Magickers have free pick of all minds. Those with talent are needed to protect the kingdom from invasion."

"Liar."

I was sluggish, stumbling. His grab snared me before I sensed his move, and he dragged me to the ground, pinning me against his side again. He smelled of river mud.

"Help me or I'll sell you to the High Sorceress in bargain for my sister's freedom."

"You're mad." My words slurred. "The High Sorceress isn't interested in me. You don't know—"

"I know what you've been stealing."

Prickling fear distracted me from ferreting strength from his touch. "I'm no thief—"

"The town criers tell of a burglar, believed to be a witch, whose head will bring bounty from Wizard College or the High Sorceress, the Magickers' Guild School, even from the Chancellor of the University of All Powers. I might well trade you for my sister's freedom. Say you not?"

"Not." I spoke without my teeth chattering and realized his body was warming mine. "Not," I said again, though the air laughed at my lie. "But I would help you for the grace of warm clothes and breakfast."

He laughed at that, the sound vibrating in his broad chest. Choose and be done, I thought; either kill him to keep his silence or help him.

"If I do this thing, will you vow to free me and not reveal me to anyone?" I wormed my chilled back against his ribs and he chafed my hands and seemed to forget he'd been holding me prisoner. How much more could I make him forget?

Nothing.

I flinched at his mindspoken answer and punched his gut. "Don't read my thoughts."

He sucked a troubled breath. "Don't splatter them all over the dawn. The magic is that you haven't been mindtrapped by a charmer or a pig caller before this."

I almost hit him again. But he was right. I'd been concentrating on trying to weasel a way through his mental defenses—a trick I'd never been good at—and forgotten to keep my own mind quiet. What was I thinking? I'd fail father right now just from stupidity.

The man coughed. "Lady, witch, charmer, whatever you be, I vow by all you hold sacred, do this thing for me and I will guard you, serve you, be your slave. Just help me free my sister."

"I want no slaves." Yet, I must get free of him, and it seemed the only way to do that was to cooperate.

But how? The Citadel, Wizard Keep, all the magic colleges and fortresses were positioned atop mine shafts excavated to fire-stone bedrock, and centuries of digging debris, littered with chips and bits of fire stone, clogged the college basements. The high magickers no longer needed more power stones; they needed more minds and bodies through which to work their magic. That was a thrall's fate, to give soul energy to her/his master, and they took great exception to anyone stealing a soul back from them.

I breathed in shuddering gasps and tried to drag my mind from blurred wandering to the task at hand. But it was hard to concentrate with the man holding me closer and closer, my face against his shoulder. Was he trying to steal strength from me? I didn't have any, was convulsed by shivering, helpless . . . me the master thief.

A giggle jiggled out of me. I wasn't the first to think of stealing raw fire stones from the magic colleges' tailing heaps, was just the first to steal the stones without ever going into the colleges' basements. I couldn't use the stones' powers, yet had learned to float them through the air, up stairwells, out windows into my hand. My secret was father's secret spell, by which he'd resisted subjugation to mightier magickers for two centuries. I couldn't use the spell's full power until I mastered the use of a powerful fire stone, but I was still a great thief.

My captor breathed heat down my neck, and my thoughts crystallized. He asked me to perform a task for which I was both skilled and sympathetic. I was a thief, and he wanted his sister stolen back. I was a free soul and wanted nothing more than to save all children from enthrallment, me being first on that list.

I cleared my raw throat. "Who are you?"

"Stone."

"Your mother named you f–for power?"

"She expected me to be a child of magic. But as it turned out, she now calls me Stone for stone-cold, stone-stubborn, stone-dumb. I have no magic."

"You mindspeak as if you do." I couldn't tell if he regretted not having more talent or regretted having any.

"Mindspeaking isn't magic. Will you help my sister?"

"How d–do I get inside?" I was not unfamiliar with the citadel. I'd stolen from it before, but during broad daylight, when I gained access from the college's public wing. We didn't have time now for that, nor could I tuck a whole girl inside my boot, even if I still had boots.

Stone chafed my arms and every stroke of his hands bled sweet strength into me. Did he know I could lap up all his energy given the opportunity? I remembered how he'd held me away from him before by the collar. He knew, and was either taking chances with me now or being kind.

He said, "The Daemons Bridge gate opens at first bell for deliveries. The last three mornings, I've bribed a carter to let me ride in with him and help unload. Today we'll send you. The guards are used to him bringing help."

"I'm soaking wet." I felt the long night's labors weighting my limbs, could drift away to sleep against his warm, muscled chest. I roused myself from fantasies I'd seldom ever indulged in all my life. What an idiot. "They'll know I'm no carter."

Besides, I carried a stolen Wizard's ring. Would the citadels' sorceresses detect its presence? There was no place sure here to hide the ring, not without Stone catching me at it, and I'd risked too much to toss it away now.

A shout sounded. Stone said, "They're here." He came

to his feet in one motion, tucked me beneath his arm, and ran.

"Wait . . ." In dizzied vision, I saw a line of carters appear out of the Daemons Bridge fog and roll toward the citadel's gate. Stone caught up to the last cart.

"Go." He flipped me atop the cart's load.

Below, I heard whispered conversation and the clink of coins. Stone was either wealthy or about to be destitute. A cloak sailed over the cart's side. I rolled on rice sacks to dry myself, then donned the carter's sweat-rank cloak as we entered a stone portal into the citadel.

Spell force and stone mass sucked my breath away. Unlike the college's public entrances, this gate was magicked to prevent such as me from entering the citadel undetected. I bunched my muscles to bolt.

Easy, calm. Stone spoke inside my mind, kept his touch so gentle that I steadied. The cart emerged into a yard, and I could breathe again. I was inside the citadel; I mustn't panic, mustn't be stupid or I'd never get out.

Stone mindspoke, *Get down.*

Down? He wasn't just riding along with me, he was looking through my eyes. I raged, *Get out,* while my skin crawled and my gut writhed at the thought that he used me like a thrall. I'd forgotten this part of his plan when I agreed to help him.

He drew himself into a tight bright spark so that I could tell exactly where he was and was not in my mind. That was better, but he didn't leave, and the sorceresses' spell energy still permeated the courtyard's air. My teeth chattered, and I felt Stone watching me with worry.

I thought, *Don't be a fool,* and slid off the cart, dragging a grain sack with me. Fear was good for a thief, it just needed direction. I caught the sack I'd dislodged, then struggled not to fall. Stone said, *Use your legs.* I spread my feet for balance, and it helped. *Center your load.* That helped, too. I joined servants and carters hauling the day's victuals into the citadel's vast kitchens. There, it was a moment's work to slip down a hallway and drop my sack.

So where would initiates be kept?

Stone stirred. *The inner courtyard. The initiates are displayed there until all are chosen. At midday, the claiming begins.* He showed me what the claiming spells involved, and my stomach knotted. But then, I already knew I'd rather die than live through enthrallment. Letting him ride my consciousness was nothing compared to having your every breath dictated.

I headed into the citadel's maze, knew of the inner courtyard because the sorceresses' College Majicka looked down on it. But how to get there from here?

"Yield ye." A barked order echoed down the shadowed torchlit companionway I followed.

Flattening against a chill wall, I forced myself to breathe, was muzzy-brained and staggering into an unknown situation with nothing planned. No smart thief worked this way. But scuffling sounded, and the object of the guard's shouting appeared: a line of sleepy-eyed, frightened girls and women who crowded a cross hallway ahead of me. The initiates. It had to be them. Sorceresses didn't wear peasant cloth, frayed skirts, or torn bodices.

"Here, now." The shout in my ear froze me. "Get you back in line with the others." A giantess in a dirty apron gave me a push.

At her touch, Stone's presence exploded inside my head. I fought him, but heard my voice say, "My mistress calls."

"Your mistress?" The giantess squinted at my face. "Bah. Get away from me, ya thing. And clean yerself fore yer mistress sees ya or you'll be flayed."

The woman lumbered off into shadow, and my mind spun back to proper focus, with just that spark of Stone's presence gleaming at me. *Don't do that again,* I shook in every nerve. He'd blocked my will and controlled me in order to convince the giantess servant that I was already a thrall and not an initiate or a thief.

Stone said, *I'm sorry.*

At his contrition, my face burned with the realization that I'd been clumsy and he'd been forced to rescue me. I needed to finish and get out of here.

Ahead, I saw two guards herding the last initiates away from me. Barefoot, I padded in their wake, hoping I wasn't making too much noise because I couldn't feel my numbed toes. My plan was simple, especially in contrast to all the spells massed in the citadel's surrounding walls. Simple was least noticeable to those on high.

Half the hallway's torches had burned out overnight. I lifted one from its bracket, grasped the charred end and bashed the torch's iron handle down on the nearest guard's neck, catching him just at the base of his skull. He sank where he stood. The second guard turned, and I rammed the torch butt up his nose, then whacked his throat.

"Tania?" Stone stole my voice to call his sister. No one answered. The girl wasn't here.

I bullied Stone back into his corner of my mind, drew breath, closed my eyes and thought nothing, only waited until he understood the invitation. Using both our strengths, he called again, this time with his mind and—

Tania! His mind shout stunned me. *Stone!*

The pair yammered inside my head, leading back the way I'd come. The girl was locked off by herself, already chosen by her future mistress. I ran, followed her mind-cries down twisting passages, up marble steps, and into the sorceresses' personal domain which smelled of potions and posies. No one stirred there yet.

I ran . . . the hallway ended. Rosy sunlight gleamed through a slit window, but I faced solid rock. It had to be a trick. A sorceress had led me here to be trapped, to become a thrall, a thing that giantesses loathed—

Stone rose inside my mind, his desperation raging. I closed my eyes and shouted at him, *Let me think.*

No guards appeared. No special magic tore at me. All the mental antics of the two mindspeakers in my head had gone unnoticed, just as Stone had intended, because such noise was common here. Thralls were mindspoken to all the time. This was not a trick to trap me . . . us . . . I just had taken the most direct route to his sister's cell, a route that didn't include a door.

Boots slapped marble. I stiffened. A servant must have reported a madwoman loose. I looked at the slit window filled with sunlight. Tiny as I was, I couldn't fit through it. I fingered the ring on my finger.

Use it.

I blinked inward at Stone. He knew about the ring?

Use them all.

He'd lied. He'd read my mind, knew everything. I spit hate at him, would hurt him. *I can't use it. Give her up.*

Use it.

I don't know how.

His presence swelled, but I was ready for him this time, wouldn't let him grab hold of me, went blank and staring, gave him nothing to snag onto.

I can help you. His presence sounded distant, muffled.

No, you can't.

Use it.

Damn him. How? The only magic anyone can work inside another magicker's spell is the spell the other magicker doesn't know yet. I only had one of those and what use was it here? The girl I could call to me like a stone, but she couldn't move through a rock wall. My mind blinked against the radiance of Stone's agitated presence while my eyes faced the sunbeams spilling through the near window slit.

I cracked open my stolen ring's cover. It was like opening an oven filled with pulsating coals. My heart thrilled

to warmth and power, but my flesh burned and my overwhelmed senses told me not one thing as to how to wield
such force. All the time, though Stone's presence swelled
and glowed, brighter and brighter, he didn't ride my consciousness under. This time, he only cradled my soul, as
he had warmed my body while we awaited the carters'
arrival, while he'd waited for me to choose to help him.

Shouts sounded at my back. The sorceresses' guards
were advancing on us. Come! I thought at the fire stone;
and an echo sounded, Stone thinking with me, *Come!*

Light flashed. My body blazed, invaded by wild ener-
gies. I'd called the fire stone's power to me.

All this time, that was all I needed, to call it—

Touching the wall before me, I summoned the rock
block beneath my fingertips. An ear-splitting crack
sounded, and the shouts down the passageway at my back
turned to stunned silence, my pursuers uncertain what they
faced in me.

The stone block fell out of the wall and landed with
a thud. I called a second block, which tumbled free atop
the first. A third shot past me, and I reached a hand through
the hole I'd created, grasped thin chill fingers, drew into
dawn light a child lovely beyond words. It wasn't her face
so much that was beautiful, but her eyes, and those because they reflected a stunningly beautiful soul.

I picked her up, faced the window slit in the citadel's
exterior wall, then thought my calling spell backward. I'd
never had power enough to try this before, but the three
stone blocks beneath the window slit burst outward.

It was my greatest magic, and I balanced on a knife
edge ready to shatter if my concentration wavered. Stone
moved my body for me. Tania and I fit perfectly through
the enlarged slit in the citadel's exterior wall. But, as there
had been no door here, there were no steps, only wind
whistling past our falling bodies.

I directed my new-made repulsion spell at the ground.

Nothing happened. We plummeted on and my back struck what felt like rock but splashed.

I was sinking into the Darn River again.

I snapped a bubble spell about me and Tania, breathed in air . . . screamed it out again as something sharp gashed my leg and my body slid across rough bars. We must have struck the river wall's base. I flung out a protection spell atop the bubble spell, but the river water trapped within both spells boiled and fizzed, burning my skin.

The ring. I yanked my hand to my mouth, kept a tight grip on Tania with my other hand, twisted the ring's cap closed with lips and teeth.

Where are you? Stone's mind presence felt panicked. I couldn't see, so he couldn't see for us.

The water about us stopped boiling, but it was blacker than I remembered it being even in the dark before dawn when I'd swam it last. Where were we? We slid over muck slick stone, tossed and . . . squeezed?

My heart thundered. We'd been swallowed.

Swim out!

We were inside a river serpent, were living a tale told to scare babes. People didn't survive being eaten by leviathans, maybe a full-power magicker did, but not stupid girls like me.

Stone hovered, silent, letting me think, yet also feeding me his panic. He couldn't see us, reach us, couldn't help us, was frantic.

My strength for my bubble spell and protection spell wouldn't last. Or else they'd kill the monster and we'd suffocate. And, if I opened the ring again, to use more power, the force would explode the monster's flesh, roasting us within it.

Me! Stone said, and I understood what he wanted; only how could I work such a spell? His presence knotted and writhed. Driven half-mad, I wished him gone.

This way. A stranger's thoughts spoke like razors in my mind.

The witch—it had to be a witch, for she used mud in her magic, soil energy not rock energy—showed me a spell. I clung to Stone's now familiar presence, gut-terrified of what he'd summoned to guide me. Magic cost the innerself, so that powerful magickers constantly stole bits and pieces of their thralls' souls to make up for that loss; yet still they were cold, hard and jagged inside, just like this witch, just like what I did not want to become.

I worked her spell anyway—had Tania to protect and wouldn't fail father—reached out and wove protection for Stone's body where he crouched atop the river wall. Then there was nothing to do, but suck strength from the monster who'd swallowed us and fight to hold three spells, one more powerful than I'd ever worked before, together all at once.

Maybe I wouldn't have succeeded, but I felt Stone coming, and that fostered unreasoning hope. The serpent enveloping me thrashed and twisted, straining my strength and focus. Then it was limp, its flesh crushing in on Tania and me while my mind grew dark—

We shot out of the monster amid a rush of spraying guts and floated upward in my spell bubble. I blinked at sunlit water as arms lifted us onto a log. Stone had dived into the Darn and cut us free from the serpent's belly.

Water drained from my ears, and I heard alarm bells ringing. The citadel's sorceresses were still after us.

Where? I thought, then sagged limp in Stone's arms as his, his witch's, and Tania's presence all abandoned my mind.

Stone picked us up. Through black-edged vision, past the pain of my wounds and exhaustion, I saw that he was young and hard-jawed. He moved, and my vision slewed, showing me that we'd come out of the river away from both Wizard's Keep and the citadel, and were on a narrow, garbage-mounded quay. Stone carried us into an alley between crumbling clay-brick buildings. The slum swallowed us as secretly as had the river serpent. The citadel's alarms rang on, and black birds filled the air, each carrying a sorceress' mind's-eye; but the birds couldn't see into the building shadows, nor did the sorceresses recognize us. We were individuals again rather than the fused being I/we had been when I/we freed Tania. Tania herself was unconscious, thoughtless, invisible to all minds, limp in my frozen arms that would not unbend. So we escaped down darker and darker alleyways, until all I saw was black.

I woke still in Stone's arms, Tania against me, my body wracked with pain and shivering. A fire burned in a shallow pit in the dirt floor on which I lay. A toothless hag crouched facing us.

Past my head, Stone said, "She helped us."

"Indeed." The hag spit as she spoke, her lips slack in her ancient face, unnatural strength burning in her eyes. Someone, present here in mind only, was using the old woman's body. "Your thief's a handy toy."

"Don't say that." Stone's words vibrated in his chest. "Don't play me for a toy anymore either."

"You think you can threaten me with your new trinkets?" I recognized the cold mind-touch of the witch Stone had summoned to aid us in the river. Using the hag's voice, she said, "The fire stones your thief has stolen are worthless scraps. Bring them to me when you bring Tania home, and I'll show you that truth. But rid yourself first of the thief."

"I can't release her." I shivered from persistent water chill and from the death-serious tone of Stone's words as he defied the witch. "We are one now, she and I. We can hold apart for a time, but not forever. The stones aren't worthless. They bind us. I hear them speak, understand what they say, and she knows how to use what I learn."

"Rubbish. No mindspeaker can master a fire stone."

"Nor can I. Nor does she. We master them."

His presence slid into my mind, not controlling, not demanding, only asking. I opened my ring with one aching fingertip, and the old woman slumped asleep, the witch banished by our joined wishes.

I blinked up at Stone's gleaming eyes, then blinked down at the child on my lap. "The witch is your mother?"

"Aye. She sent Tania to be trained the way she was trained, as a thrall, to be hardened and honed, she said."

"But not you? Your talent isn't magical—" Mindspeaking involved no spells, no power stones, only a person's born mind skill and courage.

He said, "She used me to invade others' minds. But I can block her out. She controlled me by hurting Tania."

"But she lost control of you when she sent Tania away."

"Aye. She misjudged me, thought I was tamed to hand. Now, Tania and I are both free. Will you have us?"

Have them? "To do what with?"

"Live. Learn." His lower lip trembled. "Love?"

Love. In all my life, I hadn't thought of the word except as commitment to my family, but as Stone kissed my brow, I saw so many possibilities. . . .

"You're hurt." Tania's tiny voice drew our eyes to her. Bruises covered her cheek and mottled her arms, but she reached up, rested her hand on my fire-stone–scorched lips, rested her other hand on my serpent-torn thigh, and as the child wove me back together, I remembered Stone saying Tania liked weaving. I thought of father dying. Tania could heal him. I hadn't failed; I would just bring father three magic children instead of one and return home an altogether different sort of thrall than he had ever envisioned. He had taught me deeply and well from birth to live free. Now that was the only way I could live, a free thrall to all the hope and possibilities in Stone's touch, in Tania's sweet compassion, in my own nimble soul and heart and mind. I would steal no more. I needed not another stone.

ARMAGEDDON
by Lisa Silverthorne

Lisa Silverthorne is one of the many contributors to *Sword & Sorceress* who made her professional first sale to MZB; she has four previous sales to *S&S* and two to *Marion Zimmer Bradley's Fantasy Magazine*. Since her first sale she has gone on to sell stories to many other markets. Her latest sales were to the anthologies *Quantum Speculative Fiction* and *Civil War Fantastic*.

This story is about the fight between Good and Evil, the End of the World, and other annoyances of everyday life.

SAUCHONY surged down the temple steps. Armageddon had arrived, and she was late. Of course, it wasn't really her fault, Sauchony realized as she shifted her sword hilt out of the way. All this talk for centuries about the coming of Armageddon and no one had thought to even write it on the calendar. She wouldn't have even known if the High Priestess hadn't left a note on her chamber door.

She paused on the footpath that wound through the meadow. She was the only warrior left in the temple. The others had gone away to some retreat in the southlands. Just her luck to draw temple fire duty on the weekend of Armageddon.

Pounding across the meadow, she slid to a stop behind a tree. She peered out at the rolling hills and the forest that framed the meadow. The faint breeze carried only the scent of newly cut hay and silence from the nearby vil-

lage. Sauchony sighed. What did Armageddon look like—
exactly? How embarrassing if she had to ask someone to
point it out to her.

She searched for a wave of armies rushing down the
hillside. Or fiendish creatures descending from the sky.
But only the wind whispered across the horizon.

What would it look like? From which direction had it
come? Sauchony wished she'd paid less attention to sword
wielding and more attention to prophecy. Couldn't be
helped now. She'd have to take care of this Armageddon
and get back before anyone noticed that the temple fire
was unattended. It was bad enough to face the forces of
good and evil alone, but to anger the gods . . . now, that
was something to worry over.

The sky was clear, with not even a cloud to shadow its
rich turquoise. Trees rustled and in their shadows, something coalesced in a shimmery haze. Four horsemen clam-
ored into the meadow. The pale horse rode toward her.
The rider, his face cloaked, raised a scythe. Three other
horsemen rode beside him.

Sauchony waved frantically at them. "Wait!" she
shouted. "Apocalypse is the next village over."

Confused, the rider on the pale horse glanced at the
thin rider on a black horse. The rider on a white horse
pointed toward the horizon. The pale rider scratched his
skull and then rode toward the hills. The others followed.

A horrible buzzing filled the silence and Sauchony
turned toward the forest. This was it! She crouched, drawing her sword, and waited for Armageddon to emerge.

The sky darkened as thousands of insects flooded the
sky. Locusts! Frogs chirped and squeaked as they spilled
out of the woods.

"A plague of locusts . . . that's all I need!" Sauchony
stumbled back from the menagerie that destroyed trees and
grass as it writhed toward her. If those things got into the
temple, she'd be on cleanup duty for months.

Sauchony rushed back to the temple steps and thundered inside. The insects drowned out her every footfall. She raced into a back hallway that led to the storeroom. From the wall, she plucked a torch and quickly perused the items on the shelf until she saw the wine. She snatched a bottle of ceremonial wine and ran out of the temple.

The sound of insects and frogs was deafening. They had already crossed the meadow and were nearing the steps. Sauchony poured wine around the temple steps, staining the grass a deep burgundy.

Quickly, she thrust the torch into the wine and flames erupted. Frogs and locusts flitted away from the fire. Desperate to escape the blaze, they slipped into the woods and disappeared. Maybe now she could find Armageddon and deal with it before the High Priestess returned.

Exhausted, she leaned against the stone wall to catch her breath as the fire smoldered around the temple. That's when she heard the fighting. Winged creatures, some in white robes and others in black robes, fought in the temple courtyard. Swords clashed, wings fluttered. Shouts reverberated through the temple hallways.

"Stop that!" Sauchony shouted, running onto the stone balcony overlooking the courtyard. "Armageddon is here! We need to fight it—not ourselves!"

The winged creatures ignored her and continued to fight. She didn't have time for this!

Furious, Sauchony turned to one of the fire basins hanging above the courtyard. Three ropes suspended it. She drew her sword and slammed it against one of the ropes, overturning the basin. A thick cloud of ash engulfed the fighting creatures until they coughed and sputtered. Their robes turned ashen gray. Sauchony couldn't tell the black robes from the white now.

"All of you troublemakers!" she called. "Go back to where you came from and leave us in peace!"

With bowed heads, the winged creatures rose into the air and fluttered off in puffs of ash.

"Sauchony, what happened here?"

Sauchony cringed. She slid her sword into her belt and turned to face the lithe High Priestess ascending the temple stairs. She wore the billowy blue robe of her station, and her blonde hair was swept into a knot at her nape. She paused, her entourage pointing and gasping at the silhouettes of winged creatures and the burnt grass.

"Forgive me, Priestess, but I was only defending the temple," said Sauchony. "Armageddon arrived and then there were the frogs and the locusts and—"

The High Priestess shook her head, a thin blonde curl dangling at her ear. "Armageddon *has* arrived. It's the name of a dragon that has been plaguing the neighboring village for centuries."

"What? A dragon?"

Then a smile brightened the High Priestess' face. "Four horsemen rode into Apocalypse and there was a fierce battle. They defeated the dragon, but they're very angry at being tricked into fighting that dragon."

"Tricked?" Sauchony's mouth gaped. She thrust her hands to her hips, angry now. "I only gave them directions!"

"They vowed to exact vengeance on their deceiver," said the High Priestess.

This was the wrong week to be on temple fire duty, Sauchony thought with a sigh. First, Armageddon and now four horsemen from Apocalypse. Maybe, after all that riding and dragon fighting, they were just hungry? One of them looked half-starved.

Shadows of horses rose on the horizon and she moved down the steps to greet the four horsemen. She would ask them in to supper and maybe they would forget about their vengeance. It wasn't like their detour had been the end of the world or anything.

THE LAND OF GRAVES
by Dave Smeds

Dave Smeds, a Nebula Award finalist, is the author of several books, including the novels *The Sorcery Within, The Schemes of Dragons, X-Men: Law of the Jungle*, and the forthcoming major motion picture from Warner Brothers, *Stan Lee Presents: The Guardians*. His high fantasy short fiction has appeared in six previous volumes of *Sword & Sorceress*, as well as in *Marion Zimmer Bradley's Fantasy Worlds, Dragons of Light, Return to Avalon, The Shimmering Door, Enchanted Forests*, and *Realms of Fantasy*. Other fiction—sf, horror, contemporary fantasy—can be found in *Asimov's SF, F&SF, In the Field of Fire, Full Spectrum 4, Peter S. Beagle's Immortal Unicorn, David Copperfield's Tales of the Impossible, Warriors of Blood and Dream, The Best New Horror 7, Sirens and Other Daemon Lovers*, and *Prom Night*. His work has been printed in over a dozen countries.

There is a tradition of having to perform twelve great tasks to reach a goal—remember the labors of Hercules? I suspect, however, that Hercules couldn't have managed this one.

THE runner, a halfbreed Selanese with the long legs and freckled complexion of his slave mother's people, was puffing hard as he burst from the olive groves uphill and hurried to the excavation where Tecia and her cousin's crew worked. Hair and loinclout soaked with sweat, the messenger halted at the lip of the trench. "Sorceress, you are needed!" he blurted when he had regained enough wind to speak.

Tecia sighed. "My tasks occupy me." She indicated the inscribed stone walls around her, the men with picks and buckets laboring to carry off the packed silt that had filled the hip-deep space where she stood.

"It is the headman's command. It is most dire. A revenant has been unbound. It has killed two men already."

"One victim the tomb robber, no doubt," she remarked wryly.

The messenger nodded. "You weigh the ingots correctly, Mage Helper. But the other is Gelages, your uncle's strong man."

Tecia tilted her head down and scuffed the debris at her feet, letting the twinge of loss run its course.

"Tell my uncle I will come," she stated.

The runner turned.

"Wait," she called.

He paused, forehead creasing.

"Drink some water. Rest." She pointed up at the sun. "The ghost will not venture out again until twilight. Haste is unnecessary."

The youth hesitated, darting a glance at the broken terrain through which he had to return. She could see him weigh the balance between her advice—sensible, but given by a woman—and his master's command of utmost speed. In compromise, he visited the water wagon, drenched a cloth, and wiped the perspiration from his brow and upper body. After several small careful sips from the dipper, he set off again fast enough to pretend he was hurrying, but slow enough to avail himself of the reprieve Tecia offered.

In the trench, Tecia finished making a rubbing of an inscription in the stone wall, stowed the leaf in her basket, and vaulted nimbly out of the trench.

"Another ten paces should bring us to the drain," she

told her cousin Flen, the leader of the workers, as he turned toward her, waving away dust clouds.

He grunted, which she knew meant that if she were correct, they would keep working, but if she were wrong, they would stop and wait for her return, and let her shoulder the blame for the delay.

She sighed and turned away. She slapped the grit from her tunic and took her own turn by the water wagon, cleaning her face and hands and easing her parched throat.

At this arid time of year, it took imagination to recall the point of all this labor was to restore the ancient Ladian water system and reclaim another stretch of swamp. If all went well—if Tecia had translated the old scrolls well enough—when the rains returned, water would no longer linger in pools, nurturing the young of malarial mosquitoes and other vermin of stagnant water. A new generation of farmers could till tracts of fertile alluvial soil unavailable since their great-grandsire's day.

Tecia cursed the luck that forced her to leave. It had taken much persuasion to convince the headman to devote a work crew to the project, and much goading to keep it going. The dry season would not last much longer. However, a murderous revenant was not an interruption that could be ignored.

She adopted a steady pace toward home. Olive trees closed around her, then scrub brush, relieving some of the sun's glare. By lizard's hour she was up into the hills, following the ancient track. The way was seldom steep, the gravel and vestigial paving stones flat and smooth compared to modern roads, which even in this arid season remained scored by ruts.

A low bluff rose on her left where the necropolis began. Carved columns rose at the entrances, supporting cupolas and lintels still intact in many spots, though wind and rain had worn away the glyphs that had once identified the families buried behind these entrances. The ruins went on and on, covering a parcel many times the size of Quona, the living town that ruled this stretch of the Aritis River valley.

Cresting a ridge, Tecia saw Quona itself hugging the upper edge of a shelf of land that extended into the valley beyond. Folk were crowded on the walls, gazing farther out across the plateau. Among the mounds and barrows there she spied another clump of people, their gestures and weapons directed at a house-sized crypt one hundred paces from them. Tecia made out the Selanese runner among them, and recognized the heavyset man in the center of the group as her uncle.

The path dipped, and she did not see the assemblage again until she had reached the mounds. She ventured past one last knoll and hailed the group, whom she now saw were gathered around two limp, supine forms.

Her uncle stepped forward as she drew near. For once, he actually dipped his chin in greeting, a deference to the clan sorcerer that he had often accorded Tecia's father, but which he seldom felt the need to tender to a woman, no matter how well versed in the arts she might be.

"This fool violated the tomb you see there," the headman declared, shaking his bracelet of tiny bronze skulls first toward one of the dead men on the ground and then at the large crypt. "He didn't even try to hex the guardian."

Tecia spared a brief glance at the corpse, that of a wiry, hook-nosed man she might have glimpsed scraping skins at the tannery in seasons past, but who had evidently failed to thrive in Quona. The wretch must have felt the need, like so many others, to enrich himself with Ladian tomb relics. A desperate chance, that, for though an expert thief or magician sometimes slipped in and out of crypts without consequence, it did not happen often. As her uncle had noted, the perpetrator did not even wear a fetish or talisman to distract the ghost.

She looked longer at Gelages, the strong man. Her fam-

ily and his tilled neighboring plots out in the valley, and
lived only a few houses apart within the walled town.
Though the adult Gelages had been thick of wit and too
much impressed by his own size and might to suit her,
she grieved for the childhood companion he had been. Always large for his age, he had gladly served his playmates
when they needed a strong hand to help them ford the
river, and had not minded doing so even for a girl, a
scholar's daughter at that.

He had died with eyes wide, his dagger still clenched
uselessly in his hand. His corpse showed no visible
wounds.

"Ambushed," the headman explained.

Tecia nodded. With her eyes she followed the furrows
in the dirt made by the heels of the dead men as they
were dragged away from the spots where they had died.
Her gaze came to rest on the ornate house of the dead.
Unlike the older relics in the necropolis in the hills, the
glyphs above the lintel were still deeply etched.

"The resting place of Vicedis, chief wise man of King
Tobasi," she read. A great scholar. "The revenant was a
warrior?"

"Yes. Tall, well-armored, armed with a pike."

Not the shade of Vicedis himself, then, nor the kin
buried with him. Alas, Vicedis had been so notable among
the Ladians that he had been interred with a guard of
honor. That ilk were often the restless ones, with grudges
to infuriate them, while their masters and mistresses slept
peacefully through eternity.

A blistering stream of curses rang out from the crypt,
calling for the blood of a certain man. The eerie voice
was shrill and inhuman, heard with the mind rather than
the ears. Tecia, despite her knowledge of ancient Ladian,
could make out no more than a word or two.

The men beside the headman shivered, and Tecia's uncle
himself began blinking furiously.

"Put him to sleep, Mage Helper," her uncle commanded.

"Not an ordinary labor," she commented.

One of the headman's eyebrows rose. "Eh?"

"I risk my life to do this," she explained. "I deem this another of the twelve great tasks you asked of me when my father died. The last of them. If I succeed, my boon is due."

Her uncle stared at her hard, then down at the body of his strong man, then back. "This is no time for bargaining."

She folded her hands in front of her, glancing down submissively. "The bargain was made five years ago, and you set the terms. Quelling a revenant has always been counted as a great task of a mage."

The headman glanced up at the sun. Many hours remained until sunset, but days would be needed to fetch a mage from another town. In this time and place, none but Tecia could do what must be done.

"Very well," the headman said. "This is the twelfth task. Now lay this ghost down, and be quick about it."

"As you command," Tecia said.

She addressed the headman's servants. "Be ready to seal the tomb."

The group held up pots of mortar dust and water bags, along with a sack of dried flowers for the funerary magic. They would be ready to set the slab back in place and see the ritual completed before sunset.

Tecia crept forward alone. She paused to take a deep breath at the top of the stone ramp leading down to the crypt entrance. The portal, its slab flung aside, yawned ominously wide.

She could make out the outlines of funerary stellae and urns in the antechamber. The mephitis of death wafted out, smiting her nostrils. Tiptoeing to the level of the opening, she squatted down and peered farther inside. She did not venture past the threshold, conscious of the protection of the sun at her back.

The revenant could venture into the sunlight. The flattened ground just beyond the top of the ramp where Gelages must have fallen showed it had already sprung out once. But the glare of daylight made ghosts nigh invisible. They did not care for that, because it reminded them they were dead.

The stone couch in the antechamber where the guardian slept was occupied by a skeleton, still bearing a few scraps of gray, desiccated skin, preserved by sorcery and the power of the Ladian embalming arts. Tarnished brass accoutrements showed that the deceased had once worn an ornately decorated suit of leather armor. Now he was mostly bones. His former wealth and status was proven by the dentures made of gold bands and ox teeth.

Inchoate mumbles directed her attention toward the tomb's main chamber. Here stood the central dais and its sarcophagus—the remains of Vicedis. Pacing in circles around the dais was a tall man—tall in the way of the Ladians, whose flocks and plentiful crops sustained them in a manner unknown to Tecia's people. He was no skeleton, but as his mouth issued its stream of words, she saw that the dentures matched those of the deceased warrior perfectly. The decorations on his armor were the same as the items of metal scattered upon and beside his bones.

The phantom did not seem to notice her. She waited where she was, letting her eyes adjust to the dimness, listening carefully to the ancient dialect. Finally the outbursts became decipherable.

"Where is he? Zaeghus, you child of a she-goat, come forth!"

Tecia had no doubt Zaeghus was the very enemy who had killed this warrior, long ago. Who better to wish vengeance upon? That was all the creature was—now a manifested wish for vengeance. Lethal to any who might get in his way—that being the point of placing him here to guard Vicedis and his family.

Bracing herself, she crept fully into the antechamber. On the vertical face of the stone couch where the warrior had lain all those centuries, she found a carving in relief. The artwork was a portrait of the warrior, his pike held at his side. To judge from the ghost, the image resembled the man with uncanny accuracy. Tecia wished the artisans of her age possessed such skill.

She placed her hand on the effigy and began to murmur words in Ladian. Despite the tension of the moment, she recalled the phrases perfectly. They were inscribed in every Ladian tomb. Other parts of the language were a mystery, but these were not. In as soothing a tone as she could manage, she called the spirit to its rest, to wait for the arrival of the next world, when souls would be given new shrouds and live in the light again.

The specter whirled and glared at Tecia. "Who is dead?" he cried. "Has Zaeghus killed again?"

Tecia frowned. She was not surprised that the ghost failed to realize the summons was for him, but it should have affected him nonetheless, dampening his anger and lulling him back within the skeleton on the couch.

His phantom eyes glowed as he watched her. She finished the rite. No change. All the tactic had done was call attention to herself.

"Your costume is strange," he grumbled, scanning her up and down. In life, he had probably never seen a woman in warm seasons of the year with more than one breast covered, or with a hemline reaching below the knees.

Tecia's circumstances were growing perilous. She changed tactics. She let go of the carving, stood, and began uttering the chant of exorcism in a raised voice.

The ghost staggered back. He clutched his head and grimaced.

Tecia began speaking faster, as fast as she could without stumbling over the words and having to begin again.

"You may cast out ghosts," he called. "That is no concern of mine. I have my geas to fulfill. Stand not in my way!"

Sweat drenched the underarms of Tecia's tunic. Exorcisms would not work if the subject utterly denied the fact of his noncorporeal state. But having no other means of attack, she began to repeat the chant.

"Fah!" the warrior blurted when she failed to go silent. He leveled his pike and, with the suddenness that had no doubt won him many battles, he charged forward.

The pike skewered her in the heart. She folded around it, unable to deny the illusion. Pain split her. It was as if a shard of ice had plunged inside, and at the same time, a fire roared to her extremities. She knew what warriors must feel when the battle goes against them, and they are lost forever.

She collapsed as the ghost withdrew the pike. She swayed. The world around her faded to black. She thought she heard the ghost laugh at her. Then death came, mercifully quenching the pain.

She awakened with tomb dust fouling her lips. She groaned and pressed her hands to her sternum, hoping to relieve the frigid thorniness within. The massage did nothing save to reassure her that her skin and rib cage were intact. She was as unmarked as Gelages and the thief had been.

The difference was that she was alive, kept from crossing the river of death by spells carefully woven over many years. Spells that had preserved her body while she was gone, and ultimately called her back to it.

And back to the pain. There was no escaping that. Had she been older, the spell would not have been enough protection. As it was, she would never live to be a crone—her heart had damaged itself too much for that.

She had now paid one of the prices for being a sorceress. She did not regret the choice to dedicate her life to the study of the lore. Had she chosen the alternative, she might well be as dead as her sisters, taken by childbed fever. Yet for the moment, she wished fervently she had taken a course that did not involve such pain as was haunting her chest.

She clawed at one of the pouches on her belt. Withdrawing a tiny vial, she removed the stopper and quaffed the entire draught. The medicine burned her throat as it went down, for it contained much alcohol along with the more potent ingredients. She waited for the relief to spread from gullet to her heart and to the bruises on her knees, elbows, and chin caused by her hard fall onto stone.

Darkness surrounded her, but not the lightlessness of unconsciousness. She recognized the stone couch beside her, the dusty paving stones beneath her. Starlight glinted in from the open portal.

No moonlight. Yet the moon was at first quarter and should have remained in the sky half the night. It was past midnight, then.

The revenant must have been roaming the land for many hours. She knew she had to track him down.

She leaned back against the couch. She tried to distract herself from the agony by regarding the urns, murals, and stellae across the passageway. It was her habit to glean whatever knowledge she could from the vestiges of the Ladians. No one in Quona was better at it than she. Even the minimal light could not hide the abundance of the trove.

An urn displayed a Ladian noble and his wife reclining on pillows near a fountain amid dinner guests, sharing wine and laughing. The difference between their era and that of Tecia was immediate—not only in the partial nudity, but in the fact that women could dine with men, and that the women could drink wine, an offense punishable by death in modern Quona and its neighboring provinces. Tecia had only once tasted it, in secret.

There were those who might not allow her to include alcohol in her potions, were she not the niece of a headman. There were those who would destroy "obscene" relics such as the urn, were it not housed in a tomb protected by a warrior ghost and other enchantments.

Yet however much she admired the bygone age, the living needed her loyalty more. As the pain lessened, she staggered to her feet. Only a fraction of the spasm had subsided, and the soporific effects of the potion would dull her wits for hours, but now she could function.

She stumbled out into the landscape. A flicker caught her eye. Out in the valley a fire was consuming a hayloft. Men shouted. Pigs squealed.

All the way down there, she thought. She had no strength to cover such a distance.

A pair of silhouettes separated from the lee of a minor crypt a few dozen paces away.

"Mage Helper!" a man cried. "You still live! The river be praised."

Tecia recognized the two men as Kell and Rosvoi, two of her uncle's laborers—and soldiers, when the need arose.

"You were left to watch the tomb?" she queried.

"Yes. But we dared not enter."

She waved off the apology. Even with the ghost gone, staying clear was indeed the wisest course. Had anyone violated Vicedis's resting place in search of her body, they might have fallen victim to curses she knew how to avoid.

"The revenant started the fire?" she asked, gesturing at the valley.

"Yes." It could not literally be true, for the ghost had no physical presence, but he could startle a farmer into dropping a lamp.

"What else?"

"We don't know the whole of it, because none have brought news since the moon set," Kell replied. "Early in the evening the creature frightened the headman's best stallion to death, and ran off the field slaves."

Her uncle would be fuming about the loss of his favorite breeding horse for years to come, Tecia thought. The flight of the slaves was less troubling. It was unlikely they could make it out of the province. When their terror was vanquished, most would return of their own accord, rather than risk flogging or castration.

"Does the ghost call for a man named Zaeghus?" she asked.

"He calls for someone constantly. That may be the name," Rosvoi answered.

Tecia concentrated. "Zaeghus . . ."

"Helper?"

"If he was a contemporary of King Tobasi, he would have a crypt here in the mounds. If he was great enough to slay the man chosen to be the guardian of Tobasi's chief counselor, he himself would have been chosen to guard an even more prestigious tomb."

Rosvoi shrugged, as if to say he was only a common man, unlearned in such things. And so he was. In all Quona, Tecia alone possessed the scholarship to puzzle this out.

What was the name of King Tobasi's own tomb guardian? The drugs in her belly dulled her memory, but she recalled that it was not Zaeghus. That left one likely burial site of that era: The tomb of Princess Ula, Tobasi's twin sister, and co-ruler until Tobasi's eldest son became old enough to take on his share of the ruling house's duties. The Ladians of that dynasty had never allowed a single monarch to claim total authority. The junior co-ruler was often a woman, particularly during transitional periods.

Tecia turned and gazed north at the shorter of two

prominent knolls. "There," she said. "Help me walk. We will find help there."

Kell and Rosvoi went so pale she could see the change even in the starlight. "Are you certain?" Kell asked.

"Am I versed in magic or not?" she retorted.

They took up positions beside her and supported her by elbows and armpits as she traveled. She would have tripped over stones hidden in the grass if not for their help, but with it she soon arrived at the portal of a large house of the dead.

She knelt at the door and caressed the effigy carved into it. She murmured Ladian words of appeasement.

Digging into the largest of the pouches at her belt, she withdrew her double flute. The old yellow wood gleamed in the starlight. Wetting her lips, she began to play the sacred dirge of the Ladians—but backwards, for this was not the version meant to put the dead to rest, but that meant to wake them.

Kell and Rosvoi closed hands over their ears. The music was sweet, but few people cared to hear that tune, played on an instrument that had all but died out with the Ladians.

The song ended. Tecia lowered the instrument and listened—not with ears, but with attentiveness.

A stirring came from within the tomb. It was a whisper, little louder than the susurrus of blades of grass in the wind. Though it was what she hoped for, it chilled her. Kell hiccupped, and Rosvoi backed away.

"Respectfully, we beg your assistance," she called in the old tongue.

Stepping away, she waved the two guards to approach. "Break the seal. Pull away the slab."

They hesitated.

"The ghost will not harm you," she said.

Her confidence won them over. As they worked, she waited close by with arms folded, feigning composure. In fact, ghosts were never so predictable. This one might be as murderous as the one wreaking havoc in her uncle's fields.

The tink-tink-tink of the chisels went on for some time. Finally, licking dry lips and murmuring prayers to the river, the men braced and pulled. The slab, well weighted like many of the best crypts, swung aside so easily one man would have been enough to do the job.

"Yah!" Kell called. He and Rosvoi leaped away.

A ghost stood in the vestibule. He wore leather torso armor, draped with sheaves of bronze, and held a bronze short sword.

"Guardian of Majestic Ula, hear our plea," Tecia called. "Be you the shade of Zaeghus?"

The warrior touched his collar, where a bronze disk fibula held together the corners of his cape. His fingers stroked the inscription, a traditional glyph of mourning.

"Am I dead?" he inquired.

"Yes," Tecia replied. Thank the river this ghost perceived so fully what the other denied. Otherwise she surely would have multiplied her troubles.

"Then . . . it appears I am the shade of Zaeghus, for such was my name. And now I guard that most ingenious of princesses? Why, better that than the bones of the king himself!"

"It is apparent that you served well," Tecia said. "Would you serve the living for an hour? An old enemy of yours needs killing again."

"What is his name?"

"That I do not know. But he calls for you in anger. I believe you killed him once."

The ghost grinned. "I killed many men."

"He was a noted warrior, middle-aged, with false teeth."

"Ah." Zaeghus laughed. "Ghinnis. I gutted him like a sow on feast day."

"So you will help us?"

"With delight. Promise to respect my lady's place of rest while I am absent, and I will do as you ask."

"I do so promise," Tecia replied.

The ghost of Ghinnis returned to the tomb of Vicedis in the crepuscular light of early dawn, as Tecia knew he would. The ghost of Zaeghus stepped from the lee of the edifice to meet him.

"You!" cried Ghinnis. He lowered his pike and rushed forward, as quick as Tecia had experienced.

Zaeghus sidestepped at the last moment, grabbed Ghinnis by the neck, expertly slid the sword through the laces of his armor, and disemboweled his opponent with a single wrenching motion.

The twice-slain man gawked at the intestines pouring from his belly. His eyes turned up and he collapsed. No worldly sword could have touched him, but the weapon of his known enemy was real to him.

As soon as his body stopped twitching, it melted away. A puff of vile mist trailed back to the tomb of Vicedis.

The people watching, which now included the headman and the men who had attempted to rein in the chaos created by the revenant during his excursion, burst into a cheer.

The ache in Tecia's chest eased. She smiled. But she was also quick to reach into a pouch at her belt, and close her fist around the contents.

The surviving ghost strutted before his audience and spat on the dirt where Ghinnis's phantom blood had gushed, though no stain lingered there.

"Our thanks," Tecia said. "Now, if it please you, your sepulcher awaits. Dawn is coming, and I would spare you its bite."

Zaeghus waved his hand dismissively. "Nay, it would please me not."

Tecia groaned.

Zaeghus regarded the valley and river. The growing light splashed pleasingly over the rectangles of cultivated earth. "The land is not so crowded as in my day. Perhaps I will explore it."

"Perhaps not," Tecia stated firmly. "If you do, I will take back my promise to revere the tomb of Princess Ula. I will see to it her body is stripped of its finery, and her bones scattered on open ground."

The specter bared his teeth at her and raised his blade. "You will not," he growled.

"I will unless you abide by what is right. The 'most ingenious of princesses' would admire such a decision."

Zaeghus scowled. But gradually, his swordpoint dropped.

"You are most unfair," he muttered. "You remind me of my wife."

"Death is unfair," she responded. "But it is part of nature, nonetheless."

Tecia flung out her hand, showering Zaeghus with dust she had gathered from the threshold of Princess Ula's crypt. "By the ancient rites, you are confined to your post," she yelled in ritual Ladian.

Zaeghus's scowl evolved into startlement. His "body" spasmed, became intangible and fluid. His feet rose from the earth. He was whisked back to the royal knoll like a sheet of rainwater in a gale.

Tecia finally let herself breathe. Thank the river for a ghost that could be swayed by his obligation, and therefore remained vulnerable to the old magic. She turned to Kell and Rosvoi. "Go back and seal the crypt. The sunrise will protect you."

They bowed and did not even wait for the headman to concur before they ran off to accomplish their task.

Tecia's uncle reaffirmed his authority by commanding a similar detail to close the tomb of Vicedis.

Tecia sat down on a broken column and rubbed her sternum. She let the headman come to her. He gazed down at her dusty, bedraggled self with the lordliness it had been his privilege to indulge in all his adult life. He pursed his lips and nodded. "So, niece. You have done well. I thank you."

She gazed back steadily, waiting for more. It did not come.

"The matter we spoke of yesterday afternoon?" she murmured.

"That was before I lost my horse," he said.

She straightened up, as much as the throbbing in her spine would allow. "Did I or did I not risk my life to complete this task?"

The headman sighed. She understood his dilemma. It was one thing to sanction a female to take the duties of her late father, a clan sorcerer whose son and heir had also recently expired, leaving no other viable candidates. It was another to give her the status of full mage, and enjoy the privileges that came with the rank—privileges that ordinarily came with the assumption of the duties, so long as the magician was a male. The most important of which was the ability to teach apprentices.

She had abided by her uncle's restrictions, kept the rank of Mage Helper these past five years, and undertook the twelve tasks to prove herself. Now he could only deny her her reward by breaking a sworn promise.

To her astonishment, the headman's expression softened. "Ah, girl. When I thought you dead in that tomb, it seared my throat like one of your potions. So be it. As of this moment, you are Mage. You are free to choose your students."

She rocked back. She had expected at most a begrudging concession. The elder's tears took her by surprise. With a voice gone husky with emotion, she replied, "If it please you, I will begin with the traditional candidate."

He cleared his throat, as if expecting her answer. The traditional pupil was always a younger son of the headman, if one was available. And one was. She would not only teach, but teach a male.

"As you have chosen, so it will be," the headman said.

He strode off quickly, muttering about the need to set his farm in order. Several of the observers remained by Tecia, especially the women, to help her back to her house in the walled city.

But first she stayed to watch the sun rise on a new day, the sort seldom seen since the age of the Ladians.

LIGHT

by Susan Urbanek Linville

After attending school for twenty-three years off and on, Susan Urbanek Linville received her Ph.D. in biology from the University of Dayton, with a specialty in animal behavior. She studied mate choice in the northern cardinal, and co-published an account on the cardinal sponsored by the American Ornithologists Union.

In addition to teaching biology at Ivy Tech State College, she is assistant editor for the *Journal of Comparative Psychology*. She also volunteers at Wonderlab, a children's science museum in Bloomington. Right now she is writing science articles and drawing illustrations for their newspaper publication, *Wonderpage.*

She is married to "a very supportive husband," with whom she is cowriting a fantasy novel. In addition to a fourteen-year-old daughter who is an honors student and is planning on becoming a forensic scientist, they have three cats that keep them up at night.

In addition to her literary creative projects, she has a physical one, which she described as follows: "We have an acre of property and my goal is to eliminate as much grass as possible. We created a pond in our backyard that is stocked with six-inch goldfish, have a large wildflower garden, and are adding various fruit and nut trees this spring. In the next few years we will have a wildlife sanctuary instead of the typical suburban lawn."

It sounds like a wonderful project to me—and at least they won't have to mow it.

Her story is about a young woman who is capable of far more than she realizes.

> *"He hath eaten the knowledge of every god, his existence is for all eternity and to everlasting in his sah this; what he willeth he doeth, what he hateth not doth he do. Live life, not shalt thou die."*
>
> Doctrine of Eternal Life, VI Dynasty, Egypt

NEKHTI ignored yelling from outside—children at play, most likely—and focused on her work. Her goal was to finish the day's beer before the sun's heat made the already warm ground floor of her family's brick house unbearable. She wiped sweat from her brow and pulled five molds from the fire with a metal rod.

"Abi, put these on the rack."

The servant boy, clad in loin linens, lifted the conical vessels with papyrus wraps and placed them into round holders. Nekhti scooped barley paste from a vat and filled each vessel almost to the top, just as father had taught her. The paste would be left in the molds until its surface browned.

"Cover them."

The commotion outside intensified. Now it sounded like wailing. Nekhti opened a prior set of molds and tipped out sour-smelling loaves. She tossed these into a vat filled with her own concoction of water, dates, and spices that made their family's beer the most prized in Abydos.

The wailing came closer, raising hairs on the back of her neck.

"Abi, mix this," she said. She washed her hands in a basin and walked to the open doorway.

On the stone walk leading through the garden, her younger sister Tamit knelt westward and pounded the top of her head with her palm. "Osiris Khent-Amenti, preserve us from decay."

Coldness entered Nekhti, replacing all heat. "Who has died, Tamit? Is it father?" He had gone north to the delta to find buyers for their beer.

"No," Tamit cried. "Ameni is dead!"

"Ameni?" Nekhti didn't understand. She and Ameni had eaten a breakfast of bread, beer, and fruit only an hour ago. Ameni had gone to the market with the rest of the family for linens and fresh produce.

"A terrible accident. A donkey knocked its master from the cart." Tamit pounded her head. "It came too fast and Ameni fell under the wheels."

"No," Nekhti said, "this cannot be." Ameni, the oldest of the five daughters of Djedptahioufankh and Ahouri, had reached fifteen years and was preparing for marriage to Djaou, the third son of Seti, a sculptor whose works adorned the temple of Osiris. Djaou had no talent for sculpting, but was interested in beer making.

Panic fermented the contents of Nekhti's stomach. Djaou and Ameni would continue the family business when father could no longer manage. What would she do without them? She couldn't make beer on her own.

It is a bad dream, Nekhti thought. "I will see for myself. You help Abi stir." She walked past her sister toward the market, between houses with small gardens filled with date palms, colorful flowers, and herbs. She turned south onto the main road. The houses were closer here, with no front gardens and exuded an odor of baking bread. The ground felt warm beneath her bare feet.

Ameni cannot be dead, she thought. *Ameni is my light.* "Thou art pure, thy *ka* is pure, thy soul is pure, thy form is pure." When Nekhti grew angry with her younger sisters for playing pranks, Ameni acted as peacekeeper. When Nekhti couldn't understand her mathematics, Ameni helped. When Nekhti felt unsure about helping father, Ameni encouraged her.

Nekhti entered the cramped market square. Raw gazelle and oryx meat hung from hooks beneath white tarps, watermelons and cucumbers overfilled baskets, grapes and figs attracted bees, and herbs, both fresh and dried, brought to life an exotic mix of smells. People had gathered beyond the carts, leaving their goods unattended.

Nekhti squeezed through the crowd toward the stone pillars of the temple of Osiris. In the broad avenue before the temple, a donkey pulled halfheartedly against its reins while a man examined its foreleg. Several people struggled to right a wagon from its side. Women, clad in thin linen dresses, kneeled, pounding their heads, praying and crying. Nekhti saw her mother and moved forward.

Ameni lay on a blanket as if she had fallen asleep. There was no blood, no sign of injury. *She is not dead,* Nekhti thought, but she could not make her hopes rise.

"Nekhti," her mother cried. "This is a day of bad luck. We should not have left the house. The fates have taken my oldest daughter! Gods help her to the underworld."

Nekhti bent over Ameni and touched her hands. They remained warm, but there was no movement, no life, no *ka.* Nekhti wanted to crawl into her mother's arms and be comforted; she wanted to turn to Ameni for reassurance, but there could be no solace there. The fates had taken her sister. Nekhti was on her own.

Nekhti lay on the roof between sisters staring at the starry sky, wishing sleep would come. Earlier, she had stood next to her mother in a dark temple hall, listening to plans of the Neter priest: embalming and preparation of the body, how Ameni would be placed in her parent's tomb and new inscriptions painted on the walls. Nekhti had wanted to scream that this was a mistake. Her sister should be alive. Wasn't there some sort of magic? Didn't the gods have the power to bring her back?

Her paternal grandmother had told stories about people of pure heart rising from their tombs. Her great-grandfather was said to have risen twice. In school they had been taught that King Mn, the first to unite Upper and Lower Egypt, had risen to become King Namer and then later King Aha. Even King Djet, husband of the present Queen Merneith, had returned from death because he had no son to take the throne.

A part of Nekhti wanted to curl up and hide forever beneath the blanket, but another part, an angry part, wanted to fight. If ever a person had been of pure heart, it was Ameni. Nekhti slid from under the wool blanket she shared with her sisters and walked to the roof's edge. A faint light colored the eastern horizon. Praise Ra. Soon the sun would shine down on Abydos, bringing light and life to everyone except Ameni, who lay in darkness. Nekhti shivered.

She descended the ladder to the first floor. All was quiet. She crept to her mother's sleeping room and listened. Breathing. Ti would be huddled in mother's arms, the way Nekhti had been cradled as a child. She felt a pang of regret, but made her way down cool stone steps to the ground floor, past sleeping servants and into the garden. The morning smelled of honey from hives across the cart path.

Nekhti returned to the market. Booths stood empty; white tarps hung like ghosts from the underworld. "Ra protect me," she whispered and ran to the temple.

The gate was closed, but her cousin had showed her a side entrance when he started training as a priest. It wasn't a door, but a slit in the wall. To the untrained eye, the wall looked continuous. Nekhti had learned to find the secret passage by letting her eyes unfocus.

She slipped quietly through the slit. The temple was like a small town, with houses for priests and scribes, a school, a library, and a place for the khenerit, the holy women.

An acolyte with a small oil lamp surprised her. "What are you doing here?" He was dressed only in loin linens and looked sleepy.

"I am looking for my cousin, Seti. He is kheryhebet."

"It is too early. Everyone must say morning prayers."

"My sister was trampled to death yesterday."

The young man looked startled. "Osiris Khent-Amenti, preserve us from decay. You have no mud on your face. I didn't know you were mourning."

Nekhti touched her cheek. She'd forgotten about covering her face. "This is urgent," she said, hoping to move him to action.

"Seti, the kheryhebet? Come." She followed the man to a library crowded with scroll racks. He lit a lamp and instructed her to sit on a wooden bench near the door. "I will find him."

Nekhti wasn't sure if her cousin was tired or if anger stretched his face when he entered the room. "What are you doing here?" He rubbed his hands across his shaved head. "I haven't even washed."

"I'm sorry, Seti, but I couldn't sleep. I keep remembering things grandmother said. I couldn't keep myself from hoping. And today is a day of luck."

"Hoping what?"

"That Ameni could return to life.'"

"She will live in the underworld with the gods."

"No, Seti. I know there is magic, I know there is a way to bring her back." Nekhti stood and walked to a rack of scrolls. "You are kheryhebet. You must know of this magic."

Seti covered his face with his hands and sighed. Smoke drifted from the lamp like a spirit. Shadows danced on the painted walls. "It is old magic, dangerous. It can bring pestilence, disease, and drought."

"Please, Seti. Ameni was my light."

"Impossible."

"Please."

Seti frowned and walked between shelf racks to the back of the room. He returned with a yellowed parchment, which he carefully unrolled. "The chapter of returning from the underworld. Net, universal mother, weaver of linen, thou who provides the dead with coverings. Preside over the chamber in which the dead is embalmed. Administer your unguents that were mixed for Osiris. Preserve the dead from destruction and make him young again."

Seti pointed to a list of ingredients below the glyphs. "The body cavity must be cleaned and filled with spices and natron salts. Instead of seventy days, the body rests for only thirty. It is covered with the following unguent: cassia, cinnamon, cedar oil, juniper berries, palm wine, and black coriander. It rests for two days while prayers and offerings are given to the goddess Net. On the third day, life is restored to the body."

Nekhti's soul soared. "Then only a simple unguent is needed."

"It is not simple." Seti unrolled more of the scroll. "Black coriander grows only near the gates of the underworld." The bottom of the parchment was a map. "Here is Abydos near the Nile. Here, to the west, is Kharga, and farther west, Dakhla. West of Dakhla, a natural stone obelisk marks the Oasis of the Gate."

Nekhti nodded. "It doesn't look far, not nearly as far as the delta." Her father made that trip every year.

Seti shook his head. "When this map was made, the land to the west was green and easy to travel. Now, it is desert. Ounut and even Wabou priests have gone looking for black coriander. Some said the gate is gone, others never returned. You probably couldn't even reach it in thirty days."

Nekhti stared, memorizing the map and the ingredients.

Seti touched her shoulder. "Ameni is dead. She will have a happy life in the next world. You must go on without her.'"

Nekhti didn't want to go on without Ameni. If there were a way to bring Ameni back, she would do it.

Sunset cast long shadows across the land. The house, normally bustling with activity and laughter this time of day, was quiet. Mother remained in her room and hadn't talked or eaten. The younger girls played quiet games on the ground floor. Nekhti had insisted on making beer despite Tamit's protests that she mourn properly. She couldn't just sit in the house and do nothing.

She sealed caps on beer containers with river mud, carried the heavy jars to the backyard, and slid them onto a shelf in an open shelter. Abi, eyes wide, rushed through the back gate with the family donkeys. "Nomads on the north road!" he said.

"Nomads?" Nekhti ran to the gate. To the east, land sloped gradually to the Nile, where many white triangular sails glided. To the north, on the dirt road leading to Thinis, black-clad desert dwellers with pack-laden donkeys and many goats formed a ragged line. A salt caravan. Nekhti smiled fiercely. This might be just what she needed.

Once her sisters were in bed and darkness had fully descended, Nekhti selected a container of beer and made her way to the nomads' camp. A half-moon ruled the sky, and their white tents seemed to glow with life. Shadowy figures moved about campfires, and voices talked in low tones.

Fear constricted Nekhti's throat. Ameni would know what to do, who to speak to, what questions to ask. Nekhti did not. Still, she forced her feet to carry her forward and her arms to lift the beer. Men sat on one side of the fire, women on the other with a few children. Porridge boiled, lifting a steam that smelled of soggy grain.

"I ask about trade and travel to the desert," she said quietly. A man approached, long black hair framing dark tattoos on his cheeks. He smelled of sweat and cinnamon. Nekhti wanted to run. It was said that desert people sometimes robbed travelers or appropriated women. Ameni had never believed the stories. Nekhti would not believe them either. Forcing a smile, she handed the beer container to the man and observed his unreadable black eyes. "A gift."

He smiled with large white teeth, removed the cap and drank. "Good," he said in Egyptian dialect. He passed the container. "You wish to trade beer?"

"I wish to go to Dakhla oasis," she said. "I trade beer for supplies and transportation."

The man turned and said something in his own language. Conversation and what Nekhti took to be argument ensued. He turned back.

"We leave for Kharga in two days, then to Dakhla. You must have better clothing." He rubbed the thin linen of her dress between his fingers. "The sand will eat this."

"The sand eats everything," another male voice said.

"It eats skin."

"If you are not prepared, it eats the soul." Everyone laughed. Nekhti realized they saw her youth and played on her fears. She wouldn't give in.

"I will get the right clothing, and water bags, and whatever else I need," she said. "I have an important package to deliver." The laughter subsided.

"You are welcome," one of the women said.

Good, Nekhti thought. Now, how was she going to get Ameni's body?

Nekhti removed ten jars of beer from the upper shelf. These were the smallest containers and could be transported most easily by donkey. She counted a second time and recorded the deduction on the stock papyrus. Father would not be happy, but they had had a good year and the beer spent would be worth bringing Ameni back.

Nekhti moved the jars to the back gate, next to food supplies and oils and spices she would need for the unguent.

"What are you doing?" Tamit asked. The younger girls trailed her into the garden. Ti and Hora were naked, but pretended to wear long robes and glided along the walkway as if they were in a procession. When they reached the palm, they busied themselves making baskets with dried fronds.

"I must make a trip." Nekhti didn't want to lie, but she could think of no other way. Mother would not be happy that she was leaving during the mourning period. "Father is not home yet, and we promised to deliver this beer to Thebes."

"You can't leave. We will be alone."

"Mother is here, and you have Abi and Amr to help you with the children."

"I will talk to mother," Tamit said. She rushed into the house and up the stairs.

Nekhti followed. Ameni would know how to convince mother, the exact words to make her understand. It was always a struggle for Nekhti, who went to father when she had a problem. She reached mother's room a few steps behind her sister.

"Tell Nekhti she cannot go," Tamit said. Mother sat up in bed, looking confused and sad.

"Go where?" She looked at Nekhti for explanation.

"Father promised a delivery to the temple in Thebes." Nekhti wasn't exactly lying. Father had promised, he just hadn't specified a date. "Since he has not returned, I am responsible."

"You can't go now," Mother said. She lay back and put her hand over her face. "We must mourn for seventy days."

What would Ameni have said? Nekhti had heard their conversations hundreds of times. Ameni always knew what was important to mother.

"It is for the Temple of Ra." Her mother would want to assure Ameni's passage to the next life. "I will make an offering. Ra will protect Ameni on her journey."

Mother did not speak. Nekhti felt sure she would refuse. "There is also a small temple to Anubis," she said. "I will take extra beer, make special offerings."

Mother breathed deeply. "You will dress properly and keep your face covered with mud."

"Yes, Mother."

Tamit started to complain, but her mother raised a hand. The subject was no longer to be discussed. Tamit would be eldest while Nekhti was gone. She glared at Nekhti, an angry frown twisting her pretty face.

Nekhti readied three donkeys. One would carry beer, the second water and food, the third would carry Ameni. As the sun set, Nekhti ate the evening meal. She washed and covered her body with fragrant oils, pulled her hair back and tied it away from her face. Only after her sisters had gone to sleep did she don the black nomadic robes she had hidden in the garden.

The moon lit her way. Nekhti tied the donkey to a temple post and found the side entrance, being careful this time to avoid being seen. The air smelled of meat and incense. The main walkway was covered in shadow, and she heard voices chanting.

Nekhti crossed the inner street to an alley beside the priest's apartments, careful not to go too near open doorways. She followed the edge of the building to the main courtyard where she had to hurry between stone columns to stay hidden. Before she had crossed the courtyard, several priests exited the temple, heads and bodies shaved and oiled.

Nekhti slid behind a column and remained still. The priests strolled across the courtyard, talking among themselves, but no one noticed her standing in darkness. Her stomach uncoiled.

Once they had passed, she moved quickly to the embalming chamber at the rear of the temple, a small room lit by a single oil lamp. She found only tables and equipment, no priests, and entered quickly. The sharp odor of balsam mixed with spices filled the air. Two shrouded bodies lay on stone slabs. Under the first linen cover, she found Ameni's pale, sleeping face.

Nekhti tried to lift her. In life, her sister had been lighter than a grain sack. But *this* Ameni was heavy, filled with salts and spices used to preserve her. Nekhti's heart raced. She couldn't ask for help. She couldn't bring the donkey into the temple. How could she remove her sister?

"Osiris, forgive this intrusion." She uncovered the abdomen and opened an incision below the navel through which the internal organs had been removed. She pushed Ameni onto her side. Preservative gushed from the opening, rolled across the slab and splashed onto the dirt floor. The smell was sour like spoiled meat, but balsam made it less offensive. The process seemed to take hours and Nekhti feared a priest would arrive at any moment.

When Ameni was nearly empty, Nekhti wrapped her in a dark blanket and lifted her to one shoulder. When she passed the priest's apartments, she heard Seti's voice and wished she could tell him not to worry, but he wouldn't understand.

The donkey grew restless when Nekhti placed Ameni across its back. She would have to secure her sister firmly and try to disguise the smell with additional spices.

*   *   *

Nekhti hobbled the donkeys outside the nomad camp in the cool morning air. The women greeted her and offered hot goat milk mixed with honey. The taste was strange but pleasant. She felt welcome and confident that the worst of the ordeal was surely behind her.

Her confidence evaporated as the day wore on. No roads existed in the desert and as lush vegetation gave way to a shrubby wasteland, Nekhti's sandals gathered stones that nipped her feet. The coarse clothing irritated her skin. Her legs ached and she struggled to keep up.

That evening, it took all of her remaining strength to set up camp. "Only nine days to Kharga," she said to Ameni as she slid the bundle from the donkey. She unloaded the other two animals and hobbled them near some shrubs.

After unpacking, she joined the women for an evening meal of porridge and dates, but didn't understand much of their conversation. When the moon began its ascent, she excused herself and returned to her belongings. She didn't have a tent, but made a makeshift shelter from blankets and beer jugs. Exhaustion did not invite sleep, however, and when she finally did nod off, she dreamed the man with the tattoos stole her beer and ran off with her donkeys.

One day blended into the next. The weather remained hot and dry and Nekhti felt thirsty all the time. Sand was embedded in her every pore, and she wished she could wash away the filth. Her tongue felt thick and pasty, her feet swollen and sore.

On the third night before their arrival at Kharga, Nekhti found men loitering around the donkeys; fear displaced her fatigue. Maybe the stories were true and they would leave her dead in the desert.

The tattooed man approached. "What is in this bundle?" he asked. "It smells bad."

Nekhti thought about saying "meat" but lying might endanger her life. "It is the body of my sister."

The man's eyes grew wide. He said something to the others, and they quickly backed away. Two ran toward the main camp.

"It is bad luck to travel with the dead. Very bad."

An old man approached and said something. The younger one translated. "You cannot continue with us."

"But I can't make the journey alone." Nekhti imagined two bodies lying in the sand.

"We will not travel with the dead." In unison, the men turned and walked away.

"But you accepted my beer!" Nekhti shouted. They gave no indication of having heard. "We have a bargain." She felt tears welling, but her eyes had no water to finish them.

Nekhti decided she would follow the caravan just out of sight. She had her own food and water. As long as she didn't fall too far behind, she would make it to the oasis.

In the morning she found a string of good-luck beads draped across Ameni. The caravan was already far ahead. Nekhti waited until the last nomad was out of sight before following.

After three days alone, it was a relief to see the green palms of Kharga. The soreness in Nekhti's feet seemed to vanish, and she reveled at the prospect of bathing. "We will arrive at the oasis soon," she told Ameni. "We will rest and sleep." Then she would have to find someone to guide them to Dakhla.

Kharga was a small town, but well populated with travelers. Nekhti exchanged beer for food at the market, filled her water bags, and bathed at the well. Her legs revived, but her feet remained swollen. Few people spoke Egyptian and it took nearly two days to find a guide, a fairskinned Nubian named Kush.

"Two beer and you do the cooking," he said.

"This wrap contains the body of my dead sister," she said, cringing.

"I don't care if it's the King of the Nile," he said. "Two beer and you do the cooking."

A weight lifted from Nekhti. She nodded and gave him one jar in advance. The next morning, Kush woke her while it was still dark. "Time to go," he said. "We walk while it is cool."

Kush wore a multicolored robe and brought only a walking stick, the pack on his back, and two goats bearing water bags. His long legs carried him quickly, and Nekhti had a difficult time keeping up.

It was nearing midday before they stopped on a rocky slope for their first meal. Kush tied his goats to a scraggly tree and gave them water from a metal cup. He took a blanket from his pack and propped it between his staff and a boulder for shade. "You cook."

Nekhti, having learned to make desert bread with the caravan, gathered kindling and made a small fire while Kush slept. When the fire was hot enough, she kneaded dough made from water and flour and placed it onto glowing embers. She rounded out the meal with figs and dried meat from her packs.

Kush chewed with a deep frown. "This is awful," he said. "Desert bread. No taste." He grabbed a handful of figs and most of the dried meat before Nekhti could get her share.

Kush became more irritable each day. Complaints of bad tasting food turned into tirades against the gritty wind. On the forth day, he couldn't find a well to refill their water bags and they wasted valuable time searching before Kush decided to continue. By the fifth day, he was helping himself to Nekhti's water.

"That is mine," Nekhti said, pulling the bag from his hands. He grunted and kept walking.

That night they heard jackals barking, and Kush flew

into a rage. "The smell will bring them to the camp. They will eat my goats." He flung his arms in the air and walked in circles. "We must burn that body."

"We will do no such thing!"

Kush levered a stick from the fire and headed for Ameni. Nekhti ran after him and knocked it from his hand.

"Stop it!"

"I cannot travel with this body," he said.

"Then go on your own. I will find my way to Dakhla without you!"

"Be careful what you ask for, fiery woman. If you navigate as well as you cook, you will die in this desert." Kush kicked the smoking stick and returned to camp.

When Nekhti awoke, he was gone, along with his goats, two containers of beer and half of her water. "Osiris protect us," Nekhti said. The ground surrounding camp was hard, and Kush had left no tracks. Nekhti knew they'd been heading northwest but also knew she would never find Dakhla without some kind of trail.

Nekhti led the donkeys toward a domed ridge to the northeast, hoping she might be able to spy Dakhla or a caravan from higher ground. It was almost dark by the time she reached the top of the plateau, and her legs burned from the climb. Looking down, she saw only an empty sea of sand.

Nekhti tied the donkeys since there was no vegetation for them anyway. She had no wood for a fire, so she ate dates and dried meat. Howls echoed through the night, sometimes seeming very close. She spent the night awake lying beside Ameni's stinking body, listening for footsteps and snuffling predators.

In the morning, one of the donkeys was gone. Hoof marks led down the plateau to the shifting sands, but it seemed futile to search beyond that. Nekhti packed her remaining supplies and Ameni and continued, praying that Dakhla was near.

She walked with little rest, stopping only briefly at midday. Water was running low, so she let the animals drink and had beer for herself. She had selected a rocky outcropping as her goal to keep from walking in circles in the smooth sands, but now she wondered if she might have passed Dakhla. There was no sign of other travelers, but she was afraid to veer from this path, afraid of becoming irretrievably lost.

The sun set. Thank Ra. Again, there was no wood for fire. Her grain was nearly gone, so she rationed small amounts to the animals, made a paste of beer and flour for herself, and ate it raw.

"We are lost," she said to Ameni. She buried her sister in sand, hoping to hide the smell. "I am sorry. I only wanted to bring you to life again."

Morning brought brilliant sun and hot sands. The air remained still and offered no relief. Sweat ran down her face and sides. Sand gave way to rocky ground again, and Nekhti hoped there would be grass ahead for the animals. Even if she'd missed Dakhla, the ridge would offer cover and a vantage point.

"Father is going to be angry," Nekhti said. "First I took ten jars of beer, then I let the donkey wander away. Now I am hopelessly lost."

The sun sank between a gap in the western hills. "We probably passed Dakhla two days ago." Nekhti untied the water bag and shook it. It was almost empty.

Shadows stretched from the hills like long fingers raking the ground. "Now there will be no one to help father make beer. Tamit is too young and Abi too inexperienced." She removed the good-luck beads from Ameni.

"I just wanted to save my sister," she yelled at the sky. "I just wanted to help the pure of heart. Do you hear me?"

The donkey carrying her sister brayed and pulled at its

reins. "Ptah, great god, the beginning of being, father of fathers, power of powers." Nekhti held her hands to the sky. "Ra, god of the earth, beginner of time. Osiris, god of the dead. Net, mother of the gods. Hear me, I beg of you." Nekhti fell to her knees and wept. She didn't want to die, not here, not this way.

A chill descended with the setting of the sun. Nekhti raised her eyes to the ridge and saw a thin point of stone reaching upward out of shadow, a natural obelisk. She'd passed Dakhla, but had somehow found the gate.

Reenergized, she pulled the stubborn donkeys up the incline, and around a plane of tumbled rock. Nekhti expected to find an island of green, but was disappointed. Rocks and sand spread around the obelisk just like the rest of the desert. There was no ornate gate, no oasis, no water.

"It must be here," she said. The donkeys sniffed and pawed at the ground. She knew they smelled water, but where? She approached the obelisk and examined carvings etched into its base. Some were familiar Egyptian gods and hieroglyphics, others seemed more primitive: circular patterns, unfamiliar animals, strange human figures.

"Where is it Ameni? Can you see the gate from the realm of the dead?" Nekhti remembered the map Seti had shown her. It seemed like years since she had sneaked into the temple to talk with him. The obelisk was inset into a gap between rough stone walls. Was the gate hidden like the entrance to the temple?

"Osiris help me." She let her eyes wander unfocused, and a part of the wall seemed to shift.

The gap was not a gate and the oasis not an island of green, but a shallow well surrounded by date palms and a small herb garden. Nekhti filled her lungs with its sweet fragrance. She unpacked the donkeys, stripped off sand-laden garments, and waded into the water. It was cold and she drank until her stomach hurt.

After washing and oiling her body, Nekhti dressed in loin linens and wandered among the herbs. Tall white spikes of basal bloomed, thyme formed a mat of flowering purple. She found a plant that looked like common coriander, but its thin upper leaves were dark green, almost black. She crushed a leaf between her fingers and smelled the familiar citrus aroma. This was what she had come for.

Darkness descended quickly. Praise Ra. Nekhti gathered kindling and made a small fire near the well. She cooked a large loaf of desert bread to accompany what was left of her meat and dates. Fire sparked and crackled, lighting the night sky. Nekhti felt safe for the first time since she had left home.

"May I join you?"

Nekhti started. A woman with skin as black as Nile soil stepped out of the darkness. Her short hair curled tightly, and large gold rings hung from her ears. Her dress shimmered as if woven with fibers of gold.

Nekhti motioned for the woman to sit. "Would you like bread? Beer?"

"Thank you." The woman took a piece of warm bread and filled a metal cup with beer. "Praise Ra, who brings light to the world." She ate and drank. "You make good beer. Better than your father's."

"You know my father?"

The woman set the cup down. "Why have you come here?"

"To bring my sister back from the dead. I look for black coriander."

"I see."

"I need only a small amount and have beer to trade."

"Every thing here is offered freely," the woman said. She folded her hands together and gazed at the stars. "But a price must be paid for every thing that is taken."

"I don't understand."

"You may take the coriander you need. Others have taken before you. But be aware that life does not come without cost. There are consequences for your actions. Each time one is raised, Earth must give of itself. Water is lost to the underworld."

"I must trade water for the coriander?"

The woman shook her head. She grasped Nekhti's hand with thin silky fingers and opened her palm. "The Nile brings water and life to the people," she said, following a crease with her fingertip. "Once there were other rivers and lakes and green life. Herds of antelope, gazelle, and zebra." She wiped her palm across Nekhti's. "Now there is only sand."

"You mean that for each person raised from the dead, the desert grows?"

"Yes. That is the price for eternity."

"Why don't you stop them?"

"I am only here to give warning and welcome the dead."

Nekhti looked at her sister's body wrapped in a blanket soiled by dried fluids. "Ameni always knew the right thing to do. She was strong and protected me."

"You are not strong?" The woman pulled a green stone scarab from the folds of her dress and gave it to Nekhti. "A young woman who crosses the desert alone has the strength and perseverance of a beetle."

Nekhti closed her hand on the stone and was comforted by its smoothness. The woman was right. She would never have had the courage to make such a journey before Ameni's death. She looked at the star-filled sky, a sky empty of clouds, empty of water. "We have made a desert of the world?"

"Yes."

Fire kindled in her stomach. She remembered Ameni encouraging her to experiment with the beer recipe when father was away. *You can do this, Nekhti. Do not live forever in father's shadow. Make your own decisions, too.*

Now she must decide about more than beer. Ameni's life for the life of the world? She didn't have to wonder what Ameni would say. Still, it hurt. Kings had not hesitated to choose life. Why should Ameni die?

She brought her gaze to bear on the dark-skinned woman. "I will not let the world be eaten by fire."

The woman smiled. "You have not crossed the desert in vain,. Nekhti of Abydos."

The woman stood and walked to Ameni's body. She carefully removed the soiled covering and sprinkled the corpse with sand. "Hail, thou divine one, not hath been unloosed thy garment. O unloose thy garment. Come, receive thou the soul of Osiris, protect it within thy two hands." The body took on a golden glow. "This ka is released to you, Osiris. Guide it on its way."

The rotting smell vanished; Ameni's skin lightened and drew tighter, leaving a perfect body shell. The woman moved her hands, and linen strands coalesced in the form of a burial shroud.

"Who are you?"

"I am the mother of all," the woman answered. Her dark eyes reflected stars. "I am Net and Neith, Hapt and Hathor. I am the lady of heaven who came into being at the beginning."

She wrapped the body in linen. From her gown, she brought forth amulets of gold: a hawk, a scarab, a jackal and affixed them to the shroud. An obsidian necklace appeared along with sprigs of mint and myrrh.

"Take your sister and return home," she said. "You will know the way." Her body seemed to blend into the night.

Nekhti was left with hot embers from her fire, the remnants of a loaf of bread, half a jar of beer, and a body that had once belonged to her sister. She bent down, squeezing the green scarab in her palm. "I will miss Ameni," she said. "But this is the right decision."

Father and mother would not be happy, but she would

find the words to explain. She would tell them she was the oldest daughter of Djedptahioufankh and Ahouri, she made the best beer in Abydos, and she would carry on the family tradition.

Ameni had been her light. Now, Nekhti would make a light of her own.

IN THE SACRED PLACES
OF THE EARTH

by Dorothy J. Heydt

Dorothy Heydt has been writing Cynthia stories for *Sword & Sorceress* since Volume I, and calculates that two or three more will see her done. She used to work for the University of California at Berkeley, where she learned all sorts of trivia about biochemistry and office politics. Now she stays home with her Chronic Fatigue Syndrome and her husband, two or three grown kids, four cats, and entirely too many computers.

"THE path to happiness does not consist of achieving your desires, but rather the extinguishing of desire," Zeno said. "I seriously doubt this journey will do you any good. But I think perhaps you won't progress any further until you have tried it."

"I'm certain of it," Cynthia said. She shifted her grip on the heavy staff, part of the ritual equipment, that held in a little sack her bedding and the new clothes she would put on when she reached Eleusis. "I must try at least."

The old philosopher was her closest neighbor—he lived in the ground-floor chambers of the house where Cynthia rented the loft—and the only mortal in whom she had confided. He tugged at his wispy beard and made a dubious face. "Only the good is worth seeking, and Virtue is the only good."

"My man Komi was Virtue walking," Cynthia said, "and if I can win him back from death, I will. Grandfather, we've had this discussion many times. Let's not part with a quarrel. Listen, they're starting." A song had begun to rise from many throats, raggedly at first but swelling in volume as the singers reached agreement on what note they should be singing.

> *"Come, arising out of sleep,*
> *Come, torches in either hand,*
> *Hail Iacchos, Hail Iacchos,*
> *Never-failing morning star. . . ."*

The image of Iacchos in its cart led the procession, as was its function, and nine all-holy priestesses of Demeter walked behind, each holding an ornamented basket on her head. In one of the baskets, none knew which, lay the Hiera, the holy things that the initiates would see in the course of the Mysteries. Cynthia kissed Zeno's withered cheek and said, "Good-bye, grandfather. Stay well."

"Fare well," the philosopher said, and turned to climb the hill back into Athens.

The priests and holy images rode in wagons, but the initiates walked, and their festive robes and myrtle crowns were soon covered in dust. Cynthia, warned beforehand, had worn the oldest gown she had and carried her best in the bundle on her back, but she must still pull her stole across her face to breathe. She lengthened her stride and moved up the procession till most of her fellow initiates were behind her and only the holy wagons were in front of her.

Then she heard, *Come here to me.*

No one who has heard the voice of a god will ever mistake it for the voice of a mortal. Which god, and where?

Forward and to your right, the soundless voice said

impatiently. Cynthia obediently made her way to the wheel of the trailing wagon, twined with myrtle and with the last flowers of the summer. *That will do.*

I have a task for you, mortal, and if you can accomplish it, I will make peace between you and me.

This was Demeter, then, who spoke: the Great Mother of the Hellenic pantheon, whose other selves Cynthia had crossed on the other side of the sea. She could not cross Demeter now, not when she hoped to beg her divine daughter Korë for Komi's life. "What must I do?" she whispered, hoping the wagon driver would not overhear.

There is an impious man among these initiates who means to profane my Sanctuary. Stop him, and you shall have my friendship.

"Who is he? How shall I know him?"

I cannot name him; I cannot even find him. One of my divine kindred has sent him against me, and he is veiled from me. Watch, and find him.

"I will," she whispered; and the wagon driver turned around in his seat and said in a kindly voice, "Back there, now, mother, don't hang on the cart. You'll see Her plain as day when the time comes."

And Cynthia thought, but did not say, *That's what I'm afraid of.*

She turned around and let the procession pass on either side of her, like a stream of airborne bats dividing to pass a stone at their cave's entrance. Which of these earnest-looking, dusty men—or it might not even be a man, since the goddess could not see him, and there were women and even children among the initiates. She glanced into every face, looking for—what? some kind of rage or madness? a look of avarice, maybe, from thinking of what fabulous reward the unknown other god had promised? She saw nothing of that kind.

But now four maidens, walking together, came abreast of her, their faces shaded by their myrtle wreaths. Strangely enough, no dust had fallen on their robes, the leaves circling their heads still gleamed, and a starry light shone out of their footprints, just for a moment before it faded under the dust. Cynthia bowed, and they came up and surrounded her.

Aretë glanced sideways at her, and smiled. "We told you we'd come along and speak for you."

"My thanks," Cynthia said. "Zeno tells me you are the only good worth seeking."

"Yes, he says that. He's a sweet old fellow," the young goddess said. "Careful!" She caught Cynthia's arm before the mortal could trip over a stone in the road. The young goddesses, of course, never stumbled, never sweated, never grew tired.

"Who else is here today?"

"Sophia and Elpis, and Physis, I don't think you know her. Come and meet her." The little goddesses, whose names were Wisdom and Hope, smiled as Aretë led Cynthia between them to a tall broad-shouldered lady, her fair hair braided and coiled around her head, her white hands large and full of strength. "This is the mortal Cynthia, for whose sake we are all going to Eleusis to ask Persephone to give her her husband back," Aretë said. "Cynthia, this is my big sister Physis: in Latin, Natura."

The journey westward through the hills and around the shore of the Bay of Eleusis took the entire day. A few at a time, the initiates crossed the narrow bridge over the Rheitoi and had saffron ribbons tied around their wrists and ankles to protect against evil. This took several hours, and gave everyone a chance to rest. By the time they reached the bridge over the Kephisos the sky was growing dark and the torches were lit. Here the sacred hecklers, with heads covered, hurled abuse at important citizens among the initiates, who were not allowed to answer. This protected them from the evil spirits that feed on pride, and

gave the tired initiates something to laugh at. Laughing
and cheering, the torches blazing, they came at last to
Eleusis and brought the image of Iacchos to the outer court
of the Sanctuary, not to be seen again until next year. Then
everyone sang the long Hymn to Demeter, and the
kernophoria began, when the priestesses danced with their
baskets on their heads, and the singing and dancing went
on into the night until the last tired initiate fell by the way
and went to find a bed in a hostel.

Get up.

Cynthia had gone to bed early and slept for several
hours without dreaming. The soundless voice woke her,
and wearily she rose from the narrow bed to go out and
answer. None of the other sleepers stirred as she crept between them.

Outside, the late moon hung low in the sky, and gave
her a clear view of the Sanctuary, its carven marble cold
and white as the moon itself. Two priests stood guard beside the entrance.

No, come no farther. Not yet. Look over there.

Cynthia looked, and saw nothing at first. Then a shadow
moved, half-crouched beside a low wall that ended at the
pillar marking the entrance on the south side. Slowly he
crept toward the entrance, unseen by the guards. Then he
lifted his hand and threw a stone; it fell on the far side of
the entrance, and the guards turned to look. A diversion,
to let him into the Sanctuary unseen. Cynthia picked up
her skirt and ran.

The shadow had almost reached the pillar when Cynthia caught up with him. The days when she had fought
the other children with fists and feet were long behind her
now, and all she could do was to run into him, thrusting
him against the wall. He fell, and cursed in a deep voice,
and got up again and ran. (At least she knew now that the
offender was a man.)

The guards returned and helped Cynthia get up. "What were you doing out here, mother? The dancing's over till tomorrow."

"There was a man," she said. "Creeping along under the shelter of this wall. He threw the stone. I ran up to catch him, but he got away."

The guards looked at each other. One would think this kind of thing happened often on the night of the *kernophoria*. "Go back to bed," one said. "You can tell your dream to the priest tomorrow, if you like."

"Yes, lord," Cynthia said, and turned away. As she crept into bed again, the voice said, *Tomorrow, when it is your time to take the cup, use your incantation to make it harmless. Then you will see clearly the things of earth, and be ready to stop the impious man when he makes his attempt.*

The cup, Cynthia thought groggily. The initiates, after their day's fasting, would drink from the cup before entering the Sanctuary, in honor of the Goddess who had refused red wine and drunk the *kykeon,* a ritual potion of meal mixed with water and mint. There was nothing harmful in that mixture; why did Demeter want her to disenchant it?

Unless that wasn't all that was in it.

Could she descend to the court of Korë if she did not taste of the *kykeon?* But even if not, dared she disobey Demeter's command? She lay awake the rest of the night, turning and sweating, and was glad when the morning came and the initiates' first duty was a bath in cold water.

When they had put on their new clothes, they were divided into groups and led apart to learn a strange song, about a little pig who went to market to buy himself a basket. It didn't seem appropriate, but they dutifully learned it. They also learned many verses in praise of the two Goddesses, the sort they had learned during the long months of preparation. They spent much of the day fasting and observing sacrifices to the Eleusinian gods at the hand of the King-Archon of Athens. By the end of the day they would be glad to get their share of roasted ox and barley bread, and water.

But first there was the *kykeon.*

After a long day's thought Cynthia had decided that even if forgoing the *kykeon* barred her from the court of Korë among the dead, even if she must wait another year and perform the whole ritual again, still it was safer than disobeying Demeter. But she must not ruin the drink for anyone else, and that meant going last. She feigned a twisted ankle and waited till the last moment to go up to where the two priestesses stood with the cup, a little wooden vessel built of staves like a barrel. She took it between her hands, said the words she knew, and drank. It tasted of barley-meal and mint.

When evening fell, the torches were lighted and the initiates lined up before the gates. Each was questioned and identified and vouched for by one of the mystagogues who had trained them. Each recited, "I have fasted, I have drunk the *kykeon,*" Cynthia said it without faltering and was glad when her tongue didn't stick to the roof of her mouth. The initiates' names were recorded on wooden tablets and their wreaths of myrtle were replaced by wreaths of bright-colored ribbons, to show that they would soon be consecrated to the goddesses. Then they went to sit on a bank of stepped seats within view of the shrine, a little house among the forest of pillars with a bronze-clad door that would soon open.

Cynthia could just see the door from where she sat; those on the opposite side of the Sanctuary couldn't see it at all. The holy things were kept there, and were to be shown to all the initiates; it must be that the Hierophant would take them out of the shrine and process around the Sanctuary holding them. *And if I were an impious man, and wanted to do the Goddess an injury,* Cynthia thought, *—as I have been an impious woman in my day, and done several goddesses an injury and well they deserved it— that is where I would try.* She would have to keep a close watch.

She turned a little and glanced at her neighbor, a woman a little older than herself and richly dressed. Her face was flushed, the pupils of her eyes contracted to tiny points. *And if the impious man drank the* kykeon *and is showing the same effects, he will not be able to see well at night.*

A flute began to play, and two priestesses stepped out into the center of the Sanctuary. They wore actors' masks and crowns. A chorus somewhere sang parts of Demeter's long Hymn while the priestesses danced around the shrine, miming the last day of the spring of the world, when Demeter and Korë wandered the flowery meadows of the earth together, foreseeing no ill.

Cymbals clashed, and a priest in a red robe, with a terrible mask and a shining crown, appeared in a golden chariot drawn by two men with masks like horses' heads. He snatched up the Korë-priestess and drove off, between the banks of seats in the north of the Sanctuary. Cynthia, turning in her seat, could see the chariot speeding up the Sacred Way toward the temple of Dis in its cavern in the side of the hill.

The Demeter-priestess walked around and around the shrine singing a long lament, the mother's grief for her stolen daughter. The woman beside Cynthia was in tears. Everyone in the Sanctuary except herself was watching the drama with the greatest attention; she could have bet that no one would notice her if she got up from her seat and started wandering. —Except the other priests, of course; they must be hidden close at hand, and they couldn't all be full of whatever was in the *kykeon.*

From her place in the front row she could turn back and see a great many of the initiates—a quarter of all those in the Sanctuary, perhaps. She began scanning their faces, hoping to see a face with a live mind behind it, or some other sign. She had no luck. When she turned back to the drama, some time had passed: Demeter's long wandering over the earth, her visit to the friendly house of Celeus, her attempt to make an immortal of his son Demophoon, her petition to Zeus, and the return of her daughter for nine months of the year. A priest with the bearded mask and lightning crown of Zeus was finishing up a long recitation, perhaps a blessing, perhaps a warning. Then the cymbals sounded again, and the chariot of the underworld reappeared, descending the Sacred Way with Korë riding in it, crowned as a Queen, to descend into the Sanctuary and embrace her mother.

The chorus began singing again, and the initiates joined in: it was the verses they had learned, sung to the tune about the little pig. Even for Cynthia the effect was startling, as though the song had just taken form in her mind, and for the initiates it must be as if the gods themselves were singing out of their mouths. Demeter and Korë embraced. Thrones were brought out, and they sat upon them. And the Hierophant went to the bronze door, took a key from his sleeve, and unlocked the door.

At first Cynthia could see nothing. Only a little table inside the shrine, made of marble with golden poppy flowers around its edges. And on it lay—curse it, she couldn't see. But the Hierophant picked it up and brought it out and began circling the shrine with it: a round golden platter such as was used in sacrifices. And on it, a little wooden cup, warped with age, and a knife of polished stone, and a clay figure of a woman's body, with huge breasts and belly but no head at all. Now the initiates were weeping in earnest, even as they sang, tears of joy because they saw—whatever they saw, it was dark to Cynthia. She only saw the things lying on the plate, and the sweating face of the Hierophant as he carried them around, and behind him a man who had risen from his seat and was coming up behind the Hierophant almost at a run.

Again she could only run to intercept him; she hadn't a knife and bloodshed was forbidden in the Sanctuary anyway. She leapt at him, caught him by the knees, and sent him sprawling. The Hierophant jumped back, juggling his platter of holy things, which fortunately didn't spill. The man kicked Cynthia away and ran. She followed. If he couldn't be caught, and stopped for good (probably at the hands of a dozen angry priests, if they could keep him from a thousand angry initiates), he might yet come back.

The man had hurt his knee, it seemed, but fear gave him wings and he hobbled up the Sacred Way toward the Temple of Dis. But there were priests there, too, standing at guard, and he must burst between them, Cynthia on his trail, till he came to the caves at the Temple's back. They were no vast caverns to be lost in, but mere shallow scoops in the rock, giving nowhere to hide. Here he stopped, and here Cynthia brought him down.

After a moment's stunned silence she raised her head. Why, she had been mistaken about the cave, it extended a fair way into the earth. in fact, she could not see where it ended. In fact—

There was a pillar of rock standing in the middle of the cavern, man-high and just too wide to put one's arms around. There was an inscription on it that she couldn't read.

The man got up. She could see his face now, in the faint reddish light that hung about the place. He had a blank, shocked look, such as might ripen into despair. He looked at her and turned away, and walked down into the cavern, and Cynthia followed. The cavern narrowed into a tunnel, and it began to slope downward.

She did not question where she was; she had been in the underworld before, different parts of it at least. Either that last fall had killed them both, or—possibly Demeter had smiled on her at last and sent her down to her daughter's court to make her plea.

We'll come with you, a voice said. *We promised.* Three maidens, robed and crowned, fell into step beside her. Aretë, with flowers in her hair; Sophia with the great pearl hung around her neck; white-armed Physis.

"Where is Elpis?"

I was afraid you might ask that. She is forbidden to come here.

There were others going down the tunnel, she could glimpse them ahead and behind, but they never quite caught up to her or she to them. The young goddesses led; Cynthia and the man marched downward side by side. He was tall, with black hair going gray, clean-shaven, with the skin beginning to hang in folds alongside his face.

"So what god hired you to profane Demeter's holy things?"

"How did you know—" He stopped short. His voice was very deep.

"She told me what had happened, and to watch out for you. She merely couldn't tell me who was behind you."

The man considered this for a moment. "Well, good," he said, and was silent for the rest of the journey.

The Court of Dis was painted in black and gold, and red tapestries hung from the walls. The King of the Dead and his Queen, Persephone whom mortals had called Korë the Maiden, sat side by side on thrones of onyx. The King said mildly, "Welcome, kinswomen."

The Queen glared at Cynthia, and said to the man at her side, "You wait. I'll deal with you later.

"You," she said, turning back to Cynthia. "You don't belong here. You are not even an initiate. What do you think you are doing?"

"I came here by your mother's leave," Cynthia said,

"to beg you for the life of my husband Komi, son of Endreigon."

The goddess gave her an exasperated look, like a mortal asked by the fourth peddler in a row to buy a leaky bucket. "Orpheus tried that," she said. "I made him a fair bargain and he couldn't keep it." Cynthia said nothing. "Do you think you could succeed where he failed?"

"Try me."

Korë smiled; it was not a pleasant sight. "Why should I? Orpheus offered me a song for Eurydice's life; a song worth one of your mortal cities and everything in it. What can you offer me?"

"I'm a physician," Cynthia said. "What's that to an immortal, you may ask; yet a year ago I saved the life of your kinswoman Artemis."

"I don't need a physician," Korë said angrily, and then, curiosity overcoming her, "—Did you indeed? I haven't seen her since I came back to the upper world this spring. They tell me she's found a new name and gone to other lands."

"I told her her new name," Cynthia said. "It gave her back her strength, and she's gone to places where her name is known. I could do as much for you."

Korë looked suspiciously from Cynthia to the young goddesses. Cynthia's eyes had grown used to the dark, and she could see that a face once young and unblemished had grown sour; lines had crept across the forehead and down either side of the mouth, and she looked grim and terrible, as suited the Queen of the Dead. For a moment Cynthia feared she had lost.

"She speaks the truth, you know," Sophia said. "We have come to support her offer, which is a valid one."

"Every creature has its own qualities," Aretë said, "and shows a greater or lesser degree of excellence. Some fall short; some excel. Komi was one who excelled; one of my own people."

"In the course of nature everything is born, and grows, and dies," Physis said. "Yet there have been moments when that wheel changed its course, and turned backward. You have it in your power to grant this gift."

"She changed my name, you know," Dis said quietly. His wife turned to glare at him. "She told me my new name—it's Pluto, as you remember—gave me new vigor, and a throng of new worshipers. For which reason my temple here shall now be called the Ploutonion. And I feel so much better now. You really might consider it, my dear."

There was a long moment of silence, while Cynthia had time to consider the plight of a middle-aged wife with a suddenly young husband, even in the deeps of the earth. She looked to one side, where the man still knelt beside her, gazing up into the face of the goddess; and now she knew who had hired him.

Finally Korë said, "Very well. I agree."

"You'll give him back?"

"Tell me my name; and return up the winding stair. Never look back until you reach the outside air; and if you are faithful, I will not hold him back from following you."

"Agreed. Persephonë, called Korë, far to the west in Italy, where men's hearts are still pure temples of virtue and right conduct is praised, your name is Proserpina. Not much of a change, but enough." She made a reverence and turned her back. Before her the winding stair led upward out of sight; at the level of the vaulted ceiling it was closed by an iron gate.

She climbed the stair. The gate swung open at her approach, and closed with a great clank behind her. Her friends were following her; she could hear soft whispers, soft footsteps. She could not count how many pairs of feet were following her.

They had gone only a few fathoms upward from the gate when they heard a great shout of anguish, a deep voice, full of torment. "When her tools fail her, she breaks them," whispered the voice of Physis. "It's very sad, but that is the way she is."

A faint light was shining up ahead, warm and red like firelight but steady, not flickering. Cynthia stood again in the shallow cavern behind the temple of Dis, where guards stood with torches and a priestess of Demeter stood with hands clasped. But they were unmoving; it seemed that time had come to a stop. At the priestess' feet two bodies lay, a man's and a woman's.

The young goddesses came up and clustered around her. There were tears in the immortal eyes. "Are we back in the world now?" Cynthia asked.

"Yes. "

"I can turn around?"

"Yes, but you won't like it."

Cynthia turned, fearing a changed Komi, scarred or witless with torments, but she would never let such things drive her off—

And there was no one there, only the shallow rock of the caverns and the unflickering torchlight.

"He wasn't there to begin with," Aretë said. "She lied to you."

"Why didn't you tell me?"

"So that you would go on till the end, and she would not be able to say that you had failed in your bargain and deserved to be cheated by her. It is astonishing how some of our elder kin behave. They know what's good, they advise others to do better, but they do what's worst."

"I think he's not there at all," Sophia said. "He's in some other place beneath the earth. There are several."

"I know," Cynthia said. "I've been in some of them. If I have to go back to that old hole on Phaneraia and rescue him yet again, I'm going to tear the place up by the roots."

"More likely he's in Awornos," Physis said. "Do you

know the place? The word is old, older than the language you speak now; it means 'birdless.' Avernus, the Romans call it. It's near Neapolis, on the coast of Italy. You could take ship and go there."

"I'm out of money," Cynthia said. "I need to find work somewhere. I was busy studying in Athens; I didn't have time to build up a practice. When I have the money, I'll go." And suddenly "Curse her for a liar and a cheat!" She took a step toward the back of the cavern, and now she could see the standing stone again. "We're right on the border, aren't we?"

"Yes. But you are alive and must go back to the world."

Without answering, Cynthia put her hands on the tall stone, where the carving said ABANDON HOPE. She pushed. It rocked a little. She pushed harder.

"Let me," Physis said, and joined her in pushing. The goddess had as much strength as she needed, and with one long thrust they uprooted the stone and sent it sliding down the stairs. They waited a long moment, listening to the grating sound of stone against stone; and then there was a great crash and an angry scream, faint in the depths below.

"So you've got some of your own back," Sophia said.

"I had anyway," Cynthia said. A bitter laughter was beginning to rise out of her throat, and she dug her nails into her palms to drive it back. "I kept her hireling from profaning the Sanctuary; now he's dead she'll have to find another one."

"Oh, no," another voice said, one she knew. She turned back toward the torchlight. The priestess, the torchbearers, the bodies on the ground had not moved, but one standing before them raised her arms to clutch at her hair. "Is it true? My own daughter?"

"I'm afraid so," Cynthia said. "I'm sorry."

"Perhaps I should have known," Demeter said, and began to weep. Cynthia put her arms around her and they cried together for a while; the worn old face, tanned with many summers and wrinkled with as many autumns, dripped tears on Cynthia's shoulder and left it dry.

And all Cynthia could think of was a raucous parody-drama she had seen once, performed in a part of Alexandria she wasn't supposed to go to, a twisted tale of the two Goddesses that ended with Persephonë wailing, "Oh, woe is me! I get to spend three months with my husband, *and nine months with my mother!*"

"Listen, lady," she said at last. "In the west, your name is Ceres. Use it in good health. Now I have to go." She walked away from the cavern; the torchlight began to flicker. Suddenly she could feel her bruised knees aching and she was sitting up in the cave of the Ploutonion with the priestess of Demeter leaning over her, speaking words of praise in her ear.

Two days later the initiates were dismissed to go about their own affairs, and the regents of Eleusis sent Cynthia back to Athens in one of their own wagons, to spare her knees. Zeno was standing in his doorway when she got back to the house.

"I observe you come back alone," he said. "I'm sorry."

"I haven't lost hope yet," she said, and indeed she had seen Elpis again before leaving Eleusis. "There's a place in Italy I have to find out about. For the time being, I have to earn a living. Does anyone in the neighborhood need a boil lanced, a tooth drawn, a baby delivered?"

"Any of those would be virtuous acts, enabling other people to be healthy," the philosopher said. "We can find out. Meanwhile, my housekeeper has gone off to live with her granddaughter and I have a chicken running around in my kitchen that I don't know how to cook. If you do, then we could have dinner, and tomorrow we'll find you some patients."

Note: George E. Mylonas' *Eleusis and the Eleusinian Mysteries* (Princeton University Press, 1961) gives as much information on its topic as we have, which isn't much. The Eleusinians took the secrets of the Mysteries to the grave with them. I have borrowed from Mylonas *passim*, but I have also made things up where I needed to. So if you try to invoke a goddess with this stuff and end up with a pig, don't blame *me*.

THE GLASS SWORD
by Richard Corwin

Richard Corwin is one of those people who is always moving around doing different things. He has gone from teaching early childhood education and studying architecture to educating his own son and designing his own home. He has been paid to dance on stage, work in film, perform stand up comedy, illustrate books, write technical manuals, lecture on history, program computers, consult in banking, and, yes, write short stories. He resides in Santa Barbara with his wife and son (he studied early childhood education, but has since forsaken that for being a parent). He works on restaurants, Web sites, and for four nonprofit organizations. He does sleep, but only occasionally.

This story continues a storyline that began in *Sword & Sorceress IV*, and continued in *Spells of Wonder,* both edited by MZB.

FOR THE BEAUTIFUL AMANDA

A S THE glittering new sun rose over the perfect azure sea for the first time, Kali, who in times past was called Kali the Destroyer, awoke from her sleep in the amber dunes. Once she had been a goddess; now she was human. She was this because she had asked a boon of Great Vishnu, the creator of all things. She wanted to become a human for one brief lifetime, so that she might know the joys and sorrows of mortality. Whenever this life was done, she had promised to return to her place in Nirvana, and there weave the spell that in time would end this new age, and blot out this new sun.

For a moment, though, she stood on the beach, and looked at the yellow sun. A gentle breeze rustled through her clothing. Her clothing was a drift of black silks flecked with tiny silver stars that twinkled, as though burning brightly. The soft cloth wrapped itself around her body in the simplest form of sari. She had slept in these clothes during the time in between this world and the last. It was a long sleep which had lasted through the unregarded centuries that ticked away while Mighty Vishnu himself dreamed up the new firmament. Like the Great Boar, she slept because she had fulfilled her destiny. She had snuffed out every star in the heavens. She had turned all into darkness. And now there was light all around her.

She squinted her eyes to the sun. She had never had to do this in the past. She marveled in the sensation of re-acting to the world around her, rather than the opposite being true. She bent down to touch the damp sand that ran along the edge of the sea foam. It was cold and smelled of brine. She scooped her fingers into the sand and felt a sharp pain. She pulled her hand back and saw that one of her black nails had broken off in the wet alluvium. She picked up the broken nail and examined it in her pale palm. Pain. This was new, too. She mused again to her-self that she was no longer immortal. A broken nail was proof enough of that.

She placed the sharp crescent of black fingernail down upon the sand pebbles, near the cluster of red sandstone rocks in which she had awakened. She would not need a broken fingernail anymore. She would grow a new one.

She smelled the sharp brine of the sea air. As she looked toward the rising sun, a flying fish sailed above the line of the surf. It called out her name. She smiled and nodded in its direction. Soon a dolphin poked its nose above the spray and stared at her. She smiled at it, too, and began to expect that all the creatures of the new world would come to pay homage to her in her human form. It smiled back at her with a sharp tittering giggle. The dolphin's black eyes gleamed with pleasure at seeing one of the Great Ones.

Then, all at once, the dolphin's face grew gray and concerned. Its giggle faded away, and it dove beneath the surface of the waters with great speed. Kali regarded this with her head cocked aside in puzzlement. Then, where the dolphin had been but a moment before, dark foam rose from the water. At first, it seemed to be a single cobra's head, but then it was joined by another, and another, until thirteen jet black heads arched their necks back to inspect Kali with a single stare. As the heads rose from the shimmering glare of the sea, their necks twined into a single body that was as thick about as a man's chest. The snake drew itself up upon its scaly height. It towered above the waves and looked down at Kali as she stood still upon the sand.

"Greetings, Great Kali," said the serpent. As it spoke, flames like tongues flickered out of its mouths. "Or perhaps I should not call you Great, as I see that you are no longer an immortal form."

Kali let out a nearly silent snort as she regarded the serpent. His was a sort of thinly veiled attempt at humor that she could hardly appreciate. She knew him well. He was Vasuki Kalakuta, the lord of the serpents. Neither terrestrial, nor immortal, he was of the lesser demons that existed to test noble men and plague the wicked. Rubbing her chin with her hand, she replied in an even voice, "My greetings to you in return."

Kali was startled at the sound of her own voice. It was not the voice that she had long been accustomed to having. Her voice, as she thought of it, was low, deep, and feminine. It was a voice that echoed against the mountains when she spoke. Now, as a human, her voice was firm and determined, yet it seemed so small and soft.

The serpent peered at her. Then it craned its neck down and brought its thirteen cobra faces next to hers, looking at her very closely. Its fiery breath stank of the oily and poisonous smell of decay. Twenty-six brown eyes, each the size of a fist and tinged with a sickly gold, swayed in front of her. Gently, back and forth, they swayed.

Kali folded her arms. "Do you really think that I can be mesmerized by so simple a trick?" She shook her head. "I may be human in form, my dear Vasuki, but my mind and my memory are still with me. They are unchanged. I know who you are. And I know all of the foolish tricks that you demons play on humankind. These charlatan's tricks will not work on me." The last words were spoken to the demon with cold warning.

The heads snapped away from her, startled by such a rebuke. Then they arched themselves forward again, stretching out the fans in each neck until they nearly merged into one. "I meant no harm. I merely wanted to see that it was really you. You are so different now."

His voices wove a single dark lullaby of sound. "I am so pleased that I can finally see what you look like. I am so used to that great black light that used to stream from your body. That darkness made it difficult to see you clearly."

He paused. "No, I was merely looking at you. Taking in your shape, so that I might remember it in the future."

Thirteen heads rolled out their tongues of flame and sniffed the air about Kali. "You smell of a human, but the delicate perfume of immortality still clings to you." The serpentine mouths smiled. "That is good," they said with a single sulfurous hiss.

"Good?" asked Kali, unamused. "What good might you find in a whiff of immortality? I have asked Mighty Vishnu to let me be human, so that I might know of the pains of flesh, and the joys that go along with the pain. Any immortality that clings to me is an accident." Kali pushed her face next to the nose of one of the heads, "And what would you want with me anyway?"

The demon slithered its long body back into the line of surf, retreating from Kali's advance. "Ah, you ask a fine question. What indeed could I want with you?" The thirteen heads lowered themselves nearer to Kali's level, looking her straight in the eye. The spray of a sudden wave flecked the serpent's oily black skin with white foam. "I will tell you what I desire. I want you to make a petition for me."

Thirteen heads smiled again, then spoke in a courtly chorus of entreaty. "We demons may offer up our prayers, and our demands, but it does us little good. Why? Because we are the demons. We are unfit to be heard by the Great Ones . . . unless we go to war against them. When we fight them, they hear our voices, but only briefly, and only with scorn. We are lesser beings, so when we fight the Great Ones, we lose. We always lose. So this time, in this new world, in this great new epoch, we want to find a different approach toward the Great Ones.

"We are mere lowly demons. You, on the other hand, are the bridge between the two worlds, neither immortal, nor mortal. You can die, so you are not immortal. But, when you die, you return to godhood. So you see, you straddle the two planes. One foot on the earth, one foot in Nirvana. And because you have that foot in Nirvana, we think that you may make a petition to the Gods on our behalf that would be heard. We want you to speak our desires to the Great Vishnu."

Kali's long black hair flowed like the wind as she shook her head from side to side. Her eyes met the serpent's eyes. "What makes you think that I would do you this favor?" she asked.

"Because of your greatness," the serpent replied with soft easiness. His tongues glowed like warm embers amongst his fangs.

She walked a few feet forward, into the waves where the serpent coiled. She put her hands to her hips and leaned her face close to the serpent's heads again. With an icy voice, she asked, "And what would be your petition to the Great Ones?"

The serpent rose up a little. Confident of its words, the thirteen mouths said, "We wish to drink the Nectar. We want the taste of immortality to pass our lips. Much as you want to be mortal for a moment in this epoch, we want to be immortal. It is a change that would please us all. We are certain that if the Great Ones heard our desires, especially coming from one such as you, they would certainly grant our single and most fervent wish."

Kali nodded, and moved back out of the crisp embrace of the cold salt water. She rolled her head to the side, letting her soft hair trail down her bare arm. "And if I do not grant your desire, if I do not speak on your behalf, what then?"

The serpent moved quickly toward Kali, closing the gap between them in a mere moment. He rose up in the water and opened his fans again, so that they blocked out the rising sun. The thirteen heads glowed the red of an angry volcano, and the eyes slicked into a yellow glaze. Vasuki's mouths dripped fire as they spoke: "If you will not assist us, we will take from you the one thing that we can take from you that is of value to you,"

Kali curled her lip at the demon. "And what could you take from me? I am mortal. I have nothing of value."

The snake shook its heads, and they whispered like wind in a graveyard. "No, there is one thing of value that you overlook. We can take from you your life. You will go back to being immortal, and will have learned nothing of being mortal. You will not be able to become mortal for another turning of the long Wheel of the Universe. We will rob you of the knowledge that you seek in this form."

He snarled threateningly, "That we can take from you."

He paused again, and then said in a softer hiss. "So, Great One, will you help us?" Then he reared his heads to strike.

Kali's eyes grew black as thunder clouds. "Great Vasuki," she said with a voice like cold rain, "the power that you seek flows from the dreams of Vishnu. If Vishnu has not granted this power to you, then you will not receive it in this turn of the Wheel of the Universe. It is pointless to ask of them what they cannot give. That is the way of things."

She raised out her arm and angrily pointed a finger at him, "Your fate is your fate. Accept it."

Thirteen mouths curled down into cracked frowns. "Then," the serpent mocked, "you must accept your fate, Mighty Kali." With a lightning-fast gesture, all thirteen heads bore down upon her. The centermost of the heads stretched its fangs and raked her outstretched arm.

Kali leaped backward. Blood from her arm spattered down to the sand. A wave splashed over the sand and the surf bubbled up with red pearls of foam. Pain ran along Kali's arm as she retreated from the water's edge. She backed hastily toward the shelter of a stand of gnarled trees, never turning her back to the demon.

The serpent followed her to the trees, fangs gnashing, and then stopped short. The limbs of the trees were so densely packed that the beast could not enter among them without getting caught amid the branches. Kali was small enough to find refuge in the tangle of wood.

She looked at her arm. It was already beginning to swell. There was poison in the demon's bite. She closed her eyes for a moment, and searched her mind. Recalling what she needed, she spoke the words of a spell under her breath, and the swelling in her arm abated. The skin healed, and covered itself over, leaving two long blue stripes where the fangs had torn the flesh.

Kali collected herself, and sought a way out of her predicament. A few feet away, the great snake tapped his heads upon the upper branches of the trees, seeking an easy way in. He could not make his way to her. This gave her time to concentrate on her attack. She clapped her hands three times and began to chant a simple litany. The sky began to darken, and the new sun was obscured by clouds. Her words grew louder, and the winds began to blow across the unmarked sands. Vasuki paused for a moment and looked toward the oncoming gale. Thirteen heads stared at her with golden eyes that were filled with puzzlement.

Then, with a shout from Kali's mouth, the skies opened up, and lightning fell from the sky. Sheets of lightning. Blue-and-white energy crackled from the blackness, splitting the dark clouds like the bright shards of a broken mirror. The shards spun around the sky, then coalesced into a gigantic ball of white hot anger, and finally crashed down upon Vasuki with a deafening roar.

The serpent crumpled into the ground when the lightning hit him. Then he coiled himself up, shook his head lightly, and narrowed his eyes into slivers of gold. Thirteen mouths hissed flame. "You will need to do better than that. I am not an immortal, but I am one of the lords of the earth. You, on the other hand, are no longer a goddess. Your power is that of a mortal. You are a great sorceress. But that is all that you are: a sorceress. You will need to do better than that . . ." He let out a thin laugh. "Much better than that . . ."

She grew cold for a moment. Fear crept over her. Fear was new to her. She did not entirely understand the emotion, nor was she in control of it as it climbed up her spine and clawed about her belly. Now she knew how humans felt when she addressed them. But there was little time for fear. She brushed it aside like cobwebs from an old hearth, and turned her mind to finding a way out.

She reached for a branch of one of the trees, and snapped it off. It was a mostly straight branch. She had broken it in such a way as to afford her a sharp end. She looked up at the mocking heads that hovered above the branches. She smiled. Lightning fast, she cocked her arm back, and hurled the makeshift spear at one of the heads.

It bounced off of the soft tissue just below the jaw of the head. The other dozen heads curled around to look at her. "Fool!" he shouted, "That will scarcely scratch my skin. Nothing of this new land has the taint of the eternal. Only a weapon from the immortal plane could harm me. You brought nothing of that sort with you. There are only earthly things here. I am a lord of this earth. What can you wield that might threaten me, tiny Kali?"

Kali looked at the ground. Amid the soil of the trees were flinty rocks. She condensed her mind into a single thread of thought: iron. Hot iron. The thread took shape, and a blast of heat shot from her brow. The ground at her feet scorched and melted. But the rocks would not melt themselves into iron at her command. All she had melted was the sand. That was not enough. Her powers were no longer unlimited. She now began to understand that being human had limitations. She determined to seek assistance that was beyond such limitations.

She looked up into the skies and cried out, "Great Vishnu! Old friend, come aid me!" But the skies were silent, and the dark clouds that she had summoned were beginning to drift away.

The serpent smiled a wicked smile of victory. The cowls of his heads relaxed and slimmed back into the shape of his heads. He taunted her, "Now, mighty Kali, Creator and Destroyer of all great things, now we must come to an agreement. You will bow to my will. You will speak to the Great Ones on our behalf, or you will suffer my wrath.

Bow down, or I will destroy you, as easily as you have failed to destroy me."

Kali was beaten. She knew that she had to submit to his will. There was no way out, except death. But there was the great desire to live, if only for a while, because there was so much to learn. She felt weak.

"I will give way," she said, sadly stepping out of the trees.

Thirteen baleful heads smiled. Thirteen wicked tongues darted with flame.

But as she stepped forward, something shattered under her foot. It was the ground. The sand had fused itself into glass. She looked down at the silvery slivers under her feet. Set against the ground, one tiny bit of glass twinkled black. Black like her fingernail. Black like the one thing that was a memento of the time when she was immortal. Her nails. They were not new. They did not belong to this earth.

She stepped back into the trees to think for another moment. Vasuki hunched toward the opening out of which she had run. Her hair and skin did not belong to this earth, she thought, but they would not make much for weapons. She looked at her hands. She could not hope to tear at him with her own fingernails. To come close enough to Vasuki to hurt him would put her in danger from his fangs. And she knew that his poison could hurt her. She had to keep some distance from him, somehow.

But there was one broken fingernail. One useful scrap of immortality that could be used against him. She smiled.

"Why do you smile, beaten Kali?" the beast asked with a derisive tone.

She did not answer. Her mind was focusing on a single thought. With a sudden leap, she sprang from the thicket of trees and sprinted down the beach toward the red rocks. Vasuki roared hot anger from thirteen throats and began to slither after her.

As she neared the cluster of red sandstone, her throat shouted out a single spell of a single shape. She leaped into the air and a second blast of heat exploded from her body. She landed amongst the red rocks and shook a glass sword from the sands at her feet. Straight and sharp, it was clear glass until the eyes rested upon the tip. In the tip of the sword was the black crescent nail of Kali the Destroyer. Looking at the tip, the human known as Kali stood her ground, and waited for the bilious Lord of the Serpents to close his distance.

She did not have to wait long. He came thundering down upon her in a storm of ivory fangs. His body sprouted arms, and with the hissing of a fiery spell from his mouth, a long silver ax fell from the sky into his hands. He drove the ax at her with the speed that only a striking cobra could posses.

She raised the glass sword with an upward swing and blocked his cut at the last moment of safety. When the two weapons met, lightning coursed along the length of the sword. It did not break. It *would* not break. The sword was marked with the strength of the immortal plane.

She swung the sword at him in her first attack. He beat it back with a blunt defensive riposte that showered sparks into the waters behind them. His heads roared with anger. She slashed at his heads, but he blocked her again. In a quick counterthrust, her sword traced his forearm, and opened a wound. Black drops of blood spilled from the Lord of the Serpents. As the blood touched the sand, the dappled ground sprouted with cobras and poisonous vines. The cobras skulked away, and the vines grew and twisted about the red rocks.

Kali looked at the fleeing cobras and frowned. Vasuki smiled. "You see what you have done?" he jeered. "You have unleashed a little more darkness into your new world. There are poisonous snakes where there were none before."

Kali had a new problem. She had to kill Vasuki, but she had to avoid spilling more of his blood. She could not let the world be overrun by the seeds of his black ichor.

He swung his ax down upon her again. This time she leaped aside, not defending the cut at all, but evading it instead. The ax slid down past her body and wedged itself in the rocks with a grating metallic clattering. As the stones rang with a crashing of silver, Kali struck her blow. With a single motion of the very tip of the sword, she sliced Vasuki's head from his body.

His neck began to spurt black venom as his heads fell onto the sand. Kali grasped the writhing heads and began to drink the poison before it could fall to the earth. As she drank the blood of the Lord of the Serpents, her own skin began to change. No longer fair in color, her skin turned blue, and then as black as night.

A few drops spilled away as she drained the dark bile from the heads, and snakes sprouted where the blood spilled. With eyes that were yellow with anger, the newly formed cobras slithered away from her and over the dunes. At her feet, the poison-slicked vines grew and twined their way toward the tree line and into the forest beyond.

When there was no life left in the dead beast, Kali let his head fall to the earth. She looked at the thirteen heads with an angry frown. With the sharp edge of the glass sword she cut a length of skin from Vasuki's body. Using a strand of her own hair and a broken fang for a needle, she sewed a belt and a scabbard for the sword. The casing glittered with the dark iridescence of the demon's scales. Kali smiled at her handiwork.

As the new sun rose high in the sky on its first day, Kali had accomplished great things. She had removed one of the demons from the earth. Even though snakes and poisonous plants now had a foothold on the new earth, she had constrained their powers by depriving them of a lord to command them. In limiting them, they would never rule this place that she would come to call home. She had learned of pain, she had learned of weakness, and she had learned of fear. There was much more for her to learn.

Kali slung the sword over her back and walked along the beach. A breeze from the sea filled her mind with the cool smell of salt air. She looked at the yellow sun towering in the midday sky. She wondered what else she might learn before new the sun set at the end of its first day.

BED OF ROSES
by Elisabeth Waters

Elisabeth Waters spent two decades as MZB's secretary. Along the way, she started writing. (This happened to nearly everyone who spent much time in MZB's vicinity— she was a born teacher.) Elisabeth produced over thirty short stories and one novel, plus the occasional non-fiction piece ("Death, Taxes, and the Writer" appears on the Marion Zimmer Bradley Literary Works Trust Web site http://mzbworks.home.att.net—along with several of MZB's articles about the craft of writing).

One of the hazards of being part of MZB's household was unsolicited criticism. MZB would pick up anything lying around and give her reaction to it whether one asked for her opinion or not. She found a draft of this story one day and complained that it had "too much sex." Elisabeth's indignant response was "It's got one kiss in it! And it's not intended for your magazine, so give it back." *Marion Zimmer Bradley's Fantasy Magazine* was very strict—almost puritanical—about what it printed; MZB wanted it to be suitable for younger readers while still being interesting to adults. With *Sword & Sorceress* she wasn't concerned about whether she would receive an apologetic letter from a middle-school librarian saying, "I'm sorry, but the principal says we have to cancel our subscription to your magazine."

Elisabeth would like to thank Rosemary Edghill for her help with this story.

"**Y**OU do realize, don't you, that this is entirely your fault."

In spite of the wording, Rosa knew this was not a question. She sat quietly, feet together and hands clasped loosely in her lap, in the parlor where novices of the Order of the Holy City were allowed to receive visitors, glad that there was a metal grille between her and her mother. She would have been happier if her Novice Mistress had not been sitting in the corner out of a visitor's sight, listening to every word.

"It's bad enough that your father allowed you to work in the forge with him and gave you ideas totally unfit for a young woman, but to allow you to refuse marriage to Dathan and to give in to your desire to enter the Order and become a swordswoman—well, I'm just happy he didn't live to see the ensuing disaster!"

"What disaster? Mother, you haven't come to see me in the three years since I came here. Why are you here now?"

"Don't you talk to me like that! Don't they teach you the Commandments here: "Obey your father and mother"—and now that your poor father is dead . . ."

" 'Honor thy father and thy mother, that thy days may be long in the land which the Lord thy God giveth thee.' " Rosa could easily quote the Commandments from memory—after all, there *were* only ten of them. "And I assure you, Mother, that I honor you to the very best of my ability."

"Then leave this place, go with Dathan, and save your brother."

"Garcia? What's wrong with him?"

"Abiram has taken him." Her mother's grim voice was assumed for the purpose of making Rosa feel guilty; Rosa had heard this tone many times before. She heard the Novice Mistress gasp softly and, out of the corner of her eye, saw the older woman cross herself.

"Why would such a powerful wizard want my baby

brother? And how did he get hold of him? Garcia's only six years old, and he's been baptized. I was there."

"Never you mind how Abiram got him—that's not important. Dathan says he probably wants him for a virgin sacrifice. He also says that he'll take you to the wizard's lair and help you rescue your brother."

Rosa wondered just how the rather over-confident young man her mother had wanted her to marry thought he could pull this off. "And what does he want in return for this great favor, assuming he can do it and we all survive?"

"Nothing much," her mother said complacently. "Simply one night in your bed."

Rosa gasped. "Mother, I'm a pledged virgin!"

"I'm sure the Order will release you once you're not a virgin, and Dathan is still willing to marry you."

I'll just bet he is, Rosa thought. *Dathan must still be obsessed with me, God alone knows why. But I can't very well sit here quietly and let my baby brother be sacrificed. I'll at least have to find out what's really going on here.*

"I'll have to get permission from my superiors, Mother," she said, forcing her voice to remain calm. "I'll have an answer for you this evening."

"I shall return then," her mother said, "and it had better be the right answer. We need Dathan back in the family."

"Abiram!" the Novice mistress gasped in horror as soon as Rosa's mother was out of hearing, and they were heading down the hallway back to the cloister. "How could any of your family become involved with one of the disensouled ones?"

"I think Dathan might have something to do with it," Rosa said slowly, feeling sick. "It wasn't just because of my sense of vocation that my father let me enter the Order—he didn't like Dathan. Neither did I; he always gave me the creeps, although there was nothing specific in his behavior I could point to. Mother liked him, and she was very upset when I wouldn't marry him."

"Was he upset, too?"

"*He* was livid. He cursed me and swore I'd regret it—that one day I'd learn to value him as I ought, that I'd come crawling to him. I think he was crazed; he was so totally convinced that I should do whatever he said. And it didn't help that, although he was Father's apprentice, I was better at his job."

"Pride, envy, covetousness—I can see why you wouldn't wish to marry him."

"And now we can add wrath to the list. I'm surprised he wasn't with my mother for this visit, and I bet he'll be with her tonight. With Father dead, I don't know if he found a new Master to finish out his apprenticeship. Father died so suddenly."

"Could he have sought out Abiram and asked him to take him on?"

Rosa stopped dead in the hallway. "Oh, God." It was a prayer. "Yes, I think he could have—he was never over-burdened with scruples. He broke a crucible once and told me that I had a choice: I could tell my father I'd done it, or he'd tell my father I'd done it. I told my father the truth, of course, but I don't know what, if anything, he said to Dathan about it."

"If Dathan is working for Abiram," the Novice Mistress pointed out, "then this is bound to be a trap. And, if it's virgins he wants, your going in search of your brother would give him three more."

Rosa nodded soberly. "Me, Judith, and Fatima." The sisters of the Order never went anywhere alone, and they worked in triads: one member from each of the faiths that made up the Order. Judith was Jewish, Rosa was Christian, and Fatima was Moslem. They had studied and worked together for over two years and were a good team, but Rosa would have to consider carefully before risking their lives on the chance of saving her brother's. "On the other hand, if Garcia is bait, he's probably still unharmed."

"How would Abiram get hold of your brother?"

"I think my mother might be in on it," Rosa said miserably. "I was thirteen when Garcia was born. Mother complained through the entire pregnancy and then made me attend the birth. It was really bad—I don't understand what, but something went wrong—and when the healer told her afterward that she could not conceive any more children, Mother said that was a blessing she had prayed for since I was born. She cared for Garcia even less than for me. So if Dathan came to her and said he could get me back, and then we'd live with her and it would be like old times, and he just needed to borrow Garcia for a few days . . ."

The Novice Mistress sighed. "We'll need to talk to the Council about this. Come along."

Rosa followed her along the halls to the Council room, feeling scared and sick. *Could Mother really have been so stupid? Does she care for Garcia so little—and Dathan so much?*

The Council—the rabbi, priest, and imam who together ran the Order weren't unkind men and didn't mean to be intimidating, but no one could deny that the situation was outrageous.

"Abiram!" The imam spat out the name. "Do you know what he is, child?"

"No, sir," Rosa said. "Not really. Sister said something about his being disensouled . . ."

"My brother," the rabbi said quietly, "if we are to consider this, we should have the rest of her triad join us for this discussion—" He turned to Rosa and added, "—unless you want to drop the matter now."

"No, Rabbi," Rosa said miserably.

The rabbi rang a small bell on the table. The novice on duty quickly entered the room, and the rabbi said, "Have Judith and Fatima join us here immediately."

Rosa gulped. This was getting too real. "I don't want to risk Judith and Fatima," she said, "but Garcia is my baby brother—I was the first one to hold him when he was born. I don't know if I can just stay here and do nothing." She took a deep breath. "And because I believe that our mother may have been a party to turning him over to Abiram—" the men looked grave, but none of them said anything, "—I ask that, if we *can* save him, he be taken into the order as an oblate."

That got an appreciative grin from the priest. "If the Order saves his life, it has every right to demand custody of him until he is of age. How old is he now?"

"Six, Father."

"Good," the priest said. "If he has not yet reached the age of reason, the harm Abiram can do to him is limited."

"He can kill him," the imam pointed out dryly.

"Yes, but he can't take his soul," the priest replied.

"I'd just as soon he didn't do either," Rosa said.

There was a tap on the door, followed by the novice's announcement, "Here are Judith and Fatima, Rabbi."

"Thank you. The rabbi nodded a dismissal to the young man. "Sit down, girls."

Judith and Fatima took their places on the bench on either side of Rosa. "What's going on?" Fatima whispered.

"What is going on," the imam, who had very good hearing, replied, "is that Rosa's six-year-old brother has, according to her mother, been taken by the wizard Abiram."

Fatima gasped; Judith looked bewildered.

"I see that you, at least, have heard of him, Fatima," the imam said. "Tell us what you know."

"Abiram is one of the disensouled," Fatima replied. "He is a wizard whose power comes from giving up his soul in exchange for it."

"You mean he sold his soul to the devil?" Rosa asked.

"That's probably what a Christian would call it," Fatima said, "but what he really did was seal up his soul in some sort of crystal or something. Then he probably put it somewhere he would consider safe."

"I've heard of that," Judith said. "Without a soul, he has no consciousness of good or evil, so he can do whatever he thinks will benefit him and take power wherever he can get it, without being troubled by any sense that he is doing wrong."

"That sounds scary," Rosa said.

"It is," Judith and Fatima said in unison.

"So are we going to try to rescue Garcia?" Judith asked. She was the best swordswoman of the three, while Fatima was the best scholar. Rosa was pretty much average at both.

"That is the question before us," the priest said. "Sister," he turned to the Novice Mistress, "exactly what did Rosa's mother want from her?"

"She wanted her to go with Dathan, the man her mother wanted her to marry before she came to us, to rescue the child. According to her, Dathan is willing to help Rosa get her brother back and still wants to marry her. She said that the price for his help was a night in Rosa's bed—after which she thinks we won't want Rosa and she'll have to marry Dathan."

Judith and Fatima both started laughing. "A night in your bed?" Fatima said. "With you?"

"Doesn't your mother know we sleep in a barracks?" Judith asked.

"I don't think so," Rosa replied.

The imam frowned. "Unless he's a total idiot who will get you all killed—which does not seem impossible—he intends for Rosa, at least, to survive."

"I don't think it would occur to him that Judith and Fatima would come with me," Rosa said.

"It would probably occur to Abiram," the rabbi said. "I knew him long ago. Unless his basic character has changed, he's intelligent, but sometimes he forgets about common sense. He *might* not count on getting three of you, but I wouldn't bet on it. We have to assume that this is a trap."

"So we have to prepare for the worst case," the priest said, "if you girls want to do this. You don't have to, you know that. No one will think any the less of you if you don't."

"I'll think less of myself," Judith said promptly. "Someone who could stay here safe behind walls while a small child is in danger is not the kind of person I want to be. I want to be worthy of guarding Jerusalem someday."

Being appointed to take a turn at guarding the Holy City was the highest honor the Order could bestow. Judith had never made any secret of her desire to be found worthy of the honor, and Rosa rather aspired to it herself. And Fatima, she knew, wanted to study there, which was a side benefit of being appointed a Guardian of the Holy City.

"If we have a chance," Fatima said, "I want to try."

"They handed him to me when he was born," Rosa said, "because everyone else was busy with my mother. Now she's tossed him aside. If she doesn't want him, he's mine. If she won't care for him, I will. I love him. I have to."

"Then we'd best start making plans for every contingency we can think of," the imam said, "starting with exactly what your goals are."

"To rescue Garcia," Rosa said.

"You are unlikely to achieve that without encountering Abiram," the priest pointed out gently. "What do you plan to do then?"

"Kill him, of course," Judith said. "He's evil."

"While there is certainly a great deal to be said for your point of view, Judith," the priest said, "it is a tenet of the Christian faith that God desires a sinner to have a chance to repent and turn from evil—which he can't do if he's dead."

"But can he do it without a soul?" Rosa asked. "It seems unlikely. Don't you need a soul to repent?"

"Precisely," the priest said. "If you can find the crystal his soul is in and destroy it, his soul will return to him. I don't know if that would save him, but it should certainly distract him long enough for all of you to escape."

"And it would take away a great deal of his power," Fatima added.

The imam crossed to a wall covered with books and scrolls and selected a scroll. "Study this," he said. "It contains drawings of every known receptacle for a wizard's soul."

The three girls spent the rest of the afternoon studying the scroll and the other books the Council put in front of them and listening as the three most learned men in the city told them everything they could think of about how to handle wizards and spells. In the late afternoon they went to the chapel to pray and to give each girl a blessing and an amulet to help protect her.

"We have done all we can," the imam said. "The rest is up to you.

"Go with God," the priest said.

"And return safely," the rabbi added.

The three girls bowed, then followed the novice mistress to the armory, where they put on their chain mail and gathered their weapons. One of the younger novices on errand duty found them there. "Rosa, your mother is here to see you—and she has a man with her!"

"Thank you," the Novice Mistress said. "You may go now." As the girl ran off, obviously full of excitement at this unusual event, the Novice Mistress added dryly, "It would appear that you were correct, Rosa."

They went to the visitor's parlor, and Rosa and the Novice Mistress sat facing Rosa's mother and Dathan. Judith and Fatima stayed in the alcove out of sight.

"Well, girl," Rosa's mother said impatiently, "have you come to your senses?"

"I don't believe I've ever been out of them, Mother," Rosa replied. "But if you're talking about your request of this morning, I have talked to the Council and they have granted us permission to rescue Garcia."

"And for me to spend the night afterward, in your bed?" Dathan asked eagerly.

"I told them that was your condition," Rosa said calmly, "and none of them objected."

"Good," Dathan said with a self-satisfied smirk. "How soon can you be ready to leave?"

"Any time you are," Rosa replied.

"Now, then." Dathan was almost drooling.

"Very well," Rosa said. "We'll meet at the gatehouse. Do we need horses?"

"No, we'll have a better chance of slipping in unnoticed without them."

"How long will it take us to walk there?"

"Most of the night. It should work out well—Abiram goes to bed around dawn."

"Then we'll meet at the gatehouse in five minutes." Rosa rose and left the room, noting as she did so that her mother hadn't said a word after her first sentence. *Not exactly the picture of a concerned parent*, she thought.

Dathan appeared stunned to see three young women in chain mail and dark cloaks, when he had clearly expected only one. "What's going on here?" he demanded, his voice almost a whine. "Are you planning to fight a battle?"

"Only if necessary," Judith muttered.

"The Order does not permit me to leave the grounds alone," Rosa said. "Didn't you know that? These are my companions."

She didn't introduce them; neither of them had evidenced the slightest desire to become acquainted with

Dathan, and he was trying to ignore them. He also tried to put an arm around Rosa's shoulder, but she shoved her elbow into his ribs as hard as she could, and he kept his hands to himself after that.

It was the gray light of false dawn when they reached the base of the hill where the wizard's house was located. "There's a secret passage into the cellars," Dathan said. "Follow me, I'll show you the way."

"After morning prayers," Rosa said.

"What?!?"

"We are a religious Order, Dathan," Rosa pointed out. "We say prayers every morning. And this is an enterprise we particularly want God to bless."

"Oh, all right, if you insist." Dathan sat on a nearby rock. "Go ahead and pray, for all the good it will do you."

Judith began. "Hear, O Israel, the Lord our God, the Lord is One."

Rosa and Fatima joined in, "Blessed art Thou, O God, King of the Universe, who hast made me according to thy will."

Rosa continued, "In the name of the Father, the Son, and the Holy Ghost."

The other two joined her. "Our Father, who art in heaven, hallowed be thy name. Thy kingdom come, thy will be done, on earth as it is in heaven. Give us this day our daily bread, and forgive us our trespasses as we forgive those who trespass against us. And lead us not into temptation, but deliver us from evil. For thine is the kingdom and the power and the glory for ever and ever."

Then Fatima took up her part. "In the name of Allah, the Compassionate, the Merciful!"

Judith and Rosa joined her for the prayer. "Praise be to Allah, Lord of the Worlds, the Compassionate, the Merciful, King of the Day of Judgment. Thee only do we worship; Thee do we beseech for help. Guide Thou us on the straight path, the path of those whom Thou hast favored; not of those upon whom thy wrath is brought down, nor of those who go astray."

"*Shema Ysrael Adonoi Elohenu, Adonoi Echod,*" Judith finished.

"*In Nomine Patris, Filii, et Spiritus Sancti,*" Rosa added, rising from her knees to her feet.

"*Allahu Akbar,*" Fatima said, uncurling from her position on the ground and standing tall. "Let's go."

"You do that every day?" Dathan asked incredulously.

"Several times every day," Rosa said. "Don't you believe in anything?"

"I believe in Power," Dathan said, "and I believe you're wasting time."

"You said yourself that Abiram goes to bed around dawn," Rosa pointed out. "We just gave him a bit more time to get there."

"Let's go," Judith said, adding jokingly, "how can God forgive our trespasses if we don't trespass?"

They climbed the hill and made it into the cellars without incident.

Dathan looked into the first room on the left and frowned. "He's not here," he said. "Abiram must have taken him upstairs."

Rosa tried not to think of the implications of that remark. *Hold on, Garcia,* she thought, *we'll get you out of here just as soon as we can.*

Dathan entered a room on the right of the hallway and said, "Here. These are some of his spells. Breaking the crystals will release them—we may need a distraction." He grabbed one crystal and put it in his pocket, as the girls looked over the rest.

"These," Fatima whispered, grabbing half a dozen and passing them out to the other girls. "They're illusion spells:

smoke, fire, fog, that sort of thing. Apprentice level—this must be a very old workroom."

"Are they Abiram's work?" Rosa whispered softly.

"They're not Dathan's," Fatima reassured her in an even softer whisper. "The feel is wrong. If Abiram is teaching him, these aren't the result."

"Come on," Dathan said impatiently. "There's nothing useful down here; we'll have to go upstairs." They started up a flight of narrow stairs with Dathan in the lead and Rosa immediately behind him. Judith and Fatima followed her.

At the top of the stairs there was a wooden door. Dathan put one hand on the handle and turned to Rosa as if to caution her to be quiet. But he held up his other hand instead, broke the crystal he was carrying, and blew the powdery contents straight into her face.

Rosa, tears streaming down her face, fought down the desire to cough, but it was a moment before she had control of herself again. Even through her chain mail, she could feel Judith's hand gripping her shoulder, holding her up. When she could breathe again, she looked up at Dathan.

He looked handsome and desirable, almost as if there were a soft golden glow around him. Rosa might not have been the best student in her magic class, but it wasn't hard to figure out that when someone you had disliked for years suddenly looked good to you, there was magic involved. *And from what I remember of love spells, when this wears off I'm* really *going to despise you,* she thought.

She carefully kept her face blank and said softly, "Is my brother on the other side of the door?"

Dathan blinked at her and looked puzzled.

Did he expect me to fling myself into his arms?

"Uh, yes, I think he should be."

"Let's go, then."

Perforce Dathan opened the door and stepped through it. The three girls quickly followed him and spread out so they'd have room to maneuver. The scene that greeted them, however, was an ordinary looking dining room, with two people at the table: Garcia, and a man Rosa supposed must be Abiram. He appeared to be young, in his early twenties, and was absolutely gorgeous, except for the emptiness of his eyes.

If our rabbi knew him long ago, Rosa thought, *he must have a really horrible looking picture in his attic.*

"Rosa!" Garcia jumped up from the table and ran to hug her. "Dathan said he'd bring you to visit us, but I wasn't sure you'd come."

"And miss a chance to visit my favorite brother?" Rosa smiled at him.

"I'm your only brother, silly." Garcia leaned against her. "I've missed you. It was no fun at all with just Mother. She got so sick of having me around that she told Dathan he could take me to visit Abiram." He remembered his manners. "This is Abiram. Sir, this is my sister Rosa."

Rosa took a step toward the wizard, shoving Garcia back into Fatima's arms as she did so. Judith moved to guard Fatima and the child.

"How do you do," Rosa said politely. "It was kind of you to invite my brother to visit, but we've come to take him home now."

"Have you now?" Abiram looked amused.

"Master," Dathan said, "I did as I promised. I brought the virgins to you, and you said I could have her." He pointed to Rosa. "But she's not reacting to the spell."

Abiram threw back his head and laughed. "Are you referring to that old love spell I made when I was just starting my training? The one in the old workroom in the cellar?"

"If it's a crystal that releases pink powder, he is," Rosa said. She felt drawn to Abiram; she shared his amusement without quite being aware why.

"And it never occurred to you that the spell might work better for its maker than for someone who picked it up at random?" Abiram still obviously thought this was a great joke. He turned the full brilliance of his smile on Rosa. "Come here, my love."

Rosa walked slowly toward him as if entranced, ignoring the protests behind her, which ranged from Fatima's "No, Rosa, it's magic," to Dathan's, "No, she's supposed to be mine! You promised!"

"And you believed me?" Abiram sounded mildly incredulous. He turned his head to look at Dathan, and that was when Rosa saw it. A single black crystal dangled from his left ear. She heard Fatima gasp as she, too, recognized it as a soul crystal and prayed that Abiram hadn't heard her, too.

But his head was turning toward Fatima now, and Rosa knew she had to act quickly. She stepped into Abiram's arms, pressed her lips to his, and entwined her arms around his neck. He deepened the kiss, making it difficult for Rosa to concentrate. Praying to God for strength and focusing on her objective, she ran her fingers through his hair and thanked God that she was wearing mail gauntlets. Even if they did leave her fingers free, they covered her palms and the backs of her hands. Quickly she clapped her hands over the earring, praying she was right. She wasn't going to get another chance.

The crystal broke between her hands, and a whirlwind suddenly swept through the room. Rosa staggered backward; Judith caught her shoulders and steadied her.

Abiram dropped to the floor, curled up in a ball with both hands over his head, and started screaming.

"I think it's time to leave," Fatima said loudly enough to be heard over the screaming as she moved sideways towards the door. "Obviously our host is indisposed."

Rosa and Judith followed her. As Dathan followed them, Rosa said, "Shouldn't you do something for your Master?"

"What?" Dathan shrugged. "He's no good to me now. And you and I have an agreement."

"So we do," Rosa said. "All right, let's go. We can send someone from the Order to help him."

It took most of the rest of the day to get home, and Dathan was silent the entire journey. Rosa spent it explaining to Garcia that he was going to come to the Order and live with them now, so he wouldn't have to go back to his mother. Garcia showed more enthusiasm for the idea than Rosa had ever seen from him, and she was ashamed of herself for not having done this sooner. She had every right to escape from her mother and her plots, but she should never have left Garcia behind.

Once they got back to the Order and turned an exhausted Garcia over to the Novice Master, they had to report to the Council. As Rosa had suspected, they decided to send someone to see what, if anything, could be done for Abiram.

Evening prayers that night were fervent, especially the thanksgivings, even if three of the participants were almost asleep on their feet. By the time they staggered back to the barracks, Rosa felt she could sleep for a week, even on the floor.

Dathan was just outside the doorway, smirking, standing next to the Novice Mistress. "Are you ready for bed, Rosa?" he asked smugly.

"Yes," Rosa yawned. "Are you?"

"Absolutely."

"All right; follow me." She led the way into the room. Her roommates had all been warned; everyone was in chain mail down to at least her knees, and one woman stood beside Rosa's bed holding two sets of chains.

"Here's my bed," Rosa said. "Go ahead and lie down."

Dathan looked at the bed in dismay. "But it's so narrow! How do you sleep in this without falling out?"

"Practice," Judith said with a grin.

"But you'll have help," Fatima said. She took a set of chains, fastened a fetter around one of his ankles, shoved him backward onto the bed, wound the chain under the foot of the bed, and locked the other end around his other ankle.

Judith took the other set and repeated the process with his hands: the manacles around his wrists and the chain under the head of the bed. "There, now you won't fall out."

"But Rosa's supposed to sleep with me!"

"I'll be right here," Rosa wrapped herself in her cloak and lay down on the floor between her bed and the next, carefully just out of his reach. "Good night, Dathan."

She rolled on her side, facing away from him and composed herself for sleep. He could spend the night in her bed as she had promised, and they'd turn him loose in the morning. With any luck he'd never bother her again.

With even more luck, once this story spread, he'd be such a laughingstock that he'd leave town.

SWORD OF PEACE

by Lucy Cohen Schmeidler

Lucy Cohen Schmeidler was born and raised in New York City. She is a computer software developer, and is married, with three children. She has sold stories to *The Leading Edge* and to *Marion Zimmer Bradley's Fantasy Magazine*.

Life as a mercenary is hard enough, but add in a sword that won't do what you want it to do in battle and you've got real problems—even before the sword starts telling you *its* problems.

GAVRIELLA felt the sword jerk within her grasp, and gripped it more tightly in her blood-slicked hand. *Vengeance*, as she had decided to call it, was a good sword, whether or not it was a magical weapon: well balanced, sharp of edge, and easy to wield. And it had never failed her in practice. Only now, when her skill with the weapon could mean the difference between life and death, did it seem strangely—slippery? No, not quite. It moved as an extension of her own body to block any thrusts against her; it was only when she tried to strike out against an enemy that the sword seemed to twist away, like a live thing with no love of battles. But why would anyone make an enchanted sword that hated blood?

She was still considering that paradox after the battle, as she carefully cleaned *Vengeance* and prepared to put her away. Yes, *her*. Without knowing why, Gavriella was convinced that *Vengeance* was female, like her owner.

It was a strange sword, in any case. Gavriella had gotten her in yesterday's battle from the second man she had killed, and it had been a very close thing. She had been doing her best to counter her much larger attacker, her standard issue sword against his huge blade, which glowed like pure silver, and just as their swords met, the man had let out a roar and flung his blade away. Only it had seemed to her at the time that his roar was echoed by a higher, shriller scream.

After running him through, she had picked up his weapon, judging it too valuable to lie there in the mud until claimed by some human scavenger, and had been surprised to find that the sword that had loomed so large in her opponent's hand felt just comfortable in hers. Of course, she did the only safe thing and took it to the company battle mage, who could find no spell on it, not to cause its previous owner to throw it away, nor to change size as it changed owners, nor to scream in a woman's voice.

Truth to tell, she had been looking for a good sword ever since she had begun winning occasional matches in the practice yard. Yes, she knew, if she survived six months in the unit, she'd be accounted a full member and given a proper weapon. And she understood the logic of it: If she never mastered the sword, if she remained just one more soft object to be used to slow the enemy's advance, there was no reason to throw them good steel as well. But the drillmaster had said she had a knack for the trade, and she wanted to live.

"Sweet lady," she said, addressing the sword, "let me know how best to win your help in this war."

She felt a vibration course through the sword, but the answer when it came was not spoken aloud but simply echoed within her own head: "If you want to help me, then put me aside. For, sword that I am, I have no love of blood."

"I would do that if I could. However I am a soldier, and you are a sword with good balance and a keen edge. And whatever talent I have, I don't think my chances of surviving this war are all that good if I have to make do with a standard issue sword."

"Selfish you are. Selfish and bloodthirsty, just like all soldiers."

"Selfish? When I risk my life each day in defense of my king and country? And not bloodthirsty, certainly; I am simply following my profession. Lady, what would you have of me?"

"You may address me by my name, Ilana."

"Ilana, my name is Gavriella." She swept the sword a bow. "Lady Ilana, can you tell me how so noble a spirit came to be imprisoned in a sword? For it is clear to me that this is not a form that you wished to take on."

"Indeed it is not. I was imprisoned here by a jealous rival."

"Jealous in what way? I doubt that rivalry over a mere man could have put you in such a distressful position."

"Not that kind of rival, no. A rival in sorcery. As much as I hate to admit it, he was a stronger enchanter than I."

"I am sorry to hear that, and I will gladly do anything I can to help you, if only you will serve me willingly as a sword."

"Then swear to help me, and I am yours."

"A blood oath?"

"No, not more blood. Is there nothing else your kind holds sacred?"

"Our word. But you seemed reluctant to trust mine."

"Then let us swear to each other. You to help me get free of the sword, and I to fight for you until I am free."

"I, Gavriella of Liblom, swear to be ready at all times to do whatever it might take to free Ilana—"

"Of Trandor."

"Ilana of Trandor from the curse that keeps her imprisoned in this sword. But—Trandor. That's our enemy."

"Your enemy, not mine. And only an enemy because my kinsman Hadar, who tried to arrange a truce, was killed before he could speak of it. Now my turn: I, Ilana of Trandor, swear to fight to the best of my ability in the service of Gavriella of Liblom."

"Can you tell me anything more of this enchanter who trapped you?"

"Only his name, I'm afraid: Eitan. I don't even know whether he still lives, which is unfortunate, since the easiest way to lift a spell such as this is to have the original spellcaster undo it, though I don't know what would possibly have convinced him to do that. However, as of the last I heard, he had disappeared and was presumed dead. And that implies that I am under a very strong spell, if it is strong enough to have survived its maker's death."

"Then I doubt that I have much chance of lifting it. Was it originally formulated with some kind of condition attached, so that you can free yourself if the right situation should arise?"

"Eitan said that I will return to my rightful form 'when and only when I destroy the treachery eating at the heart of Trandor.' "

"Well, that's it, then. Now I can put you away, and think of how to free you." Putting away was easy; thinking of solutions was not. Gavriella knew little of enchantments, other than the standard ones the battle mage performed regularly on the eve of battle. Or slightly stronger ones you could pay him for. But she doubted that he was good enough to undo the work of a master sorcerer. And to remove the treachery at the heart of Trandor? She would rather abet that treachery, and see Trandor destroyed. Then she could give up her enchanted sword and go back to life as—as—as a courier, a cook, even a whore—as anything but a soldier.

But like it or not, the battle mage was the only enchanter she knew, of whom she could ask questions. So she decided to seek him out first thing the next morning.

First thing the next morning they were attacked, and Gavriella had barely time to throw on some clothes and grab up her sword before the Trandorian troops had overrun the barracks. But if the only way out was for her to hack a passage through the mass of men in the doorway, then she would do it. Even if she was cut down before she was halfway there.

As she pulled her sword free of its scabbard, she felt a vibration in her hand, as if the sword was humming to itself. Or purring. "Go to it, Ilana," she whispered, meeting the thrust of the man opposite. It took several minutes before she finished him and by then, the humming had become part of her, and she knew nothing but the feel of her arm, slashing and thrusting of its own accord, as she fought her way to the outside and then to the stables, where she helped hold off the torch-wielding attackers until the Liblom cavalry were mounted and away, and then she fought her way to the ruined gatehouse and down the road, seeing nothing but the enemy soldiers and hearing nothing but the song of the sword, until a voice called out from behind her, "Hey, Gavriella. Berserker girl! Wait up."

She turned to see her friend Aryeh riding toward her on one of the horses she had helped save. "Was that 'wait up' or 'wake up?'" she called back.

"Whichever. Do you know you were running faster than I could ride?"

"Is the horse lame?"

"No. Healthy as a horse. Can you mount up behind me?"

She wiped and sheathed her sword and let him help her up.

"I didn't know you had the wildness," he said.

"Neither did I. It was the first time. But I think my sword may have had something to do with it."

The battle mage couldn't help her, though he did confirm that Eitan had last been heard from some five hundred years before, and was believed dead.

"He wasn't the sort to simply disappear," the mage continued. "If he were still alive, he'd be doing something active, and I haven't detected any powerful magic."

When she repeated his words to Ilana, the sword hummed quietly for a couple of minutes, before saying anything.

"So I've been declared dead some five hundred years as well, then. It's never easy to return from the dead, but after five hundred years at least I won't be confronting my own sister and nephew.

"You see, at the time that Eitan imprisoned me like this, I was the king's oldest child and heir of Trandor. My sister Shoshana, who had no Magic of her own, had married Eitan, who was both a prince and the most powerful enchanter of the time. So, at my presumed death, the rule passed to Shoshana, and from her to her son, and his descendants ever since then.

"I don't like the idea of bringing anyone else into the secret," she continued, "so I'll try to see what I can do, working through you. Although if it's as rough on you as I suspect it will be, you may wish you had died in battle."

"Soldiers who don't want to survive, despite everything, don't last very long. Consider me in your hands, Lady."

"Good. Now first of all, you will have to gather some supplies. Can you write?"

"I can do that."

"Then write down a list of what we need . . . and don't wake me again until you have them." She proceeded to dictate a list of magical supplies, most of which could be commonly found around the kitchen or the stables. "A hair from the beard of a mage" had Gavriella stumped, until she decided that the battle mage owed her that much help at least, and the wild plants Ilana needed she was careful to describe in detail, explaining both where they were to be found and how Gavriella could verify that she had identified them correctly. "And lay out a warm set of clothes for yourself. Now go, and let me know when you have everything."

It took Gavriella most of the remaining hours of daylight to find everything she needed. She started with the plants, so she'd have light enough to see what she was doing, and then went on to the kitchen, where the cook liked her and was happy to humor her whims, and then to the stables, where she didn't know anyone, but the men there, to her surprise, remembered her as the soldier who had sprung out of nowhere to save the horses.

She found Aryeh, who was quite happy to oblige her with a loan of the shaving mirror he had stopped using a few months back.

At the last she sought out the battle mage and requested the hair.

"What for?" he asked. "You'll not be trying to set spells on me?"

"Nothing of the sort. I'm not interested in you at all; I just needed a beard hair. You see it's a game, rather like a scavenger hunt—"

"I know what that is. But aren't you a bit old for such games?"

"Well a few of us, who don't sleep around or gamble or drink, thought it would be a good way to pass the evening."

He gave it to her, rather grudgingly.

After that she went back to the barracks, where she laid out her clothes, before calling again to Ilana.

"You have everything we need?"

"Everything."

"Then change your clothes, pack up everything else, and walk to the most deserted spot you can find that won't get you into trouble. And bring matches and firewood, unless the spot has its own supply."

The matches entailed another stop in the kitchen, and then they were headed out to the woods, but still within the perimeter of the camp. Gavriella cut wood and arranged a fire, without lighting it, in case there was something else that Ilana wanted first. She also took out the pot she had borrowed earlier, and filled it with water from the brook; Ilana had said that she'd need a pot of water, but Gavriella couldn't see carrying the water as well as the pot all the way from the kitchen.

She woke Ilana again. "Very nice," the sorceress commented. "Now set the pot to boil, and add the following things . . ."

Gavriella set the pot on the fire and lined up all the things that had to go into it, stopping only when Ilana fell silent. And then she stirred the fire to try to get the pot to heat up faster. As soon as the water came to a full boil, she added the other ingredients, one by one. When she was finished she told Ilana, "That's done."

"Now hold the mirror over the pot, but at an angle, so you can see it also."

"See what? The mirror or the pot?"

"Look in the mirror at the pot. But let it also collect steam from the pot."

She did that; at first it was just all fogged up, but shortly she could see the pot's contents reflected in it as well, with the mage's hair spinning in the center of a sort of whirlpool. She reported this to Ilana, who seemed pleased.

"Now," Ilana said, "if you had Power, I would give you the words to say, but as you have not, you must hold me up in front of your face so I can see what you see, and I will say the words myself."

Gavriella did as she was told, and for the first time she heard Ilana's voice in her ears rather than from inside her own head. Not that she understood what Ilana was saying, either because the language was strange, or because she was half-dazed, or both. She kept her eyes on the two strips of mirror she could see on either side of the blade; and gradually, the pot's contents faded away and she was looking at a bearded blond man, dressed like a Trandorian soldier, pacing an unfamiliar hall.

"It's done!" Ilana's voice came to her again from within her head.

"Now what?" Gavriella asked.

"Now I know where he is and what he looks like. I sense little or no magic in him, other than what he needs to keep his youth; undoubtedly he cast most of it away from himself, so he'd be hard to detect. But he's within the walls of Trandor, passing himself off as a common soldier."

"Can you fight him?"

"Not with magic. You must carry me there and attack him physically. It's the only thing that will work."

Gavriella pondered the advantages of getting some sleep, even without knowing whether there would be an attack in the middle of the night, over going sleepless, and in enemy territory at that. She was now wearing the uniform of a defeated soldier over her own warm trousers, and had gotten into the Trandorian keep through an unguarded back passage that Ilana told her about. They still hadn't figured out how to find Eitan, whose current name they didn't know; she had tried explaining how she had a friend in the guards, a handsome man who had somehow forgotten to tell her his name, but she remembered him as blond and bearded; and for all the teasing it got her, there were at least some men willing to direct her to her supposed lover, though they were also quick to warn her that he wasn't a man who was free with his friendship, and she shouldn't expect anything from him. Not even the acknowledgment of a child, if that's what she was looking for.

"Is this the man you want?"

She stood blinking stupidly; she hadn't seen his face clearly and had really thought him better looking than this. "I—I think so," she stammered.

"What do you want, wench?" the magician asked.

"It's a matter of honor," she said. "Perhaps we can discuss it away from your friends."

"It shouldn't take long," one of the other soldiers put in, "if it concerns what he has of honor."

"Let's go this way," he suggested, taking her by the elbow. "Now what's all this about?"

"Well, first of all," she said, "it's been about five years now since we met, and you don't look a day older. So can you explain that?"

"I don't believe you. Five years ago I wasn't even with this company. So how can you remember me?"

"Are you denying that you don't show your age?"

"I'm denying nothing."

"Then explain your secret."

"Gladly." He drew his own sword on her. "No harm in telling you what you'll never live to tell anyone else."

Gavriella drew her sword, and slunk back against the wall, as if she was too overwhelmed to think clearly. "So how do you do it?"

"Don't you want to know what will happen to you?"

"As far as that goes, I'm more curious how you'll explain my disappearance."

"No problem. I'll send your body to the outskirts of the Liblom camp, where it will be obvious that you were killed while engaging in an unauthorized raid."

"And the other answer?"

"I am a powerful mage. The most powerful alive, especially in these days of decline. But to keep anyone from detecting my power, I have put most of it into an enchanted tree, in the middle of the palace gardens."

"Whi–which tree?"

"The old oak in the very center of the king's own garden. And now, you will have to die. But first, I see you have a most curious sword. May I see it?"

Gavriella held out her sword, without releasing her grip. "Yes, it is quite strange," she admitted. "While it fits my hand perfectly, it turns aside when I try to use it."

"Show me."

"Certainly, sir. I take it up like this, and then, at the very moment when it should strike my opponent, it twists away." She swung it, half turning aside, but at the last moment she let it take control and it struck true. Only as the magician gasped out his last breath, was the sword transformed into a very beautiful—and naked—lady.

"Help me get his coat off," she said, "I'm freezing."

So Gavriella helped her. "What changed you back? His death?"

"That, and defeating the traitor at the heart of Trandor, which is what he had become."

"Do you know the tree he was talking about?"

"Of course I do. And as soon as I can get it, the power's all mine. But first, we have another task."

If it was hard for Gavriella to admit to her captain that she had thrown away her sword for another that had vanished on her, that was nothing to explaining that the rightful ruler of Trandor was in her quarters, waiting to discuss peace terms.

THE FALL OF THE KINGDOM
by Mary Soon Lee

Mary Soon Lee grew up in London, but now lives in Pittsburgh, where she runs a writers' group called the Pittsburgh Worldwrights. She has had approximately fifty stories published in markets such as *F&SF*, *Sword & Sorceress*, *Amazing Stories*, *Interzone*, and *The Year's Best SF*.

She has an MA in mathematics and a diploma in computer science from Cambridge University and an MSc in astronautics and space engineering from Cranfield University. Funny how so many people with backgrounds in hard technology write fantasy; one would expect them to write science fiction instead. Perhaps fantasy is a needed change of pace.

Her first child, William Chye Lee-Moore, was born in April 1999 and is very cute (in Mary's no doubt impartial opinion).

This story shows just how important a child can be, even if the child is dead or unborn.

TWO children lay at the heart of it. I've heard others blame ill fortune, the foreign knight, the king, the queen, the factions who opposed their sudden rise to pre-eminence. But I stood witness by the queen, and all that followed stemmed from the two children, the one that was born and the one that she longed for.

She was only a girl herself, my White Lady, when the king took her to wife, and he in the first triumph of his youth, newly crowned, newly confident, bright with vision. He married her for her connections, seeking to ally her father to his cause, as he sought to draw in every strong man to stand together against the pagan invaders.

What did she know of alliances and armies, battles or lies or deceit? Nothing then, and little more later. She never had the trick of seeing beyond her immediate circle. Father, husband, cousin, friend: these formed her whole world. Even I, her nursemaid, weighed more on her mind than the invaders' advance. When she was betrothed, she begged that I be sent as her lady's maid, even though my parents were only peasants.

After his fashion, the king loved my White Lady. Not as much, it is true, as he loved the brotherhood of knights that formed around him. But as much as he loved any woman. He bedded her with the same gentling touch he used upon his falcon.

When her monthly bleeds ceased that first winter, the circle of her world pulled even tighter. She would sit in a corner, sewing a cushion, and, after a minute, the needle would still, and then she would press one hand to her belly, lost in daydreams.

It was an April afternoon, everything green growing as busily as it could, when the cramps came on her. Short it was, but hard, that birthing, and the child born before the dusk faded. Too small to take breath, though the birthing woman and I tried every trick we'd ever heard speak of. The baby gave not a single cry, not a single kick.

When the birthing woman at length shook her head, my White Lady took her baby and put the poor dead thing to her breast. She rocked the baby back and forth, back and forth, and refused to let me take it from her, though the tiny body cooled in her arms, and the afterbirth came bloody between her legs.

She was young, my White Lady, and by midsummer she had her full health back. But not her heart. She smiled only for form's sake, an empty gesture that didn't touch her eyes. Each night after the king had left her room, she cried like an infant. I would rock her in my arms, as I had many years ago, until at last she quieted.

All that summer I grieved with her, my poor little broken-winged bird. When she cried, I thought of my own son, Brian, who died when he was three weeks old. I remembered the feel of him snuggled against me through the winter nights. I remembered his small, dry coughs. I remembered how my swollen breasts wept milk for him after he died.

The day after I had buried my son, the summons had come from the castle commanding me to nurse their baby daughter. I had never been inside the castle before, never slept in rooms kept warm even on the coldest night, never dreamed of eating meat with every meal. And that baby girl sucked the sorrow from me along with my milk, my little bird who needed me so.

So how could I not feel sad for her, my little bird, my White Lady, when she lost a child of her own?

Summer turned into autumn, and autumn into winter, and still my White Lady wept each night. She had duties, but did not meet them. Guests came upon whose good-will the kingdom's safety depended, but she would not speak to them. She left the running of the castle to a steward who shorted the lesser servants' pay to line his own pockets. She did not even wish the king well when he left to raise an army to fight the pagan invaders.

The years passed, and the king united every chieftain behind his banner. Men vied for the glory of joining the king's brotherhood of knights, then vied against the other knights to win the king's praise. For a handful of years they drove the brigands and thieves and rapists into hiding, and held back the tide of invaders.

One among them, the foreign knight, was first in every battle, first in every tournament, first in the king's eye.

But it wasn't the king the knight looked to for approval after each victory, but to my White Lady. He had dark eyes that gleamed like a falcon's, and long black hair braided with gold ribbons, and he moved as lithely as a wild cat.

And my White Lady? She ignored the foreign knight; she barely bade attention even to the king. Where she should have wielded authority, setting an example for servants and court alike, instead there was only her abstracted silence. The servants grew indolent and vicious. Their idle tongues spread rumors, and slowly, slowly, like a dark canker spreading outward from the royal castle, the rumors took root, setting knight against knight, chieftain against chieftain. The victories the king had won by blood and sword weakened beneath those bitter words.

One thing only did my White Lady crave, a living child. But none came to her, and so a fresh rumor started that the queen was barren, that there would be no heir, that the kingdom would collapse when the king died. The senior knights told the king that he must have a blood-heir, even if it meant marrying again. But the king held true to my lady, and the knights started to question his leadership.

It was then that I led my lady to the witch-woman. Down by the lake the witch lived, in a hut half-hidden by reeds, half-hidden by spells. Inside, the hut smelled of mold and damp and rot, but my lady sat heedless on the wet floor. "Help me," she said, "I wish a child."

The witch-woman fingered my lady's dress, leaving mud stains on the pale silk. She cut a lock of my lady's hair and burned it in a dish of foul-smelling liquid. I coughed and covered my face at the acrid fumes, but the witch inhaled deeply.

"Your husband will never give you a child," said the witch-woman. "Never and never, but for the one that died inside you."

My lady clutched at the witch. "Help me." She held

out an open purse of gold coins. "A potion, anything, you must know a way."

The witch-woman gave me a sideways look that my lady missed. "I said your husband would not give you a child. Look to another man."

Then the witch spat on the coins and thrust them back at my lady. "I had gold once, before your husband turned people against my craft. I lived in a fine stone house, and even the lords paid me respect. I don't like the cost of your money."

My lady left then without another word: no thanks, no questions. I wondered if she had even heard what the witch said, but soon I knew she had. For my lady looked at the knights in a certain way, appraising them, and three nights later she let the foreign knight into her bedchamber.

And I, I stood outside the king's room, pressed my lips to the keyhole, and whispered that his wife was lying with his closest friend.

When the king found the two of them together, he fell into rage. In that rage he tore apart the alliances he had striven so hard to build, and the next time the pagans advanced, he could not stop them.

And my White Lady? She never even realized that it was I who betrayed her. To her, I was only ever her nurse-maid and servant, with no past and no present except by her side. When she was a child, I had forgiven her, so small and sweet and fragile—my little bird. But she grew into a woman without growing into strength, and I found myself thinking of my parents, who worshiped the old gods, the old ways. I thought of my son, and how in all the years I served her, my lady had never even asked his name.

I said two children lay at the heart of it, but I lied. There were three, and my Brian was the third.

ARMS AND THE WOMAN
by Lawrence Watt-Evans

Lawrence Watt-Evans is the author of more than two dozen books and one hundred short stories—science fiction, fantasy, horror, humor, etc.—including the Hugo-winning story "Why I Left Harry's All-Night Hamburgers," the Ethshar fantasy series, and most recently *Dragon Weather*. He was president of the Horror Writers' Association from 1994 to 1996, has scripted comic books for Marvel, Dark Horse, and Wildstorm, and has meddled in various other things best left alone; this is his second appearance in *Sword & Sorceress*. He's been happily married for more than twenty years and has two kids and a cat.

This story proves that size *does* matter, but not always the way you think it does.

"IT'S not as if we didn't know this one was coming," Uril said loudly as he stumbled over a rock that protruded from the mud. "The books are very clear, and the astrologers confirmed the date."

"We should have done something sooner," Staun grumbled. "If we'd been sent out a little sooner, we wouldn't have to rush like this. We could have gotten there before it started raining, and we wouldn't have to hurry. Why did the Council leave it until the last minute?"

"Because they're a bunch of squabbling old fools," Captain Lethis said as he pushed aside a dripping branch that hung low over the overgrown road. "We were supposed to be here days ago, but they wasted time arguing about who should go, and how many, chosen how, and who should pay for it all, and a dozen other details, until all of sudden they realized that the prophesied date was almost upon us."

"If the Undead Lord gets loose because of their delays, I swear I'll cut a few of their throats," Staun said.

"And if he does, I won't lift a hand to stop you," Lethis agreed. "But let's not let it come to that, shall we?" He turned and beckoned to the stragglers, bellowing, "Come on, you!"

The other soldiers, with much cursing and grumbling, picked up the pace a little; behind them came a ragged little crowd of others, tagging along.

Officially the Council had chosen ten men for this errand, but all together, including friends, helpers, family, and assorted camp-followers, there were almost thirty people slogging through the Forbidden Marsh in the pouring rain, making their way toward the ruins of Haridal Keep. There had been almost fifty when they left the Citadel two days before.

Near the rear of the party, a young woman named Siria was listening to the complaints and thinking that the score who had abandoned the quest were the sensible ones. After all, if this worked the way it was supposed to, there probably wouldn't be much to see or do; the legends said that whoever wore the magical armor that the wizard Karista had given King Derebeth sixteen hundred years ago would be immune to the black sorcery of the Undead Lord, and could therefore easily strike the monster down before his resurrection was complete, sending him back to the grave for another four hundred years.

If it was really that quick, Siria doubted she would have a chance to ingratiate herself with anyone—she could be charming, given time, but she might not have that time.

And she really didn't have anything to offer other than

charm. These past two years since her father's death she had used up everything else—not that there had been much to begin with. She was too small to keep up the land her father had worked, not strong enough to work it, and the lord had sent her away, giving the land to a husky young man more suited to farming.

Since then she had wandered hither and yon, looking for a place, and had found none. What she *had* found was that soldiers were often generous with a pretty girl, especially when they had just done something strenuous and dangerous and were feeling proud of themselves.

She hoped that this particular job would qualify, that the soldiers would find errands for her along the way, and when the Undead Lord was properly dispatched that they would invite her to join their celebration.

It shouldn't be dangerous. The stories and written records from before the Extermination, left by the wizards who had dominated the world back then, were fairly clear about what needed to be done.

The earliest report of the Undead Lord dated back sixteen centuries, to a time when the world was awash in chaos and powerful magic—nothing like the quiet present day. That first time King Derebeth had disposed of the Undead Lord after a long, fierce struggle, and everyone had thought that was the end of it—but four hundred years later, when certain stars aligned properly, the creature had reappeared. After some messy delays the legendary Kurlus of Amoritan had retrieved Derebeth's armor, not to mention the sacred Sword of Light, and dealt with the problem.

Eight hundred years ago the local wizards had been ready—even though magic was already in decline, astrology was in full flower by then, and they had known the exact time when the Undead Lord would rise again. They were waiting, with a mercenary warrior by the name of Porl already wearing the armor and wielding the sword, and the Undead Lord had scarcely begun to materialize before being dispersed. The whole thing was over in a few minutes, according to the reports.

Four hundred years ago there had been some doubt about whether the Undead Lord would put in another appearance, and matters had been complicated by the Third Lodrian War, but a party of soldiers had been waiting. A Lieutenant Rusran had worn the armor and dealt the required blow.

Again, it just took a few moments.

So there wouldn't be much to see unless something went wrong and the Undead Lord was able to restore himself fully to life—and in that case, anyone in the area stood a good chance of winding up dead or ensorcelled. Siria did not care for that possibility—but she didn't expect it to arise. Captain Lethis and his men would see to that. They were the best that the Council had had on hand, and would surely handle this nasty business quickly and efficiently. They had all handled pre-Extermination relics before.

While she had supposedly come along to run errands beforehand, Siria was mostly looking forward to a time when the Undead Lord was safely gone. Once Captain Lethis and his men had the job done, no matter how easy it proved to be, they'd be feeling good, and might be generous with a woman who helped them feel better. The Council paid its soldiers well—especially when left-over magic was involved. The world was still cluttered with this sort of remnant of the bad old days before the Extermination, and the Council did not stint those brave souls who helped dispose of these menaces. Lethis and his men would have fat purses when this was done, even though sending the Undead Lord off to another four hundred years in limbo did not appear especially difficult or dangerous.

Of course, there might be unknown dangers. Siria had heard that the accounts of the previous manifestations were not as detailed as the Council might have wished—there was a mention in the record of the Undead Lord's third appearance that the wizards had had some brief difficulty in finding a suitable candidate before choosing Porl, but there was no explanation of what the selection criteria had been. The report from the Lodrian Wars mentioned in passing that Rusran was given the job at the last minute when his commanding officer, a Captain Orilik, proved unable to do it, but again, there was no explanation of why Orilik wasn't up to the task.

And of course, since the Extermination, there were no wizards or sorcerers to ask for more details—they were all long gone. Only their written records and the scattered bits of magic remained.

This lack of clear, detailed information had worried the Council somewhat, and that was why they were sending ten of their finest, rather than two or three volunteers; it wouldn't do to have no one in the party fit to wear the armor.

Lightning flashed, followed all too closely by a sudden clap of thunder; a moment later the rain turned from a drizzle to a torrent.

"Oh, enough!" a woman to Siria's right exclaimed, "If they want me, they can find me back in Splittree." She turned around and began slogging in the other direction.

As if that were a signal, a handful of the party turned back as well—but the ten soldiers kept on marching forward, and Siria stayed with them, as did a dozen others. After all, Siria had no place to go back in Splittree, no family waiting for her anywhere, and she was already soaked to the skin.

Uril, the big bushy-bearded pikeman from the Stoneford Marches, paused and looked back at the shrinking of their retinue. Siria smiled at him, and he smiled back.

That was promising—when this was done, maybe he would spend some money on her, buy her a good dinner back in Splittree perhaps. She had been thinking that the group turning back were probably the smart ones, that she was a fool to stay, but Uril's smile prompted her to reconsider. Uril would soon have money to spend, and she would not be particularly demanding; he might keep her around for quite some time, which would certainly be preferable to approaching strangers in inns and taverns.

And she was surely already as drenched as she could get . . .

That was when she slipped and fell face-first in the mud.

Before she even realized properly what had happened, Uril had her arm and was lifting her back to her feet.

"Thank you," she mumbled, looking down at the huge brown smear down the front of her frock and hoping there was no damage that wouldn't wash out.

"You're quite welcome," Uril said. "You'll want to be a little more careful up ahead—it's just as slippery and a good bit steeper."

Siria muttered something, she didn't know exactly what, and turned away, ostensibly to brush the mud from her frock, but really to hide her blush. Here she had wanted to impress Uril as someone charming, someone who would be good company, and then, right in front of him . . .

Well, there was nothing to be done about it now.

Uril turned away and marched on through the marsh, and a moment later Siria followed, ignoring the snickers of the others. She kept to herself after that, apart from the rest of the group; she had no desire to turn those snickers into open laughter by letting them see her take another tumble.

Half an hour later the trees thinned enough to give them a clear view of Haridal Keep, former home to assorted necromancers and monsters. Captain Lethis and his men marched on, undaunted, but some of the others stopped and whispered.

Siria couldn't hear what they were saying, but she could imagine. Haridal Keep, even after sixteen hundred years, was impressively forbidding. The castle had been built atop a huge mass of bare stone that thrust up from the earth, and some of the walls had not been built atop the outcropping, but carved directly from it. The towers had long since crumbled, and the battlements were broken and uneven, but most of the walls still stood straight and strong.

"I think I'll wait here," a plump woman declared loudly. "It'll all be over by sundown, won't it?"

A chorus of discussion arose, reached a quick crescendo, then died away as most of the party began to settle down under the trees, spreading canvas from branch to branch to keep off the rain.

Siria hesitated—it would be good to get under the shelter—but then slogged on, following the ten chosen soldiers. Staying with the others, constantly displaying her soiled frock, would be too embarrassing.

Besides, she was curious to see the inside of Haridal Keep, and what the famous magical armor and sword looked like, and whether the Undead Lord would actually appear.

It was only when the party reached the long crumbling stair up to the castle gate that she realized that she was the only one besides the soldiers who had come this far. She hesitated before setting foot on the steps. Maybe she shouldn't be here. She didn't really belong with these professional heroes when they were going about their job.

"Come on," Uril called, waving to her from a dozen steps up.

"Captain Lethis won't mind?" Siria asked.

"Why would he? Come on and get out of the rain—assuming there's any roof left in this drafty old ruin!"

Quickly, Siria scampered up the steps.

If nothing else, this got her feet out of the clinging,

slippery mud that had made the journey so miserable. That alone made it worth the effort.

The main gate was a heap of broken stone; the soldiers simply marched over it, but Siria, with her much shorter legs, had to clamber awkwardly. Uril glanced back at her and hesitated, as if he might come to her aid, but she determinedly didn't meet his gaze as she picked her way through the mess.

Past the gate was an empty stone courtyard, and then a gap in the yard-thick wall that had once divided the courtyard from the great hall. That gap had once had an archway and door in it, but they were long gone, the arch crumbled, the stones above it fallen away, leaving an opening that was as broad as a farmer's wagon at the base, widening to three times that at the top.

There was no roof, no shelter from the rain, in the great hall. Siria brushed wet hair from her eyes to see Captain Lethis standing there, consulting a document, with the other nine men gathered about him.

"The entrance to the crypt was behind the high table," Lethis said. "That would be *that* way." He pointed to one end of the room, but how he made his choice Siria could not guess. She followed along as the men marched across the ruined hall and began poking through the rubble that filled one end.

"Here," Staun said, as he uncovered a black opening.

"Right," Lethis said. "We'll need a light."

"Light it once you're inside, out of the rain," Uril suggested.

"Good idea," Staun agreed, and Lethis nodded. Then they began climbing down into that lightless pit, one by one. Siria heard a splash, and quiet cursing, and muttered comments, as the ten men vanished into the hole.

She hesitated. That opening did not look inviting at all—but she had come this far, and what was the point of standing in the rain?

And then a faint orange glow appeared in the blackness as someone got a light going, and she realized from how brightly it shone that the daylight, not very strong to begin with, was fading—the afternoon must be almost over, the sun nearing the horizon. She would be waiting in the dark soon no matter where she was; she might as well go on.

Cautiously, she climbed over the stones and lowered herself into the hole.

Strong hands reached up and grabbed her waist, and she yelped with fright before realizing that it was Uril, helping her down.

A moment later she was standing in a tunnel with the soldiers, a tunnel where the low spots in the uneven floor were flooded to various depths. Three of the men held lanterns that thinned, but did not fully disperse, the surrounding gloom.

"This way," Captain Lethis said, pointing. As he started walking, and the others fell into step behind him, he asked, "Did anyone get a look at the sun before we came down here?"

"Couldn't see it through the clouds," Staun grumbled. "I *tried.*

"It was getting dark, I think," Siria said timidly.

Lethis threw her a glance. "Was it? Then we need to hurry—the Undead Lord is due to rise as soon as the horizon pierces the sun's heart, which I suppose means when it's halfway below the horizon, and we still need to get someone into that armor."

"I *told* you we waited too long," Staun said angrily.

The captain did not bother replying; instead he broke into a trot down the passage.

The others followed him through what seemed to Siria a senseless maze of passages and tunnels, dark corridors of rough stone with broken floors and barrel-vaulted ceilings. She had to run to keep up.

At least, she thought as she stumbled around the fourth or fifth corner, she was out of the rain.

And then they were in the chamber they sought, and she almost fell down the half-dozen steps that led into it.

The soldiers were already arranging themselves around the contents of the chamber—a black stone sarcophagus that gleamed as if freshly polished, and beside it a dusty, sagging wooden chest.

Staun prodded the chest with the toe of his boot, and one side caved in.

"Rotted through," he said.

"It's four hundred years old," Uril pointed out. "That's from the Third Lodrian War."

"Get it open," Lethis ordered. "If it's not the armor and sword, it probably says where they are."

"You think the Undead Lord is in this?" Fellan asked, pointing at the sarcophagus.

"If he's not, then we're in trouble, because I don't know where else he could be," Lethis replied, as Staun knelt and tugged at the lid of the chest.

The lock pulled free of crumbling wood and the chest opened, revealing a long, narrow oilcloth bundle, a rolled and tied parchment, and a tangle of rotting wool threads and dully-gleaming metal. Lethis promptly snatched up the parchment, while Staun prodded gingerly at the mess of wool and metal.

"This is it," Lethis said, as he unrolled the parchment and read it. "Someone had terrible handwriting, and it's in Old Mardish, but it definitely mentions King Derebeth, and that's the word for armor." He turned to one of the other soldiers. "Grulli, you know some Old Mardish, don't you?"

"A little," Grulli said, accepting the parchment. He squinted at it and held it closer to a lantern as he read, then nodded. "It says the Undead Lord will rise today, and must be stopped with the Sword of Light wielded by a person wearing the armor of King Derebeth." He lowered the parchment and gestured at the box. "That's the sword and armor, and the Undead Lord will appear in the sarcophagus."

Staun lifted out the bundle of metal and unfolded it, tearing away the desiccated remnants of the wool to reveal a mail shirt of bizarre and ancient design that somehow, despite centuries of neglect, showed not a speck of rust or corrosion.

Other than the odd pattern of links and the lack of aging, it was a very ordinary mail shirt, with no magical aura that Siria could see. She hoped whatever spell was on it still worked.

"Captain, it's up to you to choose who wears it," Staun said. He looked at the shirt. "I don't think it will fit me."

The others gathered around and stared at the mail shirt; Siria, who had been watching from the bottom step rather than setting foot in the crypt itself, came forward as well, peering around the soldiers for a closer look at the miraculous garment.

"It does look a little small," Uril said.

"No one ever said Derebeth was a big man," Lethis said. "I suppose ancient heroes came in all sizes."

"Captain," Uril said nervously, "maybe ancient heroes came in all sizes, but *we* don't. We're all big men. I don't think *any* of us can get that thing on."

Lethis looked suddenly worried. "Maybe it will magically expand on the right person," he said. "Staun, try it on."

Staun obeyed, pulling the mail over his head, but his ham-like hands would not fit in the sleeves, and the tunic would not fit over his broad shoulders. He lifted the metal shirt off again and passed it to Grulli.

While Grulli struggled with the garment, Staun unwrapped the Sword of Light from the oilcloth bundle. Siria stared in awe at the gleaming, ivory-hilted weapon; it shone in the dim glow of the lanterns as if it were in direct sunlight, sparkling like freshly-polished silver. This weapon clearly *was* magic; it had all the glamour the mail lacked.

"There's no problem with the sword, anyway," Staun remarked, as he hefted it.

Grulli had no more success with the mail shirt than Staun had; he passed it on to Uril.

After Uril came Lethis, then Mokor, then Fellan, and so on. By the time the eighth of the ten was struggling unsuccessfully to don the shirt, everyone in the room had become aware of an odd whistling sound.

"It's coming from the tomb," Uril said, stepping back.

"We have the Sword of Light," Staun said. "Why don't we try to dispose of the Undead Lord with that, even without the armor?"

"It doesn't look as if we have much of a choice," Lethis said, as Orpac gave up and passed the armor on to Kael—who was the largest of them all, and the armor had shown no signs of any unnatural expansion.

"At least now we know why Porl and Rusran got the job," Uril said. "They must have been runts."

Siria, unnoticed by the men, grimaced at that. As a "runt" herself, she suddenly felt a new empathy for those heroes of old.

"Captain, maybe if we open the coffin and I go at whatever's inside with the sword . . ." Staun suggested.

"Do it," Lethis agreed, as Kael handed the shirt to Worna, the last of the ten carefully-chosen warriors. Staun stepped up to the side of the sarcophagus with the sword in his right hand, and reached for the lid with his left.

"Captain, I don't know . . ." Uril began.

"Do you have a *better* idea?" Lethis demanded.

"Maybe," Uril said. He pointed at Siria, who was trying hard to stay well out of the way. "It might fit *her*."

The whistling sound was growing louder and deeper and suddenly the lid lifted from the black sarcophagus, rising unsupported into the air. The whistling turned into the roar of a great wind, and the three lanterns flickered and dimmed. To Siria, it seemed not so much as if the light faded as if darkness poured in from somewhere, like oily smoke.

"Worna," Lethis ordered, "throw her the shirt."

Worna struggled to get his right arm out of the shirt so he could obey.

Staun thrust the Sword of Light into the darkness beneath the sarcophagus lid—then screamed, and snatched it back. Siria stared in horror—something black, like an animate liquid, was crawling up Staun's arm, wrapping itself around his wrist and elbow.

Staun's grip loosened, and the Sword of Light fell from his hand, to bounce on the edge of the sarcophagus and land ringing on the stone floor.

The sarcophagus lid fell away to the other side and landed with a deep, thick thump that shook the stone floor.

"Oh, blast," Lethis said. "All right . . ."

And then he stopped and stood motionless and silent.

Staun, too, was now frozen, and Uril, and Fellan.

And Worna finally had the mail shirt off.

"You, wench!" he called, "here!" And he balled the shirt up and flung it at Siria.

She ducked, letting it hit the wall behind her. She turned, snatched it up, and by the time she turned back a shape was forming in the air above the open coffin—a shape that was black and vaguely manlike, but not quite human. The only distinct feature that was visible as yet was a pair of red eyes that seemed to glow as they scanned across the men in the room.

"Oh, Holy Mother," Siria gasped, clutching the mail shirt to her chest.

At that the red gaze suddenly swung in her direction, and she lifted up the shirt to cover her face.

Even through the protective mail, she could feel the thing's displeasure.

She began bunching up the mail, struggling to get the shirt over her head.

"I can't believe this," she said to no one. "We're all as good as dead—*I'm* no hero! I'm just a poor orphan girl. Even if I get this thing on, all I can do is run for help, and by the time anyone gets back here . . ."

She didn't complete the thought.

She pulled the shirt on—it fit fairly well, in fact. Her arms slid easily into the sleeves, and her head popped through the neck.

And she almost wished it hadn't. All the ten men, the Council's ten best warriors, were turning toward her now, their expressions dazed and flat. The shape in the air was thickening, becoming more solid.

"You can't hurt me!" Siria said, but her voice trembled.

Staun bent down and picked up the Sword of Light, but he did not use it against the Undead Lord; he didn't even look at the black thing. Instead he hefted it and took a step toward Siria.

She swallowed. Maybe the Undead Lord *could* hurt her—he couldn't harm her directly while she wore the armor, but the Sword of Light could probably hack right through the mail.

And even if it couldn't cut the magic armor, it could cut her exposed throat, or split her skull.

"Staun," she said, "drop the sword! *Please!*"

"Woman," Staun said, in a strained and unnatural voice, "you are all that stands between the Undead Lord and his freedom."

Siria swallowed again.

It was true, she knew. The Council had left it until too late and had sent the wrong men, and the Undead Lord was materializing—had materialized, really. In a few moments he would be completely revived, and it would probably take a war to stop him—if anything in these wizardless post-Extermination times *could* stop him!

Staun took another step toward her, and another—and to either side others were joining him, forming a line, trapping Siria against one wall of the chamber.

She had no weapon, no way to fight them—and even if she could, what good would that do against the Undead Lord?

But if she just stood here, Staun would kill her, and the Undead Lord would be free. She looked up, over Staun's shoulder at the thing hanging there, at the red eyes that watched her every move.

She was no warrior—but she had fought a few warriors, in her own way. She had never been on a battlefield, but more than once she had been face-to-face with drunken soldiers who wanted their way with her.

She had been defending herself from rape then, not death, but the methods she had used then were all she had.

Staun stepped forward, sword rising to strike—and she slid suddenly down the wall until she was sitting on the floor, her legs thrust out before her, knees bent.

Startled, Staun checked his thrust and pulled the sword back. Puzzled, he lowered his gaze.

He was moving very slowly and stupidly, Siria saw. That was surely, she thought, because he was doing what the Undead Lord wanted, rather than what *he* wanted.

She flung herself forward, between Staun's legs; before he could react she had rolled over onto her back and taken aim.

"I'm sorry, Staun," she said. Then she kicked as hard as she could, with her leg fully extended.

Her foot hit soft tissue, and Staun's breath came out in an astonished and agonized whoosh. He crumpled forward, dropping the Sword of Light.

Siria whirled and grabbed for the Sword, snatched it away and pulled herself out from beneath poor Staun's crumpling form.

The others were turning, trying to surround her, but

they, too, were slow and stupid, as if wading heavy-laden through deep water. She rolled clear, still clutching the sword, then leaped to her feet and ran toward the sarcophagus.

The Undead Lord glowered down at her, and a voice spoke from nowhere, inside her head.

You will not defeat me, it said. *Not again! I will not be . . .* Then she plunged the Sword of Light into the black shape above the sarcophagus.

It exploded; black vapor swept over her, snatching her breath away, and she fell backward, gasping. She landed sitting on the floor, legs splayed, left hand behind her hip but her right hand still held the Sword of Light, and she still wore King Derebeth's armor. She did not lose consciousness, or collapse further; instead she sat, dazed, for a moment, while the vapor dissipated and the menace of the Undead Lord passed away for another four centuries.

And then it was all over, and she had a bruise on her right hip and had skinned several knuckles. Her foot hurt, and her eyes stung. Somewhere behind her Staun was rolling on the floor, moaning.

"Well," Captain Lethis said at her left shoulder, "I suppose we had better get the lid back on that thing, then pack up the sword and mail for next time."

"And *this* time," Uril said, "I think we had better make sure everyone knows just what a skinny little fellow King Derebeth was!"

Siria looked up at Uril, but could not yet find her breath to speak.

"You were very brave, young lady," Lethis said. "And clever, too."

"You probably saved our lives," Fellan added.

Still looking at Uril, Siria managed to say, "Then perhaps someone could buy me a dinner when we get back to Splittree."

"Well, it won't be Staun," Orpac said. "I don't think

he'll want anything to do with *any* women for a while, and I'm *sure* he won't want *you* around!"

"I'm sorry," Siria said, turning to look over her shoulder. Staun was now sitting with his back against the wall, still breathing raggedly.

"Don't be," Uril said. "As Fellan said, you saved us all."

Siria looked up at him again. "Then you'll buy me that dinner?"

Uril laughed. "You can buy your *own*," he said.

Siria shook her head. "No, I can't," she began.

"Yes, you can," Uril said. "Once we get back to the Citadel, anyway. You've just earned yourself full pay for this errand—hadn't you realized?"

Startled, Siria looked at Lethis, who was helping Grulli and Worna lift the stone lid of the sarcophagus back into place.

"Of course," Lethis said. "And you'll be offered a place at the Citadel. It's the usual reward for disposing of dangerous magic. The Council prefers to keep anyone who can handle themselves that well where they can watch them."

Siria's mouth opened, but no sound emerged.

That meant no more begging. No more cozying up to men she didn't like in order to scrounge a meal.

Her mouth closed; then she said, "But that's at the Citadel."

Uril laughed again. "Fine," he said. "Then *I'll* buy you dinner in Splittree. And maybe we'll talk a little, get to know each other. Here you've saved my life and I don't even know your name!"

"Siria," Siria said, with the broadest smile she had allowed herself in ages. "And I think I'd like that."

THE STONE WIVES
by Michael Chesley Johnson

Michael Chesley Johnson has had stories published in *Marion Zimmer Bradley's Fantasy Magazine*, *Between the Darkness and the Fire*, *Absolute Magnitude*, and other magazines and anthologies. He is currently working on *The Dogs of Spring*, a fantasy novel set in thirteenth-century Wales.

He began his studies as a biochemistry major and ended with an MA in English Literature. He has had the usual collection of strange day jobs: pushing wheelchairs for a hospital's radiology department, landscaping Burger Kings, and bartending (during which he invented the Chocolate Cheesecake Frozen Daiquiri). For the past twelve years he's been a computer systems analyst, which is not as glamorous as it sounds; he's run cable, pulled (very gently) jammed labels out of printers, cobbled together networks and software out of whatever was available, and "reminded people that computers aren't everything." (I think that may be the tech version of "Get a life.") In that spirit, he recently quit his day job to write full time. He lives with his wife, Trina, in New Mexico.

But the old job has left its mark. Here's a story about a king dissatisfied with his current system and the princess he brought in to fix the problem.

"LOWER your eyes before the king!" the knight said. But Princess Tiwa of Elaan did not submit. The knight had shoved her down, and as badly as the paving stones sliced her knees, she refused to let the pain make her any less indignant. Instead, she glared at the sorcerer-king who had kidnapped her so that he might conceive an heir.

Ancient King Brald sat perched on a golden throne floating magically six feet above a slab of green stone. Around him spun hundreds of brilliant crystals that shot rainbows into his legendary, dark hall. Their light pricked hard at the princess' eyes but with her hands tied, she could cast no spell that would let her see through that blinding swarm to the face of her abductor.

Through clenched teeth she said, "I will not bear your child."

"I have been lord of Amantithi for over a hundred years," King Brald said sadly, "and now that I am failing, my heir must prepare himself for kingship while I yet live. However, not one of my wives bore me a child! Each was as barren as a desert."

"Perhaps the problem wasn't with your wives, but with Your Lordship."

"Such insolence, my Lord!" the knight said.

"She is right, in a sense," King Brald said. "A powerful curse has been thrown on me, a curse I cannot break alone. But I believe a union with another like myself will overcome it. And this, Princess, is why I have stolen you. My kingdom doesn't have such a powerful sorceress, and I genuinely regret the loss of the people of Elaan."

"I will not have any child," she said.

"Your reward will be your life and your freedom. By first snowfall next year—one year from now—you must be with child."

The knight fetched a woman, a midwife, who came and led the princess out of the hall to her new chambers. There she flung herself onto the fine silk coverlet of her bed and swore at her situation.

The midwife, who was called Adria, coughed gently. "My Lady, I am told that a sorceress requires both her hands and her tongue to cast spells. My Lord has asked me to give you a choice. You may either keep your hands tied, or your mouth gagged."

"I would like my hands untied."

"Very well. But first I must bind this cloth around your mouth," she said, taking a silver strip out of a pocket. "It is some of my Lord's magic. You may eat and drink through it, but you will not be able to speak. Nor, of course, will you be able to untie it."

"Wait! How many wives did—or does—the king have, and what happened to them?"

"Do you see the chess set over the hearth?"

On the mantle sat a collection of stone figurines, some black and some white, the largest no bigger than a fist. The princess got up to examine them. Each was crudely carved: Some had warped noses, others misshapen heads, and each wore a sad face. "The carvers of Elaan are better artisans than the one who made these," the princess said. "And it's not even a full set—one piece is missing."

"He's had thirty-one wives. Each was given a year, just like you. Each failed. And each was magicked and trapped in a lump of stone. I suppose it is you, my Lady, that he expects to finish the set with."

King Brald had only told the princess what her reward would be, and she had failed to ask the penalty. Now a chill crept through her—as if she were already becoming stone—and she gasped. "But why does he leave them here?"

"He won't lock them up, for he says they aren't of any use to him, and they won't be of any use to anyone else. They are, after all, only chalk and coal."

"I would have turned them into emeralds," the princess said. "But put them away—I can't stand to look at them."

Adria, who was not delicate and had large hands, swept

them up in her arms and went to a corner wardrobe. She opened the door and tucked the pieces in as far back as she could. "I didn't like them either, my Lady," she said. "Now, if you please—"

The princess sat on the bed, and Adria gagged her and freed her hands. Then Adria whispered, "Pray that you have the strength to resist him, for he will visit you tonight," and she locked the door as she left.

The princess decided that was a curious statement. Why was the midwife on her side? she wondered, rubbing her wrists to work out the red rope marks.

The princess didn't know how long she had slept, but when she woke, moonlight was spilling across her bed like a silver scarf.

Suddenly, the lock turned with a snick, and in shuffled King Brald, this time without his attendant swarm of crystals. He tied her hands and removed her gag.

"Any sorcerer worth his salt," she said, "would have just transported himself here."

The king's knees creaked as he sat on her bed. "Any sorcerer worth his salt wouldn't have to make a personal visit to get done what I need to do. As I said earlier, I am failing. But believe me, I've still enough power to finish my chess set. Shall we get started?"

"I am sure my countrymen are on their way even now."

"Amantithi cannot be breached, much less even stumbled across, by your soldiers." The king smiled. "A little magic I put in motion when I was younger."

"Then we are at loggerheads," she said.

He shook his head. "I have given you one year. Why will you not agree? All I ask is a single child—not even a boy, necessarily—and you can go. Scot-free. You won't even have to nurse it. What is one year to a sorceress-princess such as yourself, who can weave a spell to extend her life beyond that of ordinary mortals?"

"I don't need to justify my reasons. That's one of the benefits of being princess."

The king's face flushed red. "One year! I can give you no more than that." Then rising with effort, he began to gag her.

"One moment," she said, and he paused expectantly. Without a doubt, she knew, he was going to keep her custody for the full term. But she also realized she did have a choice: Either she could twiddle her thumbs for a year and then get magicked into a chess piece, or she could devise a plan of revenge and, perhaps, eventual release.

"It's clear that we don't get along," she continued, "and that I do think you are as ugly as sin. However, if you could help me conceive without sharing my bed, I would be more amenable to your proposal."

"As I told you, I am failing."

"But as you also said, with our powers combined—"

He nodded slowly. "Some people believe sorcery is nothing more than skill. They are wrong, of course, for there must also be natural talent. So, hobbled as you are, you do contain a germ of sorcery with which I might work. Perhaps with that and our very proximity—"

"When the old moon lies in the new moon's arms, collect me a cup of your blood. It will be a symbol of your presence, and may help."

He raised his gray eyebrows. "Very well, but no tricks, now. The midwife will make sure you stay hobbled. And remember, this is your suggestion, not mine. I will do what I can, but whatever the outcome, you have one year. One year!"

He finished gagging her and untied her wrists. Then he pointed to a heavy brass bell on a small table. "When you notice a change, ring that bell, and your attendant will fetch me."

*   *   *

Days passed. Every morning, Adria laid out new dresses on the princess' bed, dresses enchanted with colors that flowed like water and clusters of gems that danced like clouds. The princess, however, would try none of them. After the dresses, Adria set before her a breakfast of buttery pastries, fruits, and spiced meats. The princess would only give the platter a cold eye and nibble at the crumbs. After breakfast, jugglers came to toss and balance, courtiers to sing and prance. But always, she would roll her eyes and, with a wave, send them packing.

By the end of the week, this entertainment had worn her patience thinner than King Brald's blood. And she knew just how thin his blood was, for that very morning Adria had brought a goblet brimming with it.

The princess hid it under her bed and decided to start her plan of revenge the very next day.

Slate and chalk had been given to her so she could communicate her desires—no magic would come of it, for Spells had to be spoken—and when Adria came in, huffing and puffing with her load of dresses, the princess scrawled: No jugglers today.

"Yes, my Lady." Then she studied the princess' belly. "Forgive my insolence, but my Lord wants a daily appraisal." Then, as she turned to leave, she added in a whisper, "I see nothing yet. Between you and me, that makes me very glad!"

The princess' eyes followed her out the door, and again she wondered why the midwife maintained such a curious attitude. But she had things to do, so she buried the question and got started.

Quickly, she went through the dresses. Each of them had enough fabric to clothe a small village. Taking one of the less gaudy ones, she examined it closely. Yes, it would do. With some pins, she fashioned a large, hidden pocket and then put the dress aside. Next, she pulled out the goblet of blood and retrieved a single stone wife from the wardrobe. After wetting her index finger in the blood, she carefully painted the figurine's belly with it. Finally, she bundled up the piece in a silk stocking, stuffed it in the hidden pocket, and slipped on the dress.

On one wall hung a long mirror made of polished silver. Although its surface was uneven and added a variety of new bumps to her figure, she could see that one particular new bump was quite real. She ran her hands lightly over it, tugged at the dress where it pinched her, and smiled.

She knew she could do no magic until she could both speak and use her hands, but until then, she would rely on unmagical stealth. The single stone wife made just the tiniest difference in her figure. So tiny, in fact, that no one would really notice unless she pointed it out. But it was important that the change came gradually. One stone wife every week, and she would let the dress out a little at a time—

She lifted up the big brass bell with both hands and shook it. The clapper sent a shiver deep into her bones. Adria came to see what was the matter, and then ran to fetch the king.

It took King Brald a good half hour to make it to her bedside. Hesitantly, he lifted a hand. Blue veins stood out in relief like the grain in a weathered plank. "May I?" he asked.

The princess nodded. His hand trembled as it touched the belly of her dress. "Our magic together must be very strong! You have done well, Princess. If you can take your child to term, I shall return you to your people in nine months."

Behind the king's back, Adria wore a pained look. Her lips moved soundlessly: I'm so sorry.

But the princess lay back and smiled.

Weeks passed, and the king came every week to feel the swelling of her belly. The last crust of ice melted from her window sill, and down in the inner motte the grass greened. A pair of swallows built a nest of mud just under the sill, and soon the young were testing their wings in the hot, hazy afternoons. Storms rolled over the hills, and rain beat at the panes. But before long, dull-colored, autumn leaves filled the wind, and she had to keep the fire going in her little hearth all day and night. Then one morning, the clouds let fall a quick burst of snow.

On that day, she took the last of the stone wives and added it to the thirty others in her hidden pocket.

When Adria came in, she threw herself at the princess', feet, sobbing. "My Lady, I cannot bear to see you suffer in this way any longer, so I must confess to you and help you, if I can. I have a secret—I was once the wife of the king."

Surprised, the princess put her hands on Adria's shoulders. Then she took her slate and chalk and wrote: Free me, so we can talk.

Adria wiped her eyes. "My Lady, you know I must—"

The princess nodded impatiently: Yes, get on with it, she thought. Understanding, Adria tied her hands and removed the gag.

"You said he'd had thirty-one wives," the princess said.

Adria sobbed some more. "I was to be the last."

"But why didn't he simply turn you to stone, too?"

"Because I went to him willingly and did not fight. As impossible as it might seem, none of the others wanted a child by him. They all knew he was wicked and would make them bear griffins or chimeras or somesuch. But it did not matter to me—I so desperately wanted a child, I would have been satisfied even with a monster."

"And what happened?"

"The king worked his magic, but he had become too old, and it wasn't enough. I never conceived." She hung her head. "And it is my fault that you are here, my Lady. For I suggested that he find himself a powerful sorceress to lie with. Yet there were none in our kingdom powerful enough to—"

"But he kept you alive."

"Yes, to tend to you. And that is my punishment, the cruelest of all—to see a woman succeed where I failed. I am told that after you bear his child, I will be set free."

"So you hate him now."

"I want to help you, my Lady."

The princess grunted. "Don't you think it's a little late for that? After all, I bear his monster."

"There are things we can do for that, my Lady. I know an herbalist, who—"

"Never mind that. But there is a way you can help me. When we are alone, free both my hands and my mouth." She looked into the midwife's eyes and saw true regret. I will reward you with your freedom when I gain mine."

"Can it be so, if I free you?"

"You will have everything you desire. But first, I will require a few things."

Gladly, Adria began work on the princess' list.

Shortly the king's surgeon, a thin, gray man, came to examine her. But the princess, who had asked Adria to gag her again and fearing that her plan would be discovered, reached for her slate: *I can tell just by looking at you that your hand is colder than a fish. It will make the child phlegmatic, and the king won't want that.*

The surgeon saw the good sense in this, and when he went to report to the king, he recommended that he, too, stay away from the princess until the baby was ready to be born.

The king then sent a message back to the princess: *Fine, but the child must be born within the week. Otherwise, I will have my surgeon force it—or you will suffer the same fate as my other wives.*

But the princess was prepared: *Come tomorrow at dawn.*

That night, she asked Adria to sup in her chambers. Adria came obediently, freed her Lady as requested, and then sat with the princess at a little table to dine. In her Lady's presence, she slurped her soup as delicately as she could and kept her lips clean with the back of her hand. To her great curiosity, the princess didn't eat a bite, but just looked out the window as if waiting for a sign.

At last, the princess said, "It is time."

"For what, my Lady?"

"For the magic, of course. Satisfying any desire that requires magic also requires a sacrifice. The soup we have shared tonight is the easy part of the spell."

The princess cleared the table and laid upon it a sheet of white silk and then, upon the silk, a small silver knife. Beside the knife she laid her piece of chalk and, taken from the edge of her hearth, a chunk of coal.

Adria watched curiously as the princess performed a strange ritual. Singing softly to herself, the princess rolled up the sleeves of her dress, unbuttoned her blouse and then hiked up her skirt. Next, she took up chalk and drew a small circle on each forearm, one on each calf, another between her breasts and, finally, one in the middle of her forehead. Then she took up the coal and filled in the circles. Each of them looked like the old moon in the new moon's arms.

"Now I need your help again," the princess said. She handed Adria the tiny silver knife. "From each of these circles, cut a small piece of my flesh and put it in the center of the silk."

Adria's eyes grew wide with horror. "My Lady! I could not harm your person in such a way."

"You want your freedom? I want mine, too. We can both have it if you will just do as I say."

Perspiration glistened on Adria's brow. With trembling hands she took the knife and pressed it against the circle on the princess' left arm. The point made a dimple, and she paused.

"Please," the princess said.

Adria pressed harder, and a drop of blood welled up. The knife, sharp as a tiger's fang, cut without effort and freed a plug of flesh. Adria plucked it like a flower—wet with blood, it nearly slipped from her grip—and laid it in the silk.

Then she went to the circle on the other arm. . . .

When Adria had finished and set the last bit of her Lady's flesh in the square, she dropped the knife to the floor. Her hands trembled and her voice shook as she said, "Is there anything else, my Lady?"

"One last thing." The princess went to the silk square and, again singing softly, wrapped up the flesh and folded the square into a long sash. She laid it across the width of the bed.

"Now it is time for sleep," she said. "And you will sleep soundly, Adria. You won't have to worry about any nightmares from what you have seen here. In fact, in the morning, you will remember none of this. Come, lie with me on the sash, and put your belly against mine."

Adria followed her into bed. As asked, she lay on one side, atop the wet and bloody sash, and faced the princess. The princess then tied the sash around them, pressing their bellies tight.

She began to sing . . . and they both drifted into sleep.

The next morning, the princess woke first and undid the sash. She examined Adria's belly—it was as round and full as a haystack, while her own was as flat as a bench.

Suddenly, Adria woke with a loud groan and slapped her hands against her belly. "It's time," she said. "Please call the midwife!"

The princess smiled. Her spell had worked so well! Clearly, Adria had forgotten it was the princess who was supposed to be in labor, not her. "I will be your midwife," she said.

"You, my Lady? But—" Then she stopped. "What has happened to your face?"

"A carbuncle, but never mind. And as for my helping you, midwifery is an important part in the training of a sorceress." Then she shook the brass bell with a loud clang. While she waited for the king to come, she went to work.

First the surgeon burst in, and then the king. They quickly saw that the princess was free of her bonds, and that it was the midwife who was in labor. The king said, "This is sorcery!"

"This is what you wanted," the princess said. "This poor woman said she tried to help you, but failed. Well, now I have helped her. She bears your child."

The surgeon pushed the princess aside and took over. With a grunt, he held out the infant. "It is small, my Lord, but it will make a suitable heir. I mean, she will make a suitable heir."

The king fell to his knees, hands clasped, eyes rolled up to Heaven. "After all these years—"

A note of alarm sprang into the surgeon's voice. "My Lord, you will have two heirs. No, three. No—"

Soon thirty-one babies lay swaddled in the bedsheets beside Adria, each of them squalling healthily. The sharp, coppery tang of childbirth filled the chamber. The surgeon rinsed his hands in the wash basin and wiped them dry on his breeches. "This is indeed sorcery, my Lord," he said, scowling.

"These are your thirty-one wives who disappointed you so terribly," the princess said.

The king looked at her with an angry glare. "They are not my children."

"In a very real sense, they are. With your blood I have freed them. They are of your blood." She rubbed the pink cheek of the first child. "In fact, I think this one has your eyes."

The king studied the children, and the fire died in his face. "Will they remember what I have done to them?"

"They will have a second chance to live their lives as they wanted, for by the time they come of age, you will have long passed from this world."

Adria, who had lain silently catching her breath, rose up. "My Lord, thirty-one daughters!" She sounded quite pleased.

The king lowered his head. "I will keep my word—you are both free to go."

"I want to stay and raise them," Adria said.

"Very well, but as for you, Princess—"

The king ordered his men to take her safely to the border of Elaan before winter gathered its full strength. On the night her escorts left her, she camped at the foot of dark mountains and watched the sparks from her fire fly into the air and die among the stars. In the west, a new moon shone, a tiny, hooked sliver.

Just within its crescent, the old moon lay sleeping.

She smiled to herself. She didn't want to have children. There were just too many other equally wonderful things to do in the world. And besides, if she ever did get wistful about having children, once a month she could always look for the old moon in the new moon's arms, and remember. . . .

TIGER'S EYE
India Edghill

India Edghill's interest in fantasy can be blamed squarely on her father, who read her *The Wizard of Oz*, *The Five Children and It*, and *Alf's Button* before she was old enough to object. Later she discovered Andrew Lang's multicolored fairy books, Edward Eager, and the fact that Persian cats make the best paperweights. She has sold stories to *Catfantasic IV*, *Marion Zimmer Bradley's Fantasy Magazine*, and the *Magazine of Fantasy and Science Fiction*, and has just published *Queenmaker*, a historical novel of King David's court. She and her cats own too many books on far too many subjects.

"A boy and his dog" is a bit of a cliché; really tough situations may require a girl and her cat.

THE scrying bowl was very old. Time and the touch of many hands had smoothed living jade until the bowl's sides only hinted at shapes carved long ago. Yellow jade; yellow as a tiger's eye.

Rātrichāyā balanced the bowl in the hollow of her cupped hands, staring into the liquid filling the ancient vessel almost to its brim. Red liquid; red as heart's blood.

Her blood.

Despite bright pain from the fresh knife cut across her wrist, Rātrichāyā held the scrying bowl steady. Within the confines of yellow jade, her blood remained motionless, a crimson mirror.

A mirror to spy upon the wide world; the world Ratrichya had not set living eyes upon since the day she had returned from the Pavilion. The day she had been imprisoned within the palace walls by her brother.

When she had seen the metal circlet waiting in her brother's hands, Rātrichāyā had known what would befall as clearly as if the future had been scribed in new ink on ivory tablets. Coveting the treasures she now possessed, fearing both her power and his own weakness, her brother had clasped the band of gem-studded gold about her slim throat—and with the closing of the iron padlock, had usurped the magic that rightfully belonged only to her husband.

Her brother had asked little enough of her since that shameful day, fearing her skills as much as he coveted them. But today he had demanded service of her, for today her jailer feared something more than he feared his sister's powers. Sworn to obedience, Rātrichāyā had little choice but to submit.

And truth demanded she acknowledge curiosity; she wished to know what worried her brother so greatly he would ask blood-service of his sister. His Pavilion witch.

But curiosity, too, must be smoothed aside, for emotion distracted from purity of will. Rātrichāyā forced rebellious thoughts from her mind, concentrated upon the task of creating a mental twin to the crimson mirror within the scrying bowl.

Her mind a calm reflection of the crimson mirror created from her blood, Rātrichāyā stared into the bowl within her hands. At first she saw nothing but blood, a crimson veil between her and the world beyond. Then, slowly, an image began to form, taking on life from her still-warm blood.

A man, tall and stern-faced, walked through towering deodars. A stranger, odd-looking and exotic; a foreigner with pale eyes and hair as tawny-golden as a lion's mane.

Behind the golden man, others followed, dressed as he was in short tunics and stiff leather armor. The men carried spears in their hands and wore swords belted at their waists. . . .

They were lost. For the hundredth time, Leander squinted into the setting sun, vainly trying to ascertain their location. The attempt was useless; mountains surrounded them like armed guards, and the narrow hill-track the native guide had unwillingly led Leander's patrol along had vanished half a league back.

Soon we will reach World's End, Leander thought. And for what? It was hard, now, to remember the eagerness with which he had once followed Great Alexander, zealous for adventure and glory. Half the world had fallen before Alexander, and still it was not enough. Now Great Alexander yearned to add the hot mad lands east of the River Indus to the foreign jewels in his hero's crown. To that end, Alexander had sent men out, as a hunter might loose a hound, to spy out the country and carry back its secrets. Leander had been ordered to take a squad of men north, into the hills; oddly uneasy, he had obeyed Alexander's command.

I am tired of fighting and marching and killing. I am too old for this life. Leander glanced back at his men and met half-sullen stares. The men, too, had long since wearied even of conquest; only heroes despised the comforts of a trade, a home, a wife.

Great Alexander is a hero. I am not.

For a time that fire had burned bright, fed by Alexander's own ardent inner flame. Now Leander knew he had obeyed Great Alexander for the last time. Knew that he would never leave this exotic wilderness of cedars and briar-rose and streams like liquid glass, this alien dream-world where monkeys ran on two legs like silver ghosts and huge striped cats prowled, ebony-and-amber shadows, through singing grass. A land where mountains vaulted in cruel beauty from dawn's horizon to dusk's, marching in ice-crowned glory to the far end of the sky.

It was when he had first set eyes on the snowfire of those faraway peaks that Leander had understood why the ranges he and his men climbed with such effort were only the High Hills.

But hills or mountains, we shall never leave them. We have gone too far—Leander scanned the vista intently, and for a moment thought he saw a flash of dull gold, as if sunlight struck stone—or fiery eyes. But his tired eyes blinked, and when he looked again, the golden glint had vanished.

But he remembered where the golden light had been; it made as good a goal as any, now. Forcing a smile, Leander turned and, with a sweeping wave of his arm, summoned his men to follow as he headed down the ridge.

"Strangers? Foreign soldiers? Who are they, and where do they come from? And why?" Cāruman added, almost as an afterthought.

"I do not know why they come, brother." Rātrichāyā deliberately invoked their relationship, knowing such reminders troubled Cāruman. *As they should; no brother should treat a sister as he treats me.*

Once her brother had been fond of her—at least, Rāitrichāyā thought he had been. But that had been long ago, before she had been sent to the Pavilion to learn women's arts.

Now she owned skills of magic polished smooth as gems; precious skills meant to serve as her dowry. But those hard-won powers now served as chains, for during the years she dwelt at the Pavilion, her father had died and her brother had become king in his turn.

Her brother commanded her often, to flaunt his

mastery—but he did not command her to perform great deeds, for he feared her skills as much as he coveted them.

Ensure a good supply of game for the hunt; reveal a courtier's inner thoughts; bring a reluctant woman to his bed. Rāitrichāyā used only the smallest summonings when her brother demanded a woman's yielding of her; herself coerced, she would not constrain her sisters against their will. But few women truly objected to a king's notice—and of those whom small magic could not compel, Rātrichāyā need only murmur, "Sorcery is powerless against true virtue, my lord brother."

Which was true enough, and hint enough to silence King Cāruman. Rātrichāyā's brother was not a total fool.

But still fool enough to hold her, when he might have become rich on her bride-price. Twice a fool enough to waste what he so shamefully held, from fear of commanding her skills as he might have done.

And thrice foolish to fear redressing all error by releasing her into a husband's hands.

Fool and coward, too. Rātrichāyā knew her brother would never release her now, no matter what bride-price might be offered for her. *Not after what he has dared; in my place he would take petty revenge, and he thinks me no better than he.*

She did not trouble herself to explain his error, for he would never believe her truth. She had been carefully taught never to waste effort on impossibilities.

"Strangers," her brother repeated, his brow furrowed beneath the gemmed circlet he wore about his head. "Strangers—coming here?"

"I cannot tell, brother." Her words were true enough; she did not know the foreigners' planned destination. But she knew where that narrow path led, should they follow it across the High Hills: To the valley of the Tiger Palace. *And to me.*

"Perhaps they come here," she added. "They carried swords and spears, and seemed men hardened by war." There; that needle should prick her brother, perhaps draw blood.

Through lashes demurely lowered, as befit a modest maiden, she regarded King Cāruman keenly. Engrossed in his own fears, he paid his sister little heed; her patient submission to his will had ripened poison fruit. Set beside new danger, awe of his sister's Pavilion training dulled; its keen edge blunted against the threat posed by the foreign warriors.

"Men of war." King Cāruman paled. "They must not reach the valley." Cāruman stopped abruptly and rounded upon her. "You must stop them."

"But, brother—"

"I command it," he repeated. "You must obey."

"I must obey." Rātrichāyā bowed her head, then murmured, "But, brother, this concerns men, and war, and I can do nothing here, encircled by iron and ancient women's magic."

Her brother knew no better than to believe her. "Where, then?" he demanded.

Rātrichāyā lifted her head, opened her eyes wide to catch the light. "Outside the walls. But these foreign warriors seem savage, violent—no one can touch me here within the tower—"

"Do you think only of your own safety?" her brother demanded. "You will do as you are told, sister—did they not teach you obedience at the great Pavilion?"

Again Rātrichāyā bowed her head. "Yes, brother," she whispered. "If you ask it, I must venture from my tower's safety and try what magic I can summon for you." And to remind him of what he had done, she lifted her hand to the cold iron of the lock closing her jeweled collar.

Under her gaze Cāruman shifted, uneasy. "Go, then," he told her, and could not meet her eyes.

*   *   *

Freedom intoxicated; Rātrichāyā bounded through the forest like a living flame. It had been long since she had summoned this power, conjured this freedom. Too long, for she could not control the fierce desires that flowed like hot magic through her blood.

The tigress Rātrichāyā struggled to retain memory of why she raced through the sunlight and shadow of this wild forest. A man; she sought a man, a stranger—

But tiger's form held tiger's nature, and it was long since Rātrichāyā had been permitted to practice her more arcane skills. The battle to retain consciousness of her goal distracted her, granted the tiger's nature the opening it craved. With a coughing sigh, the tigress wrenched control from the sorceress; a moment later the tigress fled nearly mindless through the cloud forest, fleeing the taint of man. A fallen log barred the way, and the tigress tensed. So simple; a leap—

—and a crash through forest floor that was not solid ground at all, but a cunningly woven mat of grass and branches. And then she was falling, falling to land with brutal force upon the hard-packed earth floor of the tiger pit.

As they approached the next stretch of forest, growls echoed through the slim pines, the grim sound seeming to encircle the soldiers as they huddled close in the center of the clearing. "A panther," one man said.

"A demon," another corrected as the growls lifted into a wild wail that rang through the surrounding trees.

Leander looked at his men. Good men, brave men, pushed by this insane quest past the point of endurance or sense. "There are no demons," Leander said. "Nor does the beast sound like a panther. And it comes no closer."

"We must go back," Perdicas said, sullen. "It'll eat us all if we go on."

"Go back where?" another demanded. "Across those hills again to be eaten by something just as evil?"

"Panther or demon, we can't go on while it bars our path," Perdicas said, stubborn.

"I'll go see what the beast is," Leander said, "and where it lairs. Wait here—and if I am not back by sunset, Glaucis takes command. And may the gods have mercy on you all."

Like everything else in this accursed place, the beast's lair proved farther than the echoing disembodied snarls had hinted. Leander walked away from his men, pausing at the tangle of bushes edging the next stretch of tall trees. Refusing to look back, he pushed through a thicket of gleaming leaves, into the silent forest beyond. Once through the bushes, he glanced back, only to find himself unable to see the clearing in which his men waited for him; green darkness barred his view.

Another snarl. The sound no longer seemed to encircle him; Leander listened, and then strode forward, seeking the source of the wrathful noise.

His long strides took him rapidly through the open ground beneath the tall trees, the pine needles that lay thick upon the ground silencing his footfalls. Once he had taken a dozen paces he paused, listening; there was no wind, and the angry growls had ceased. Now the only sound was a quick heavy panting, frightened breaths sighing through the still cool air beneath the pines.

Another dozen paces, and an opening in the earth yawned before him. The panting grew louder, overlaying a steady, rhythmic padding. A catch-trap; a pit dug deep enough to imprison even a large beast. *Let's see what manner of creature has fallen to its doom.* So thinking, Leander strode cautiously to the edge and stared down.

In the pit below, a tigress paced, muscle silk-supple beneath fire-bright pelt. Hearing Leander's approach, the tigress paused like a dancer between one step and the next, and looked up.

Leander stared down into the tiger's eyes. Eyes like hot fire . . . *eyes I have seen before*. But that flashing image was folly born of this eerie land. Below him was only a great cat that had met its fate at last—and in its misfortune lay deliverance from this trackless forest. Men had dug this animal-trap, therefore men would return to see what prize they had captured. Leander and his soldiers need only wait beside the tiger pit, and sooner or later they would have the native guide they so desperately needed. Relief weakened Leander; he sat down upon the mounded earth at the pit's edge and stared down at his unexpected savior.

"Thank you," Leander called down to the tigress, who had resumed her restless pacing. At the sound of his voice, the beast once again paused, and this time doubled back to stalk toward him. As Leander stared, the tigress lifted her forepaws, resting them upon the dirt wall of the pit. And as she lifted her great head, Leander saw the jeweled collar circling the tigress' neck.

Random sunbeams kindled green fire in emeralds set evenly about the supple gold that collared the trapped tigress. Clearly the great cat was some noble's pet gone astray; even better, for certainly someone would soon come seeking an animal valued to the extent that its very badge of ownership was formed of precious metal.

"Well, cat, shall we await your owner together?" Leander asked, smiling at the beast that would prove his men's salvation.

In apparent answer, the tigress growled and shook its massive head. And as the trapped cat lifted its chin, Leander saw that its jeweled collar was held closed by an iron padlock.

That was odd; why should a pet tiger's collar be held shut with a lock? No beast could unlatch such a collar; what need, then, for a lock? To prevent a human thief from removing the valuable collar?

From a tiger? A robber must be bold indeed to dare such a theft. Bold, or desperate . . .

Desperate, as I am, to attain what he desires. Staring downward, into the tigress' hot eyes, Leander found himself speaking again, as if the great cat could understand as well as hear.

"So here we are; trapped, both of us. You by earthen walls, and I—I by mountains such as I never dreamed of, by a wilderness flung before me by the Lady of the Crossroads."

Below him, the tigress paused, then sat, gazing intently up; the collar's iron lock swung slowly back and forth beneath her white-furred chin.

"There is no escape from our fate," Leander said, and a cloud-shadow fell across the pit below; in the shifting light, he fancied the tigress frowned. "You do not agree," Leander said. "Well, perhaps you are right. Does not Great Alexander say men make their own fates?"

As he spoke, Leander looked again at the iron padlock closing the tiger's jeweled collar. Something was wrong; every instinct warned him, and Leander had long since learned to heed such warnings. Abruptly rising, he strode around the deep pit imprisoning the waiting tigress, pacing its bounds as if he, too, were trapped by its earthen walls.

At last he stopped, and turned away; behind him a low moaning arose; the great cat protesting her abandonment. "Be patient," Leander called, and the sound ceased.

Despite the vast tract of woodland surrounding him, it took Leander precious time to find what he needed. But at last his increasingly wide search yielded a fallen tree not yet rotten.

The log was too large for him to shift alone; Leander returned to the tiger-trap and called down, "Wait a little; I must call my men to help. Patience, striped one."

The fire-gold eyes blinked once; perhaps the tigress understood. Leaving the pit, Leander began to retrace his footsteps, seeking the clearing where he had left his men.

"You wish to do *what?*" Glaucis demanded. The grizzled sergeant plainly thought Leander had run mad, as mad as Great Alexander.

Leander looked at his men, and saw the same thought reflected in each man's face; he laughed. "No, I have not gone mad. Look—see the beast's collar? It is tame, and such a valuable pet must be greatly sought after. Releasing it will gain us favor with its owner."

A low growl from the tigress in the pit; Leander glanced down and smiled. "Or perhaps the beast is hungry, and will lead us to its home."

"Or perhaps it will eat us," Glaucis said, and shrugged. "At least that would end our troubles swiftly."

That finished the grumbling; the men put their strength willingly to the task of hauling the fallen tree from its resting place on the forest floor over the thick-laid pine needles to the rim of the tiger-pit. "Stand back, cat," Glaucis called, "we've brought you a fine ladder."

"Aye, and try not to be too hungry for Greek meat when you come up," Akhilles added.

Heartened—it had been long since any of the men had the heart for jests of any sort—Leander directed the sliding of the dead tree into the pit. "Careful—and once it's down, stand back to give her room."

"As much as she cares to take," his sergeant agreed.

As soon as the makeshift ladder slid into place, the soldiers moved hastily away from the tiger-trap, expecting the great cat to spring to freedom in a snarling rush. Instead, the tigress climbed out with quiet dignity, placing each thick-furred paw upon the slanting log with the graceful deliberation of a rope-dancer. When she had reached the edge, and stepped from the log to solid ground, the tigress paused and looked slowly around her, as if studying the waiting men.

And then the great cat stalked with elegant, sinuous grace toward Leander.

Common sense urged him at least to draw his sword, however little good the weapon might do against such a beast. But another instinct kept Leander still, waiting. The tigress stopped before him, and Leander found himself once more staring into tiger eyes. Eyes like hot fire. . . .

Slowly, Leander knelt before the tigress; slowly, he reached out and touched the jeweled collar circling her throat.

Her fur was sleek as a house cat's, soft as a woman's hair. Long contact with her body had heated the collar's gold; Leander's fingers slid under the warm metal and the tigress leaned into his hand, purring. And when Leander stood, and began to edge away, she followed, twining her sinuous length about him, curving to keep him near her.

"She likes you," Akhilles called, and Leander glanced at him, taking his eyes from the tigress.

As he did so, he felt a heavy tap upon his thigh; the tigress wished his attention upon her. Oddly taken with the beast, and unwilling to try its unknown temper, Leander stooped again, and the tigress came to his outstretched hand.

Purring, she nudged against him; Leander found himself staring once more into her fire-gold eyes. "What is it you want, tiger-lady? If it's food, we've none for ourselves; perhaps you will hunt for us."

The tigress made a trilling noise that might have been anything from puzzlement to assent; Leander found himself smiling again. "Or perhaps you wish to return home to your pleasant cage? Alas, I know not where that may be; I am only a poor lost traveler, like yourself."

His own idle words sparked an idea; Leander closed his fingers over the tigress' collar. The tigress stared fixedly at him: Leander sensed a strong will struggling behind the beast's eyes. A sad thi ng, to shackle such a beast. . . .

Once more Leander's fingers sought the tigress' collar, slid along the curve of blood-warm metal. But this time his fingers sought the iron lock that bound the collar closed.

The iron was cool to his skin, and the lock itself an oddly flimsy thing, as if cold iron were merely adornment for the collar's gold and gems. A swift twist snapped the padlock's clasp as if it were forged of glass. The tigress stood frozen, a beast carved of ebony and amber, as Leander slipped the broken lock from jeweled collar circling her neck.

Free. I am free. The word burned through Rātrichāyā like wildfire. *Free.*

Thanks to a barbarian warrior who does not even know what service he has done me. But he would know; she would make sure of that. *And he will be rewarded beyond his dreams for his kindness.*

The tigress Rātrichāyā could not smile, but that did not matter. Once more she leaned against the golden-haired stranger who had unlocked her collar, pushing her head against his thigh. Cautiously, he laid his hand upon her head; Rātrichāyā caught his wrist between her white fangs—gently—and tugged. Then, releasing him, she sprang away, only to pause at the clearing's edge and look back.

Come. Follow me.

For a moment tiger's eyes met warrior's.

Follow me, Rātrichāyā willed at him. *Trust me.*

The tigress led them eastward, through trackless forest at first, bounding forward out of sight and then slowing, circling back and urging them on with cheerful chirps and purrs that insensibly heartened the weary men. At last the trees thinned, and suddenly Leander looked down to see a narrow path, its dirt hard-packed as if by many feet. And not half a league ahead the cool green light vanished in a ruddy curtain of sunglare.

Forest's end, at last— Nevertheless, Leander forced himself to keep his hand on his sword's hilt, and his eyes alert, as he followed the narrow path through the last cedars. At the treeline's edge, Leander stopped, almost afraid to look for fear of seeing yet another forest, another range of mountains—

But the tigress had not deceived him. Leander found himself staring at a broad valley like green velvet, a narrow river rushing through it like liquid crystal. And at valley's end—

Leander narrowed his eyes, challenged his perception. But his tired eyes did not deceive; what he saw was no sunglare-illusion vanishing under a steady gaze.

At valley's end, a city huddled against the rising hills; a city guarded by a fortress and crowned by a tower, walls amber fire in the rays of the westering sun—

What he saw was real.

With a tangible goal at last before them, Leander's men cheered instantly, readying themselves to march upon the city in good order, as befit Great Alexander's soldiers. Only Leander held aloof from the sudden good humor; something about his encounter with the collared tigress disturbed him. The beast had been too—too what? Too tame? Too helpful? *Too good to be true,* flashed through Leander's mind, and for a moment he wondered if the tigress had in fact been a god, or a god's messenger, sent to guide them safely from this endless forest.

He dismissed the thought; why should the gods trouble themselves with him and his men? No, the encounter with the trapped tigress had been chance only—and good luck for both of them.

*   *   *

Her brother was not pleased. Even knowing how useless mere words were to alter what was past, he berated her. Falsely meek, Rātrichāyā stood silent as he ranted, her bowed head hiding the triumph glowing in her eyes.

"I trusted you! And this—is this all those Pavilion witches taught you? *Failure?*"

At that, Rātrichāyā slowly raised her head until her hot eyes met her brother's fearful ones. "Oh, but I have not failed, brother," she said, and lifted her chin still higher, until he could not fail to see that the iron padlock was gone.

When he saw the iron lock no longer rested against her skin, his face took on the color of ash. Swiftly he fumbled at his sash for the padlock's key, and Rātrichāyā smiled.

"A key is useless without a lock, brother."

"I will have another forged! I—I order you—"

Still smiling, Rātrichāyā shook her head. "Too late, brother; I am no longer bound by that command." And as her brother stared, faded by fear, she added, "If you wish the city or the palace defended, you must take up your sword and do it yourself.

"I am no longer yours."

When the alien warriors stood before the palace gate and demanded admittance, King Cāruman panicked; Rātrichāyā had known he would. In panic he ran to his sister and dragged her from the Fire Queen's Tower, through its iron doors and past the Queen's Maze and the Concubines' Pool, past the Tiger Court and the Poison Garden, the King's Hall and the Great Court, until at last he hauled her up the steps beside the West Gate. Only when they reached the top of the wall did her brother slow his breathless pace and release her hand.

"Look!" he ordered in a voice made unsteady by the terror he himself had summoned to rule him. "Look be-

fore the gate, sister, and see what you have done. You
have doomed me."

Rātrichāyā smiled; an expression her brother had not
seen since the day he locked her collar with iron and imprisoned his sister and her magic in the Fire Queen's Tower.
"Your greed doomed you, brother, when you grasped that
which is not yours to hold. You might have asked anything for me, once; now you will have nothing."

As her brother stared at her, she moved past him, to
the wall's edge. A low parapet of stone edged the drop to
the street below; Rātrichāyā set her freshly-hennaed hands
upon the sunwarm stone and looked down at the armed
men waiting below the palace gate.

Tilting back his head, Leander studied the top of the
wall before him. A few men armored in padded leather
cuirasses and holding small bows peered down at him—
gawked, as if they were schoolboys faced with an African
giraffe. *Sloppy soldiers*, Leander thought. Sloppy soldiers
meant an unfit general; Leander searched among the dis-
mayed men for their leader.

There, that plump fellow in silk and pearls staring down
at Leander and his dozen men. Even from the ground, Leander spotted telltale signs of fear as the man gestured
frantically at the young woman beside him. *She* showed
no alarm; instead, she placed her hands upon the wall and
leaned forward, as if seeking a beloved face below.

Shadow-thin silk fluttered, drawing Leander's eye to
her face. She was younger than he had first thought her;
barely past girlhood. But there was nothing girlish in her
intent eyes as they met Leander's gaze.

To show himself harmless, Leander smiled up at her,
and waved. She regarded him steadily a moment before
smiling back, and lifting her hand as if to wave in turn.
But instead of waving, she pushed back the heavy tresses
of black hair half-veiling her small body.

And sunlight glinted fire from the jeweled collar circling her slender throat.

Once Leander had seen his opponent, he had known there would be no battle. He was barely surprised when the massive gates were opened to him, and not surprised at all to find the plump prince and the fire-eyed girl awaiting him. Leander stood within the gateway and she walked toward him, moving with the same supple grace as the tigress who had led him here. Just before Leander, she stopped, staring at him with eyes as fire-hot as those of the collared tigress. Then she smiled, and her painted fingers caressed the golden band about her throat.

"Ask him for the key, lord." Rātrichāyā touched the collar and then gestured at her brother, and the stranger who had freed her shot a keen glance at her, as if he knew all she could not yet tell him. But he obeyed, holding out his hand, palm upward, toward her brother. And then he waited, regarding Cāruman with the steady, intent eyes of a hunting cat.

Her brother could not hold against those eyes; three breaths later he submitted, fumbling in the folds of his embroidered sash for the key that lay there. Eyes averted, King Cāruman dropped the iron key into the golden stranger's waiting hand.

Leander stared at the iron key; a small, plain thing to be so highly valued. But that the girl valued it was clear; her eyes glowed like hot coals as she looked at the dull metal key lying on his palm. *An iron key—* Suddenly Leander knew what lock matched the key he now held.

He reached into his pouch and closed his fingers on the iron padlock he had broken from the trapped tigress' collar. He laid the lock beside the key on his hand, and looked once more into Rātrichāyā's eyes. Then he walked over and held out his hand to her.

Does he know what he offers me, this stranger? Rātrichāyā stared down at the iron-hard key to her collar's lock. Slowly, she touched the lock and key, then delicately lifted them from his hand. The key to power—

—a key she alone now possessed.

A key the stranger lord had given willingly into her hand.

Her eyes never leaving his, Rātrichāyā pulled a tress of hair forward over her shoulder, braiding the small key into the long strand. The metal dulled against the midnight brilliance of her hair.

"Well?" Cat-pale eyes regarded her with a cat's keenness. "Have I passed your test, Queen of Tigers?"

Touching the cool iron key, Rātrichāyā smiled. "If ever you wish the key, you have only to ask," she told him. "Now follow me, lord, and I will show you the limits of your new domain."

RAVEN-WINGS ON THE SNOW

by Pauline J. Alama

Pauline J. Alama, a professional grant proposal writer and former medieval scholar, is indebted for the seeds of this story to two great medieval scholars, the Brothers Grimm. Pauline's first published story, "Heartless," appeared in *Marion Zimmer Bradley's Fantasy Magazine*, issue 22, and she will always be grateful to Mrs. Bradley for giving her this start. Her poetry has appeared in *Pandora* and *A Round Table of Contemporary Arthurian Poetry*, and she is hoping to find a publisher for her first novel, *The Eye of Night*. She lives in Lyndhurst, New Jersey, with her husband, Paul Cunneen, and several thousand books.

Here is a story of a well-nigh impossible task carried out against great obstacles.

FROM my earliest years I remember the king, my father, looking at me with a hunger that I did not understand but feared. When he looked thus, my mother would gather me out of his sight, without a word to him or me. Then I would sit in her chamber for hours, watching her ply the needle in silence. I, too, would work my little embroidery, trying to pour all my feelings into the flowers I stitched into linen, trying not to let emotion rise to my mouth, knowing it would avail nothing to ask. My mother doted on me most of the day, but whenever my father looked at me so, it turned her cold against me, so that though she protected me, I scarcely knew whether to be thankful for it. I was heir to the crown, bowed to and begged from like any princess, and yet everyone from my mother to the lowliest beggar seemed to look at me with a kind of horror, as though I were mysteriously guilty of something I could not know. That was before I heard the story.

Only once can I remember breaking the silence of our retreat. My mother embroidered twelve ravens circling a tower with one high window. Looking at it, I felt a memory stir. "Those ravens," I said. "They came from inside the tower. I remember them: young men turning into ravens and flying out the window."

My mother smiled, but I saw no mirth in her eyes. "It was a dream you had," she said. "You told it to me long ago." I believed her then, and went on stitching my aster-flowers. Years passed before I knew more.

As I grew, it seemed my father watched me more avidly and I, shy by instinct, retreated to what secret haunts I could find. Once, hiding between a tapestry and a wall, I found a ring of keys wedged between the wall-stones. Cautious beyond my years, I hid them elsewhere and waited, watching my parents for signs of alarm to see if the keys were missed. Only after long watching did I dare try them, testing them one by one on doors I'd never seen opened. I came at length to a garret at the top of a tower. Sunlight from a high window illumined twelve long boxes, the largest the length of a tall man. Upon their lids were carved images of sad-faced boys. Twelve burial effigies stared up at me from twelve coffins. I gasped, then saw a movement in the shadows at the other end of the room. In real terror now I turned to run, but heard a voice from the shadows: "Have no fear."

Slowly I turned to her. She stepped into the light, and I saw tears shining on her face. "Mother," I said, "whose coffins are these?"

"Your brothers'," she said, "but fear not: they are not inside them."

"What do you mean?" I said. "My brothers? I never had any." But then I caught a glimpse through the window and memory flooded back like dawn. "That window," I said, "there, it was *there* I saw the ravens flying out—in my dream. The young men taking wing—"

"Most were just boys," my mother said, "But they would have seemed men to you; you were so young. You remember rightly. You must not speak of them anywhere but here."

"It was no dream, then," I said, "But what was it? What happened?"

"Once upon a time," my mother said, "there was a king who had twelve fine sons, more than many a man could wish for. But when his queen brought forth a daughter, late in life, he formed an evil plan. With the maiden growing up in his house he need not wear out his years tied to an aged wife. Instead, when the girl reached womanhood, he would take her in her mother's place, against the law of God. He knew his sons would not allow it, so he trapped them in a tower, planning to murder them. So certain was he of his plan that he had twelve coffins made for them.

"But the queen knew his plans through a secret art, and she did what she could to save her children. As they awaited death in the tower, she changed them one by one into ravens. They flew far from sight, but she herself remained to protect her daughter."

"I am that daughter?" I said, still uncertain. I had drawn closer to my mother as she told the story. Now she reached across to me, touching me more gently than she had in years.

"Yes," my mother said, "and I have protected you as well as I could. But I cannot protect you forever. When I die, you must leave this place. Seek out your brothers and restore them to their proper shapes."

"What can restore them?" I asked.

"Shirts sewn of aster-flowers and silence," she said. "You must not speak from the first stitch to the last, until your brothers stand clothed in your handiwork."

"I will restore them," I promised her. "I will set it right." She may have thought I meant years later, after her death. But I left the castle that night.

As I traveled, I sold my jewels to buy food, and asked everyone I met if they had seen twelve ravens with human eyes. No one had. I wandered to the wastes, where there was no one to ask but the four winds. And so I asked the winds, but one said "Go north," and another "Go south." At last they told me to ask the Sun, which sees all things by day.

"How can I climb up to the sun?" I asked. "No mountain reaches so high."

"Doesn't the Sun descend at close of day?" said the West Wind. "At night she lives in dreams. Sleep with your face to a fire and a sun's-heart blossom in your mouth." He made a patch of small red flowers wave. I thanked the winds, plucked one of the flowers, and readied myself for nightfall.

When the last trace of the sun had vanished from the waking sky, I did as the West Wind directed. With the heat of the fire on my face, I dreamed I saw a woman in the flames. "Why have you come so close? Foolish child, leave me: you will be burned." Her hair was pure flame. A spark flew toward me and stung my face.

"Help me," I stammered in confusion. "The winds said you see all things. I seek twelve ravens who are my brothers. Tell me, wise Sun—"

"I have seen them," she said. "They are imprisoned in the Glass Mountain. Now go, or I will surely do you harm."

"Wait!" I cried, "Where is this Glass Mountain?"

"I will make it shine, and my light will guide you," said the Sun. "Now be gone!"

"Wait," I said once more. "How will I open their prison?"

"I have the key," the Sun said, "but if I reach out to give it to you, you will die. I will give it to the Moon. Ask her instead."

"But—"

"Now wake!" cried the Sun. Light blazed in my face, and I woke. The fire before me had flared up and my left hand, which I had stretched toward the Sun in entreaty, had been singed. I quickly rolled away from the fire, spat out the blossom, and doused the flames. My hand blistered. I soothed it with moist leaves and waited for the winds to rise. When the West Wind stole into my camp, I asked him where I could find the Moon.

"There is a tree far to the east," he said, "so tall it catches the moon in its branches. Build a boat, and I will take you there." I built the boat as he taught me. When it was done, the West Wind carried me to the Isle of Moonrise, where the Tree of the Moon lifts its branches. "Wrap your cloak well around you, and do not touch the Moon," the West Wind said. "The East Wind will return for you tomorrow."

I climbed the Tree of the Moon as high as I could go and waited for moonrise. A little after dark I felt chilled; then I knew the Moon was near. I looked up and saw her in the branches just above me.

"Fair moon," I said, "By your mercy, give me what the sun promised: the key to the Glass Mountain."

"And was that key for you?" the Moon said languidly. "I can't hold fast to anything she gives me. I gave it to the earth. My sister should know better than to trust me." Then the indifferent Moon began carelessly brushing back branches, preparing to leave.

"Wait!" I said, "I came so far for your help. Can you give me nothing?"

"What help can I give? I am not strong," said the Moon.

"Even my light is borrowed from the Sun. But I have one gift for you," she added. "Take this knife. You may need it."

At the first touch I shrank back. The curving silver blade was cold as the edge of winter. But at last I drew up the courage to grasp it. "What will I need it for?"

"Who can tell? A woman must often defend herself," the Moon said.

"I am not yet a woman," I said.

The Moon smiled. "You are." Then she drew blood from me, and I was. "I must leave you now," she said.

"But the key—?"

"Ask the Earth," were her parting words. I coaxed my frozen limbs down, branch by branch, to the sand. Then I built a fire of wind-fallen twigs to warm myself till the East Wind came for me.

When the East Wind had carried me back toward the lands I knew, I thanked him, but this time I did not ask what to do next. The cold Moon must have taught me more than she seemed to, for I knew.

In that wind-swept plain I dug a grave and lay in it. On my breast I placed the keys to the hidden rooms in my father's house. Then, as one throws earth on a dead body, I took a handful of soil and scattered it across my chest. Walls of earth loomed over me; a thousand times I expected them to crumble and close upon me. Still I waited as the patch of blue above my eyes turned black. Blood pounded in my ears; there seemed too little air in the burrow. I could lie here all night but never rest, I thought. Nonetheless I did sleep or, at least, pass into a dream. I heard the voice of the Earth ringing in my ears: "How much you have dared, my daughter!"

"The Sun called me fool for facing her," I said. "Now that I've dug my own grave and lain in it, will you not call me twice the fool I was then?"

"I will not!" the Earth said. "You have learned much.

But there is more yet to learn, if you would finish your quest alive. The key to the Glass Mountain I will put in your hand. But the key alone will not deliver your brothers. I will give you better things: a loaf of bread and piece of meat that, however much you eat of them, will never diminish; an apple from the Western Islands; and a golden bridle. The bread and meat will sustain you until you reach the Glass Mountain—a long journey through barren lands. The apple you must keep till you reach the feet of the mountain. There you will find a wild horse who can tread the Mountain of Glass as well as any road. Give him the apple—he will not be able to resist it. While he is eating it, slip the bridle about his neck and mount. The horse will have no choice, then, but to carry you. Still, there is more: the mountain is guarded by a monstrous dog. He devours all travelers that pass by, because he is always hungry. Throw him the undiminishable meat and he will be satisfied. Then you can ride up the mountain and free your brothers."

I thanked the Earth and would have said farewell, but she interrupted: "I am not done. One more counsel must I give you: be not too trusting of your brothers' gratitude. To restore them, you must endure years of silence, sewing shirts of aster-flowers. Do not be too eager to do it. Make them promise you their loyalty."

"I will remember your counsels, good mother," I said. Then the ground convulsed beneath me, bearing me up to the surface, where I lay panting on the turf as dawn broke. The keys from my father's house were gone. Instead I found clasped in my left hand the key to the Glass Mountain: a tiny white bone. In my lap were the bread, meat, and apple the Earth had promised. The golden bridle I found about my neck. I rose and saw the Glass Mountain gleaming in the distance, red in the dawning light. I traveled many days toward its splendor.

When I reached the foothills, I did not forget the Earth's

advice. I fed the wild horse with the apple and tamed it with the golden bridle. As I rode on, the great dog accosted me, but I threw it the meat and appeased it. The slick glassy slopes were no hindrance to my mount; we flew like eagles to the summit. But in that wild ride I must have dropped the key: when I reached into my pocket, it was gone.

I had come too far to turn back. I could not search the Glass Mountain on foot, nor could I hope to see a tiny bone from horseback. I must either force the lock or find a substitute. The key had seemed an ordinary bone—small, like a finger-joint. There could be no other way, then: praying for strength and clenching my teeth, I took the Moon's knife and cut off the little finger on my left hand.

The pain nearly overpowered me. I slumped half-dazed on horseback until the fear that someone or something would come to stop me overcame all other sensations. Stifling repulsion, I fit the bone of the severed finger into the lock. It opened, and I rode through the portal.

Inside, I found myself in a room rich enough to grace any palace. Brocaded couches, patterned rugs, a banquet table set with golden goblets and a fragrant feast——if my brothers were imprisoned, at least their prison was comfortable. But not, perhaps, fit for them in their present shapes. Twelve enormous ravens, ill-at-ease in human-made chairs, pecked awkwardly in half-human, half-bird-like manner at the feast on the table. At the sound of hoofbeats, a fork clattered forgotten from one raven's claw as all twelve turned to stare at me with human eyes of blue, gray, or green.

"Welcome," said one of them, his sea-green eyes glowing with pleasure.

"Why?" squawked another, the biggest of the lot. "For a maiden's sake, we were banished, almost killed. Why should a maiden be welcome to us?"

"Why indeed!" I cried. "A woman gave you wings to

escape your deaths; a maiden has opened your prison; and a maiden will restore you to your true forms, if you are not too insolent to accept it. Earth's Blood! What greeting is this? Must I listen to your grievances, when I have withstood the sun's fire and the moon's chill, dug my own grave and lain in it, even cut off my own finger for a key," I waved my still-bleeding hand at them, "and for what? To atone for the sin of being born? Or to rescue ingrates?"

"Listen, Caradoc; listen, all of you," said the green-eyed raven, the one who'd welcomed me. "This can only be our sister, Brangwen."

"That I am," I said. "I have come a long way to free you."

The green-eyed one fluttered toward me and, as well as he could in raven-shape, he bowed to me. Then he gave me a clean napkin from the table to bind my wound. "My thanks to you, sister," he said. "I am Brannoc, your youngest brother. I remember you as a baby; I always loved you. Whatever the others say, I am with you."

With my uninjured hand, I stroked his feathers, the only embrace possible. Then I turned to the others: "What of the rest of you? I thought to free you, but perhaps I should think better. You are my elders, and men. If I restore you to your true shapes, you will be knights. Will you then lord it over me, treat me as your chattel, marry me to an old lord as it pleases your purse? It will be a fearful task to restore you: making twelve shirts of aster-flowers and silence. If I do this for you, will you repay freedom with bondage?"

"Can you believe us so disloyal, so dead to honor?" said the one called Caradoc.

"Why not?" I returned. "You are my father's sons. I have no more reason to trust a man than you to welcome a maiden."

The raven only glared at me with his strange, human eyes till one of the others said, "Let go this foolish quarrel, Caradoc! We have waited long for this day. For Myself, I would give the kingdom to be out of this birdcage, and lifelong service to be free of the bird-form as well. Brangwen," he said to me then, "I am Hanvon, your third brother, and I will pledge you my fealty if you free us and restore us. Let the others do as they will: I cast my lot with you."

"And I," Brannoc said.

"So be it," said Caradoc suddenly. "I, Caradoc, first-born heir of the kingdom, swear by the blood that binds us to do your bidding if you can release and restore us. Whoever defies you defies me. Now let us leave this prison."

We plundered the mountain cell before we left it: though my brothers had been ravens for a dozen years, they still craved human comforts—as did I. Then I fled on the wild horse, and my brothers on the wing. In the depth of the forest we built a fine rookery with room for us all. There the ravens hunted and scavenged our food as I began my sewing.

I was well trained for the task by the hours I'd spent with my mother, silently plying the needle. I worked quickly and neatly, scarcely needing to think where to place each new flower as the shirts took shape. Only scarcity of asters hindered me. I made longer and longer journeys to find them, a basket of unsewn flowers on one arm and a bundle of sewing-gear and shirts on the other. It was in those travels that I met my young king.

Of course, I did not know what he was when I first saw him ride through the forest with his men. I thought they were a robber band. When I heard the hoofbeats approaching, I fled to the top of the tree I'd been sitting under, leaving the basket of flowers, but taking the bundle of sewn shirts with me.

Below me I heard slowing hoofbeats and the laughter

of men. "That was no stag we glimpsed," said one of them.

"A stag picking flowers?" another laughed. "Here we are with arrows ready, hunting a wench."

"No—a bird," said a third voice. "See where she's flown?" I trembled then in my high perch. They were armed, and might shoot me down if they chose. But no arrow rose to greet me: only the third man's voice. "We mean you no harm," he called. "Won't you come down and meet us?" I made no sound, and moved no least limb, hoping he would give up and leave. Then, below me, I heard leaves rustle and felt branches sway. He was climbing after me.

How should I make him turn back? Half forgetting that a man could want more of a woman than some garment or other, I dropped the mantle I'd taken from the Glass Mountain, hoping that a thief might be satisfied with a bit of good brocade, the only thing I had of value. The mantle fell over his head, blinding him for a time; he struggled under it, but did not fall. At length he cast it off and climbed almost to where I sat.

"Fair bird, forgive me if I invade your nest," he said, half gasping for breath. He was not the climber I was—I who had climbed to the Moon's perch. From a higher branch, I met his eyes with a stern gaze and watched his eyes fill with wonder. "Raven wings on the snow!" he breathed, and it was my turn to be astonished, wondering how he saw through me so readily. But then he added, "Do you know how lovely you are?" and I understood that he only saw the wings of raven hair against my white shift. Ashamed of my ill-covered body, I took up the shirt I'd been working on and held it in front of my breast. Then I noticed a seam unraveling, so I hastened to knot it, gripping the branches beneath me with my legs while my hands worked at the thread.

"What's this?" the man said, "a shirt of flowers? Who's to wear it?"

I looked into his eyes again, wishing I could tell my story.

"You don't speak?" he said, answered again with silence. "You can't be deaf; you look up at the sound of my voice." Little by little, I began to notice his quickness to scent out the truth. "I'd wage my horse you are not mute by natural means. This strange work of yours tells a more ghostly story. Are you bewitched?"

I shook my head.

"Are you fulfilling a *geas?*"

Close enough. I nodded eagerly, pleased with his eager mind.

"I see—you are bound to sew this shirt without speaking," he said.

I nodded, but signaled that there was more, showing the bundle.

"Many shirts, then. Will you ever be done?" he asked.

I nodded, hoping I was right.

"When that day comes, will you speak again?" he asked me, and I nodded again. "On that day, I would like to hear you," he said. "I am Runemon. Look for me at the king's hall."

"Sire!" called the men beneath him. "Will you rejoin the hunt?" And so I learned he was a king.

"When you have a voice, ask for me," he said, and climbed down. As they rode off, I, too, came to earth to find my mantle carefully folded and laid on top of my basket. The hunters' trail was fresh; I wanted to follow them, but to what avail? I could say nothing, and I had asters to pick.

I needn't have feared losing him. Some days later, bent over my work, I heard a footfall and a voice: "White Raven! I've found you."

I looked up in confusion, for he had hit upon my name: Brangwen, "white raven." How had he known?

"Have no fear, sweet bird," he said. "I mean you no harm. I only followed you for wonder. I am forever seeking riddles, and you are the loveliest riddle I've ever met. I followed the trail of broken aster-stalks to find you. But if I frighten you, I will leave."

I shook my head and sat gaping at him, wondering if he'd truly divined my name or stumbled upon it in praising my hair and face. There was nothing otherworldly about his appearance. As I stared at him, trying to search deeper, my hands continued their practiced movements with the needle,

"How fast you work," he said, "as though you'd been doing this forever. Will you soon be done?"

I shook my head.

"I wonder who they are for, these shirts," he said. "I have heard of women sewing a charm into a shirt to bind a lover. But love-charms are singular, and you make many shirts. This must have another purpose. Am I wrong?"

I shook my head. It was good I could sew without looking; I could not tear my eyes from him. I wanted him to go on reading me till he knew me as no one had ever known me.

"They are not for a love-charm, then," he said. "What might they be? To clothe is to shelter—or perhaps to disguise, to change?" He fell silent a while as though awaiting my answer. Then he said, "No matter. It must be weary work. Can you accept any help?"

I shook my head.

"Can I at least cheer you now and then with idle talk while you work?" Rapturously, I nodded yes. I'd been lonely, avoiding society so no one would tempt me to talk. Here was a companion who understood my need. He sat by me, telling me stories until the afternoon tired. As I watched him depart, I knew that I wanted him more than

I'd ever wanted anything for myself. But for all that, I could not abandon my task and speak to him.

Runemon came again, as he'd promised, on many a summer day. He told me quaint tales of ancient heroes and long-dead lovers. He told me, also, his own tale: how his father had died in battle long ago and he, the only child, had been crowned as a boy so small that the weight of the crown pained him. After that, his mother had been regent until he was old enough to rule—and a little longer, he said with a rueful laugh. He had not ruled long. He was young, still: older than I, but younger than my brothers. And every day he grew handsomer in my eyes.

One autumn evening, the trail of wildflowers led me almost to the gates of the castle. Had Runemon planted them there? As I knelt to gather them, he came to greet me. "The cold is coming," he said. "If it will not break your *geas* to dwell within walls, why not come in and warm yourself in my house? I will save a place for you at the table and a bed among my guests. You may come and go as you please. Otherwise I will fear for you, sleeping outdoors in the autumn rain."

With no words, I could only slip my hand into his. He kissed it, and my heart melted. I let him lead me into the hall.

He set me among his noble guests at the meal, with a bard on one side and a scholar on the other. He introduced me as "the White Raven, a riddle I found in the woods. She hears, but does not speak; she sews, but without cloth. Let the wisest among you work out her story and the meaning of it. A ring of gold to the first who tells her true tale!" But the bard and the scholar had no answer for him.

The Queen Mother, however, had enough to say. "You're too eager to see wonders where there are none to find. Look how her left hand is scarred with burns, and one finger cut away. She is someone's runaway bond-servant, maimed for stealing. If she does not speak, why then, her tongue was cut out as well. There's no mystery here but why you brought her in, my son."

I poured fury out the corners of my eyes, trying to mimic my mother's burning, basilisk glance that had discomfited even my father. The Queen Mother saw it and understood well, I believe. Our enmity was fixed.

Nevertheless, I came back often, undeterred by the dowager's hatred. The castle was warmer than my brothers' rookery, and when Runemon was home, he was better company than the best of the ravens. When he left his home to ride circuit of his lands, I, too, stayed away, whatever the weather, finding shelter where I could until the king rode home at last. Then I would join the welcoming procession, silent among the bards that sang his fame.

Bards flocked to Runemon's court, recognizing a kindred spirit in the quick-witted king. If I'd thought he'd told me all his wealth of stories that summer, I'd underestimated him. Above all other tales he loved riddles—and few could match his skill at that game. He was skilled, too, in the knotty riddles of justice. I watched him hearing pleas from subjects, teasing out the strands of truth from the most tangled cases, judging with a wisdom rare in the young and a compassion rare in the powerful. And every judgment, every riddle, was a thread stitching my heart to him.

I lived there long, following him like a silent shadow, watching him rule as he watched me work. Saying nothing, I heard everything at his court. And as I stayed a second year, I began to hear of a king whose army threatened the border of Runemon's land. That king was my father.

Ambassadors were sent to reason with my father, but they returned disregarded. And so Runemon prepared for war. As he raised his army and consulted with his generals, I saw little of him—and when I did see him, he was somber and uneasy. His bards now sang only of battle. He had no time for riddles now—yet still his dark eyes would drift to me across the hall. His mother noted this and was not pleased.

"You're no longer a boy, my son," she said one night, before my very face. "Your mute wench is a toy that you should have discarded long ago. Better to seek out a princess who can bring you good alliance."

"You might have married me off in childhood," he retorted, "but I am a man now and no boy, as you rightly tell me. Now the choice is mine."

"A king chooses a wife for the good of the kingdom," she replied.

"For the kingdom's good I am planning a war," he said, "I have no time to plan a wedding."

"Then let me plan it," the Queen Mother said. "The King of Eil's widowed daughter—"

"—is twelve years my elder," Runemon said.

"Better an old wife than no wife and no heir," said his mother. "Who's to rule this land if you fall in battle?"

"My steward is of good family and good character," he said.

"What! Let the crown pass from the family?"

"If I fall, what else could be hoped for?" said Runemon. "Even if I wed tonight, the only heir I might have by spring would be an unborn child. Can a baby hold the throne if I cannot? I'll hear no more talk of marriage until the war's done."

"I see," his mother said coldly. "No marriage till the war is ended—and perhaps till the earth cracks or the mute wench speaks, whichever comes first. She bewitches you. What do you think she sews, but bonds to hold you? I see you stare vacant-eyed at her, ignoring any woman fit to marry. She keeps you from choosing a bride and getting an heir."

"She is an honorable woman, faithful to a hard *geas*. If I set her before me like an emblem of constancy, what concern is it of yours?"

"You dote drunkenly on a beggar and ignore your duty," she said. "I will not tolerate it."

Runemon sprang to his feet. "*You* will not tolerate it? *I* rule here. If I choose to marry the White Raven tomorrow, who's to gainsay me? I am king."

"You scarcely rule yourself," his mother said, and stalked out.

We were alone then. My heart pounding, I looked to Runemon, desperate to read his thoughts. His eyes were downcast at first, as if ashamed. At last he met my gaze. "I do love you, White Raven. God knows how you slipped into my heart without a word, but I love you."

Tears spilled from my eyes. With the gentlest touch he brushed one away. I caught his hand and held it against my cheek. I had longed for this—but if only it had waited till I might speak! I must not wed till my work was done. I had heard that in the marriage bed, both husband and wife sometimes cry out uncontrollably. One cry would ruin my work and my brothers' hopes.

But he did not then speak of marriage. Instead, his fingers still clasped in mine, he said, "Is it true? Have you wrought a spell on me?"

I shook my head. What else could I do?

"I feel almost bewitched," he said, "but no: I don't believe it. You fled from me when you saw me. I was not what you came looking for with your baskets and bundles, half your shirts already sewn before we met." Releasing my hand, he reached for my sewing bundle and picked up one shirt, then another. "You don't make these shirts to my measure. You don't even make them all to the same measure: this one's long and narrow, and that one broader, as though each were for a different man. As though, perhaps, you were clothing a whole battalion." He sighed. "If only you were! I will need that, come spring."

He left me then and returned to his generals. As he crafted his strategies, his mother planned her own war. If the king would not heed her, others would: lords who'd hoped to see their daughters crowned queen and priests who'd urged Runemon to marry as a stay against fornication. To these ears, she slandered me as a traitor who beguiled the king by sorcery, stealing his manhood and his judgment. I heard her whisper, "It's not only for herself that the harlot works her charm; no, she has a master, perhaps a kinsman, in the enemy's camp. She weakens Runemon as prey for his enemy. Why, she even looks like the tyrant—for I saw him, you know, in my youth. She is very like him indeed."

I knew then that I should flee—but where, on the eve of war? Back home, to be captured by my father's army? Besides, to flee would seem a confession of guilt. No: why deceive myself? I stayed, not for such prudent reasons, but to see Runemon again before the war—perhaps for the last time. My work was nearly finished. Might I speak to him before he left? Oh, God, I prayed, let my needle fly. I worked like one possessed; and many believed I was.

Fitting sleeves to the last shirt, I hid myself in a disused closet—but no crevice of this castle was unknown to its mistress. She burst in with two guards. "There's the traitor! See how she hides her trickery in the darkness. She shall do so no longer! Destroy those shirts, and our king will be himself again."

One of the guards seized my bundle of shirts. I resisted, but he held fast and, rather than tear them in the struggle, I let go. The other guard would have dragged me out, but he had no need: I would not lose sight of my work. Clutching the last shirt, I went willingly.

In the courtyard I saw my enemies assembled: the courtiers who envied me and the priests who misjudged me. In the midst of them, servants kindled a fire. Among the crowd I heard hurried footsteps and shouting—Runemon's voice, panting with haste: "What's this? What's going on?"

"We are here to expose the traitor you've harbored," the Queen Mother declared. "She has bound you by the spells she sews. Destroy her handiwork, and you will see her evil unmasked."

She threw the bundle of shirts on the fire. At once I dove after it: better my life than all my work lost. Flames caught my clothes, my hair; I rolled to extinguish them in the dust. For a moment I thought I had screamed and wasted all my long labor—but it was Runemon's cry that I heard. He beat out the last of the flames with his cloak, half-praying, half-cursing. I was not much hurt; perhaps the Sun had inured me to fire. Steadying myself on Runemon's arm, I rose to stand before the crowd. Then, with trembling fingers, I made the last stitch in the last shirt.

Wind seemed to churn around us from every direction. It was the beating of great wings—ravens' wings. One by one they came to earth around me. As they landed, I cast a shirt over each raven's head.

As the shirts enfolded them, each raven became a tall warrior, black-haired and brawny. And as their human forms filled the shirts, the links of flowers became links of mail. I had sewn them coats of armor. Their transformation was as perfect as it was timely.

Turning to Runemon, I spoke at last in a voice harsh from disuse: "Sire, answer me this riddle: what sort of king would put his wife aside and force his daughter to fill her place?"

For a moment he only stared at me. Then, his wit reviving, he answered: "Whoever wants to be more than a father to his daughter will want to be more than a king to his people. He will be a tyrant."

I asked on: "And what would you say of a king who would murder his own sons to have his will?"

"Whoever would slay his own sons will hold all life cheap," he said. "He will ravage the land like a wolf."

"Well have you named your enemy," I said. "That tyrant, that wolf is now poised at your border. I, Brangwen, am the daughter he would have defiled. These knights are the sons he would have killed, but for our mother's cunning. They have waited long years to punish their father and reclaim their land. These princes are loved and missed by the people of my land: they could turn aside half my father's army without a blow. And they are sworn to follow me." I paused to read Runemon's reaction. His eyes shone as they would at a bard's best riddle-mastery; his parted lips looked ready to smile. I spoke on: "Twelve princely warriors should be an ample dowry in time of war."

Runemon's look of astonishment stretched into a smile. "White Raven," he said, "you know I'd marry you with no other dowry than your story. But this help is welcome."

"Then you shall have both," I said.

And so, after the battle was won, I told this tale at our wedding feast. I delighted my beloved and amazed his bards, for I had mastered words as well as silence.

LITTLE ROGUE RIDING HOOD

by Rosemary Edghill

Rosemary Edghill has sold stories to MZB for years, both to *Sword & Sorceress* and to *Marion Zimmer Bradley's Fantasy Magazine*. Strictly speaking, this story doesn't fit the *S&S* guidelines—which forbid modern settings, but Marion always said she'd ignore her guidelines if the story was good enough. (I used to beg her not to say that in public, because it would inevitably produce slush from wanna-be writers who were convinced that their stories were wonderful. They were wrong.)

This story has already suffered the fate of several stories first published in *S&S* over the years—it has grown and become a novel: *Vixen the Warslayer*, which will be published sometime in 2002.

VIXEN McArdle did somersaults for a living . . . on prime-time television.

Just six months before she'd been Glory McArdle, ex-Olympian, red-headed teacher of English and girls' gymnastics at Ned Kelly High School in Melbourne, Australia, and called Vixen only by her closest friends.

Good enough to be on the Australian team that went to Seoul. Not good enough to medal and garner tempting offers from top coaches and sportswear manufacturers. She'd always been a little tall for a gymnast, but when her final growth spurt hit late that summer, it thoroughly put an end to any possibility of ever competing again, and she'd been wise enough to know that coaching was a mugg's game. She enjoyed teaching—molding and shaping impressionable little minds and bodies—but found herself still hungry for . . . something.

She'd gone to an open audition for a straight-to-cable series called *Ninja Vampire Hunter* out of sheer boredom. Full Earth Productions had just been looking for extras to stand around in the background, but a six-foot-tall redhead who could do backflips, layouts, and walkovers had gotten their attention. She'd been hired on the spot, and when *Ninja Vampire Hunter*—rechristened *The Incredibly True Adventures of Vixen the Slayer* (TITAoVtS for short) had gone to series, Barry Doherty and Full Earth had offered her the lead.

"Doreen doesn't want to spend a year in Melbourne, and anyway, you look a lot better in a black leather corset," he'd said winningly.

It wasn't one of Life's Tough Choices. Playing "Orcs-and-Bush-Rangers" as Vixen the Slayer (even with a whoppingly sexist leather corset) was more fun—and more lucrative—than teaching high school. She'd signed a three-year contract with Full Earth and entered the glamorous world of show biz on the spot. Now *The Incredibly True Adventures* captivated millions of UPN Network viewers every Friday night, as the ninja-raised traveling do-gooder wandered the villages and hedgerows of Elizabethan England with her sidekick, the doughty ex-nun Sister Bernadette, to seek out supernatural evil and religious intolerance.

The Australian exteriors gave viewers a peculiar idea of the English countryside, not that anyone particularly seemed to care. By the time the first six episodes had aired, *Vixen* was international front-page news, its star usu-

ally portrayed in mid-backflip beneath a banner headline
saying something like: "Is this Today's Woman?"

*Well, only if today's woman needs to be able to slay
trolls and vampires at need,* Glory thought, and kept her
thoughts to herself. *Vixen*'s producers, of course, realizing
they must strike while the *zeitgeist* was hot, had quickly
booked the regulars for a promotional tour of the US during hiatus: interviews, photo layouts, talk shows, personal
appearances, the whole enchilada. Glory, Anne-Marie
Campbell (the long-suffering and constantly-imperiled Sister Bernadette), Romy Blackburn (the show's regular vil-
lainess and a veteran of American soaps), and Adrian the
Wonder Horse (a burly chestnut with a tendency to over-
act) were all shipped Trans-Pacific to fame, frenzy, and a
general blurring of the lines between fantasy and reality.

The whirlwind publicity tour had been even more ex-
hausting than *The Incredibly True Adventures'* six-day-a-
week, eighteen-hour-day shooting schedule, and that had
been the worst grind Glory had endured since her com-
petitive days. At least while they were filming, the only
risk was of broken bones. On tour, the risks seemed more
subtle.

I wonder what city I'm in? Glory thought idly to herself, staring broodingly into her dressing-room mirror. *Hell,
I wonder what COUNTRY.* She gazed around the room.
At least its contents were familiar. It was crammed with
the good-luck totems she'd traveled with since she was
six: a Raggedy Ann in workout sweats, the big blue elephant named Gordon. Added to them was an ever-growing
collection of licensed tie-ins: the eighteen-inch stuffed
Vixen doll; the full set of action figures (including the very
rare Lilith Kane, the Duchess of Darkness); the Franklin
Mint limited edition sword and stake (of genuine English
rowan!); the cups and mugs and keychains and T-shirts and
caps blazoned with the show's logo and her picture.

In short, Glory McArdle had Arrived. But whether she was where she wanted to be was a question it seemed increasingly urgent to find the right answer to.

Not that she was going to find it today.

She sighed, and began to put on the makeup that would hide thousands of pale-gold freckles. *Everything they've ever told you about fame is true*, Glory told herself sagely. She'd known it wouldn't be all gravy—but somewhere deep inside she'd assumed it wouldn't be that much different from the Olympics. She'd been right . . . and wrong. The Summer Games only lasted two weeks, and a promotional tour went on forever.

But didn't everybody want their fifteen minutes of fame? She'd hoped for it when she'd gone to the Olympics, after all. How could she complain about getting it now?

Flounder, flounder, in the sea . . . Glory muttered, staring into the mirror. There were deep circles under her tiger-yellow eyes, and she looked haggard. *This isn't what twenty-six and famous is supposed to look like.*

In the past four weeks she'd done ShoWest, *Letterman, Leno, Oprah*, and dozens of local shows. She'd signed copies of tie-in books at chain stores across America. She'd been interviewed by everyone from *Movieline* and the Sci-Fi Channel to *Cosmopolitan*. She'd been a guest at half-a-dozen conventions and schmoozed with every UPN executive they threw at her. Every single one of the people she met wanted a little piece of her, just one little piece. But a million little drops added up to an ocean, and a million little pieces added up to more than one Glory McArdle.

She picked up the copy of the script that was on the corner of the table and flipped through it desultorily. Enlightenment dawned. She was in Malibu, California. Today was an MTV special. Christina (her personal publicist, and, as far as Glory was concerned, personal devil) must have explained it to her last week, but she'd managed to forget. Still, she knew just what Christina would have said: *Hey, Vix, easy money. Show up, do some shtick, a few back-flips, everybody's happy.*

Everybody but Vixen the Red, scourge of the sound-stages. Glory looked toward her costume, neatly laid out on the couch.

It's show time.

She'd just finished dressing when there was a knock on the door.

Oh, bleeding Christ!

She opened the door in a rattle and creak of armor, and her mind went blank. She stared.

There were three figures of indeterminate sex standing in the doorway. The tallest of them barely came to her shoulder. They were all wearing floor-length robes in vir-ulent candy-colors, and the one in front was carrying a large stave with a glowing purple crystal on the top.

"We have come seeking Vixen the Slayer," he said, when it became obvious to both of them that she wasn't going to say anything.

"Yeah, sure," Glory said, stepping back. Just like Christina not to give her all the gory details. She turned back to the dressing table, reaching for her script. If it in-volved little green (and pink and turquoise) men, she'd better actually read it.

"We have journeyed far from the plains of Serentho-dial, through many perils, seeking you, O great warrior," he continued, stepping into the room. His companions fol-lowed, shutting the door behind them. "I pray that we are not too late to seek aid for the Allimir."

"What the fu—*heck* is the Allimir?" Glory demanded, dropping the script. She had a terrible suspicion that this little delegation wasn't from the show, and when she saw what the little one in the back was carrying, she was sure of it.

"We are," the little one in the back piped.

"Look, I really love meeting fans," Glory lied, "but—" *But how the hell did you get back here dressed like that without anyone stopping you? I thought Americans were all paranoid.*

Short as he was—even wearing mascara—there was something enormously *dignified* about the leader of the little delegation, and tired as she was, Glory couldn't bring herself to step on that. Besides, it would only be for a few minutes. When they were ready for her in front of the cameras, Christina would certainly appear to drag her out there. And Christina had a ruthless streak to which Glory could only aspire.

"Okay. What can I do for you?" she asked, stifling a sigh. *If this is one of Barry's practical jokes, I'm going to ruin him straight.*

The little man drew himself up proudly.

"A terrible power has been unleashed in the land of Erchanen. Long was it prisoned upon the peaks of Gray Arlin, until foul mischance freed it once more. Now it stalks the plains of Serenthodiel, and Great Drathil is no more than an abode of shadows. We are a simple and gentle people, without the arts of war, and we knew that only the greatest warrior who ever lived could help our people in their hour of greatest need. You are she."

Great grammar, Vixen thought automatically.

"I'm really sorry," she said, as gently as she could. "I'd like to come to your . . ." Convention? Asylum? She abandoned her search for *le mot juste*. "But I'm afraid I don't have any free days this year. If you want to write to the Publicity Department at Full Earth, Barry could . . ."

She stopped.

The little man was crying.

He did not argue or beg. He accepted her words. The look on his face was one of utter despair.

"You're really serious, aren't you?" she said helplessly. Though the situation was incredibly weird, she found that she was upset for them rather than irritated by them. She couldn't believe that this display of grief was faked.

But if it was not . . .

Deep inside, a tiny spark of trepidation woke to life. If it was not, then this was the utter sincerity of madness.

She'd been famous for six months—long enough to know the dark side of it: the obsessed, the stalkers, the people dazzled by the bright images on their television into believing those images were real people who could see them back. So much belief could twist people in ways they never would have chosen for themselves: twist them and change them into weapons pointed at the celebrities they worshiped.

That these three were honestly sincere was something she did not doubt for a moment. They truly believed that they needed Vixen the Slayer, but what they'd found was Vixen McArdle. When they realized the difference—when they realized there *was* a difference, things were going to get . . . ugly.

"I'm not who you need," she said, very quietly.

"You were our last hope," the little man in pink answered, his voice choked. "We have sought through all the worlds, and always the answer is the same: they are too busy, they will come later. *But there is no later for us, Slayer! We are dying now!*" He, too, began to weep, turning to his turquoise-clad companion. She enfolded him in her arms.

"We will go," the man in green said with quiet dignity.

Oh, God, yes. Just open the door and go.

The intensity of her fear made her feel angry and ashamed. How could they do this to her? What right did they have to do this to her? Being Vixen was a part, a role, a really expensive *game*. It wasn't life. Glory clenched her hands at her sides and concentrated on what she was going to say to Christina when she got her hands on the lazy little tart.

She flinched back as the leader raised his staff.

"*Neddhelorn, Hambrellorn, Gathrond Megnas!*" he chanted in a deep impressive voice. He thumped the staff on the floor as he did, and with each blow the purple crystal glowed brighter.

"Hey, Vix? C'mon, you're up next." Christina's voice, calling through the door. There was a rattle as she tried the knob.

Locked.

"Yo! *Vixen!*"

Glory lunged for the door. Christina could set things right. Everything would be fine, now.

As long as none of them had a gun in those robes.

"*—Lergethil, Gwainirdel, Algoth-Angras!*"

Just as her hand touched the doorknob, there was a loud pop, a flash, and a wave of intense scent like burned perfume. Glory screamed and flinched, but an instant later she realized she wasn't hurt—yet. She struggled with the knob until it slipped from her hands.

She blinked.

The door of the dressing room had fallen off into the hall.

The hall was full of yellow leaves.

A wave of cold, damp, foresty air rolled in. Glory stared. There was no sign of Christina—or for that matter, the green-painted hallway outside her dressing room. Through the doorway, Glory could see trees—a birch forest that stretched into the infinite distance. She could hear the rustle of the branches as the wind passed through them, and watch the flicker of sunlight. The forest floor was covered with bright yellow leaves; as Glory stared in wonder, the leaves rustled and disgorged a chipmunk. It dashed up to her feet before realizing where it was, then turned and dived into the leaves again.

"God's teeth!" she gasped, and just-too-late remembered it was a line from the show. Vixen's favorite oath.

She turned back, still blinking away afterspots. When her vision cleared, she saw all three of the short guys still standing in the middle of her dressing room, staring at each other in confusion.

"This wasn't supposed to happen," Greenrobe gasped. The purple crystal on his staff was slagged and melted, like the remains of an old-time flashbulb. "This is the forest of Arondir—beyond it lies Serenthodiel the Golden—home!"

"It *has* happened," said the woman in turquoise. "The magic went awry. But she hasn't agreed to help us. We have to send her back."

"*How?*" the man in green cried in anguish. "The stave's power is expended, and the rest returns to Erchane's embrace." He let go of the staff. It hit the floor in pieces, crumbling into a line of dust as Glory watched in disbelief.

This is real. This is all real, or . . . or I'm going to break Barry's jaw, is what. She leaned against the doorway, fighting a wave of dizziness borne of pure panic.

"We'll have to get more," Pinkrobe piped up bravely. From the way the other two looked at him, Glory got the impression getting more wasn't going to be all that easy.

"I think that I— I just— I'm glad this is all . . ." If she didn't sit down soon, she was going to fall over and probably squash a couple of her guests. Glory staggered over to the couch and collapsed, breathing as deeply as she could under the circumstances. George tumbled from his perch, and she clutched the stuffed elephant reflexively to her chest.

She felt a pang of relief so strong it was almost surprising. These people weren't nutters. She knew what special effects could do, and they couldn't drop a Malibu dressing room into the middle of a birch forest, even for a goof. The forest was a real forest. But that meant a delegation of wizards really had come to her for help.

"What do you think *I* can do? It's not like I— You shouldn't believe everything you see on television," Glory muttered weakly. "I mean— You got the wrong person. I'm an actress. Not even all that good an actress, I guess. Romy's better. She plays Lilith, and . . ." *Quit grizzling, Vix.*

"Of course we did our research," Pinkrobe said, sounding affronted. He thrust the book he carried toward her.

Glory looked down at the well-worn paperback copy of *Vixen the Slayer: The Unofficial Journeys* by Greg Cox. She'd spied it when they'd first entered and thought it meant they were fans, but if they were, they weren't the same kind of fans she'd been meeting all summer. Not by a long chalk.

"Your life imitates art," Greenrobe said with forlorn dignity. "We have read it."

"Yeah, I guess it does," Glory said with a sigh.

Because this is wackier than all of last season's scripts put together. But here she was, and here they were. And she was their last hope. That much you could take to the bank.

Glory McArdle was a closet romantic. She believed in heroes. She knew what heroes were, and what heroes did, and she knew there was no way anything she did could possibly measure up. Vixen won every week because she had the scriptwriters on her side. Glory had no such advantages. She knew that her life had been a patchwork of compromises, false starts, and mistakes. She was stubborn, but not brave. Faced with one real-world monster, she knew she'd run like a rabbit.

But there wasn't anybody here but her. Maybe she could actually do them some good. And she owed it to these people to at least try.

Because they believed in heroes, too.

"*C'mon, Vix! Yer wanna live forever?*" her coach always used to say whenever she tired. She knew the right answer, the real answer. She'd lost it once, growing up, but now she had a chance at it again.

I choose everlasting glory over length of days.

Vixen McArdle—Vixen the Slayer—rose to her feet, set down her stuffed elephant, and hitched up her matched set of chrome baby-moon hubcaps. "Okay, fellas," she drawled in her hard-learned American accent, tossing her hair back over her shoulders. Her armor rattled, and she touched the sword at her side to make sure it was there. "I'll see what I can do for you. Lead on."

It was a cool fall day in the land of Erchanen, and Vixen moved through the woods in a small symphony of creakings, clickings, squeakings, and jingling. Her arms and thighs tingled with the cold while the rest of her sweltered under several layers of leather, buckram, and steel, and she was starting to get a raw place under her right arm where the shoulderpiece always rubbed. Her armor was still a pain in the ass to march in, but at least the boots were comfortable.

She wished she'd changed back to her T-shirt and jeans, but she hadn't even thought of that until she'd followed the other three through the doorway. And after that, it was too late. Door, doorway, and room, all were gone. Nothing was left but the forest, her strange companions, and her idiotic bravura.

This is a stupid idea. Was a stupid idea. God's teeth, gel, doesn't your mouth ever get tired of writing checks your body can't cash? She couldn't help these people. It wasn't that she had any nonviolence issues: if there was a monster running around her, she was perfectly willing to shoot it, but it didn't look like anybody was going to loan her a shotgun. All she could do was . . .

(die)

. . . get into real trouble, and let down the—what was it? Allimir? She still wasn't quite sure they knew they had a TV actress to help them instead of a warrior ninja, but if you couldn't go back, you had to go on, right? And if somehow this still turned out to be a joke, at least it was one of the elaborate interdimensional kind.

She now knew that the others—their names were Belegir (in green), Englor (in pink), and Helevrin (in turquoise)—were disciples of the Great Mage Cinnas the Warkiller, who had apparently been dead for uncounted generations and so was of precious little help now.

"Died in the moment of his greatest achievement, Slayer, but his works live on!" Englor had piped cheerfully.

"That's reassuring," Vixen muttered.

It had been early afternoon when the door fell off her dressing room. Now it was later. As the sun dipped toward the west the trees thinned, and grass took the place of leaves. Then long grass. Then there were no more trees. That was as good a sign as any. She'd had it. Vixen stopped.

She'd thought she was in good physical shape from the show, but cross-country hiking used unfamiliar muscles. She could feel the tendons in her legs thrumming like a plucked guitar string, and her back ached. In fact, *everything* ached, but at the moment, looking back the way she'd come, she forgot all that.

Bright autumn gold against midnight green—birch and pine—stretched for miles, climbing the lower slopes of mountains that thrust blue and jagged into the evening sky. The setting sun turned the patches of snow on their higher slopes a pale shell-pink.

"Behold, Slayer—Serenthodiel the Golden!" Belegir said.

She turned back and really looked at where she was going for the first time in hours.

There was nothing before her but kilometers of flat open grassland, so vast and featureless that for a moment the sky seemed close enough to crush her like an open hand. She staggered back, throwing up an arm to shield her eyes from the glare of the westering sun. A grass ocean, stretching on until it passed over the shoulder of the earth, with no place to run to, nowhere to hide . . .

"Slayer?" Englor said. "Are you well?" The others had stopped and were looking back at her.

This is really real. This is really happening. You're not in Kansas anymore, Dot, let alone Oz. Christ—what was I THINKING?

"There is the camp of the Allimir," Belegir said, pointing. "Since the destruction of Great Drathil, we have become refugees, outlaws in our own land, hunted for the sport of Cinnas' once-prisoned foe."

The trouble with Belegir was that he talked like a script before rewrite. When she untangled his speech, Vixen squinted in the direction he was pointing. Halfway to the horizon she could see the smudges and dots that might be a caravan. A thin spiral of white smoke rose into the sky, the only vertical in a horizontal landscape.

"Ah," Belegir said with satisfaction. "They have seen us. We should reach the camp before dark—and tomorrow, you will save us from *Her*."

Yeah, right. Vixen thought she might sit down right here and wait for the moon to rise so she could howl at it. The camp she'd seen was miles away. Even if she managed to walk that far, she'd never reach it by dark—never mind getting up bright and early to save Belegir's folks from *Her*.

Whoever *Her* was.

Her feelings must have shown in her face, because Belegir smiled. "Fear not. Ivradan will bring horses, and we may ride back to our people in state—bringing a hero."

Even the sound of the word made Vixen's stomach flinch.

But her eyes were beginning to adjust both to the light

and the enormous scale of this place. Now she could see a disturbance in the grass arrowing toward them like a speedboat wake. Ivradan—and the horses.

Ivradan must be an ordinary Allimir instead of a mage—he didn't wear a robe like the others, but a soft cap, tunic and leggings, and high soft boots that looked as if they were made of heavy felt. The garments were violently colorful, and Ivradan looked like a jockey who'd been dressed by a color-blind bag lady.

He was riding a fat buckskin pony, and leading four more that looked like its clones. As he got closer he slowed down, and Vixen could feel him staring at her. If the three wizards were any indication, she must be the tallest person he'd ever seen, not to mention the best dressed.

"Behold!" Belegir boomed in theatrical tones. "For it is written in the Prophecies of Cinnas, that there shall come . . . a hero!"

Ivradan touched his forehead, bowing deeply from the back of the horse, but Vixen sensed she hadn't claimed as much of his attention as he would have hers if their situations were reversed.

"*She* came again last night," he said.

Belegir seemed to shrink, as if someone had stuck a pin into him. Though he had never looked like a young man to Vixen, in that moment he looked terribly old.

"How many are left?" Belegir said.

It was only much later that Vixen realized what had struck her as so odd about the question. Belegir didn't ask about dead or wounded or whether their side had won the fight—only how many were left.

"Four great-hands. Of all the Allimir nation!" Ivradan buried his face in the pony's mane.

"Four hundred," Helevrin whispered.

Four hundred people? Out of how many?

"I think—" Her voice squeaked, and she took a deep

breath and tried again. "I think you'd better tell me what you brought me here to do."

This is stupid, Vixen thought to herself, four days later. She rode—alone—in the direction of Gray Arlin, where once upon a time Cinnas the Warkiller had chained the Warmother.

Apparently the bitch had gotten loose.

And none of the Allimir, laymen or wizards, could do a damned thing about it. They were farmers, and beyond that, the Allimir were curiously nonagressive. They didn't even smack their kids. They just weren't . . . stroppy. When trouble came, they hid until it was over and then picked up the pieces. And against a fire or a hailstorm, that strategy worked fine.

It didn't work against the Warmother.

So Belegir had done the most belligerent thing one of the pacific Allimir could imagine, and searched for somebody with a small brain and a big sword to save them. And while he searched, the Warmother had driven the Allimir out of their city and cut them down by the hundreds.

Vixen wasn't entirely sure what the Warmother was, and she suspected the Allimir weren't either. Even Belegir admitted that he hadn't thought there was much truth to the old story—all he knew for sure was that the peaks of Arlin had been taboo for a thousand years, and the Allimir were great respecters of tradition.

Yesterday, Belegir had brought Vixen as far as Great Drathil. According to the Belegir, it had once been a sizable stone-and-timber city at the foot of Gray Arlin, surrounded by sprawling fields and orchards. It was now a sizable charcoal-and-large-rocks wasteland surrounded by scorched earth and tree stumps.

Maybe their problem's just a dragon, she thought without any sense of irony. A dragon was just a big poison-spitting lizard that could fly. She could deal with a dragon—or (more what she had in mind), if she saw that it *was* a dragon, she could go back and tell Belegir, and they could all work together to coordinate some kind of ambush or trap.

But first she had to see the dragon. Belegir said it laired at the top of Gray Arlin, and the ancient path (followed by who?) up the side of the mountain was still easy to follow, even after three years had done their best to obliterate it. When they'd parted, Belegir had assured her that the pony knew the way, and she had to admit that the little beast had been slogging determinedly along as if he had a mileage quota to make and a destination in mind. She tried not to think of where she was going, or why, or what she might find when she got there. To tell the truth, she wasn't completely sure *why* she was going, but every time she told herself this wasn't her problem, she couldn't quite make herself believe it. If there was one thing she did believe, it was that the remaining Allimir were going to be dead soon if someone didn't do something.

And once all of them were dead, what would the Warmother go after next? Other than the Allimir's imported hero?

"Let's not even go into where that's going to leave me besides stranded," Vixen muttered, just to hear somebody talk. "What do *you* think I should do?" she asked her mount.

The pony flicked his ears at the sound of her voice and forged steadily on up the trail. Vixen sighed, trying to pretend she wasn't entirely out of her depth here. She didn't know what was at the top of the mountain, but so far it had been easier to go on than to go back. That was probably going to change sometime today, and she didn't know what she was going to do about it. There was only so far that living up to other people's expectations could take you.

"C'mon, Vix! Yer wanna live forever?"

I choose everlasting glory. . . .

To distract herself, she looked back. Beyond the burned scar that had been Great Drathil, the vast prairie that Englor had called Serenthodial the Golden stretched outward to meet the sky. Somewhere out there were the last of the Allimir, counting on her to save them.

The pony stopped, and a moment later, Vixen realized why. The trail was gone, leaving an eight-foot gap in the middle of the trail.

She dismounted to look at it. Landslide or earthquake or enemy action, it didn't really matter. She thought she could probably jump it, but she doubted the pony could. It was Shank's Mare from here on, providing she didn't break her neck in the next few minutes.

Provided she made the jump.

She walked up to the edge to gauge the distance again, then spent a few minutes doing stretches, not really making up her mind. She knew she could cover the distance, but it was one thing to cartwheel between two markers with CGI to be added later, and quite another to make the same jump in real life.

She *could* just turn around and go back. She was almost all the way to the top and hadn't seen anything yet. Maybe there wasn't anything to see. If there wasn't anything here, she'd have to go back and ask Belegir what to do next, wouldn't she? Of course she would. In fact, she didn't really have to go to the top now. She could turn back here.

She *could.*

No, I can't, she admitted with a sigh. *I have to go and make sure.* Vixen the Slayer would, after all. Without a single second thought.

But I'm not her. Or she isn't me. Or . . . hell.

She shrugged off her thick wool cape and folded it neatly, then set it at the edge of the trail, and added the small sack of provisions she carried. Before she could give

herself any more time to think about it, she flung herself
forward and into a handspring.

There was a confused moment of flight—long enough
for her to regret what she'd done—and then her feet hit
the trail again with a jarring thud. Her sword banged
painfully against her leg, just as it always did. She dusted
herself off, grinning in spite of herself.

One hurdle down. One to go.

She waved cheerfully to the pony—it was cropping
grass, paying no attention—and strode on up the trail,
whistling merrily.

Her lighthearted mood ceased abruptly when she
reached the top of the mountain. It was flat and open, as
if someone had decided to construct a scenic car park in
the middle of nowhere, and in the center of the space
someone had placed a monument-sized slab of black basalt
with four large rusty manacles sunk into the four corners.
The shackles were bent and twisted, as though something
had torn itself free in the not-too-distant past. It looked
remarkably like one of the sets from TITAoVtS's "For
Whom the Belle Trolls" episode.

She walked forward slowly, reaching out to touch the
stone.

::*Have you come to chain me once more, little mortal?*:: a voice said in her head.

She froze, part of her mind waiting for someone to call
out and tell her they had the shot, fine, cut for lunch. The
light faded from the sky as if the sun had gone behind a
cloud, and then it went right on getting darker. At the same
time, cold rolled toward her as if someone had opened a
freezer. She turned, slowly, telling herself desperately that
it didn't matter what she saw, she wouldn't scream, she
wouldn't.

The sound she made emerged as a desolate moan.

Cinnas' triumph was no myth. It wasn't even an allegory. This was the Warmother—the essence of War Itself—and it looked like every nightmare Ridley Scott had had for the past twenty years.

The monster was a crusty glistening greenish black, and there was something horribly insectlike about its movements. Vixen's gaze stumbled over its unfamiliar contours, unable to figure out what she was seeing.

::Well?:: the Warmother said. It opened its mouth. Black teeth glistened with venom.

Vixen threw herself sideways out of sheer expectation, and a moment later a fine mist of venom sprayed the stone where she'd been standing. Her sword slapped her leg and she grabbed it, dragging it from its sheath because, dammit, that was what she usually did after a forward roll and she was too scared to think straight. Prop it might have been, but it was live steel: durable and looked great in close-ups. Surely enough to take out any dragon.

"Easy money," Vixen muttered to herself, hunkering down and brandishing her sword threateningly. It was that or run, and there was no place to run to.

::No warrior born of woman, no weapon forged in the world, can unmake my form, for I am made of all warriors and all weapons. Prepare to die, Vixen the Slayer.::

The Warmother reared back, and its body seemed to stretch, its contours crawling and changing until it resembled another sort of insect: a mantis. Vixen stared in amazement, her terror dissolving in the face of this fresh impossibility. Then the monstrous head dipped toward her and she scrambled back out of the way. No matter what it looked like, it was still trying to kill her.

She managed to avoid its next several lunges—long enough to get cocky, long enough to think she had a chance.

Hey, this isn't as hard as it looks!

The wind was picking up, and the first fat drops of rain had begun to fall. It was getting harder to see, but there wasn't much up here to trip over.

Then the monster darted forward—much faster than it had moved until now—and seized her sword in its jaws. Even over the sound of the rising storm, Vixen could hear the faint pinging as the Warmother crumpled her sword in its mandibles. The glass jewels in the hilt sprayed between its jaws, catching the fading light like drops of flame. It lashed at her with its foreleg, and Vixen flung herself out of the way, automatically catching herself on her hands and popping a forward rollout.

But she was getting tired, and the ground was getting treacherous as dust turned to gritty mud. It was only a matter of time before she wasn't fast enough.

::I don't need this to destroy you:: the monster sneered, as it finished eating her sword. It reared up again and began to melt away in the rain, dwindling until it had taken the form of a naked woman, impossibly old, her mottled skin hanging in folds and only a few wisps of white hair clinging to her waxy scalp. Her face was fallen in, her cheeks hollow over toothless gums. She drooled. Only her eyes were alive, black pits of malignant fire.

::This is what you fear most.::

Age. Death. Incapacity.

"Everybody dies," Vixen said flatly. And everybody got too old to be what they wanted to be. It was the prevailing fear of an actor, but Vixen had already faced it as a gymnast. She wasn't afraid of it anymore.

She groped around her back for one of the row of stakes sheathed there. While her sword had been made of honest steel, these stakes weren't wood. They were plastic. She gave herself about ten seconds, max. Her fingers closed over the stake.

The Warmother reached for her.

::You're dying now.::

"Up yours, Granny!" Vixen howled in helpless defiance.

Cold where it touched her, and she felt her heartbeat

slow as she was gathered into the hag's embrace. Then suddenly there was a yelp of pain, and something hot and thick spurted over the back of Vixen's hand. Vixen recoiled, staring at the thick black blood.

No warrior born of woman, no weapon forged in the world....

But the plastic stake was a prop, not a weapon. It had been cast, not forged, and in another world than this. And she wasn't a warrior. She was a gym teacher. Exultant with sheer terror, Vixen stabbed again ... and again. The stake began to dissolve in her hand, and she reached for another, but the first had already done its work.

::You'll live to regret this, Slayer!:: the hag squealed, sinking to her knees.

"Yeah, yeah, yeah," Vixen muttered. *I guess bad villain dialogue is the same everywhere.*

She was jittery and exhausted at the same time, watching the Warmother closely for further signs of life. But the creature seemed to be finished. *It can't be that easy....* As Vixen stared, her opponent withered away to a skeletal bundle, then began to *melt,* a thick mist rising skyward from her huddled form.

Vixen risked a glance toward the massive stone behind her.

Manacles.

Broken manacles.

The penny dropped.

"A terrible power has been unleashed in the land of Erchanen. Long was it prisoned upon the peaks of Gray Arlin. . . ."

Long was it prisoned. . . .

"Uh-oh," she whispered. Cinnas might have been named the Warkiller, but he hadn't killed the Warmother. You couldn't kill War. Cinnas had *bound* her, removing the threat of war from Erchanen. Then somehow she'd gotten loose, but she'd still been in corporeal form. Vixen had managed to take that away from her, but that didn't make everything roses. She hadn't slain the monster—all she'd done was force the Warmother to return to her original form from eons before, the form out of which she'd been summoned by the Mage Cinnas so that she could be chained. Once more, the Warmother was a red spark in the heart of every man . . . and in some hearts more than that. A flame.

"Well, fu— um, drat," Vixen said feebly. She took a few steps and sat down on the edge of the basalt slab. She'd been out to do a good deed, and it looked like all she'd done was reintroduce the concept of not-very-original-sin into a world that hadn't had it.

Of course, alternatively, they could all be dead.

The sun appeared through the fast-dissolving clouds as Vixen brooded, not even cheered by the fact that there was no one around to yell at her for losing two props and mucking up her leather. She wasn't dead. She wasn't any closer to getting home. She'd lost a really expensive sword. And it looked like there was going to be plenty of work in Erchanen for Vixen the Slayer.

"Cut. Print. Save it for the day, kiddies, we'll go again tomorrow." She got to her feet, muscles already starting to complain. She hoped her pony was still there. Otherwise, it'd be a long walk back to Belegir's camp.

She wondered if he'd think the news she brought was good.

Thanks to Doris Egan, Sylvia Kelso, and Bennett Ponsford, for invaluable criticism on an early draft of this story. No, really.

THE QUEEN IN YELLOW
by Gerald Perkins

Gerald Perkins was born in central Minnesota far too long ago. His family moved a lot which undoubtedly encouraged his itchy feet. He graduated from St. Cloud State University, Minnesota, and immediately left for California, Guam, New Hampshire, Kodiak, Alaska, Australia, and other foreign places. He has worked in aerospace, hardware quality assurance, been a freelance technical writer, and is currently pursuing a certificate in technical communications at a community college in San Jose, California.

He took up science fiction reading and writing in third grade, but made a sharp left at photography. He returned to writing in time to make his first professional sale to *Sword & Sorceress V.* He has since had several short stories published, primarily in fantasy anthologies. He currently lives in San Jose with more books than he has room for and a collection of photos that badly need sorting. Unlike most SF and fantasy writers, he is not currently owned by a cat.

For the benefit of those readers who may not be hardcore science fiction addicts: there is a well-known story by Robert Chambers called "The King in Yellow" about a book which has a strong effect on anyone who reads it. Judging from this story, I'd say that Mr. Perkins has read the story, though hopefully not the book.

KATANÉ, mage queen of the Finger Lands, caught the invading horseman's downward strike on her light cavalry shield. She used what little magical strength she had left to bind his saber to her shield, digging her boot heels into the trampled earth. His horse danced away, pulling him half out of his saddle. Blood splattered her dark yellow surcoat as she cut off his hand.

"Milady!"

One of the queen's horse guards shouldered aside the whimpering soldier. Katané threw herself onto the riderless mount he brought. He spurred forward to intercept another of Zareetha's cavalry, then tumbled as a foot soldier disemboweled his steed. Man and horse screamed as they fell.

The queen urged her mount away from the melee. The invading forces, drawn from all the lands Zareetha had conquered, swarmed up the five broad valleys. Soon they would meet at the ramparts of the low plateau that held the Finger Lands' last pastures and the royal town. She turned as she broke free of the press.

"Katané!" Hallwin, royal consort, mage, and warrior without equal, fought his way toward her. His escort surrounded him, even as hers tried to reassemble itself. He bounced an invader's long-handled ax off his shield with such force that the wielder staggered back into the sword of an escort. Half-plate armor gleamed through rents in his amber surcoat. His ruddy face shone with sweat and a lock of his unruly black hair hung nearly over one eye. Katané tucked wisps of her light brown hair back under her helmet.

"We must retreat!" He raised his sword, pointing over his head at the plateau where the Finger Lands abutted the Great Eastern Mountains.

An arrow sprouted in his side where light mail links joined breast and backplate. Shared pain nearly unhorsed Katané.

Surprise washed over Hallwin's face. He let go of his

sword and shield, but pressed his charger into a momentary gallop.

"Beloved," he said as his mount crashed into hers.

Amidst the clash of arms and screams of dying men and beasts she heard his glove thud on the grass. He raised his bare hand, slowly, slowly, as through thick oil. Katané let her blade fall on its lanyard as she pulled off her glove with her teeth. Their flesh met, pale square hand and one slender and tanned.

Power surged into her as Hallwin made his death gift. His body tumbled to earth.

Katané pushed back the miasma that had been slowly suffocating her as Zareetha, her mages, and her armies marched up the five valleys. Katané turned her horse, lifted her hands in a beginner's focusing gesture, and cast the simplest, most powerful death spell that she could summon at the invading queen-general.

Darkness hit her like a war hammer.

"I should be most disappointed if she *didn't* live, even after two days." The pleasant voice of a middle-aged woman came to Katané through waves of pain and weakness. The smell of laundry soap tickled her nose. "After all, she must marry Tliden if I am to legitimize this latest conquest. I'll undoubtedly have troubles with the locals even so."

"Her children, Your Majesty?" said a man somewhere in her darkness.

"Dead before her consort. Give me credit for some subtlety. Or maybe not; turncoats are so disgustingly easy to find. Now hush, she'll be waking soon." Clothing rustled and male footsteps left room. Moments passed as Katané struggled to regain control of her senses.

"You may as well open your eyes, dear," Zareetha said.

The small room in the servants' quarters swam before Katané. Wearing a plain blue dress, Zareetha sat alone on a stool near the queen's pallet, smiling kindly. The smile did not reach eyes as steel gray as her hair.

Katané gathered dregs of power and lurched toward Zareetha. The conqueror did not even twitch as a hot needle of pain drove through Katané's skull.

"Oh, dear, I was afraid you would try that." Zareetha shook her head. "I admire your spirit, but that *was* foolish.

"Katané, child, you are almost as powerful a mage as I—almost. I cannot destroy your talent without killing you, so I have made a little spell that surrounds you like a mirror. Any spell you try will reflect on you as pain—up to the point of death. I cannot let you die, not yet."

Sickness made Katané's stomach churn as she realized how short "not yet" could be and how long it could seem.

"You can live long and well as my son's wife. He has some talent and I'm sure you will produce beautiful children.

"I *am* sorry, but one of your servants ran off with your children. Probably in a foolish attempt to use them as rallying points for rebellion." Zareetha *tsked*, shaking her head.

Katané tried to reach Zareetha with her clawed fingers. *Liar!* she cried in her mind. She fell back as darkness edged her sight.

"If you wish," Zareetha said, not smiling, "you can live for a year as a slave—just long enough to bear me an heir.

"Whatever your choice, you will surrender the rule of the Finger Lands as soon as my chamberlain returns with the scroll and witnesses. You will marry Tliden within a week, and bear him a child so that my blood will rule here in perpetuity."

Katané tried to speak.

"Why? My dear, I should think it's obvious. I intend to bring order to this world; if not by myself, then through my offspring. Why do you think I went to the effort of bearing all those children? I expect to birth many more. Between my talent and their love, I can guarantee they will not rebel."

The door opened.

"Ah, here comes my chamberlain. Now just sign the scroll and swear fealty to me. As soon as my mages have cleared the castle of your spells, you can have your rooms back."

A man in dark tunic and trousers, carrying a rolled up scroll, led five servants and six soldiers into the room. One of the servants set a folding table between the queens. He retreated to stand with the others against the far wall, under the scrutiny of five of the soldiers. The only woman soldier helped Katané sit up.

The Queen of the Finger Lands sat slumped, staring at the document of abdication the chamberlain laid on the table. She made no move toward the pen he placed next to a traveling scribe's inkwell.

"My dear," said Zareetha with a sigh, "with no little effort I have bound the lives of one hundred of your people to each of the five behind me. It would be a great relief to end that strain." One of the soldiers drew a long knife.

The woman soldier blotted Katané's tears before they could stain the document.

Katané found the body servant Zareetha had assigned to her mewling at the foot of great-grandmother's wardrobe. The girl crawled away from the defeated queen as fast as she could while keeping her right shoulder pressed against the wall. She flinched as she passed through a spill of late afternoon sun.

Katané blinked in surprise. A flash of hope made her shiver.

Great-grandmother's massive wardrobe stood against the wall, only the glow of many years of polish differentiating it from those on either side. One had to have mage talent to see the silvery runes woven deep in the wood, but *seeing* required no spell. She pulled the heavy door, now shorn of its locking spells, all the way open.

The dress hung askew on its form, alone in the dark space except for matching low-heeled shoes. Puffed shoulders bracketed the wide neck, ending in tight upper sleeves that kept the indecorously low neckline and loose bodice in place. Cloth fell in billowing folds from the embroidered waist to the floor. So tempting to a servant who expected no punishment.

How could Zareetha's tame mages have missed it? Katané's lips pulled back in a feral smile. The spell on the dress was subtle and old, very old. And they were looking for *her* touch.

Hopelessness yielded to the slow deep rage in her.

The sound of cloth on stone, then wood, then stone again as the servant crawled past the barred door between Katané's suite and the hall drew her attention.

Damn the conquering bitch! Because of Zareetha's mirror spell, she could not even give painless mercy to a girl made mindless through no fault of her own.

Katané took three steps from her robing room to the spacious sitting room. She knelt in the path of Zareetha's tool and guided her into the queen's sleeping chambers where no one entering the suite would see her. The girl tried to avoid her, but was too terrified in her madness to even cry out.

Voices of men and women preparing for the wedding feast in the great hall this evening came faintly through the window. The clean smell of wisteria outside the tower window tickled her nose. Katané hurried back to the robing room.

She dropped the unadorned dress that was the only garment she had been allowed since her defeat on the floor in front of great-grandmother's wardrobe. At least they had let her wash in the servants' quarters under the watchful eyes of women soldiers. She took undergarments from a drawer.

The Finger Lands queens were neither short nor boyish. Katané knew perfectly well how she would look, nearly as tall as Tliden, athletic figure set off by the artful design of the dress. That would help keep the gaze of everyone in the chapel—with luck, none of them friendly—on her.

In the fading light, the dress appeared an ordinary yellow.

Katané took the garment gently from the form that helped it keep shape in the wardrobe. Grandmother had altered the dress so that the wearer needed no help donning it. Had she not tried to steal, that would have saved the unfortunate servant girl's sanity. Katané lifted and stood, arms above her head.

The dress slithered down her body like a lover's caress. Her arms slid through the tight upper sleeves without hindrance. The neckline fell perfectly into place. The waist seemed to fit even before she fastened the hidden hooks. She padded over to her dressing table in the last of the day's light.

The thin silver of the mirror behind her table was darkening now that the maintenance spells had been removed from her rooms. The tarnish did not account for the slow changes visible in the dress as she lit four oil lamps.

Katané combed out her light brown hair; only shoulder long since it had to fit inside a war helmet. Piping on the dress brightened to nearly metallic gold. She blackened her light brows. The bodice took on a butterscotch hue. She bruised her eyelids with powder until they were nearly as dark as her irises. The skirts darkened, light amber at the top, dark at the hem. She reddened her lips with berry color in oil. The dress colors shifted, blended so that no one could say where one shade ended and another began. The shadows in the folds seemed darker, somehow, than

they should be. As she added rings, necklace, a brooch—
everything but the coronet that was hers by right!—faces
came and went in the stitchery between bodice and hips.
She stepped into the shoes and nodded at her reflection in
the mirror.

Nathanau, a powerful mage of the time, had demanded
the hand of great-grandmother. When she refused, he
wrought a subtle revenge and gave it to her in the form
of the dress Katané now wore. The spells in it would steal
the mind of anyone but great-grandmother or her blood
heirs who looked at it for more than a few moments.

Nathanau underestimated great-grandmother's talent—
and her will. She and her intended mage husband displayed
Nathanau's mindless body in a cage until it died.

Katané smiled again and quickly composed herself
when she saw her reflection. It would not do to look sav-
agely triumphant.

The magic in the dress was not *hers*, not caged by Zareetha.

"Milady?" One of her guards banged on the hall door.
"Milady, Queen Zareetha requires your presence."

"A moment only." How calm she sounded. Katané took
a long, light evening cloak the color of dusk from another
wardrobe. The shadows in the dress swirled as the cloak
hid them.

Katané kept her face composed as she entered the small
family chapel. Nearly three dozen people, mostly the cream
of Zareetha's military aristocracy, filled the small chamber, though she saw the barons of two valleys among them.
The opportunists had the grace to look away.

Many candles lighted the chapel. She was surprised to
see that family portraits still hung on the pale wood pan-
eling.

People stirred as Zareetha, Tliden, and Zareetha's chief
priest entered the chapel. Zareetha and the priest wore

plain, but elegant robes. Tliden's tunic and trousers boasted elaborate embroidery and jeweled medals decorated his left breast. He was handsome, no doubt, with red hair and smiling blue eyes. He looked like a kindly man despite his upbringing. Katané almost felt sorry for him.

Two of the generals stood on either side of the only door and fighting men maneuvered subtly to be near the two windows as the crowd drew aside, all eyes on the royal trio.

"Good evening, Katané," Zareetha said. She and Tliden stopped next to the queen and her escort as the priest continued to the small altar at the opposite end of the chapel.

Katané said nothing as a soldier took her cloak.

The priest cleared his throat. Almost no one turned to look at him.

"Before the gods of the Empire and of this land," he said, "we are gathered here . . ."

Then the screaming began.

Courtiers foamed at the mouth, clawed their clothing or their faces. One scarred general plucked out his eyes as Katané watched. Others convulsed on the floor. The priest fell to his knees, eyes lifted to heaven, his face contorted with visions of hell. One of Katané's woman guards drew her knife, lunging at the queen. She stopped, staring at one of the faces in the gown's stitchery and cut her own throat instead.

Tliden curled on the floor, smiling peacefully as he sucked his thumb. He soiled himself.

Zareetha fought. Hate filled her eyes as she struggled to look away. Her hands twitched in aborted focusing gestures. Slowly the knowledge of defeat seeped into her expression. Katané knelt before the conquering queen during that moment of lucidity, her skirts spread around her.

"I could probably save your mind," she said, "but your mirror spell prevents me."

The candles burned down two finger widths before the mirror spell failed. Katané hastily raised her own barriers to keep out the madness around her. Silence filled the room except for a few moans.

Katané, mage queen of the Finger Lands, stood, donned her cloak and stepped outside to announce victory.

MAGIC THREADS
by Pete D. Manison

Pete D. Manison, thirty-nine, lives in Houston, Texas. His fantasy and science fiction short stories have been published regularly since 1989. He's currently writing full-time, though a fortune cookie recently told him "You will soon make a long overdue personal decision," which he interprets to mean getting another day job.

Of "Magic Threads" he writes: "My girlfriend gave me the idea when she was knitting a blanket for her sister's impending baby. She said she wondered if the child would be able to sense the warmth and love she felt while knitting it, if the emotion would be transmitted through the blanket. I'm always listening for stuff like that, and there's always a pad and pen handy."

MELIKA blushed as she told Kyreen the Weaver her problem.

"It's my husband. He hasn't been able to . . . rise to the occasion, if you know what I mean. It's eating him up inside. And the worst part is that I'm enjoying the break. Before this, he was at me every night. I never got any rest. Only now he's depressed, and I fear our marriage may not survive."

Kyreen smiled encouragingly. People usually sought her out only as a last resort. She'd known Melika since childhood; she knew this couldn't be easy for her.

"I think I can help you," the Weaver said at last. "But it isn't cheap. The cost of thread alone . . ."

"I'll pay anything," Melika pleaded. "As long as it works."

Kyreen went to her cabinet, opened a lower drawer. Inside, the many garments she had created sparkled with magic. She lifted up a cloak of bravery, and beneath it she found what she wanted.

Melika's blush deepened when Kyreen turned to show her what she held. "I call these the Undergarments of Passion. They were an early effort, I admit, and until today I never thought I'd find anyone with a use for their . . . particular effect."

Melika reached out timidly to touch the yellow threads of the garment. "Oh," she sighed when she felt the whispering tickle of their power.

"Nineteen rellas for you, my dear. Only the cost of material."

The girl took out her coin purse. "Will they really work?" she asked.

Kyreen nodded. "Oh, they'll work well enough. As long as he's wearing them, he'll be stiff as a battering ram."

"And when he removes them?"

Kyreen smiled. "He'll wilt like a week-old celery stalk."

Melika giggled as she counted out the money. "Perfect," she said.

Kyreen worked at her loom, closing her eyes to tune into the flow of her emotions. Focus. Let the feeling fill you, let it spill from your fingers into the thread. Safety, comfort, warmth. Another vest today, for a regular client. He spoke of mindless fears that grew stronger with the passage of each day. How he longed for the peace of security!

No. Don't think. Don't drift. Focus. Safety, comfort, warmth. You are safe when you wear this vest. Nothing will harm you. I weave security into every strand. May these magic threads bring you the peace you so desperately desire.

The stranger arrived at her cottage the following morning, the dust on his clothes speaking of a long journey.

"You are Kyreen the Weaver of magical garments?" he asked. His voice was deep, yet hard, as if he'd seen terrible things.

"I am," she answered, wrapping herself more tightly in her Shawl of Confidence. She wasn't about to let herself be intimidated by this tall stranger.

"My name is Talian Krin. I am . . . was . . . a knight in the service of Queen Lochuria. Now her kingdom has fallen, and I alone have survived to seek your help."

Kyreen looked him over more closely, noting the gauntness of his cheeks, his bandaged shoulder, the smell of infection. "What has become of the queen?" she quietly asked.

Haunted eyes regarded her. "A darkness has come to our land. A man . . . a monster . . . has spread his corruption to every border. Those he has not slain he has enslaved. He boasts he will continue until the whole world lies within his domain."

"Terrible news, indeed," Kyreen said. "But what has this to do with me?"

Now a flicker of anger lit the darkness of the stranger's eyes. "This man, this conqueror, wears a magical cloak. I believe it to be the source of his power. And in all the land, there is only one Weaver who could have produced it."

Kyreen shivered. "Certainly not! My garments are designed for good, imbued with only the gentlest of magic."

Talian arched an eyebrow. "And it has always been so?"

Kyreen glanced down at the stranger's boots. They were finely crafted, though worn from long use. It always fascinated her how much one could deduce from a person's clothing. Talian came from wealth, but he'd seen much hardship of late. "Not . . . always," she finally answered.

"The cloak is black, with borders of silver and gold. It seems to give Sinmara total domination over all he encounters."

Kyreen's heartbeat quickened. The stranger must have noticed a flush in her cheeks, for he nodded once, squinting.

"Yes," she confessed. "Though it shames me to admit it. In my youth, I wove such a garment. But I have it here, under lock and key."

"Show me."

Kyreen went to her cabinet, unlocked the secret drawer, and opened it. She was not surprised to find the drawer empty. She had recognized more than the description of the cloak.

"Oh, Sinmara," she moaned. "What have you done?"

The stranger made a small sound in his throat. "Then it's true?"

Kyreen turned to face him, her shawl supplying her with the strength she needed. "Alas, yes. Sinmara and I we . . ."

Talian nodded.

"He left so suddenly. I had no idea he'd taken the cloak." She considered. "He was such a gentle man, so kind and giving. I refuse to believe he could have become this abomination of which you speak."

Talian arched an eyebrow. "You seek proof?" he asked quietly.

Kyreen shuddered. There was menace in the stranger's tone.

"Then proof you shall have." He reached into his pocket and withdrew a small pouch. Before Kyreen could react, he opened the pouch and spilled its contents—a fine dust— into one hand.

"No—" she started, too late. He blew the dust from his hand, and as it sparkled in the air before her she felt a rush of movement. Her cottage had vanished. She stood on a hilltop overlooking the smoking ruins of a city.

"Gods protect me," Kyreen muttered.

In the desolation below, dark shapes moved among the whimpering wounded. Women and children were forced to watch as their husbands and fathers were beheaded, their bodies spilling blood onto the ground while their heads were mounted on pikes and planted in a circle surrounding the smoldering chapel. Carrion-eaters hovered, their eyes aglow with the orange light of the many fires.

A man on horseback appeared out of the smoke. He wore a necklace of human teeth, and though his face was distorted by an evil sneer, Kyreen recognized him all too readily.

"Sinmara."

The lone horseman raised his sword, beckoning to his followers. "Quickly now! The rest of it!"

The followers obeyed, moving as if controlled by a single mind, and what they did to the women and children sickened Kyreen so deeply that she closed her eyes.

When she opened them again, she saw the familiar walls of her cottage.

"Now do you believe?" the stranger asked.

Kyreen looked at him as if for the first time. "I only wish I could deny what you have shown me. Can my work have spawned this madness?"

Talian eyed her solemnly. "It could. It has."

"Tell me, then, how you managed to escape, if the cloak makes him impossible to resist."

Talian glanced down. "That is not important. What matters is that I am here. Now that you have seen the truth, you must help me to stop him."

Kyreen noted the desperation in his eyes. "Surely you don't need my help. You are not without magic yourself."

Talian nodded. "True. But my powers are useless against him. Only your magic can undo what your magic created."

"What am I to do, alone, to stop this horror?" she pleaded. "I am only a simple Weaver. I'm no warrior."

"But I am. Together we may prevail. Together we may be able to retrieve the cloak and end his domination."

"You propose that we travel into his realm together? How will we get close enough to act, if he dominates the will of everyone around him?"

Talian looked toward her loom and the spools of magic thread that sat on the table beside it.

Three days later, the two travelers approached the border of Sinmara's kingdom. The journey had been arduous, and Kyreen felt stabs of protest from muscles she hadn't known she possessed. But troubling her more was the stranger's silence. He seemed never to sleep, and in those times when they sat beside the fire at night, she saw him watching her, his dark eyes unreadable. Mourning for his queen? Or filled with vengeance for her slayer? It was difficult to be sure.

Only the small case she carried in her knapsack brought her any comfort. It was her secret, of which she had told Talian Krin nothing. If their plan failed, if something unforeseen occurred, she would have that last, dreaded resort.

On the fourth day, they came to the ruins of a city. Houses had been burned to the ground. Charred bodies littered the streets, and the smell of death was heavy in the air.

"It is time," she told Talian when they had crossed the doomed city and stood looking out on the dark country ahead of them.

The stranger grunted, once, and removed from his pack the garment she had woven for him. He seemed to hesitate, but then he removed his riding cloak to reveal a lean, muscled body crisscrossed with scars both old and new. Kyreen averted her eyes. When she looked back, he had donned the shirt and was replacing his riding cloak over it.

"Don't worry," she comforted him. "It will work. As long as you wear that shirt, you will see him clearly for what he is. His powers shall hold no sway over you."

Talian looked at her, his eyes sparkling as if seeing into her very soul. She expected him to speak, but he only grunted again, once, and said nothing. They mounted their horses and began the final leg of their journey.

"Hold!"

The border guards had emerged from behind a small copse of saplings where they'd waited in hiding. Kyreen fell into character, bowing her head submissively as the three riders encircled them.

"And what have we here?" one asked, chuckling.

"I am Talian Krin, in the service of Sinmara the All. I bring our master a new slave."

Kyreen risked a look, saw the riders appraising her suspiciously.

"I have no word of—"

Talian started to reach into a pocket. Instantly, swords crossed in front of him.

"Careful, Brother. The killing grows habitual."

Talian eyed him coldly. "For Sinmara, too, I hear, when one of his men acts capriciously."

The swords remained, but the captain of the guard motioned with his chin for Talian to proceed. Kyreen watched as he withdrew a small scroll and handed it to the man.

"Everything appears to be in order," the captain said a moment later, a trace of disappointment in his voice. "You may pass."

Talian glanced at her, and together they started forward.

"And Missy?"

She turned her head just a fraction. "Give my regards to the All."

The three guards roared with laughter. Kyreen held her tongue. So far, the deception had held. But the worst was yet to come.

The Palace of Sinmara was a great structure of gray stone that sprawled over many acres and stabbed skyward with its pointed spires. The two travelers were met at the outer gate, and again Talian gave them his story and showed them his scroll. The palace guards were more cautious, consulting among themselves for many minutes before escorting the two inside. Two guards each accompanied them with weapons drawn as they made their way to the All's private chambers.

"Wait here," Talian instructed her as they stood in the anteroom. "This won't take long."

With a grim smile, Kyreen nodded. Only as Talian vanished, unarmed, into the next chamber did she realize how much faith she had placed in her work. If the power of the shirt failed . . .

No. She had woven clarity into every strand. Even the Cloak of Dominion would have no power over him. Vision would give him the freedom to act as he chose, without the mind-killing power of the cloak to distort his senses.

Then why did she feel so uneasy? Long minutes dragged by, the guards watching her with amused little smiles on their faces. This was taking too long. It should have ended by now. With Talian in possession of the cloak . . .

At last, the door swung open. Kyreen held her breath. Out of the darkness emerged two figures. The first, Talian Krin, moved aside to stand motionless as the second person entered the anteroom.

"Sinmara?"

The tall man smiled. He still wore the cloak, and despite herself Kyreen felt the compelling tug of its awesome power.

"So, my dear, we meet again."

She looked at Talian, back at Sinmara. "But . . ."

Sinmara laughed. "Such an innocent you are, Weaver. You trust far too easily—back then, when you told me your secrets and showed me the cloak, and now, when you allowed a stranger to deliver you into my grasp."

"Talian?" she moaned. "Is it true? You do this of your own free will?"

He only smiled, looking down at her as he might a child. It was Sinmara who answered.

"Yes, lovely Kyreen, it's true. Clarity of vision is such a subjective thing, isn't it? Apparently your shirt only succeeded in making Talian see that my power is too strong to oppose, that it's far better to fight beside me than opposite me. I suspected you might try such a trick. That is why I sent Talian Krin, my finest warrior, to bring you to me."

"But why?"

"Once my power made me the All, I realized that only one person could ever threaten me. You. And I knew my cloak would hold little sway over she who had created it. Forgive the deception. It was the only way to bring you here."

She felt a sinking sensation in the pit of her stomach. "Then you mean to kill me?"

Sinmara laughed, a sound dripping with venom. "Kill you? Why, Talian could have accomplished that easily enough. No, dear Weaver, you are far too valuable for that."

"Then?"

"You will serve me, of course. I know your work of late has been rather . . . mundane." He stroked the hem of his cloak, dark fingers against the gold and silver. "But you have the capacity for so much more."

"Never. Sinmara, what's happened to you? What's become of the kind and gentle man who once shared my bed?"

He laughed, tossed his head imperiously and looked down at her with eyes that seemed to peer out from some other dimension. "That Sinmara is dead. Behold now the All. The ruler of this kingdom, and soon of the entire world."

"You're a monster!"

"Perhaps. But I'm a monster of your own making. Surely fate guided your fingers when you wove for me this Cloak of Dominion."

All was lost, Kyreen thought. Or was it? Suddenly she remembered the other thing, the last, terrible thing.

"You win," she moaned. "I cannot resist you any more than your subjects can. Tell me, then, what it is you wish of me."

Sinmara smiled, his face glowing with triumph. "You are a Weaver. You shall weave for me. You shall weave such garments that will make me a god. We'll start with omniscience, perhaps, or a pair of socks to make me immortal. Such work have I planned for you."

Kyreen looked down, feigning submission while she actually concealed a tiny smile.

"You're in agreement, then? My dungeons are really no place for a lady of your stature."

Kyreen looked up, knowing it had to be just right. "I'll need my instruments, my materials. I'm afraid I came illprepared for this."

Sinmara squinted, turned to Talian.

"She lies, your Allness," said the traitor. "She carries a case in her knapsack. I have seen it."

Sinmara looked back at her, a scowl clouding his features. "So, you seek to trick me! What a pathetic little creature you are. Now, girl, remove your knapsack. Take out the case."

She hesitated.

"Do it!"

"Very well," Kyreen muttered, unbuckling the straps

and removing the knapsack from her back. "I have no choice, it seems." She opened the sack and removed the case, began to open it.

"No! I fear you may be deceiving me."

Kyreen held her breath.

"Give the case to me."

She did.

"Now, my Weaver, your work shall begin." Gloating, Sinmara the All opened the case. When he saw what it contained, he screamed.

It was after midday that Kyreen the Weaver accepted a visitor into her tiny cottage.

"Melika. How good it is to see you again. How fares your husband?"

The girl's face grew red, not with a blush but with anger. She reached into her pocket and removed the Undergarments of Passion, which she thrust toward Kyreen in a clenched fist.

"I want a refund," she said.

Kyreen blinked. "Refund? I never . . ."

"Nineteen rellas, I believe it was. The gods know I'll need the money now, with another mouth to feed."

"Another mouth? What are you talking about?"

As quickly as she'd angered, the girl broke into tears. "You said these would fix the problem, that his potency would last only so long as he wore them, that he would be unable to consummate his desire."

"Yes," Kyreen said gently. "Removing them would negate their effect. A useful paradox, I thought. His ego would remain intact, and so would your night's sleep."

"Well, think again!" Melika shouted, the pendulum of her emotions swinging back to anger. "He wore them as a cap!"

Kyreen took the briefs in her hands, looking down. "Oh, my," she said.

"The money . . ."

"Of course, my dear. And you have my apologies. Surely you see I could never have anticipated that this would happen."

Melika said nothing as she counted the coins, twice, and then stashed them in her purse.

Kyreen repaired their friendship over lunch.

"Excellent sandwiches," Melika commented. "And this tea, it is heavenly."

"Thank you."

"Oh, Kyreen, I'm so sorry I shouted at you. But you understand my disappointment."

"Such a reaction seems quite natural, child. Think nothing of it. Here, let me tell you a story that'll take your mind off your coming difficulties."

They ate pastries while Kyreen recounted her adventure, beginning with the stranger's arrival and sparing no detail of their journey and eventual confrontation with Sinmara the All.

"By the stars, Kyreen, can all this be true? You were betrayed and captured. Powerless. You were to be the servant of evil . . . forever."

"It is so. Or would have been. But you're forgetting the case."

"Ah, yes. The case you said contained your instruments and materials for weaving." Melika smiled, a gleam in her eye; clearly, she knew it couldn't have been so or Kyreen would not be here.

"Care for another pastry?" Kyreen asked.

"No, thank you. And stop teasing me. The case didn't contain your instruments, did it?"

Kyreen smiled. "No," she said.

"Then what did it contain?"

Kyreen sat back, the glass of tea cool in her hand. "Moths."

MARION ZIMMER BRADLEY

THE DARKOVER NOVELS

EXILE'S SONG

A Novel of Darkover

by Marion Zimmer Bradley

Margaret Alton is the daughter of Lew Alton, Darkover's Senator to the Terran Federation, but her morose, uncommunicative father is secretive about the obscure planet of her birth. So when her university job sends her to Darkover, she has only fleeting, haunting memories of a tumultuous childhood. But once in the light of the Red Sun, as her veiled and mysterious heritage becomes manifest, she finds herself trapped by a destiny more terrifying than any nightmare!

- A direct sequel to *The Heritage of Hastur* and *Sharra's Exile*
- With cover art by Romas Kukalis

☐ **Hardcover Edition**   UE2705-$21.95

Eluki bes Shahar

THE HELLFLOWER SERIES

☐ **HELLFLOWER (Book 1)**　　　　　UE2475—$3.99

Butterfly St. Cyr had a well-deserved reputation as an honest and dependable smuggler. But when she and her partner, a highly illegal artificial intelligence, rescued Tiggy, the son and heir to one of the most powerful of the hellflower mercenary leaders, it looked like they'd finally taken on more than they could handle. For his father's enemies had sworn to see that Tiggy and Butterfly never reached his home planet alive. . . .

☐ **DARKTRADERS (Book 2)**　　　　UE2507—$4.50

With her former partner Paladin—the death-to-possess Old Federation artificial intelligence—gone off on a private mission, Butterfly didn't have anybody to back her up when Tiggy's enemies decided to give the word "ambush" a whole new and all-too-final meaning.

☐ **ARCHANGEL BLUES (Book 3)**　　UE2543—$4.50

Darktrader Butterfly St. Cyr and her partner Tiggy seek to complete the mission they started in DARKTRADERS, to find and destroy the real Archangel, Governor-General of the Empire, the being who is determined to wield A.I. powers to become the master of the entire universe.

OWLSIGHT

by MERCEDES LACKEY
& LARRY DIXON

Darian has been living in the temporary encampment of the Tayledras Hawkpeople for nearly four years, working as liaison between them and the survivors of his own ravaged village. But as he is about to return with the Tayledras back to their home Vale to continue his magician's apprenticeship, Darian suddenly learns that his parents, missing for five years, are alive.

☐ **OWLSIGHT (hardcover)** UE2802-$24.95

And don't miss OWLFLIGHT, *the first novel of Darian, now in paperback:*

Apprenticed to a venerable wizard when his hunter and trapper parents disappeared into the forest, Darian is difficult and strong-willed—much to the dismay of his kindly master. But a sudden twist of fate will change his life forever, when the ransacking of his village forces him to flee into the great mystical forest. It is here in the dark forest that he meets his destiny, as the terrifying and mysterious Hawkpeople lead him on the path to maturity.

☐ **OWLFLIGHT** UE2804-$6.99

Prices slightly higher in Canada. **DAW 172X**